Outlander Page

First Book of the Aethereal Knights' Tales

William Cornelison

Warring Magic Books

The Aethereal Knights' Tales

Outlander Page

Mountaineer Page

Seafarer Page

* * * * * *

* * * * * *

* * * * * *

Outlander Page

First Book of the Aethereal Knights' Tales

Chapters

There are those with spirits unbound by the qualms of their fellow man,

and faith in what lies beyond what is told,

and minds that seek what is past the horizon.

Undeniable, to even the mightiest mountains or roughest of seas,

they are as majestic swallows dancing in the boundless skies.

Such boisterous whims can never be caged.

But even the spriest swallow must take rest

and return to the sanctuary of their nest.

Sad it is when what is meant to be their homes falls into shambles

when ravaged by the ravenous snake, leaving them without home

... or family.

Instinct to return home cannot be denied, whether it is to search for it

or to make one anew.

~ First Chapter ~

Change

Autumn was a favorite time of year for those on the southern outskirts of Vermalio. An abundance of crops had grown from the bountiful soil. The crisp snap of the wind uplifted the farmers working in the fields. The sun blanketed the earth in a comforting radiance.

They were signs of the coming Harvest Festival.

The village of Russalin held festivities at the dawn of autumn to commemorate the success of their crop production. The farmers were some of the most important people around; they labored in growing the fruits and vegetables that supply the southern half of the kingdom. Their hard work kept their humble village on the map and the villagers well protected from brigands.

But among the great men in life, there were those who were beloved by all, including the farmers: those people were the knights of the realm.

A young Vandelas Kronas of Southern Valley looked up to the knights more than anyone. He always went to the village in hopes of seeing them.

He, along with the rest of the village, always remembered the gallantry they displayed two years ago. At the time, many of the knights had been called to the neighboring merchant town to quell a revolt. In their absence, the village was attacked by brigands. Half of the village had been burned, their crops stolen for the brigands' ravenous appetite. And when it seemed like all would be consumed by the flames, the knights returned and cleared the mess.

The incident left many children afraid to leave their homes, and Vandelas was no exception. Even on the most peaceful days, he required his father's escort to feel at ease.

"Van, come on now!"

Vandelas answered the familiar call immediately. He ran to a man thrice his height. This man had blue eyes that glimmered a courage once lost and a crescent scar dug up to his tattered blonde-gray hair from his right eye. He donned plain, rustic clothing that accentuated more muscle than he had.

Vandelas' father, Jerrell Kronas of Southern Valley, was one of the knights who fought to protect the village two years ago. He was enjoying a leisurely stroll during his day of rest. He was without his armor when the chaos erupted and entered the fray after stealing a sword from the first pirate he saw. Although he fought bravely, after killing fifteen pirates, he had been caught off guard and sustained terrible injuries that left an arm and a leg crippled. He was left with little choice but to retire after the doctors told him he would never fully recover. Ever since then, he always wore plated armor underneath his clothes to protect himself.

To Vandelas, as well as many others, his father was a hero.

"We don't want to keep your mother waiting, do we?"

Vandelas shook his head vigorously. He remembered how his mother got when she lost her temper—vividly.

His mother was also a knight; her name was Victoriah Kronas, and she was even better a knight than her husband. Victoriah was a knight admired for her beauty, although that was often overshadowed by her savage strength and wily wits. She once fought in a war when she was a squire and saved her meister knight from being impaled. Although reliable, she had an aggressive personality and was quick to anger. That was why the kingdom called her Victoriah the Wolverine.

She had been away for three months patrolling the north, but she came home for a week's rest, and for a special day. The Harvest Festival was none of her concern. She wanted to tend to something of greater importance to her: her son's ninth birthday.

Victoriah might be a frightening woman at times, but it meant a lot to Van knowing she came back for him.

Van walked beside his father on their way to the grocer. His mother asked him to stop by the market to pick up some beef and vegetables for her special stew, a filling and flavorful dish that provided those who partook energy and stamina. Not only was she a renowned knight, but her cooking skills were sublime. Van tagged along to see if he could see what the villagers were doing for the festival.

A banquet was being set up in the square. With the surplus of crops grown this year, everyone would happily fill themselves with the fruits of their labor. The village children made colorful and vibrant decorations to be hung all over town, as they did every year. The mayor supervised the whole thing to make sure no mistakes were made.

And the boy made sure to avoid his sight.

Vandelas tried helping decorate once but somehow ended up setting back progress five hours and ruining half of the food. He was not quite sure how it happened himself. The mayor wanted to declare him a public menace; he was either very bold or incredibly foolish to tell that to Victoriah's face. She would have knocked all of the remaining teeth out of his mouth if not for her vow to protect the people of her country, not attack them—and her husband holding her back.

Their trip was supposed to be a quick one, and it would have been had the grocer not gone missing. They should have seen it coming. He never stepped foot away from his place of business, but today was a special day for everyone.

His father figured the man was discussing meat prices with the mayor. "Van, I'm going to find the grocer. Stay here and wait for me."

"Yes, sir."

Van was scared to be without a knight to keep him safe, but he knew his father would not be gone long.

Everyone loved Jerrell for what he did two years ago, and the many efforts he made in the years past that earned him a noble status from the king. Of course, he also had it taken away after marrying Victoriah, who was a fallen noble. Van never understood how that worked or why his mother was considered "fallen" nobility, and he never thought to ask since the subject of noble titles always bored him.

The grocer would give Jerrell a moment of his time if he could break away from the mayor.

The only thing that bothered him was how he would spend the time. "Hey, Van!"

Many of the village children avoided him after he nearly ruined the festival once before. They thought him too different to get along with. But there were a few that had not taken caution to some unfortunate slipup; to be exact, there were four. A small group of two boys and two girls took a liking to his uniqueness.

Van went over to the brunette girl in a blue cotton dress who called him. Dominique Drevenr had her own unique quirks—her irrational fear of little birds, for one. They got along rather well with each other.

"You here to help decorate for the festival?"

Van groaned. She also had a rare tendency to overlook the obvious. "No. Don't you remember what I told you last time, Mini?"

He liked to call Dominique by that nickname because she was so petite. Most girls were usually shorter than boys, but she was two years older than him and he outgrew her by a head's height. She usually liked being called that.

Her cheeks bloated like a red puffer. "You told me it was an accident." She was much more forgiving than the adults. "Well, if you're not here to help, then what are you doing?"

"Mother wanted Father to buy some ingredients for the special meal she's going to make tonight."

Mini's face deflated. "Your mother is making dinner on the night of the Harvest Festival? Doesn't she know there is going to be a banquet?"

"She ... doesn't get along with the mayor too well. And she's rarely home, so she doesn't get to cook for the family much."

"I didn't think knights liked to cook."

"Me either, but she likes cooking for us. And she likes to make her special dishes on our birthdays."

Mini looked up for a moment in thought. It did not take much convincing for her to speak her mind—it never really did. "Does she cook yummy food?"

Van closed his eyes and thought of his mother's cooking, nearly making his mouth water. "That doesn't even begin to describe it. Everything she makes is beyond belief!"

"Then you can invite me to your birthday dinner tonight?"

Her words surprised Van. She and the others always went to the festival with their families. Music was played, games were hosted, and knights even came to compete in a tournament in a vacated area.

The festival's food was nothing compared to what his mother could make, though. Everything she made tasted better, but the festival had more to offer. Van was not sure about the choice Mini made, but he saw no problem with it either. "S-Sure. You can come to dinner if you want."

He thought she would be happy, but her childish expression spoke anything but gratitude. Even though she seemed upset, he admitted that her red puffer face made her look cute.

"That's the best invitation you can give?"

Van blinked. He never thought Mini to be the kind of person to expect such extravagant things.

She was going to visit the home of two famous Vermalian knights. Perhaps it would be ideal to give her a proper invitation. So Van put a flat palm over his chest, aligned his spine to give perfect posture, then bowed saying, "Lady Drevenr, it would be an honor and a privilege to have you over for supper this evening."

That should have been proper enough. It was the best formal invite he could give with the education he had.

Mini had always been a complicated girl. Just when Van thought he had her figured out, she started laughing like his father when someone tried to catch the thieving rabbits in the crop fields. "You crack me up, Van. You don't have to take everything so seriously, you know?"

As odd as she was, her uniqueness always made Van smile. It was something he enjoyed.

Father and son left the village after getting what they needed. It took forever for Jerrell to pull the grocer away from the mayor, but he managed to buy some of the freshest ingredients. He got a kick out of telling his son about how the mayor looked like an angry, sweating grapefruit when he barked orders to the villagers. His bald head had so many rough veins that he looked ripe to split. They had fun laughing at the village leader over this. Is that why a huilo monkey attacked him once?

As much as the villagers abhorred him, Van was glad he decided to go. It was a chance to be around others. His family lived up on the tallest hill overlooking Russalin, so a trip down took some time and effort. No one went up there willingly because there lived a tall, black-haired monster capable of snapping a grown man in two. It was not a bear, but the Wolverine everyone came to both love and fear.

She rarely left her den, for she returned for rest, and only stepped outside whenever needing to tend to chores she decided to do while her mate was away.

Van returned to the fortified cottage near the edge of the cliff. There, a slender woman with modest yet well-formed muscles filling her curves was breaking a pile of chopped wood with her bare hands. Her full lips gave a pout portraying a brash bravado. Her black hair had been tired into a ruffled ponytail, and her hazel eyes looked at the wood she split fiercely.

"You could have asked me to cut the wood, you know," her husband openly teased.

The cold woman turned, darting a glare at him and quickly threw in a curt smile. "What's the matter, Jerrell? Feeling threatened now that your woman is back?"

"I don't feel threatened by you, Victoriah. I just thought you'd have your hands full preparing for dinner tonight."

Victoriah gave a snide laugh. "Please. I've made all of my dishes more than a thousand times. I can take my eyes off them for a few minutes."

"So you know when it'll all be ready then?"

"It'll be ready when I say it's ready!"

She almost enjoyed the way he flinched. The way his calm demeanor crumbled when she bore a few teeth always baffled their son. Van admired her, but he could not help fear her as well. He was almost afraid to tell her about the extra guest they were going to have tonight.

"Oh. By the way, Van invited one of the village girls to dinner."

That did not last very long.

Was he eavesdropping on us? Van thought.

He explained the invitation he made to his friend so she would not get angry. It was not until nearly completing his long-winded story that he noticed his mother had a smile to her face. She kneeled down to him, keeping that very same smile, and fluffed his blonde hair.

"Is it that sweet girl— You call her Mini, right? I'd love for her to come over."

The stories of Victoriah the Wolverine depicted her as a menacing beast that would crush anyone who dared cross her, but when her son held her attention, she was kind and affectionate.

Van loved his mother, but she was still very scary when upset. He never liked thinking of what she might do if he would upset her.

"Jerrell, darling, can you finish chopping the wood for me?"

"So now you want me to chop the wood?" Jerrell thought to tease his wife a little more, but he understood she was not in the mood for that when Victoriah shot her stern glare his way. "I'll go get my axe."

He settled when his wife traded that glare for a pleased grin.

"Van, come help me tidy up so I can tell you about the ambush I was in." She always did that. Her son usually did not like to clean, so whenever she needed something done, she told him of her exciting tales while they work. It was the same old trick, and he always fell for it.

A loud neigh grabbed the boy's attention. Van had almost forgotten about Timberhoof, Victoriah's noble steed. The light amber warhorse living in the stable built just for him and Arrowhead, Jerrell's mount who fell deceased the last year, had immediately been visited by the excited little boy. Timberhoof happily lowered his face to greet him. He loved to see Van's bright face after coming home from months of riding. He always missed the way his little hands massaged and gently tickled his snout.

"I wish I could ride you, Timberhoof. But mother says I'm too small."

Ever since he could remember, he wanted to learn how to ride a horse. Victoriah would have gladly bought him a pony more appropriate for his size were it not for her costly debts—she always caused a lot of damage while on duty.

She smiled at her child and her mount, reminiscing when the five-year-old Timberhoof met Van as a baby. "You'll ride someday, Van."

"Yeah, I know."

"He already had his oats. You can feed him before dinner if you'd like."

Victoriah leading her son inside their home. Van waved at Timberhoof before she took him out of view. The stallion flicked his left ear, which had a small scrap bitten off at the tip. He always did that to say bye to the boy, flicking it again in case it went unnoticed.

The cottage's interior looked as cozy as the outside. The family room was decorated with fluffy fur pelted furniture around an exposed fireplace barely protected by the gothic iron shield. A family portrait of Jerrell with Victoriah holding a little russet-skinned baby with what looked like red paint under his closed eyes hung over the wall. It was parallel to the smaller portrait hanging in the dining room of a grinning teenage girl with a long, whipping black ponytail leaning an elbow on the shoulder of a shorter young man of blonde hair just like Van. The dining table was a fancier design made by an artisan from Ederea, a kingdom to the east.

Victoriah began unraveling the bandages from her wrists. Van, as if to mimic his mother in some way, removed the red pendant from around his neck. Upon doing so, while hanging it on the hook by the door, his entire appearance shifted into something anew—ruffled hair from gold blonde to pure white, lively eyes from skyline blue to a red matching the pendant's, skin tone from a peach to a deep russet, even small red marks had been printed under his eyes—matching the baby in the painting.

When Victoriah turned to see if her child followed, she simply smiled at Van coming her way as though never noticing his transformation. He was completely different from how he was seconds before, but she was not daunted by it.

"So Mother, what happened to you while you were away?"

She was so glad he asked. The entire trip was a tiring rush, barely a moment for her to rest.

On day thirty-five, Victoriah had been ambushed by three brigand parties banding together. From their squabbling and bickering, she was certain that none of them enjoyed working together but united to get rid of the lone famed knight. But the brigands took her much too lightly. Victoriah gave a surly grin in remembrance of the assault. For every ten men she took out, one managed to graze her; the battle only a nice workout for her, despite her body being covered in scratches and bruises.

Some of the methods she described to Van sounded rather unchivalrous. But the famed Wolverine once taught him something after telling him a story where she beheaded three raiders in a sneak attack: "Sometimes, it only matters if you leave the battle alive."

No knight would ever admit to agreeing with such a thing. Even compared to other female knights, Victoriah was incredibly different from the rest of the crop grown in the capital.

But then again, she was up against three hordes of savage fighters all by herself. Even she could not have fought them all off without a few underhanded tricks.

Five days after the bandit attack while she was transporting those who had survived her with a company she messaged, another group attacked in hopes of freeing their comrades. Only when they reached the bottom of the canyon they ambushed them in had they realized the famed

Wolverine had been with them. Van nearly passed out laughing after she told him they tried to run away from her only to be captured in the end.

Then ten days later when she arrived at Csekentil, a vibrant town with a proper prison to contain the bandits, Victoriah discovered something truly outrageous. As it turned out, the head of Csekentil's patrol guard was in cahoots with the bandits and the brain behind their unification. Obviously, she brought him in. However, it was difficult to believe in Victoriah's statement in the king's court at the capital. Fortunately for her, she relieved the patrol guard head of a little evidence before exposing him to the crown. A few of the bandits were questioned as well. No one expected them to tell the truth.

Even the king was skeptical, but to ensure their words be true, he threatened to have the dreaded Victoriah the Wolverine interrogate them if they spoke any false details. The sight of her cracking her knuckles in preparation for the fun made them all sing like a flock of little birds in spring, as expected.

Van admired his mother's prowess greatly. She never ceased to amaze him. Before he even realized he was helping her clean, they already wiped the shelves of dust, removed the soot from the open fireplace, disposed of the rat they found living under the floorboards, fixed the gap in the gnawed-up floor, polished the fancy dining table, and cleaned all of the filthy dishes as she finished telling her tales. He never realized just how much his mother's stories give him a motivation boost.

"Van, would you like to brush Timberhoof while I get dinner ready?" His mother had already tossed the warhorse's grooming brush before the boy could say yes.

Van raced for the front door to put on his leather sandals again while his mother reminded him to brush Timberhoof's scalp where he likes it the most. "Ah! Van, don't forget your Shift Pendant!" the motherly she-devil frightfully called to her adored child. He had nearly forgotten the red pendant, propping the beautiful gem around his neck again—reverting his appearance to how he appeared when entering a while ago—before placing a finger to the doorknob.

The auburn warhorse acted hysterical when he saw Vandelas with the stylish grooming tool in his hands. Van tried not to laugh so hard at the gelding's excitement and waited for him to calm down enough before getting too close. Since he was still short in stature, he had a difficult time brushing the overgrown horse. From attempt after attempt to brush Timberhoof without falling over, Van learned to climb the wooden gate and plant himself firmly in place so he could get a better reach. Timberhoof seemed worried for him, but he settled down after the boy found his place so he could brush. A simple stroke over his mane made the wild warhorse mewl a quiet murmur of relief. Van loved animals, and he loved Timberhoof more than any other. Ever since he first met the beautiful creature, he never knew a moment where he did not smile around him. Timberhoof was always so friendly to him, entirely affectionate even. Thinking back made Van realize the mount was a lot like his mistress.

Van found it very easy to talk to Timberhoof even though he never said anything back, though his ears did twitch whenever the boy spoke. He knew the horse really listened to him. "Mother goes all over the kingdom. You must have been on tons of adventures she doesn't tell me about, huh?" Sometimes, he thought Victoriah held back on a few vivid details she did not want him to hear. "Father was very strong before he retired. And Mother is still the best knight alive."

Timberhoof retorted with a low neigh.

Van smiled and brushed Timberhoof more vigorously. "And, of course, you are the best gelding out there. It must be hard work carrying Mother for such a long time and going to dangerous places."

Facing dangerous perils and vile brigands, the life-and-death situations, carefully caring for sharpened steel, visiting new places and experiencing new ways of life, meeting different people, finding new animals—each thought excited the boy all the more.

Jerrell walked into the stalls with a heap of chopped wood as Van worked his way over Timberhoof's back. The man kept his eyes onto his son, impressed with how stable he kept himself on a fence pole; he did not even wobble. "Having fun there, Van?"

He lost focus of the glorious images in his mind when his father interrupted. Turning around to meet his gaze, Van nodded, then turned back to work on Timberhoof's short fur.

"Meet me when you've finished. We've still got a lot of work to do before dinner is ready."

With the moon's ascent to the twilight sky, the Harvest Festival came to its most anticipated event: a tourney where the knights competed. In Vermalio, the moon was considered a beacon of peace and harmony, so many celebrations were held at night, even the ones involving conflict and heavy weaponry.

Van would have loved to watch the tourney in the village down the hill, but celebrating his birthday was more important—or so he came to believe after hearing it from his parents. They were not the only ones to think so either. Just like she promised, Mini left the village to visit Van for dinner. It took her some time to figure out where he lived since she never visited. Everyone knew the beastly Wolverine dwelled atop the tallest hill overlooking their fair village, but somehow she still managed to get herself lost along the way.

Still, it was nice of her to come, Van thought.

He greeted his guest at the door, wearing his best clothes—a cotton shirt and coal-black trousers, and of course, the Shift Pendant under his shirt. The village girl dressed up for the occasion, too, in a pretty pearl dress and a matching bonnet.

Victoriah gave the girl a hearty "Good evening!" and, with a bright smile, beckoned her to the dining table. It was almost amusing seeing Mini eye what had been laid on the table. A buffet of scrumptious dishes had been arranged neatly before them—smoked corn, yams, bread made from the freshest wheat, two jugs filled with juice and wine, and Victoriah's special stew. The main course was made with the most succulent beef, onions, carrots, and potatoes dripping with flavor, and a touch of tomato juice and spices.

It was hard to believe she had time to prepare such a bountiful feast.

Mini spaced out at the sight of the food and the exquisite smells making her mouth water. She barely heard Victoriah pull out a chair next to hers for the guest to sit in, but she accepted it after getting her focus back. The kindly mother pushed in her chair with a beaming smile, then went on to serve the food.

Everything tasted better than Van earlier described. It all had tastes and sensations Mini never before experienced and never thought she would. Compared to Victoriah's home cooking, the food at the festival was as appetizing as horse dung.

"Lady Victoriah, your food is to die for! I've never eaten anything so delicious."

Victoriah beamed with pride hearing her guest's praise. "I'm glad you like it. Feel free to eat until your belly bursts."

Mini gladly took her up on the offer. It was all much too delicious to let go to waste.

When everyone had their fill and the food was gone, they leaned back in their chairs and just took a minute to let it all settle. Such good food. Van's mind nearly drew a blank. His taste buds were still dancing.

It was a shame the comforting mood started to fade. A faint chill permeated the air as the fire was starting to go out.

Mother and Father have already worked so much today, Van thought to himself. *They deserve to rest.*

"I'm going to get more firewood." Van jumped from his seat and headed to the back door past the kitchen before anyone objected.

Jerrell took the wood he and his wife cut into the stables earlier. It had to be somewhere in there. Van spent no time trying to think it over and just went to find out for himself. He circled his home to the stables resting at its side. Timberhoof was already sound asleep, so Van tried to look quietly, not wanting to disturb him.

It did not take long to find what he came for. In the corner. Behind the bales of hay.

As he was returning to the back door, Van stopped halfway. Another cold chill cut through the already crisp air and crept over his skin. There was something different about the atmosphere. He took a careful look around just to be sure. Nothing changed. Everything was exactly as it had been since morning, although now veiled in the nighttime glow.

If everything was the same, then why did nothing feel right? He could hear it. Van swore he heard something relative to a voice in the wind. He decided to investigate, leaving behind the pile of wood and taking with him only one thick, broadly cut piece.

He followed the voice into the woods, disobeying the one in the back of his head warning him to go the other way. The voice in the wind kept telling him to follow. Van was not sure which one to listen to with them saying such different things. The boy's curiosity took priority above much else. He could not deny wanting to know where it came from.

Perhaps it was a mistake. All of the voices now hollered at him to get out of there. Regret and fear guiding his legs, he moved to turn back.

"The child of the Wolverine wench..." Now the wind's voice suddenly sounded strangely deep, craggily even, almost like—

No, it's not the wind!

Someone had found him, and it was not anyone good. Van, holding his breath from the tension, turned back the way he came and burst through the forest debris frustratingly. Other animals and insects were doubtlessly living in the lush greenery, but he could not bother with that now. He needed to clear everything out of his path.

It only mattered that he got away alive.

He was almost home. He would be safe there. Van thought he had actually gotten away; his pursuer thought otherwise. A broad figure leaped out from the foliage to intercept his prey just before it could break through the trees, revealing himself to be a large, burly man in torn leather clothing wielding a thick battle-axe.

Van could not stop trembling. He thought to turn back and run, but instead, against his better judgment, took his wooden plank in both hands like a knight would a sword.

When the burly barbarian moved in to split him in half, Van leaped down and slipped past his blind spot, then bolted for the stables.

"Timberhoof, help!"

The barbarian pivoted, allowing him a good look at his prey, then leaped after him with axe firmly in hand. A wild neighing had broken out the moment when he missed and struck the ground. The warhorse knew there was trouble.

Now that Timberhoof had gone into an uproar, Victoriah would know something was wrong. He only wailed out such wild cries when there was danger.

I just need to keep running for a few more—

But Van had already run out of time. The burly man had caught him after seeing his guard was down, taking him by the arm with his burly hands, and struck.

* * *

It hurts... It hurts... What's going on? Where am I? Why can't I move? Why is my chest so wet? Why...? Why am I so cold? ...No. I don't like it. I don't like the cold. It makes me feel so tired. I don't like feeling tired.

Wait— What's going on? I couldn't see a thing just a moment ago, but now ... there's so much to look at. Ice. Snow. A barren land of nothing except that. But there aren't any people, animals, plants, or houses or anything. Where is everything?

This isn't right. I feel my eyes are closed, but I still see so much? This is so strange. I want to move. The ice under my arms is starting to burn. Can ice even burn? ...And where are my arms? I can feel the cold, but my arms aren't there. I can see everything happening around me, but I can't see myself. Where did all of this come from, and where am I now?

How long has it been since I came here? It feels like an eternity since I awoke to this accursed place. How much time has passed? What are my friends and family doing now? Are they worried about me? Sometimes, I feel I can hear their voices in my head ... which isn't there.

It is so creepy not knowing where my body is. And feeling things without it is so bizarre. Can I even find it the way I am right now—without any limbs to move?

Without a body, what am I?

I have been cold for so long I don't even mind it anymore. It's actually starting to feel nice. In my aloneness, in this frigid place, it's the only thing that keeps me company.

I'm starting to treat the cold like it is a person. Do people act like this when alone? I guess it is not so bad. It keeps my mind off of the bitter silence. Without it, I probably wouldn't feel alive anymore. It's like ... like it is hugging me, protecting me.

Hey, wait! What's going on? Why is the world moving? I can't see the sky anymore. Am I standing? Am I walking? But I don't feel my legs moving ... or whatever it is I'm using now. This could be good. Maybe I can get out of this place and find somebody, anybody who can help me... But this place is surrounded by water. Is there anything around here to build a raft with? Can I even build a raft?

Thinking like that won't get me anywhere. I may as well look. At least I don't feel hungry or thirsty or tired. None of that can stop me from looking for supplies.

Oh! There is something over there!

Maybe a branch. No, bigger—it has to be a log. That can float me off this iceberg. This is— This is... This— What is this!? I finally found my body, but ... it's not moving. My skin looks so pale I think it is starting to turn white. Is that ... blood? Blood is staining the ice ... and it's coming from that crack in my chest. Is that really me? Am I—

* * *

A gaggle of irritated voices woke Van from his slumber.

"Are you sure he is still alive?"

"Shut up, Jerrell!" That threatening snarl was unmistakable. "He's going to be okay. He ... he's going to be okay."

There was another, a third. "As unbelievable as it is, Jerrell, this boy is still with us. But the man who did this struck him with an axe. He will, at the very least, be unconscious for some time."

"Excuse me, Sir Knight... Are you sure he will be okay?"

"Yes, child. He is just tired and needs rest."

"I still can't believe Van was actually attacked..."

"I can't believe you attacked the man in a manner more barbaric than he. No, perhaps monstrous is more appropriate."

"What in the seven hells did you expect, Charlie? He tried to kill my son! If you're going to criticize me in my own home while he is like this, you can just get out of here before I throw your sorry arse—"

Four people within ear's reach. Jerrell. Victoriah. A third man he did not recognize. And then there was Mini.

They were all in one place watching over him.

Van's eyelids flicked open unsteadily. A wooden ceiling was over his head; they brought him back inside. And judging by that familiar patch in the ceiling, he was in his room—in the comfort of his bed.

Everyone scrambled over to his side after they heard him groan.

His mother clung to Van's head tightly like a steel trap. "Thank the gods you're okay!" she exclaimed. The waver in her voice revealed she tried to keep her composure.

"M-Mother, I ... I can't breathe..." Van felt he would split in two from the pressure of her death grip.

Victoriah did not want to harm her son more than he already had been and let go quickly, careful not to drop him hard.

"Boy, you are tough. Don't scare us like that again."

Victoriah then slugged her husband at the back of his head. She thought he meant it like their child tried to get attacked.

Van barely noticed what everyone around him did. A tearing pain kept his mind on his chest and prevented complete thoughts from forming. Everyone could plainly see he was suffering from his light, broken exhaling. It hurt so much he could barely keep his eyes open, and he shivered terribly. "S-So ... so cold," he groaned under his breath. It felt ridiculous saying that when his body was buried under three heavy blankets.

Victoriah left the room when Mini asked if he needed anything. Van could not say much more; his throat was sore and dry. He was worried his throat would crack and fall apart if he did anything but breathe.

A middle-aged gentleman in armor stood across the room examining a collection of tiny bottles, knives, and needles. His dapper blonde hair and pure red eyes had been exposed without the helm at his side to cover his head.

Under normal circumstances, Van would be thrilled to meet a knight, but now he did not know how it would be possible to feel glee.

"Charleston, how come he isn't saying anything?" Jerrell inquired.

The knight continued to pack away his supplies into his leather case after inspecting them. "He may be trying to cope with that new scar."

Van was too disoriented to understand how he got a scar. Hearing he had something he did not have before disturbed him. He had to see it for himself. Mini tried to keep Van from squirming, but this Charleston person intervened, wanting to see how well the boy's body could operate.

Every move Van made was agonizing. The slightest twitch made him want to stop moving altogether, but he had to see what happened to him. After mustering the strength to sit up, he noticed his skin returned to its true russet color. He looked down, noticing the Shift Pendant had been removed and something new had been in its place: a long, deep scar gashed across his abdomen from his right hip to the left shoulder. Looking down at it made him remember faint seconds when he saw the thick axe cleave through his body.

Victoriah returned carrying a cup. She hurried to her son's side. "Here, love. Drink this. You'll feel better." The cup had been filled with water— just what he needed for his dry throat.

Solaced by the promise of cold liquid, Van reached his shaky hands for the cup. Upon grasping it, he thought he had lost his mind. A white vapor suddenly covered his hands, and the water in the cup froze solid from his touch.

~ Second Chapter ~

Determination for Strength

Van lay lifeless in bed for what was left of the night. All his energy had been reserved for heavy breathing. He still could not believe how his shaken touch froze a cup of water. He tried to convince himself it was a wild dream, but he did not wake to the reality he desired.

He slipped into a bizarre half-sleep state, a blank gaze on his face. The pleasant feeling of being carried off into slumber never came. When all sight had abandoned him, sounds from every direction—near and far— filled his disoriented mind. A babbling brook from a far-off forest. Winds both gentle and stormy. The chirps, shrieks, and caws of birds. Cries of the shifting earth. The harrowing roars of beasts clashing with one another in endless battle.

The awful sounds raging in his mind overwhelmed him.

When he thought he could not take any more, a few familiar sounds suppressed and purged the thundering dissonance. Muffled though they were, Van easily recognized the voices of his parents. Whatever focus he had left was diverted to catching every word he could. Upon stilling his rapid breathing, cryptic masses of color filled his vision. Human silhouettes had taken form from the shimmering colors—a couple uneasy dark blue, the third flaring in an aggressive scarlet. An unknown word sounded from the calm silhouette with the voice Van did not recognize. He wished it repeated, but a brief gagging followed instead as the scarlet silhouette closed in and converged its arms around its neck.

He did not need to be fully conscious to know what occurred.

The other blue silhouette, now jolting yellow in alarm, attempted to pull Victoriah's from her victim. Victoriah might whack, smack, flip, tip, and restrain her husband on occasion, but she would never choke him. He remembered another came to visit earlier that evening, though not who it was. The silhouette retreating farther from the Wolverine had to be that same person. Since the voices were scattered, he needed to keep in mind who was who as the silhouettes occasionally changed color.

"If you *ever* call my son that again—"

"Calm down! This isn't helping anything."

"Do I look like I care?"

The burning silhouette grew more intense with each attempt to pounce at the one picking itself up. Had it not been for her husband holding her back, the stranger's silhouette would have disappeared before long. Slivers of fear and anxiety formed within him. He must have been attempting to keep his composure, hiding his apprehensions inside.

"Give me one good reason why I don't gut you right here!"

"Other than your shield will be revoked and you will be imprisoned for the murder of a fellow knight?" the stoic silhouette retorted. Even with the Wolverine acquiring her thirst for blood, the stranger acted as if he were in control of the situation. "I can tell you what happened to the boy."

That was reason enough for Victoriah to calm her fury, the intense flare from her silhouette diminishing. She wanted to understand what it was plaguing her child, and although he was not with them, so did he.

"You are ... with ... correct?"

No use. Pieces of the conversation slipped past him as he began forgetting what was happening. Van's focus began to break, his mind falling into the black.

Focus. Focus! he demanded of himself.

"—can only ... the ... he bears ... a Second—"

His strength faded. The connection he kept with the silent plane was severed. And he once again fell into a deep slumber.

*   *   *

Ugh ... why now? Why couldn't I hold on just a little—

This place seems ... familiar. Have I been here before? These roaring winds, blistering ice, fluffy snow, thick fog. There was no ice or snow at the cottage, so why did the air feel the same as this place? Where am I anyway? Why am I here?

Why so distraught?

W-Wha— Who said that? Where did those voices come from? ...Is there anyone else here? That bulge in the snow, is that one of them? Could he be the reason I am here?

All right, you, don't try anything. I won't be ambushed a second ti— No... No way. He looks just like me ... when I wear the Shift Pendant. But what's this? It looks like he's been living here forever: pale, snowy skin, faded blonde hair, gloomy blue eyes.

Aagh! W-W-What is wrong with you? Where did you get that scar? A-And why is your right arm frozen over? And your leg! What in the gods' names happened to you?

Wait a minute! Don't come any closer.

You have a look of curiosity in your eyes. Tell me, are you always so inquisitive, or is it merely because you've found yourself suddenly in this foreign plane of ice and snow?

He seems ... friendly? Go on, coward. Say something! Standing silent won't do you any good. "W-Who are you? Where am I? Why do you look ... sort of like me?"

This form does not please? Pity. I took it in hopes of easing your anxieties.

How is that supposed to make me feel better in any way?

Wait. Why are all of those voices coming from him? How are they all coming from him? How are they all speaking at once? What is he?

You are in my realm, mortal child. This is a place for the formerly dead to take refuge and recuperate before their revival. I believe your people once called it, and myself, Pruina.

"I have never heard of this place before..."

Out of touch with your culture? Quite a shame, truly. The Kindhrin were naturally proud of their heritage, or so I have seen. I am afraid I know little of your realm as it appears a blur from my—

"Wait, wait! You said 'formerly dead?' ...So that means I really did die."

Yes. You died, and you were dead. Hence the origin of this fine trophy—which, I must say, does not suit you.

My scar, a trophy?

Although, given time, perhaps it may. But that is beside the point. Listen well: you were dead, but now you live, thanks to my power.

"Well ... I appreciate it. But why did you give my life back to me?"

Even I cannot say for certain. Perhaps it is fate. Perhaps mere happenstance. The reason I encounter you passing souls has always escaped me. Only the strong connection you have to nature makes sense to me, as it is a rarity amongst humans. It is something most desirable indeed.

This spirit is an unusual thing.

Now then. Feroxis Maveronyn, kindred spirit yet to break free of deceptive shackles, I bestow my gift of mastery over the frigid nature to you. May it bring you to the truth.

Hold on. What are you doing? Take your hand off my— Agh! My ... my heart... My—

* * *

Sunlight from the window woke Van from his slumber to the reality he belonged in. This time, he remembered everything—from being spirited away to the frozen alter ego.

Morning had come, and Van finally felt he could move again. His body lost all numbness in his muscles and bones, thawed from the witch god of death's embrace. Yet even with the comforting rays of sunshine draped along his body, he still shivered.

How can I still be so cold?

Apparently, the "gift" Pruina bestowed came with a price. He hoped there was not much more to it than that.

More than ready to get out of bed, Van sat up but remained where he was after seeing his mother. She had taken a chair, probably late at night, and fell asleep sitting in it, her head resting against her shoulder.

How worried she must have been for him. Van crawled over to her on his knees, then gave her a gentle nudge. The frustrated Victoriah deeply grumbled a word of hostility under her breath. A wayward arm flung at Van and would have knocked him off the bed if he had not ducked.

"Jerrell ... not now. I'm still tired..."

Did she actually think she was in her bed sleeping like that?

"Mother, wake up. It's morning."

Victoriah thought herself still asleep. She could have sworn her husband's voice lost all masculinity and had taken the sound of a youngling's pleasing small, quiet—

Only when the thought that it belonged to her son reached her did she open her eyes. She drew them toward him, a look of mixed shock and elation in them.

The overjoyed mother took her child in her arms. She held him close and stroked his dapper white hair, and only released him when she realized he had been struggling for breath. "I'm sorry, love. Did I hug you too tight again?"

Van grunted upon feeling air reach his lungs again. The strength Victoriah wielded was more suited for crushing the skulls of her enemies rather than a motherly embrace. "I'm okay. I just need to get used to this new gash."

The freshly carved scar reminded its bearer of its presence. The fleshy marking pulsated irritably after the pressure applied to it. He had not forgotten it was there; it was like a chunk of him that used to be there was no longer. But after the hug, he felt as though what had been ripped away could still feel pain, pain which he received.

Van's stomach broke the awkward tension regarding his small body's new feature. His mother chortled. The only time she heard a stomach growl in such demand was when it came from her. When they heard her stomach snarling with his, they started to laugh. It had been a while since either of them had eaten.

Mother and son walked to the kitchen and dining room to see what they could fetch for themselves. With the oats, water, and fresh milk she earlier got from the village cows, she prepared a large pot of piping hot porridge over the burning hearth. Van loved her porridge. She crushed fresh berries and mixed in the juices to the porridge right when it was ready to eat. He tried to keep his mouth from watering while he waited, its tart scents teasing his nose.

Van looked across the homey room to distract himself, constantly eyeing the roof, and stopped when something seemed out of place. A brightly decorated cake with creamy white frosting, crowned by rich berries, sat on the counter where the mixing spoons used to be. Victoriah was never known to buy complete dishes when considering her loved ones. She only cooked food made with plenty of heart.

She made that just for me.

And not a dab of frosting was out of place.

His mother interrupted his dreary thoughts before he could go too deep, offering a wooden bowl full of porridge. Van accepted the dish into his hands with glee, a glee that slowly faded upon noticing the food's warmth never graced his palms. While the hands felt less frigid while holding the bowl's round bottom, his body was still plagued by the intense freeze. A tense chill startled him every few minutes, and he constantly breathed a white vapor upon exhaling. Van ate his meal with gusto, hoping to forget about the disturbing changes for just a minute, scarfing down all his spoon could take.

Was he unconscious for only a night? It felt like ages passed since he last ate.

Victoriah tried to contain her laughter while they ate. Seeing her son like this was a treat; he never ate so heartily before. It warmed her heart.

He would not pull away from the bowl after a single spoonful. Everything in the dish tasted much better than he remembered. Van loved berries and came to memorize the flavor from each one, but never had he savored such a sweet taste. His nose tingled too; he could smell every flavor inside the milk. His senses were so tantalized that he failed to notice his father's return.

Van only managed to put down his spoon after scarfing all of the porridge down. He saw his father at the door sighing in relief and starting to laugh after seeing the bits of porridge on his face. "It's good to see you up and about again, Van." He spoke in a boisterous tone. Jerrell normally kept his emotions under control, restrained, as many Vermalians did. Even if it did not show as well as his wife's, Van could tell he was genuinely concerned. "Your mother was up all night worrying if you would ever wake up."

"A mother worries for her child, Jerrell!" retorted Victoriah. "You should be more concerned for his well-being too."

Were his bowl full, Van would stuff his face to ease his guilt. He regretted ever stepping foot into the forest.

Van stared down at the table and wiped his face clean. "Mother, Father, I'm sorry. I heard something behind the house and thought to see what it was. This happened to me because I got careless. Please forgive me." For a child of nine years, he sounded prim and proper—thanks to the lessons on manners Jerrell gave him.

Neither parent knew what to say. Their child was blaming himself for the attempt on his life.

Victoriah stood from her chair and walked up to Van, giving him her gentlest hug. "This is nowhere near your fault, love. You didn't ask to be attacked. We don't blame you ... do we, Jerrell?" She leered at her husband, almost thinking he would believe otherwise.

But he agreed. "I only wish the barbarian was still alive so I could sentence him myself. But your mother took care of that."

Were Van not a child, Jerrell would have told him of the terrible scene in copious detail. Guided by rage and malice, Victoriah the Wolverine drew her sword and immediately dug the blade into the man's flesh, his rancid blood flying everywhere. He survived the impalement, only to suffer more. The enraged mother's iron fists battered the barbarian until they were covered in crimson. The only thing to snap her out of it was Timberhoof breaking out of his stall to trample the corpse with the hooves that gave him his name.

"I still feel I'm to blame..." Van sighed under his breath. "I wish I could have heard what that man told you last night."

Victoriah and Jerrell, alarmed, tried to assess what they heard. They thought Van had been asleep the whole night. When they asked what he meant, he told them about the strange half-conscious state he was in. He failed to tell them he did not hear everything, though. He began to feel discouraged by the disturbed looks they shared.

"Van ... do you want to hear a story?"

A strange time for one of his mother's tales. But they were always entertaining.

"A story? What kind of story is it?"

"A true one." For a moment, Victoriah seemed unsure, hesitant, but she looked away from her child and shook her head. She looked back to him with a more reassured expression, or rather one feigning sureness. "There was once a kingdom said to have existed at the center of the world. It was a prosperous nation, its people knowledgeable and resilient. Everyone there had this insatiable love for music and art, and worshipped them as if they were the voices of the gods." She paused for a moment, almost dreading to continue. "But despite this kingdom's prosperity, it had fallen into ruin. The people could not sustain their greed and lust for power, and became as demons. Their civilization collapsed and the people died out. Those people were known as the Kindhrin."

Kindhrin... That word sounded very familiar, but Van was too fixated on the story to recall why.

"One day, after the kingdom fell, a cloaked stranger appeared before a beautiful Vermalian woman. The stranger was weak and frail, but what the Vermalian paid the most attention to was the baby in her arms. It was adorable, a precious jewel. This baby ... was a Kindhrin, a survivor. The stranger pled for her to take care of the baby before thrusting it into her arms, and vanished into the dark of night.

"She could not go after her, not with the baby crying out in need. She did not know what to do. Though it was a stranger, she could not leave the precious thing alone, nor could she take it out into the open. When the woman's husband returned home, he went to track down the one who gave her the baby." Victoriah hesitated, unsure whether or not to leave something out, but came to a decision. "He managed to find the stranger, but ... he found her dead, beaten and beheaded.

"They couldn't abandon the baby to its fate. It was so small, so pure. It needed them... So they became parents to the Kindhrin baby, hiding it in plain sight from the rest of the country. And after the father got his new child a present, they decided on a name for him: Vandelas Kronas."

Vandelas ... Kronas? ...But that's my name.

The world before him began spinning with the confusing concepts of what was right and what was not. They were not really his parents? This was not really his home? It hit him hard enough that he bent over and glanced down at the floor.

Never once had he questioned why he was different from everyone else, nor why he had to wear that pendant. It was just a part of his life, a never-changing occurrence, something as normal as changing his clothes.

Unease shivered up Van's body and gripped it tightly. Had he not been sitting when told the truth, he would have fallen over. He tried to keep his breathing steady, but his frightened heart beating frantically against his chest riled up his burgeoning anxiety. Terrifying thoughts began plaguing him the more he came to terms with what reality became. He wanted to shut them out, shut the whole world out.

"Van, love, look at me."

Although he did not want to, Victoriah's tender voice beckoned to him. When he picked his head up, he caught a glimpse of a white vapor permeating the air around him. He looked back down at his chair when he thought he heard something, and saw a patch of frost slowly building beneath him. The frigid air parted and the frost crumbled upon his notice.

"H-How ... how is this happening?" Van's voice trembled.

Victoriah brushed her hand softly against Van's cheek. "You are living something called a Second Verse," she replied. "Try to stay calm, okay? I know this is scary, but you didn't escape the attack unharmed. You've already died once."

"Died once...?" Van exhaled a puff of white air when he spoke.

"The man from before is an old colleague of ours. He told us everything he knew," Victoriah continued. "The gods smiled upon you. They resurrected you and made you a Nascitte, a being with strong ties to nature and the power to control it with the Second Verse."

Resurrected? A strong tie to nature? Second Verse? There was too much happening at once for Van to keep up with. So many questions swarmed in his mind that he feared it would shatter.

Instead of trying to figure it all out, he hobbled back to his room for some more rest, a hand against his pounding skull.

Van did not rest soundly after blacking out. A terrible icy sting pestered him while he was under.

Learning that he was not related to his parents tortured him. It never dawned on him to question the differences in his skin or eyes, nor had he thought anything strange of the brands on his face. He never argued about wearing the Shift Pendant to appear like an average Vermalian. Now that he knew, he felt like a complete fool.

After a while, he realized he did not have the Shift Pendant on his person anymore. He spent three days searching high and low for the magic charm without any luck.

Van did not know why he bothered looking for it. He did not want to hide who he was now that he knew he was Kindhrin. Even so, he searched. He had been trying to avoid looking outside until there was no other place to check. Fear made him tremble when he reached for the door after his parents told him it was dangerous to be without the Shift Pendant. If anyone were to see him without it...

Rather than focus on that, Van put his efforts to finding the pendant and decided to seek help from Timberhoof.

He kept out of sight in case anyone decided to make their way to the home of Victoriah the Wolverine. Although unlikely, it was still a possibility.

Timberhoof was as happy to see Van as ever. To him, there was no change in the boy without his Shift Pendant. It made Van happy to see that. He stroked the gelding's nose and scratched his black mane as thanks, then asked Timberhoof if he knew anything about the pretty rock he usually wore. The warhorse waved his big head to the exit a few times.

Outside? Maybe it flew off into the grass when he was attacked. It would have been a good idea to start there.

It had to be somewhere. The gem on it was so bright a red it would not blend into the grass well. Van carefully searched the area outside the stall, careful to avoid getting too close to the hill, then reluctantly went over to the side of the cottage.

Going back to the spot he died was arduous. Fear lingered in his muscles, weighing them against the hesitant pull of his thoughts. There was still blood dried on the blades of grass. Was it his? Or his killer's? Either possibility made Van want to turn away and go hide in his bed.

But he needed the Shift Pendant. He might not like that he did, but if he was going to live his life as he had been, he could not be without it.

"You're finally awake!"

Van went rigid when he heard a voice suddenly speak up, and only relaxed when he realized it was a familiar one. He turned to find Mini walking up to him, wearing a red dress with pink floral patterns.

"Oh. Hi, Mini."

"How come you haven't come back down to the village? Are you still hurt?"

"Sorry, but I am not allowed to go to the village without my Shift Pendant. I shouldn't even be outside without it on."

Mini blinked, staring at him while he resumed his search. "Is this it?"

The rattle of an old metal chain stilled Van's hands combing through the grass. He turned back and was so surprised he jumped to his feet. In her hands rested the very crimson pendant he lost.

"I found it down the hill when Sir Jerrell walked me home."

It travelled that far? How was that possible? And how did Jerrell never notice the jewel in her little hands?

I suppose that doesn't matter.

He gratefully accepted it and again propped it around his neck. The pendant then glowed a faint yet noticeable light that slowly rippled along his body, instantaneously changing Van's appearance to a young Vermalian's, resembling his father. The girl's eyes dazzled at the transformation. "Wow! It really is magic," exclaimed Mini pleasantly. "That's amazing! I never thought I'd get to see something like this, what with magic disappearing from the land." She still remembered something a scholar that once visited the village told everyone. Not everyone believed him, but the village children took his words to heart. "And you can freeze water too. Why didn't you tell me you were a mage?"

Because I never could before I died, Van thought sullenly.

The familiarity between the two children allowed her to discern Vandelas from the change in his skin, the hue meant to be left unseen. He felt so confused. He was of a race of demons, yet Mini did not fear him.

"Mini ... why weren't you afraid of me?"

To that question, she laughed. "And why should I be? You're too ... quiet to be scary." She did not seem too sure of what she had said.

Not wanting to amuse the idea of being a demon, Van told Mini of the Kindhrin and his coming to be in the Kronas family quickly. The short girl listened curiously and paid close attention, and at the end of the story, she laughed again, treating it like a joke.

"If you wanted me to keep this a secret, you should have just said so," she put bluntly. "Your parents told me about you that night." When she noticed the uncertainty still written on his face, she stopped jesting and offered him sympathy. "We've known each other long enough for me to never think that of you. Relax. No one else will know about this, 'kay?"

Again, he felt very foolish. Had his mind become so distraught by the passing events that he would believe his friend would give him away?

She was as cheerful as ever until she gasped, pointing at Van's feet. Van, too, felt like jumping after seeing the grass around his sandals coat in frost. Once again, he used his power without intent, without control. It infuriated him enough that he thought to kick the frozen grass. But he stopped himself and stared into space instead.

That settled it.

That evening, Victoriah prepared a big dinner to celebrate Van's recovery and distract him from any talk of brigands.

Four more barbarians had been discovered scouting the area around Russalin. The knights have been on high alert as a result.

After sending word to the capital of the increasing brigand activity, Victoriah knew she would soon have to return to her duties.

Before the cake was served, Van made his announcement.

"Mother, Father, I want to become a knight."

His parents fell silent and their faces lost the joy they earlier showed. They looked to each other, appearing discouraged. Then Jerrell turned back to his son. "What is this about, Van?"

"My power won't be something small for long. I can feel it. It'll grow and grow and go out of control if I don't do something. You both told me how you learned discipline through your training, right? Mother, you told me it helped you control your anger? If I learn that discipline too, maybe I can keep my power under control."

Throughout dinner, Van froze three pieces of tableware, five drinks, and even the vegetables on his plate. In that brief moment of silence, another cold chill ran through the air, freezing the candles on the table.

Victoriah reached over to cup her son's hand. "Van, I know you're worried about your power, but this isn't the way to go about it. Being a knight is serious business—serious and dangerous. There are far worse things you would have to face than that monster who attacked you."

"That's why I want to do it!" Van stated firmly, enough to startle his mother. "This isn't just about the ice. I've been thinking a lot about this. Knights keep people safe when they are in danger and help those who need it. And I want to do that too. Please let me do this. I want to be a great knight just like the two of you!"

The day had finally come—the boy wished to follow in his parents' footsteps. Hearing that, neither of them could find the will to deny him any longer. He always liked helping people, and work as a knight would provide one of the grandest services to the people and the country.

But work as a knight would not be easy. The training needed to become one was an extensive trial. And Van already put himself under such strain just to control his power.

Jerrell, worried for the worst outcome, made a decision: before beginning his training to become a knight, he needed to learn better control over his Second Verse. For as long as it would take, Jerrell would teach him to forge the concentration capable of bending the ethereal power to his will. He would teach Van control of his power until they would not have to fear him freezing things unintentionally in the presence of watchful eyes. While it seemed a bit unfair to him for a moment, Van agreed to his father's terms.

A week passed.

As Victoriah predicted, she had been called back to duty to discuss the sudden rise in brigand activity in southern Vermalio. More places have been pillaged besides Russalin, each sustaining much more severe damage than the loss of a single child.

She and Timberhoof had to leave immediately. But she refused to head for the capital without seeing off her son.

Jerrell had sent for a coach to transport him and his son to the Sperov Mountains up north. Since that was on the way to the capital, Victoriah joined as an escort for as long as she was able.

Van occasionally looked out the window to say hello to Timberhoof. The gelding always tried to get close whenever he saw him. He was all too fond of the boy, and wanted to keep close to protect him.

After the sun began to set, Van watched the light gilding the sky, looking aloof. He had never been so far from home. It made him uneasy.

"What's the matter, Van?" Jerrell leaned closer to the boy. Thinking he knew what was going on in his head, he grinned. "You disappointed you couldn't bring Mini along?"

Van flashed him a glare remarkably similar to his mother's, the very glare she used to imply "Shut up, meathead!"

"Mini goes to faraway cities to help her mother sell clothes all the time. She told me she's kind of sick of travel." His answer almost sounded cold. He did not yet understand romantic pursuits, but he was not unaware of them—at least he thought.

Van had been quiet for much of the ride. He felt distant from his parents since learning they adopted him. The unwilling way Victoriah described the nameless stranger forcing him upon the young couple made Van believe they never wanted him and had no choice but to raise him.

Ridiculous, Van scolded himself for having such thoughts. And they kept returning.

Focusing on that was discomforting. He needed something to distract him. "Father, what was it like being a knight?" A rather vague question, but it was something. "I mean, what were all the bad things you had to see and do? What regrets did you have?"

Jerrell had a hunch he would ask that eventually. His son became more inquisitive post-death. "Where to begin?" he sighed. "You are right to assume being a knight isn't all glory—many people do, and they could not be more foolish." He paused before continuing, perhaps hesitant to speak of his blunders. "I have regrets aplenty, but ... if I had to pick one, I'd say it would have to be from a battle with those damned Pternites." Jerrell spoke of the war against the empire of Pterna often. It was a critical time when Jerrell was a squire, the Pternites threatening to lay waste to Vermalio and enslave its people. Had it not been for the drastic action taken by the crown prince of the time, Vermalio would have lost the war. "My meister knight was in charge of protecting the fort not far from Starscape. Though the enemy feared our army's strength, they were bold and daring. They attacked us in elaborate raids. Our stronghold was well fortified, but the enemy managed to find several ways to penetrate our walls. Casualties were inevitable, I knew that well. I regret not being able to help those who have fallen. I regret that others gave their lives to protect mine. Above all else, I regret failing to follow my duty.

"So many died in the surprise attack, many I knew well. They looked after me like a second family. Even my meister knight, Sir Pinesglen, fell to a most atrocious death—five swords impaling his mighty girth ... to protect me, his squire." Van's thoughts froze. He tried making the man's words into a portrait in his mind so as to better understand his father's point of view. The suffering, carnage, and gruesomeness were nonexistent to him, having never witnessed any of that, but the dim way Jerrell described the event and the dreariness in his eyes gave Van a faint understanding of the weight it left on him. "It was my fault. Since Pterna began attacking, I have been relentlessly training my mind and body to be more useful to my fellow soldiers. My body gave out in that battle because I exhausted myself—because I couldn't keep up." It was harder to hide his guilt and how it still plagued him the more he talked about the story. Soon, he stopped talking altogether, then tried to distract Van with something he pretended to see out the window.

It was something of an awkward ride for much of the way. If Van was not the one to keep himself to his own thoughts, then it was Jerrell. Apart from the father teaching his son about the geography or weather or the kinds of animals that were likely nearby and the potential places for them to hide, they rarely spoke to each other.

When it came to rest, Victoriah and the coachman competed to see whose stories were more entertaining, which put a little more life back into their listeners.

And on one quaint midday, it came time for Victoriah to leave.

Time for her to leave again.

Van stepped outside the coach when it came to a halt to say goodbye to his mother.

"Do you really have to take him there?" Victoriah asked her husband. "Those mountains are dangerous this time of year."

"The blizzards there will help his training," insisted Jerrell. "Having him in his element is the best way for him to learn control of it."

"Can you at least wait for midwinter?"

Asking that now only served to delay their parting. One could hardly blame her. She had not long ago seen her child dead on the ground.

Upon relenting, she sighed and kneeled down to her son's level. She brushed his false blonde hair aside, giving his forehead a light peck. "Just be careful. Don't go dying again, okay?"

Van nodded. "Promise."

With a heavy heart, Victoriah mounted Timberhoof again and rode off into the horizon with a tap of her boot against the steed's side. Van watched as his mother fled from him yet again.

Does she really feel bad about leaving...?

Days of uneventful travel followed Victoriah's departure. They took the safest possible route to the Sperov Mountains, the coach steered down a flat, hard path. They kept their guard up whenever they stopped for rest, on the watch for any predators or rogues that braved the jagged pass.

Soon, the coach came to its final stop. The sun was making its descent over the horizon. Van watched the scenery around them pass by from the window most of the way, grasping the only sense of relief he could find as time passed.

"We have reached our destination, sirs," the coachman hollered back to them. That was their cue to get off.

Van was nervous about being in this new environment. A certain vibrancy in the air put him at ease, though. He was not certain what shackled his nerves but chose not to question it. He wanted a good look around. The window only offered so much of a view—a rugged earth with few trees rooted into it and flecks of white falling from the sky. When he stepped out of the coach and onto the rough ground covered with snow, he got a good look at the stone giants clad in the silver cloaks. The Sperov Mountains stood over them in divine majesty, serene beauty, that reached the heavens and very nearly penetrated the clouds. Groves of thin yet broad trees bristled along the backs of the giants, seemingly random at the higher altitudes but were gathered along their bases, laying out paths for daring souls to begin their trek.

Quite the monument, wouldn't you say?

Van jumped. He heard voices like those before, cryptic and flowing harmoniously together. They were the voices that Pruina spoke with. He had not encountered the spirit since that fateful night. It seemed he could make himself known whenever he desired. Invasive as it felt, Van quickly lost the will to protest. The spirit revived him, gave him power; they were likely connected through that very power.

"I am sorry, sir." That voice, belonging to their chauffer, firm yet timid, was more welcome. "I'm afraid this is as far as I can take you. The horses are exhausted and... Well, they simply cannot tread mountains of such scale."

Jerrell handed a sack of lev to the coachman as payment. "This should do us fine. It was very kind of you to take us this far."

The adults still had something to talk about, so Van let them discuss their business while he took it upon himself to visit the horses.

The coachman was right. They did look tired. The two beasts of burden that pulled the coach—a white mare with a spotted black mane, a gray stallion with umber streaks along his back—were breathing heavily. Sweat trickled over their bodies. The cold air offered them some relief. Approaching them calmly, Van pulled out a few carrots from the satchel his father had given him. Pamela and Quicksilver, he remembered the coachman calling them, flicked their ears up in delight. "I don't know if you can have these, but you worked really hard. I won't tell your master if you don't." Regardless of their feelings toward the coachman, both horses gladly accepted the gift. The looks across their long faces had not changed, but somehow Van knew they were grateful.

"Van, come on!"

He gave both horses a gentle stroke on their noses when they finished eating, saying he would see them again. Pamela called out when she saw the boy rushing toward the mountain, sounding worried. She recognized this part of the region, and feared it.

Van smiled at the mare. "Don't worry. I'll be fine."

Their trek up the mountains began without delay. The paths steep and the snow thick, it promised to be a challenge. Van and Jerrell wore the thickest winter clothing they could find available from Mini's mother, the village seamstress. The protection restricted their movements, making it more difficult to trudge through the layers of snow, but it would keep them from freezing to death—or at least one of them.

Their hike continued for several hours, and even though they had gone a great distance, high enough that the clearing they began at was barely visible, there was still a long way to go. If they continued at the rate they moved, they would reach the first summit in a matter of days.

His training would begin then.

As sundown came, the snowfall grew into a blistering storm. The frigid winds did not tire Van, rather the force with which they blew. He felt ready to surrender to the snow's embrace.

"Keep moving, son!" Jerrell called out to him. "We need to get out of the wind. Bear with it a little longer. Show some of that spirit you always have!"

Spirit? What spirit? This isn't exactly a game I played back home. Van's thoughts spun in a vicious whirlwind, but then calmed when he thought of the reward to come. *It doesn't matter,* he decided. *So long as I can get stronger, I don't care what I have to do.* The wish for strength bolstered Van to force himself through the snow. Adopted or not, being the son of two renowned knights meant he had to be strong. If Jerrell could get through this even with his injuries, then so could he.

The mountain winds grew savage, threatening to throw the climbers back down to the earth where they came from. But they did not waver. Both braved the winds and defied the screams of the wraiths hiding within them, focused on only advancing farther.

The bellowing winds were impossible for Van to put out of mind. They almost made him believe that lost spirits did haunt the mountain.

Then, from the vortex of bellows, an innocent scream broke through.

The snow spoke, he was sure of it. A weak yelp reached him. It was small, feeble, and helpless—a cry for help. Van turned to the direction it came from, worried. The cry became clearer, the fear it carried too great to ignore. Upon picking up where it came from, he quickly followed it.

"Van!" Jerrell yelled through the winds. "What are you doing?"

"I can hear something. Someone is crying!" Maybe it did not make sense, but that was what was happening. Whoever or whatever cried out was in trouble. He had to help.

"Hey! Van, come back!"

He would not stand idle. He ran back the way they came to locate the voice. It pierced through the winds—an arrow of sorrow wavering and dwindling the farther it travelled. He took the pitches deep inside his mind, narrowing it further to the point it originated from.

Making a sharp turn, Van slid down a steep hill. The cries came directly from the heap of snow at the bottom. He dug into it the moment he reached it.

Van cringed, a sharp pain sprinting over his hand. Three small fresh cuts opened around his palm, the snow beneath him becoming stained in speckles of crimson.

The crying turned into a light growl reverberating from the hole that he dug. Inside lay a small white fox glaring at the human child with dimming blue eyes. On its claws clung the blood snatched from him, but much of the crimson staining the fur on its foreleg was from its own.

Van crouched down to get closer to the injured animal all the while blocking out the winds that would have buried it again. He said nothing and sat there with an inspiriting smile.

The sounds of the world around them faded. For a time, there was no blizzard, only the two of them as Van conveyed the wish to help this poor creature. The fox did not seem convinced, still giving off a vile snarl. Van understood how frightened it was, how it feared he had come to harm it, how it would not be able to struggle for long. He simply looked at the fox, remaining calm.

The fox kept its guard up, its body trembling. But as they kept looking to each other, it began to quiet its growls and hide the fangs. Soon, it relaxed, and its bristled fur fell back into place. The fox stood and attempted walking out on its own, but its legs wobbled and shook. It fell safely into Van's outstretched hands before brushing its still bleeding foreleg against the snow.

In that moment, they connected.

Van got back on his feet while bringing the fox to his chest. Even in his intent to shelter it, the fox seemed just as ready to surrender its life as it was in the snow.

"Van!"

Jerrell's voice ruptured the silence that captured the boy and his new animal friend. He was aflame with rage over his thoughtless actions, but once he saw what rested in his arms, Jerrell lost his infuriated composure. The same thing happened when Van returned home late one night with a hungry cat. He even looked at his father with the same innocent eyes he had used when pleading to help the cat.

Not bothering with a gruff tirade like last time, Jerrell instructed his son to follow him, promising to patch its wounds after they found shelter.

Their fates seemed bleak as the night. Nothing suitable for shelter presented itself. The path slowly became gray, blending with the sky. Predators would likely be on the prowl looking for scarce prey, and would relish sinking their fangs into rare humans and a wounded snack.

Lady Sundralla, the goddess of luck, granted them mercy when they climbed to a cliff that towered mightily above them. It was ideal for hiding from the winds, but the wall itself was not enough for a decent shelter.

And they were out of time.

Taking advantage of the desperate situation, Jerrell decided to make it an exercise for Van. His idea was sound, but Van was uncertain he could do it. His powers had been erratic up to this point.

But he did not have the time to worry about what he could and could not do. He had to.

Entrusting the wounded fox to his father, Van hurried over to the side of the cliff wall and began by piling snow up with his hands. As slow as the progress was, it started speeding up when he froze the snow over, making a rising wall of ice. He stopped a moment, unaware of how his ability was triggered at first. He just kept sculpting the ice while listening to his father's words about maintaining focus and feeling the power inside him. It was hard to ignore as it was; the Second Verse coursed through him like blood, pulsing through him with an eerie force that fluctuated with his focus. He pushed himself to keep building the snow upward and mounting the peaks with ice until the deathly cold winds were closed off from Jerrell and the fox.

Van fell to his knees when the task was finished, gasping for breath. It took more energy than he anticipated. He did not fall unconscious after a single use this time, which made him feel empowered, although his fingers did burn with hypothermia.

Jerrell built a fire with the dry wood he brought from the foot of the mountain while Van rested with the fox. The fox's injuries were wrapped in bandages he thought would be used on himself or his son. The entire time, Van acted as the poor thing's guardian protector, keeping it safe in his little arms, and kept from freezing it further by wrapping it securely in his coat.

"Van, take your coat back!" Jerrell ordered upon noticing. "You'll freeze to death!"

"I'll be fine." It was hard to reassure his father with his voice sounding so tired, almost emotionless. "This will keep it warm. I'll only make it colder if I don't hold it like this."

Jerrell cupped a hand over Van's shoulder, ready to force him to obey, but jolted backward when he felt his exposed skin. It was like ice.

Van's body core temperature had not dropped even in that frigid climate. The cold weather could not harm him anymore, ever since he reawakened with the Second Verse. The gift came with a few advantages, perhaps more than he realized. It was still too early to tell.

Jerrell dropped the matter after realizing that and pulled out a large blanket for him and his compassionate son. Their bodies drooped with exhaustion from the climb, but they could not yet rest. Neither would say to the other how Van's new abilities troubled them. They both feared some tragedy befalling someone, somehow, because of it.

~ Third Chapter ~

It Begins

Two years—that was how long Van spent in the Sperov Mountains honing his control over the Second Verse.

Every month or so, they climbed down the mountains to test Van's capability to keep from unconsciously freezing anything. It was not so simple when the temperature was always so low. It became unnecessary after the third month, their efforts paying off, but Jerrell proposed taking it a step further and find out how much control he could muster over the Second Verse. Van made no objections out of respect for his father and kept his grievances about wanting to train with weapons sooner rather than later to himself.

Mastering control over his power was not easy. That night he crafted a shelter for him and his father without flaw was pure luck and desperation. After that, he could scarcely control what he froze and when.

Fortunately, he had his father to guide him.

The way his Second Verse worked was similar to magic.

An ethereal energy flowed through, with, and around life itself—an energy that occasionally caused alterations to simple elements on its own. That energy was bound to all of nature and refined to be more powerful by the hands of those who wielded magic. And upon use, the energy returned to the world stronger than before. In order for a person to possess magic, they must possess something about their souls that was especially strong. Although similar, the Second Verse did not abide by the same principles. Van became more aware of that the more he used it; the energy he controlled did not change, as opposed to when a spell was cast, yet contributed to the cycle regardless.

As promised, upon his return home, his parents wrote in a request to the most reliable noble family they knew to train him as a page.

The wait was excruciating. He had to be patient for so long already. His parents commented on how patient he could be, but Van always laughed on the inside.

His only thoughts were on his acceptance or denial into a page training facility. He spent the time practicing swinging a stick like one would a sword outside. His father attempted to teach him the basics of swordplay. He showed the least improvement there compared to the other exercises given to him, and kept striving to do better.

Mini and his other friends sometimes went up the hill to see how he was doing, but Van pushed them away in pursuit of training. He agonized over his poor swordsmanship, allowing that poor decision to be made. He wanted to beat the ice out of himself for shooing them away and to go play with them while he could, but something held him back.

He changed after deciding to better himself, to seek further control of his power and test his limits. The changes were small and gradually appeared with time, but he recognized them. They did not really concern him until it affected how his friends looked at him.

A week more of waiting was all he had to put up with. A message arrived via a trained carrier bird.

Surprisingly, Van paid more attention to the pigeon than to his father reading the letter aloud. It had been staring at him since he came into his parents' bedroom, as though seeing something that set him apart from the other humans. It seemed dreary and lethargic. As strange as it was, he understood what it was feeling from just one look at it.

It's hungry.

Van slipped away for a minute without notice, rushing to the kitchen to grab a slice of the bread Victoriah made the morning before. By the time he returned, the hungry bird had already flown off.

He was disappointed, but his parents seemed thrilled.

"Van—" Jerrell took a breath for a moment of suspense, which Victoriah quickly broke going to her child, kneeling to his level, ruffling his hair. "They've accepted you, Van! Come autumn, you'll be a page at the Estrine Chateau in Brigadier."

"The capital?" Van uttered. Brigadier was even farther from his home than the Sperov Mountains. The Vermalian royal family lived there, something he had been taught at a young age.

More waiting, huh? At least now I know I have my chance.

Throughout the summer months, he became less tense, as he was the years before, and went to visit his friends in the village. He could not afford to let his body grow soft because he had been accepted, but that did not mean he could not be with the children he grew fond of over the years.

They were easy to find. Everyone made it a habit to meet at the southern edge of the village near the flower beds. Van went to meet them as soon as he heard the news. There, he found Mini showing off a chromatic caterpillar she found to the others—Davern, Brute, and Marina. She thought it was cool, as the boys had, but the ever-snippy Marina cringed and gagged at the sight of the insect.

Davern Lyone never got along with anyone his age. He preferred harvesting knowledge from books over playing with the other children. Everyone tried avoiding him because he was so pale and scrawny, thus leading him to stay enclosed at home. But he began to slowly open up when he met Van, the only child to take an interest in his knowledge.

An especially burly child, Brutus Terrin often bullied other children for being ostracized for his unusual size. It began when he lashed out at the other children out of anger for the oldest ones bullying him. The vicious cycle had no end until Van saw the bullies terrorizing Brute and attacked them, waving around a stick like a maniac. The two have been friends ever since.

Marina Fleuriau of Rivièredell was an occasionally prissy Ederean girl who settled in the village not long after her mother, a servant, became employed by a Vermalian noble who enjoyed travelling abroad. Since her mother did not want to constantly rove from one country to another without her precious daughter, she set Marina up with a trusted foster home in Russalin. Marina often got herself into trouble because of her attitude, but she eventually found her place after befriending Mini.

With everyone being an outcast in their own way, it made sense for them to come together.

"Hey!"

The excitement they all shared died down when Van announced his arrival. A few of them seemed glad he finally came out to play, but other than that, they were surprised.

Marina, who sat in the flowers, stood and smirked. "Finally decide to come down from your palace, Vandelas?" she taunted.

Van did not blame Marina for her ill-tempered reaction, though Brute nudged her, and Davern fell over in Marina's place when the bully knocked her into him.

After helping the frail Davern up, Mini approached the Ederean girl. "Mari, what was that for?" Though Mari was prickly to a fault, her friends knew her well enough to know the difference between her playful teasing and her being rude.

"What? Do you expect me to treat him any differently? The lad goes off with his father for two years, leaving my host family to look after his home upon Sir Jerrell's request, and comes back without so much as a 'Good day.' You all saw that haughty attitude he brought back with him—practically sent us away. He thought himself too good for us."

Van made no excuse. No one should treat their friends so coldly regardless of what transpired. "I may have been under some stress, but I shouldn't have treated you all so rudely. I'm sorry. Truly."

Brute scoffed for a moment, folding his arms. "Well, that wasn't any worse than how Mari would have treated us, I say."

"Wha— You oaf! Such talk isn't proper when speaking of a lady."

"Since when have you been a lady?"

Mari gritted her teeth and spread her claws like a wildcat reaching for her prey. It took both Van and Mini to keep her from gouging Brute's eyes out she lashed at him so angrily.

She calmed down quickly, much faster than her temper normally allowed. After remembering who she was first upset with, Mari looked to Van and mumbled, "At least you have more class than this lout."

They let go of her when they were certain she would not attack anyone else.

As they saw upon his return a month ago, Van had grown from the journey he had taken. He grew nearly ten inches in height, and his muscles formed. Those changes seemed appropriate after he told them he would be a page come autumn.

After everyone settled down, he explained everything to them about his admittance into the Estrine family's tutelage and how tense he became worrying over if his efforts were not enough. Everyone was ecstatic to hear the news, whereas Mari remained apathetic.

"You're never happy for anyone, are you?" groaned Davern.

Mari pouted as she turned her head from him. Her disapproval had been greatly accentuated in her narrowed eyes. "As honorable a desire it is, wanting to be a knight, 'tisn't very profitable work. Any lev you earn will only be put toward weapons, armor, mounts—anything a knight needs. Only the most esteemed knights can afford to use their lev to make a difference for themselves or others."

Mari knew as much as she did about knights and everything they required from her mother, a woman who learned enough from the men in her country to know the finer points of knighthood without sugarcoating anything.

"And Van, I mean this in the kindest possible way—" which meant she thought of this in the harshest way possible "—but being a noble raised as you have been, you can't handle the training like others our age can. Your parents coddled and sheltered you in this quiet province. You never had any training to protect yourself when you were younger. Have your parents even taught you about the life a knight leads?"

His friends spoke up to defend him, but what Mari said left its weight on Van. Those words were blunt, forceful, and unrelenting.

"I'm thinking about more than the stories and the promise of glory; I'm thinking about what is real. You should try it."

While the others took Mari's attitude as scorn, Van did not. Her rare personality sparked a fire in his spirit. The snippy responses that left her did not demean him. What she told him about the realities of knighthood did not smother his determination. Instead, his passion burned brighter with the attempt to dissuade him.

"If it will be so hard for me, then it'll mean all the more when I do become a knight."

His retort earned him a stern glare from Mari. How he took her blatant negativity into a positive made her hair stand up. But she lightened up and traded her frown for a smirk. "I know how stubborn you can be. Fine then. I support you too. Happy now?"

Van grinned. "Very."

That summer, Van spent all the time he could with his friends because come autumn, he would not see them for a long time. The five spent their days having so much fun they lost the strength to keep up. Friendly competition helped motivate their pastimes: hide-and-seek, catch the witch, climbing trees, shooting targets with Davern's slingshot.

Van tried not to overexert himself too often. During his training, he learned that a thin vapor wafted from his body whenever he was hot, almost like sweat. He even exhaled it when he breathed too heavily.

Sometime in the late summer, Mari returned to Ederea after her mother's service with the nobleman had suddenly ended. As harsh and direct as she was, she was a part of their group. It was sad to see her go.

Despite the loss of their friend, the summer was a memorable one.

The adults have been offering advice and showing them new things. One of the blacksmiths in the village offered to show Van and his friends how he forged weapons and armor; it brought a wide smile to Brute's face when he saw the sparks fly from the man's hammer falling onto hot metal. The chef at the inn showed them how to prepare a variety of simple dishes. Mini's mother, the village seamstress, demonstrated how to stitch and sew together unsightly tears in cloth.

"I know this isn't something a lot of men like to learn," the seamstress told the curious Van specifically, "but this will come in handy when you are out on the road as a knight."

Van was grateful for everyone's advice, but their kindness left an uneasy weight in his chest. He did not remember any of them, aside from Mini's mother, being so nice to him before.

They must be eager to get rid of me.

The next Harvest Festival was nearing before they realized it. Page training commenced a week after the festival. If Van planned to make it in time to settle in, he needed to leave two days before the festival.

That day came sooner than anticipated.

While his parents made preparations for the trip, Van decided to go into the village and say goodbye to his friends. He did not know how long he would be gone or whether or not he would see them again when he returned. After all, Mari left. The others might as well.

While Davern and Brute hid their emotions well, as young men were expected to, he knew they would miss him. So they would not part with sad thoughts, Van promised to teach them both how to wield a sword when next they met.

Saying goodbye to Mini was much harder. Although she supported his choice, she kept saying how dull it would be without him around and worrying about what would happen to him. Van promised to write often to ease her concerns. The quirky girl smiled and joked around saying she looked forward to seeing his penmanship improve, but she still seemed distraught.

It could not be helped.

His parents were already waiting for him by the time he climbed up the hill. Everything was ready for them to leave. While Victoriah went back into the cottage to retrieve her sword, Jerrell reinstructed their son how to mount a horse.

Timberhoof's body looked lower to Van than he remembered. He had grown a little more during the summer—already four foot nine.

So much time has passed, he thought fondly.

Soon, he would be able to ride a horse of his own, like Timberhoof, maybe even bigger.

"Time to mount up, Van," Victoriah called from the stable entrance.

The eager dreamer led Timberhoof outside. For a moment, he thought he forgot his Shift Pendant, but saw his skin was as pale as his father's. That stone was the only thing he must never be without.

As Victoriah circled her mount and climbed aboard its wide back to show her son how it was done, Jerrell clamped a hand over Van's shoulder. "You'll make us proud, son. I know it."

It was rather unlike his father to disregard instructions and put encouragement in its place. It was different from what he expected, and it meant the world to him. For him to say that, he knew he would.

He went up to Timberhoof and readied to mount him. Though he was not as tall, he managed to get up top on his first try. The decision was immediately regretted, as his legs nearly split apart. Van gritted his teeth and forced himself to keep from crying out, the pain excruciating.

"You'll get used to it. I felt that way when I first mounted a full-grown warhorse too," Victoriah reassured.

With goodbyes already said, the family split apart once again at Victoriah cracking the gelding's reins. Movement only made the pain between Van's thighs worsen, the tear between them slowly ripping until he felt it etch his spine. He tried taking deep, slow breaths to distract himself from it. Taking in the surroundings and keeping focus only on what he saw and heard allowed him to disconnect his senses from the pain, working wonders, if only for a while.

They were not riding very fast, but the wind brushing against Van felt refreshing all the same. It calmed him down enough to forget the pain he was in.

After they rode some distance outside the village, he began to hear someone's voice. It was strange considering they took a route away from the village to avoid drawing attention. The voice belonged to someone he could not ignore.

"Van!"

Victoriah must have heard it, too, because she pulled Timberhoof to an abrupt stop.

Looking back, Van saw someone running their way. He almost could not believe his eyes, but after hearing the voice again, he could not deny it. It was Mini. She ran his way as fast as she could until tripping over herself on top of a small hill. She got back on her feet, panting heavily, then cupped her hands over her mouth.

"Van," Mini called out to him, "become the greatest knight ever!" When the message reached him, she took her hands from her mouth and gave him a great big smile.

Though he felt a strong chill from hearing her say that, his chest briefly brimmed with a strangely comforting sensation. He smiled and waved back, exclaiming, "Count on it!"

Victoriah brought Timberhoof to a trot when the children said what they needed. Van kept waving to Mini until she was completely out of sight. Seeing her go through the trouble of chasing him down to give him her support made him feel all the more confident. Everyone important to him believed in him. Now he knew nothing would stop him from becoming a knight.

Victoriah and Van had crossed many acres of land by the time the Harvest Festival began. They visited a few quaint towns fairly larger than Russalin to rest and stock up on food.

Timberhoof was fast, superior in speed to any gelding. Running at a full sprint made his passengers never worry about making it to their destination on time, though riding atop him made enjoying the lush terrain incredibly difficult. So much passed their eyes that it blurred together in a smear of vibrant color.

There were days when they never reached a settlement to rest at. When that happened, they camped, which Van found enjoyable. Many of the towns were much bigger than Russalin and more crowded than the little village. The change left Van a little uncomfortable. Victoriah laughed when he compared their home to one of the towns. "Just wait until we get to Brigadier. You'll be more than impressed." He would have asked what she meant at the time if he were not distracted by a squirrel he saw perched on a branch and looking down at them curiously.

There were only a few days left until the Estrine family expected them. Fortunately, they were making good time. With all the running Timberhoof did, they only had a hundred miles or so left to go. If they continued as strongly the next day, they would make it by sunset.

That night, the serene twilight sky was clear, and the stars shone brilliantly. While Van set up camp, Victoriah cooked dinner. Since they could not celebrate his eleventh birthday like they always had, they made do with his favorite dish, her special stew.

Van had no complaints. He was too eagerly scarfing down the stew once it was finished to care how they spent his day.

It made Victoriah smile to see her child have such a hearty appetite. "How about I teach you how to make it the next time you come home?"

Van nodded and sealed the deal by asking for a fourth serving.

Victoriah happily took his bowl and returned it filled to the brim. "Try not to be so voracious when you're a page, okay, love? They're not going to give you more food just because you ask for it."

He promised not to cause too much trouble in between messy slurps.

It was surprisingly easy for Van to sleep that night. He was normally restless when he tried to sleep, always tossing and turning and never finding the perfect spot to get comfortable. Something about the shift in the seasons put him at ease, though, as though nature itself wanted to comfort him. Van had only a moment to ponder on the many mysteries of nature before drifting off into a deep, dreamless sleep.

The weather was breathtaking the next morning. The wind blew crisp and warm with the aroma of dying leaves. Not many obstacles blocked their path on the way to the capital. As they rode, Victoriah looked toward the sun. Judging by its angle, they were ahead of schedule.

There was a river down the road with a few trees slowly going dormant for the coming winter. Victoriah stopped there to water her horse and had her son fill their waterskin. Van checked the water beforehand, then followed his mother's instructions.

As his hands neared and occasionally touched the water, Van constantly took slow, deep breaths. He needed to remain calm to prevent the Second Verse from reacting and freezing the water.

Victoriah took the opportunity to clean her armor and wash her hair and face. Their bodies were still covered in dirt, but taking a proper bath never crossed either of their minds.

While they rested, Van and Victoriah lay back in the grass completely relaxed, eating strips of dried, salted jerky. Timberhoof trotted around the area, careful not to waste energy, and remained in his mistress' sight while he regained his energy.

"Mother," spoke Van, breaking the silence, "did you train with the Estrine family too?"

She chortled lightly. "That I did." Her eyes sparkled from the memories returning at that simple question. "Only the toughest, strictest mentors for me. It was a lot of hard work and studies without much time to rest. For someone like me, the training was a little dull. But it wasn't all bad—met your father there during my second year."

"You met Father there?"

"Yeah. The meathead was aiming to be more of a tactician than a knight, but that didn't sit too well with the Estrines. He sought me out for a little advice about combat after he saw me throw three boys on their arses. My studies were slipping, so we helped each other; I whipped him into shape, he helped me cram for everything I didn't understand. He wasn't that big a man, kind of like you, but he was pretty tough. He even tossed me off my training horse after just one try at a joust."

It was difficult to believe at first, his father besting his mother.

"Father was a great knight, huh?"

Victoriah nodded. "Put me to shame on a few occasions. You wouldn't believe how disappointed I was when I heard about his retirement." She paused a moment, seeming to regret her words. Her voice became a bit rushed and distressed when she tried to rephrase her thoughts. "Don't get me wrong: I'm glad that your father kept you safe, but it's never easy hearing that a good knight hung up his shield."

Van felt the same way after the attack back when he was five. Seeing Jerrell admit he had to give up his role as protector made something crack inside him, but seeing the terrible injuries to his arm and leg hurt even more. After his father's retirement, he learned Jerrell mainly accepted so he could limit his responsibilities to protecting Van instead of an entire country, putting less strain on his crippled body.

He began to fear attacks on his village. Jerrell, without something to look after, might follow his old sense of duty and jump into the danger if it showed himself. "One thing's for certain: we don't have to worry about your father, even if he is a broken knight," Victoriah added, stretching out her arms. "He may not be a monster like me, but he is not a force to be trifled with."

As an imposing knight or nurturing mother, Victoriah knew how to put her son at ease.

With clothes dried, Van redressed himself in his plain tunic and dark auburn pants, a vibrant red sash wrapped between them over the waist. Those were his best clothes. Suddenly, he began to worry if the nobles would find him improperly dressed.

The thought quickly left his mind when he saddled back onto Timberhoof again with Victoriah. The pain burned through his legs as it had whenever mounting the massive war-beast.

You lied, Mother. I'm not used to this...

Pain became the furthest thing from his mind when he saw a great stone body rising steadily over the horizon. A blot of tall structures appeared not long after they went on the move. And as it grew more by the passing second, Van grew all the more excited, and could soon hardly breathe when the walls of the city loomed overhead. They were enormous, perhaps as big as the giants his parents told him of from fairy tales. For a moment, he worried they would fall on him.

"Good day, Vicci!" Before Van realized it, they had already passed the gates—a stone arch leading inside the gargantuan wall. A man in chain mail and a helm holding an inornate spear waved to Victoriah the Wolverine. Unlike the other knights who stood guard, this one seemed a rather friendly sort.

"Oh. Good day, Gervall," Victoriah greeted. "Keeping the peace?"

"Just like always," the guard replied in an upbeat tone. He seemed oddly welcoming for a disciplined member of the city's militia. The air about him was rather docile, but it tensed up a little upon seeing the new face. "Oh. You finally pick up a squire?"

"Nah," Victoriah replied, taking a quick pause to dismount from her fierce mount. "He's my son," she finished when he dismounted to the other side.

Van looked up to the guard. His eyes were buried beneath the thick helm, so he could not tell if he was surprised or intrigued. Van only recently learned to read the emotions from the energy flowing around and within people—their valsara—using his magic sight.

"So he's the one I heard whisper about. I always wondered when you and Sir Jerrell would plan on sending a child off to be a knight."

"I have nothing to do with it. This was his idea." Victoriah took Timberhoof's reins, petting his thick skull, to lead him. "Van, this is Gervall Canvast. He's an old friend from my squiring days."

Van straightened his posture. This man was probably of high society despite his casual speech. His mother used a form of speech almost like a common northern highlander, but he could not help thinking he expected something from him. "Hello, sir. I am Vandelas Kronas of Southern Valley. It is a pleasure to meet you." Van struggled to keep his spine straight while bowing.

The guard laughed, his armor rattling.

Did I do something wrong already? thought Van.

"I see he takes after his old man. You couldn't have taught him how to be that polite." He had to have been familiar with Victoriah in some way. "Glad to meet you, Vandelas. I'm part of the Estrine family's guard. You need anything, just come find me, okay?"

"That is very kind of you, sir. Thank you." Van could not help being formal. His body, tense from the freeze, kept him cautious of new people.

Gervall returned to his post, and Van and Victoriah continued onward to the Estrine estate. Immediately, Van's attention turned to the large stone buildings surrounding them on all sides. The cabins and huts from the towns and villages were old, run-down shacks compared to these monstrous foundations. Most buildings appeared to be involved in one business or another: jewelers, armories, grocers, tailors, and dress shops galore. For a moment, he seemed startled and a little worried the buildings would all come crashing down, but he calmed quickly and prepared to adapt to this change in his life.

While they marched through the street, Victoriah handed Van Timberhoof's reins. She told him how her mount got lost if she took her eyes off him for too long while staying in the big city. Van had the feeling his mother was not worried about her horse getting lost, though.

"Not as glamorous as you'd expect, Van?"

He begged to differ. While they were in the fields, he would not have thought such tall structures could be so impressive.

"I bet you a silver lev you can figure out where the royal palace is."

If it was as monumental as his parents described, it would have to be the largest, most heavily fortified building there, and the most impressive as well. With all the other buildings in his way, though, Van was not sure whether or not he would be able to spot it. It took him a few guesses, but when he turned to the north, he found it—a grand palace made up of several towers with an immense, round structure past its center.

"Are pages trained there too?"

"No, but squires are knighted there after their meister knights recognize them."

Timberhoof yanked Van over to his side every now and again. It looked like the burly horse tried to keep him from the approaching people for the most part. This was a side of Timberhoof he had never seen. He was being cautious about treading near others, keeping a sturdy gaze on everyone. Victoriah seemed aware of her mount's attentiveness, walking close and cupping a hand over his head. "A lot of crooks like to pickpocket around these parts."

Van looked around the area, unsure. The people around them seemed normal enough, just going about their business. When he closed his eyes to uses his magic sight, the air throughout the area asserted an unsettling presence—a swarming avarice.

Suddenly, he began to miss Russalin.

After working through the streets and crossing two long oak bridges, they came across an enormous manor near the west of the city. It was not as extravagant as the royal palace, but still very illustrious. An air of might and prestige resounded from the emblem of a diving falcon carved into the top of the gate.

The Estrine family home, definitely.

The guards, already high-strung, were quick to raise their spears to any incoming presence, but as soon as one of them saw Victoriah, every one of them stood at ease.

In place of the tense men, a gentle maiden wearing frilly clothes left the confines of the building through the giant doors opening powerfully. "Good day, Lady Victoriah. Welcome back to the Estrine Chateau." She graciously greeted the guests and took Timberhoof's reins while another came to escort them inside.

The maiden guided them through the halls, unfazed by the many different matching paths. Every direction looked the same to the young page-to-be. He hoped he would be able to find his way through the chateau like the kind maid after meeting the head of the family. She guided them through three long flights of stairs and several long halls, bringing Van and Victoriah before a massive pair of solid doors.

She stepped up to the doors and knocked, a tremendous *bang, bang* resounding. "Beg pardon, Lord Estrine. Lady Victoriah is here with her son."

"Send them in."

The deep, ragged voice behind the door spoke with tempestuous force. It sent a tremor through Van's spine. Whoever it was on the other side had to be a great mountain of a man stronger than a raging ox with an unforgiving rage. As the servant opened the cage for them to enter, Van began to have second thoughts but cast out all doubt and followed his mother inside. He kept his shaken composure under control, feeling his wits weaken at the *creak* of the closing door. The owner of that booming voice sat at a tall desk at the end of the room, cutting off light from the glass wall behind. The Lord Estrine sitting there did indeed appear as fearsome as Van predicted, but he soon felt ridiculous after laying eyes on him. When he approached his visitors, Lord Estrine's true physique revealed itself—a scarred, chiseled brunet head prompted atop a body not much taller than the child. Although diminutive in stature, his muscles rippled wherever hard plated armor did not cover.

"Long time no see, gnome. How's the family treating you?" Victoriah nonchalantly patted the tiny lord on his back.

A vein formed from his right eye up to his straightened hair. "Must you address me so crudely in front of your child, Lady Victoriah?"

Van blinked, still amazed the man's voice made the air shake.

Could so much forceful energy really come from such a small man?

He cringed, fearing he could read minds, as Lord Estrine's narrow eyes slanted back onto him. Van forced himself to straighten his posture again when meeting Lord Estrine's outstretched hand. "Lord Dragnal Estrine of Everspeak. It is a pleasure to make the acquaintance of the child of such a noble warrior."

"I'm surprised, gnome. Flattery usually isn't your strong suit."

The small lord's hand tensed up from Victoriah's interruption. "I was speaking of the man foolish enough to take you for his wife."

"Vandelas Kronas of Southern Valley, sir!" The boy made haste to interrupt them before their pestering turned into a fight to the death. "It is nice to meet you, milord." Lord Estrine smiled upon taking his hand back, likely glad Van better resembled his father instead of his mother.

He was glad the nobleman took the hint.

Lord Estrine invited his guests back to his desk to get comfortable while they discussed the arrangements. He offered them cups of elderberry tea and had one for himself.

"You come from an excellent line of military lineage, young Vandelas. I know your mother and father both very well. Perhaps they had some influence in the decision you have made?"

Van held back a small laugh in the back of his throat, pondering how Lord Estrine would act if he told him they tried to talk him out of it. Taking a sip of his tea, he took the time to think of how to respond, not wishing to lie while keeping it simple and brief. "They have told me many tales of their exploits."

"I see. Did they tell you of the time they and I helped to defend our shores from the Pternite invaders?"

"No, milord." Van hesitated to respond out of respect. "I was not aware you and my parents knew each other ... until now."

"Sorry, gnome. I only told him of my greatest battles. In all honesty, the only one we fought together was a little ... lackluster."

They heard no outrage from Lord Estrine even after he stopped sipping his tea. When he tried to bring it up, various details slipped his mind. The tale must not have been so impressive after all.

"Well, the reason you chose this path in life is no business of mine." Lord Estrine had to have lost interest in further formalities after being offended by his guests. Nevertheless, he kept to the subject without appearing offended. "I am to merely inform you of our regulations before you attend our lessons."

"And here comes the boring part."

"Lady Victoriah, if you continue to interrupt, I can have someone escort you out."

A worried glance from her son was all it took for her to bitterly accept being silent.

Appreciating the interference, Lord Estrine cleared his throat and continued. "Firstly, the boys' bedchambers are on the second floor's east wing and the girls' in the west side. Boys are not allowed in the girls' wing and vice versa. A bell will alert you to wake in the morning and warn you of curfew three times—breakfast begins immediately after the bell sounds. After training and lessons, you are free to go by the rest of your day as you see fit, but you will be expected to keep up in your studies. Tardiness for anything will result in disciplinary work. Weapons are not permitted for use inside the chateau except during an emergency or unless instructed. My orders and that of the instructors here are expected to be followed without question. Your uniform, which you will be scheduled to be fitted for tomorrow, must be worn during lessons and training exercises—we expect our pages to be presentable and professional. You are permitted to explore the city when not busy with your duties, but you must return by sunset unless accompanied by one of our knights. Animals, aside from our training horses, are not under our jurisdiction to care for; we will not house anyone's pets. Furthermore, acts of violence outside of training exercises are inexcusable and will result in harsh punishment however we see fit."

Those were quite a number of rules to follow, but Van paid close attention to Lord Estrine, knowing this to be but a brief explanation.

"Do you have any questions?"

Van was about to say no, but then a certain thought crossed his mind. He glanced back at his mother, eyes curious, then looked back at the nobleman. "Do you allow visitors?"

To his disdain, Lord Estrine replied, "We do accept visitors for our pages at the beginning of every month and on holidays as well as when the page is chosen to be squire to a knight."

He was satisfied with just that. "I have no further questions, milord."

With the formalities and rules out of the way, Lord Estrine offered another handshake, "We expect great things from you, young Vandelas," then excused Van to the maid waiting patiently outside. A curt laugh filled the lordship's quarters not long after the doors shut behind him. A tense air vibrated inside. The maid kindly offered to escort Van to his new living space while he left his mother and Lord Estrine to discuss other matters.

The halls of the boys' wing had an unusually soft atmosphere Van found comfort in, but something told him the state was only temporary. The tension would pick up when more arrived to train together.

"Are you nervous, Young Master?"

For a moment, Van had forgotten the maid's presence. She was so calm she blended in with the space around them. "No, miss."

"Quite the brave young man. And your mother is a lovely woman."

"Your master does not seem to think so."

She grinned. "Oh. Those two just have an old history together. You can probably understand Victoriah the Wolverine made as many enemies as she did allies."

Van nodded in reply.

"I am sure you will make quite the history here as well. Being the child of Victoriah the Wolverine and Sir Jerrell, you will undoubtedly have a fine experience."

What she said excited Van while concerning him all the same. The possibilities he might uncover and the obstacles getting in the way made him think of how he could encounter and deal with them all. "The life of a page can be just as difficult as a knight's. With all of the work, studies, and training you will undergo, you may not have time to keep your living space neat and tidy. My job is to take care of that issue while keeping this mansion spotless, so you need not worry about it."

Van would have told her she did not have to worry so much over him had the maid not told him it was her job.

Just don't make a mess, and you won't trouble her.

The maid excused herself after leaving Van at the last door farthest down the hall and bestowing him a key to its lock, instructing not to give it to anyone under any circumstances. The inside was already been occupied, a package resting on the floor beside a bed. Curiosity overcoming him, he inspected them before his new living space consisting of the bed, windows, a small chest next to a desk, and a wooden wall with a tub behind.

He used the knife provided with the delivery to cut loose the ropes keeping the package contained. He did not expect much. Despite that, he expected what he found the least of all: an old, dusty sword with some unusual wording engraved on one side of the scabbard.

The weapon came with a note written in a penmanship he recognized which said,

> I used this practice sword during my training. Maybe it can give you the strength it gave me.

A gift from Father.

Van unsheathed the blade from its scabbard. While the hilt and all else grew old and dull, the blade inside still kept a slight shine. The blade was shaved, not intended for killing, rather for practice. He tried swinging it in front of the mirror on the wall to check his form.

Still sloppy and shaky, as it had been for as long as he was training.

Van growled. No matter how hard he tried, his form was never acceptable. His father would be disappointed in him.

He sheathed the sword and laid it beside the mirror, and noticed something was rather off. He leaned in closer to get a good look. His eyes were different. They held a certain glimmer he never noticed before. For a moment, he tried telling himself there was nothing wrong, that his imagination was merely playing tricks on him. But that glimmer was unnatural, almost eerie.

An idea popped into his head. No one was coming by that he knew of, and if they did, they would likely knock on the door before entering. Relenting to his weary mind, he took the Shift Pendant around his neck in hand, letting the magic in it rest.

What he saw in the reflection gave him a fright.

His eyes were still blue. Only when he wore his false colors did he have blue eyes, as his real ones were a fiery red. But the ones looking back at him were still an icy blue.

Then instantly did he notice what it really was—not a glimmer, but a glare, a glare flashing off a bright, smooth surface. The longer he stared, the more he thought they resembled cracked ice.

"How long have they been like this?"

A knocking at the door alerted Van to reawaken the magic in his Shift Pendant quickly. There was nothing for him to fear. It was only Victoriah, entering without a word and shutting the door from behind at once. He sighed and let the magic his charm rest once more. If it was just the two of them, he preferred being his true self.

"I see your father sent you his old practice blade. He must be worried about you." Though Van had a difficult time believing so, it did give him something to think about. "I just came by to check on a few things before I left. What did your father tell you to do while you're here?"

"Only two things: be careful of overexerting myself and keep from using my Second Verse."

His mother's mouth hung ajar, unable to believe he was ordered to do that. "Why doesn't he want you using your power? Magic isn't frowned upon here. The pages greatly admire it. You'd be very popular." Victoriah acted milder than Van had expected. His father usually had a reason for things; she knew that better than him.

"When I use my Second Verse, it negates the magic in the Shift Pendant. My disguise will come undone if I use it."

And everyone will see I am one of the demons they despise. He kept those thoughts to himself. His mother never wanted to hear that from him, and he did not want to say it.

Victoriah sighed. "You spent all that time training to keep that power under control, and now you can't even use it. That's a real shame."

Van chose to focus on something else. He did not wish to think of it more. Victoriah seemed to take careful notice of that and looked to the window, looking over to a tree growing from the ground two floors downward. "Say, they gave you a nice room. I bet you'll like it here." Her words sounded strong at first, but they dimmed as she drew on. She always had that same disheartened tone whenever she had to leave him.

Despite knowing they would see less of each other, Van's heartstrings were left untouched this time. He turned back to his mother, seeing her kneeling to his level, and gave her a big hug.

"Thanks for asking if I could come visit," Victoriah said while brushing her hand through his hair.

Van smiled warmly. "I knew you would want to."

The goodbyes Van made with his mother the past few years never made a gap in his heart once, and that bothered him. He used to feel so open and warm toward the woman who raised him, but since death, he noticed her warmth reaching him even less and less. The cold had frozen him to the point where the feeling of such warmth became a fading memory.

What happened to me?

~ Fourth Chapter ~

Friends and Foes

Van woke early the next morning, though not of his own volition. A raucous *gong* gave him such a fright he jumped out of bed, falling onto the floor headfirst. He doubted he would get used to the bells very soon.

What do the bells mean again?

Lord Estrine said the bells served a purpose, but the pain ringing in his head made it difficult to keep his thoughts straight. A second bell gong—further agitating his headache—rang, reminding him it was time to get dressed and head for the banquet hall.

Lessons would not begin for a few more days, so he was permitted to wear his usual clothes. His favorite set needed cleaning, so he made do with the pale laced-sleeve shirt and the brown trousers belted together with his second favorite earthy green sash.

It had not even been a day, and Van felt guilty for troubling the maids. The one who escorted him yesterday, Alicalyn Feroste, informed him to leave any clothing that needed cleaning on the dresser. He promised himself he would cause the servants as little trouble as possible.

He decided to relax and forget about that while he bathed, the tub having been filled by someone without his notice. If his emotions ran amok, he would freeze the bathwater. The last time that happened, he was stuck in ice until his father broke him out with an axe.

The one thing he did not mind troubling Alicalyn with was asking her to guide him to the banquet hall. Growing up the way he did, Van felt uncomfortable having some stranger do his chores. And he told her that.

She seemed to understand but could not help laughing when he finished speaking. "I will not be much a stranger if you know me for some time. Give it a while, and you will be accustomed to a servant helping you. You are a noble, after all."

Yes, but a fallen one, Van thought to himself. *Do all nobles really have people do everything for them?*

The way he thought about it made him think nobles were lazy rich people for a moment. But nobles served their purposes as well. They did deeds that allowed them to attain their power, somehow.

Van began to see why his father said he asked too many questions; the more he learned, the more he had to know.

While sorting through the mess in his mind, they came to a vast hall occupied by rows of tables and benches spread across the entire room. A finely crafted table made from the sturdiest wood sat at the center. That had to be where the Estrines ate.

Very few people were there. Most of them were servants who gave food to the children. The children had to be the other pages training there.

Alicalyn had placed a gentle hand onto Van's shoulder. "The pages gather here for mealtimes and to listen to Lord Estrine's words of wisdom." The boy looked up at her, finding an odd comfort in her glossy blue eyes. She seemed glad to see him loosen up. "It is all right to be nervous, Young Master. These are new people."

Van clenched his fists. Hearing words like nervous directed at him was upsetting. "I'm not nervous. I'll be fine."

"Well, go on then."

Van toppled over. The maid's hands were held out in front of her before clasping them before her to appear more ladylike.

"We must get you fitted for your uniform after breakfast. I'll be waiting for you in the maids' chambers." After leaving him that reminder, she bowed to him and returned to her duties.

What she said surprised him. He assumed she rested in the opposite corner of the manor along with the girls who would attend lessons. Lord Estrine explicitly said anyone who crossed into the wrong wing would be expelled without question.

Considering her position in the massive mansion, it might be safe for him to follow her instructions.

With that in mind, Van went to get something to eat. There was plenty of food prepared to welcome the pages there. There were many savory dishes, many of them far fancier than Van had ever seen. He stuck with a simpler selection: a bowl of porridge, a banana and an apple, and a mug of tepid ivory juice.

He was eager to meet the other pages, but now he seemed more focused on finding a comfortable place to sit. There were plenty of tables available, but one sitting directly in front of a stained glass window caught his eye. The array of colors beaming over the table was strangely soothing. No one occupied the benches there, so there was plenty of space for him.

He dug in as soon as he sat down. As he sank his teeth forcefully into the peeled banana, he felt its smooth, soft texture spread over his tongue. Its flavor reminded him of home, but it had a peculiar sweetness unfamiliar to him. It made him think about where it grew. He savored the sweet flavor a little longer as he picked up the spoon and brought some porridge to his mouth.

"Judging by the clothing, I'd say you're from the south."

Van stopped chewing a moment, looking up to find a tall blonde boy taking a place across from him. He set down a tray of carrying thick slabs of ham and heaps of eggs. The way he addressed him made him curious. He assumed, from the kind glimmer in his umber eyes, that he was friendly enough. The boy's pale teal clothing was a bit frilly, much less than the stuck-up man he saw roaming the streets the day before, though. "I've never met any folks from the south before. A lot of you are responsible for our grocers always having food, right?" he asked before a slice of ham slapped into his teeth. The way he ate was appalling. Greasy fat slathered over the rest of his food, dripping from the meat hanging from his lips as he tore it apart like a voracious animal. He only calmed down after taking a swig from his mug. The boy, who acted so lively and boisterous, suddenly seemed bothered. He gave Van a mixed leer that further drove his curiosities. "You don't talk much, do you?"

Van felt he was being rude for not saying anything for so long. *He is giving me the time of day. The least I can do is give him a response.*

"Wallace Alivvrn of Illuascove. Good to meet you." The boy held out his hand past the table without delay. Van felt oddly comfortable with this unusually friendly stranger. "You can call me Wally if you want."

Alicalyn's words about making friends and foes ran through Van's mind. Forming a few friendships would definitely come in handy in the long run, and this one seemed rather interesting.

Van reached to grab Wallace's hand before he decided to pull away, giving it a shake. "Vandelas Kronas of Southern Valley."

Wally lurched back in surprise. "So you can speak!" he jested. "Thank the gods. It would have been weird if I befriended someone who can't keep with a double-sided conversation." His sense of humor was rather odd, but it made Van smile and laugh. "I think I'll call you Van."

"Everyone does."

Now Wally laughed.

Earlier cold and stern, Van now began to loosen up. He thought making friends in the city would be harder than in the countryside. Perhaps it still would be—this boy seemed rather outgoing. But it was comforting to know he had at least managed to make one.

Van did not say anything when Wally asked about his family name sounding familiar. Wally seemed to think he was teasing him. He gave up quickly, though, likely finding it none too important.

"So, is this your first year here, Van?"

"Yes. I arrived the night before."

"Same. My father told me it was best I arrive quickly. 'A knight is to respond to any and all tasks quickly and without delay,' he says. I think he was just eager to get me away from the manor."

Parents like that were a mystery to Van. Despite his conflicting thoughts about his family, he knew they cared for him unconditionally. If they could accept a demon as their child, then other parents should be able to do so with their own.

"He was probably worried I'd try to get involved with his business with the neighboring village's mayor—worries I'll promise too much on their behalf."

"Too much?"

"Money, protection, arms—you name it. I got into the habit of offering more than my father could allow. He's got heaps of lev in his coffers, but he barely spends a fraction of it for his people."

So it was true. Nobles looked out for themselves more than they did the commoners. The sour look on Wally's face mirrored Van's disgust. Lending a helping hand to anyone if in it was in one's power seemed to be natural, but nobles must have held their own limits to that. It made no sense to him, but he had no intention of getting involved with such things. It was difficult enough remembering the names and lands of the nobles and what they did for their country. What went through their minds seemed like something he could not understand.

"What about you? What are your parents like?"

"Well, Father is a retired knight who spends his time supporting our village—basically with manual labor. But he has to be careful not to agitate his injuries."

"What happened to him?"

"His arm and leg were crippled after a raid several years ago. He can still use them, but putting too much pressure on them makes it hurt so much that he can't. It happens more often than it should."

At least once a week, he caused more trouble than help pushing himself to finish a task anyone could do. Van had to nurse his father back to health on more than one occasion because of that. To that, Wally actually laughed.

He tried containing himself, but his snorting laughter could not be held back so easily. Van supposed that would be amusing in some way if he was not too worried his father would run himself ragged or completely ruin one of his scarred limbs.

When Wally managed to find the breath to speak again, he asked, "What about your mother? What is she like?"

The advice Alicalyn gave him did not seem so frightening anymore. This was a subject he always enjoyed. The quiet boy lost restraint on his mouth, spilling every detail he could about his fierce parent without speaking her identity. Wally seemed to enjoy a good guessing game. So many marvelous and occasionally frightening tales had been told of her exploits: fending off an entire group of bandits with only a worn lance, skinning a gazelle with just her teeth, playing a major part in the previous war against Pterna when she was a squire—

When his stories came to that point, Wally finally realized why his family name sounded so familiar. It was a wonder he could forget the realm's most famous female knight, famed for her strength and brutality.

"You here by choice, or did your parents make you?"

"By choice, of course. Why would— Wait. Your parents forced you into this?"

Wally shrugged. "They say it is to bolster our family status. My older brothers—Siron, Dougdin, Fredrick, Ezekiel, and Oelius—are all knights already. They're even making my little sister train once she reaches a certain age."

"You live with all those people?" Van interrupted, sincerely surprised a family could grow so large.

"Yeah. Just them, my parents, my auntie and uncle, grandparents, even an old family friend."

So many people to live with! Having so many packed into one living place must have been madness even for someone as laidback as Wally.

"What? You don't have any brothers or sisters?" The truth came as a shock to him.

"I don't know why you are so surprised," Van blurted out. "Your family is the one kept at such a full stock."

Surprised as he was with Van being an only child, he laughed at his reply.

This one peaked Van's curiosities. The carefree way he spoke put him at ease, leveling his tension with a sense of joy. Wally did not seem to care about much or at least kept his stress well maintained. He had an interesting nature.

For a moment, Van was considering second-guessing his decision to befriend Wally when he saw how fast the boy scarfed down his food with an appetite more ravenous than his own. His plate cluttered to the rims had been cleared in less than four minutes. Did he even chew his food? Seeing as there would still be more surprises to be had about him, he reconsidered his reconsideration.

After chugging down the contents in his mug, Wally collected his dished and stood. "Well, I'll see you around, Van. Good luck here."

It was a little disappointing to see him already leave when they were having a good time. But Van also had his own plans to keep. It was best to settle everything before making any alliances.

The uniform fitting came next.

He went to look for Alicalyn after eating. The chateau's halls were expansive and difficult to navigate without a guide. Whenever believing he took a wrong turn, Van let out a muffled grumble, wishing he had earlier stopped the maid when he had the chance. A growling stomach was hardly an excuse for being distracted.

He wandered the halls, hoping to interact with the maid or one of her cohorts as they passed by from one of their duties.

At least she remained in one place. He just needed to find out where that place was.

The halls were uncomfortably empty no matter which direction he turned to. With so much space, there should be a multitude of servants scuttling all over the place in preparation for arriving pages. Then again, the halls already sparkled from constant shine and polish, nary a speck of dust hanging among the gaudy décor.

There should be more than just his lonesome lingering about.

The lonely atmosphere had no effect on Van. The cold that followed him since he awakened as a Nascitte felt like an atmosphere of loneliness. He grew accustomed to it after a time. In a way, it was not all bad. It almost felt like it was cradling him. Van never could explain how else to put it. Though he attempted to, the sensation was much too complicated.

Lost in thought, Van barely noticed when he had fallen from a strong blow to the skull. He quickly made sure the Shift Pendant remained in place beneath his shirt before anything else. After making certain it was secure, he caressed the bump on his head and looked up, wanting answers on who attacked him. A girl in unkempt clothing sat parallel to him, her red hair tied in a long ponytail. She looked like she had fallen too. Neither of them was looking where they were going and bumped into each other, it seemed.

"Hey, watch it!"

Her demeanor and coarse voice agitated Van. He stood ready to state that she rushed into him, but he remembered how his father stressed the importance of manners, especially toward a lady.

"I ... apologize. Do you need a hand?"

The girl slapped his hand away when he offered it. "I can handle myself."

Not another word was spoken. She bolted off in the opposite direction after getting back to her feet. Van thought her oddly energetic, influenced by some sort of adrenaline. Whatever she was up to, he could not help but wonder.

One mystery at a time, he reproved himself.

He could not find Alicalyn, but thankfully, another maid noticed he had lost his way and escorted him to her associate. As it turned out, the maids' chambers resided near the edge of the hall where the boys' and girls' wings linked.

Alicalyn took the measurements right away. Van tried staying perfectly still as she ran the tailor's strap over his body, but he felt much too perturbed about a stranger touching him.

Sensing his unease, Alicalyn did her best to treat him with the utmost care. After laying hand on his icy skin once, she attempted to avoid direct contact as much as possible. She thought he had fallen ill at first. No one's skin should have such a stinging chill. It was difficult for her to believe Van when he said that was natural for him. "Are you any comfortable wearing such frigid skin? You feel so tense."

He only became stiff after feeling the maid's constant flinching. Every time she pulled away, it felt like she was handling a beast instead of a boy, something much less flattering than he thought when others enthusiastically addressed his mother the same way.

"You admire your mother greatly, don't you?"

Van became stiff as a board, and his eyes shot wide open. He looked up at the woman, who suddenly stopped measuring and recoiled. She acted surprised but knew what he thought by the look he gave her.

"Please excuse my rudeness. I did not mean to invade your thoughts," she bowed respectfully. "I have Praecur: a magic which allows me to read people's thoughts ... and I do not have the best control over it, so I have a tendency to use it without trying."

Hearing someone else possessed an unusual power allowed Van to loosen up. The shroud of anxiety held by the cold grew thinner.

"You read people's thoughts? That's ... amazing."

Alicalyn smiled and proceeded to finish Van's measurements. She did not feel so timid to touch his icy skin with the cold having thinned. As she worked, she told him a little story. "I came here when I was but a girl for an honest job, but after the others heard I have magic, I ended up aiding in interrogating prisoners at the royal palace." That would not have concerned Van as much if she had not said it with such lively enthusiasm, as if she enjoyed what she was a part of. She did not appear the type to enjoy harming others. Her valsara matched her gentle appearance. "It was a little frightening at first. I never wanted to go near the people kept there. Many of their thoughts were revolting to listen in on. But since their minds were so ... loose, it was impossible for them to hide whatever secrets they had tucked away in their heads."

Alicalyn finished both the intriguing tale and the measurements quickly, rolling up the tailor's strap in one hand. Van went to retrieve his sash—he needed to keep the bundled cloth out of the way so it did not interfere with the measuring.

"Your chain mail will be delivered to you before the lessons begin."

After wrapping the sash firmly around his waist, Van turned to bow to the maid. "Thank you, Alicalyn."

The maid kept her professional composure for a moment, then laughed, letting joy show. "You may call me Lyn, if you prefer."

Had she felt some kinship that incited her to be more familiar with him? Van did not understand it himself, but he felt comfortable with her too.

With plenty of time to spare, Van explored his new home for the next year, wanting to get to know everything about the facility.

The Estrine Chateau had much to offer, even an observatory located past the fourth floor's north wing. He had taken a liking to the training grounds behind the chateau more than anything. There seemed to be no limit of space. An expansive, empty field spread over the horizon, dirt roads stretching into the tall grass and disappearing, and a small woodland sprouted at the very edge. Past the expanse stood a massive wall that met with the city's border, but it was so far away it looked to be a region away.

While he explored the outside, he noticed a tattered old shack built by a bed of wilting flowers, unlocked and unguarded. How could he resist taking a peek inside? While there were no windows, the gaps in the roof drew in the outside light for Van to see. Further investigation showed the shack was a weapons stockpile. There were swords, axes, lances, bows and arrows, javelins, and even hammers. All of the blades were shaven down to the point where they would cause as little injury as possible.

It had been some time since he last practiced his swordplay. He took the dull sword he kept strapped to his side—which Lord Estrine permitted him to keep—and went outside to find training dummies stabbed into the ground like scarecrows behind the shack. He held the sword in both hands and began swinging.

His form was, as always, a complete mess. His arms refused to stay steady and, swipe after swipe, flew in different directions. Fifty swings to the bucket head, and if anything, his form only became worse.

Why can't I keep do this right!?

"Doing a few exercises, young one?" a strong voice stated from behind.

A knight of regal blonde in shimmering armor was standing behind him. He had a stare that could petrify any spirit.

Van tried straightening his spine to show proper posture. Making direct eye contact proved challenging; this man's presence disturbed him, as though he looked to a predator ready to pounce. "Y-Yes, sir. I thought keeping my body conditioned would keep me fit for training once it begins."

And I really want to get a grasp on using a sword...

"You've certainly proven how eager you are in how you attacked the dummy. But your technique is deplorable and your focus just as poor. Were the dummy alive and breathing, there isn't a doubt it would be laughing at your incompetence."

This man was infuriating already. It was obvious how pitiable Van's swordsmanship was without him blatantly pointing it out. Saying so seemed completely unnecessary. How tempting it was to ignore the formalities and decide on a new training dummy. But this man was a knight, and unless treated with respect, his troubles would only get worse.

"Self-control is essential for every knight. ...Although, perhaps I should not assume you would know that given your mother's tutelage."

"My mother? What does Mother have to do with—" Something about this man's presence made Van choke on his words. He felt such a vague sense of dread, but one that left him frightened to make any sudden moves or speak. When he blinked, in those brief flashes of darkness, he noticed the intensity of the man's valsara and remembered. "You were at my home. On the night I was killed."

The knight raised an eyebrow. "So you noticed me after all," he said undaunted. That assured voice did not ease Van's concern even with his suspicions confirmed. "I must say, I'm surprised. From the way Victoriah sheltered you, I assumed she would never allow you to take this path. Yet here you are, amongst the other children with the bravado to strive for knighthood."

He had a disdain for pages? The air thickening around the knight boldly spoke it. Perhaps even someone without Van's sixth sense could notice as much. But all knights were pages once. His dislike of the youth seemed redundant.

"If I'm not mistaken, your name is Vandelas?"

The new page nodded. He was not sure whether to speak or not.

"I will be brief. You will address me as Sir Charleston, and you are to pay myself, my relatives, and our subordinates due respect. During your stay here, I trust you will be on your best behavior, as any knight should. If I hear you cause any trouble, you will answer to me, not Lord Estrine."

The knight stepped over to the dummy. His stare was harsh and intimidating, and soon became riddled with hatred. "Know that out of respect for Victoriah, I will safeguard your secret with my life. However, I am no saint, boy." A strong malice reverberated off the man's valsara and connected with the sword strapped to his back. "If you prove to be a danger to anyone here—" Words were no longer necessary once Sir Charleston drew his sword and—Van flinched—buried it into a training dummy's upper-left abdomen nearly in the instant it would take to blink. "Am I understood, Kindhrin wretch?"

It baffled Van that he managed to nod after seeing what he did, unintentionally picturing himself where the dummy was. His throat closed upon understanding another wished to take his life.

Ever since meeting Sir Charleston that afternoon, Van constantly looked over his shoulder out of sheer terror. His parents' fears were true: knowledge of his true lineage promised death.

It was luck alone that kept him alive for so long—being left in the care of a protective couple, resurrected by an ethereal being, healed by someone repressing his murderous urges for another's sake.

A day of surprising encounters left him exhausted. Blissful sleep in that lonely plane of ice and snow seemed pleasant all of the sudden. It was no luscious bed of snow, but the one in his bedchamber felt rather comfortable, much too comfortable. He could not sleep a wink.

He lay back in the bed, taking deep breaths to calm his frayed mind so he would drift away from the world for the night. He kept the windows' upper shutters open, letting in the cool autumn breeze to soothe him.

The wind played childishly with the leaves and trees outside.

Now they were raucous, shaking a bundle of leaves. He ignored it, knowing the small ruckus would soon die down. But it picked up instead, the winds deciding to play with him too.

Something brushed against his leg. Van leaped from his covers and reached for the knife Victoriah left behind. Something slid into the shadows before he could see it. Whatever creepy night crawler chose to raid his new home, he would not back down.

It appeared small and vulnerable, not much to take as a threat. The bright blue glow peering through the darkness made him lower his guard. He knew that affectionate stare anywhere, and could not hold a knife to it. A small white-furred creature glowing with affection stepped from the shadows as soon as Van hid his fangs. "Snowflake?" The small fox pressed its paws against the bed the human child sat in, leaping up aboard at his call. It was the same snowfleece fox he saved from bleeding to death at the Sperov Mountains.

Ever since the fox's injuries healed, she followed Van everywhere he went as though thinking him her new parent, or perhaps her new possession. It was not surprising, considering the time and effort he took caring for her, but to still follow him, after three months of separation, all the way to the capital nearly sent him into shock.

The fox cuddled up him, rubbing her head and body against Van like a cat claiming its territory. She missed him.

"I'm glad to see you too, Snowflake." Van choked a tad. "But you can't stay here. Lord Estrine doesn't permit animals inside the chateau."

Snowflake did not care for the human's opinion. She made that clear after making herself comfortable in the boy's lap. Van knew his body was cold to her, but she never seemed to mind. Snowflake often did that to share her own heat when not seeking her own comfort. Though he never felt anything given, Van always appreciated the sentiment.

It was already late. There was no certainty how far she travelled to reach him again. The poor thing had to be exhausted.

Although intent on following the rules laid out for every page, he could not turn her away. Seeing the lovable fox return to him after leaving her behind to live a life away from humans touched him deeply. She could have forgotten about him and lived the remainder of her life in the mountains, but instead she tracked him down like a bloodhound and kept out of sight until they were alone.

Unable to resist her, Van brushed a hand over her plush fur and brought her into his arms, welcoming her back. "All right, you can stay the night." He carried the fox up to the pillow with him and covered her gently with the blanket. "But you have to leave come morning. I'm serious. I don't want anyone skinning you."

Snowflake licked his cheek after finding where she was most comfortable: against his chest. She knew how to work Van without much effort. Cute little animals were always a weakness of his.

Heat became a foreign sensation he would likely never feel again. But with Snowflake's fluffy white fur brushed against him, he did not mind as much.

Again he heard the bell ring, and again Van leaped from his bed.

The animal that shared his bed had not made herself known among the blankets or nearby furniture. Although unlikely, she must have taken his advice and left at an earlier time for her safety. Van knew she would be safe. Kit-sized though she was, Snowflake was very elusive, as he learned during his intense training in the mountains, and could not be captured so easily. How else could she have escaped whatever unfortunate fate that befell the rest of her skulk? The question rose quickly, though, as to where she hid in this new environment. Anything white would stand out, and the entire city was a spectrum of color.

She will find a way, Van reassured himself. *Tougher threats than humans have given her a hard time before.*

Thought of the fox eluded him after enduring another loud gong from the bell. Every ring of the bell sounded louder and more menacing than the last.

"All right, all right already! I'm getting up!" Van exclaimed, getting back to his feet before the third bell rang.

While he searched for something to block out the rattling noise, he found a new crate placed in his room with him none the wiser. Snowflake must have fled upon its arrival. He looked inside to see its contents: a set of small gray chain armor along with a few sets of red tunics and black pants. At the gong of the final morning bell, he donned his new uniform and chain mail instead of dressing in his normal garb.

Equipping the armor did not require much effort. It weighed about as much as the dull sword he carried and went on as simply as his regular clothing. A look at the full-length mirror brought a slight boost to his mood. Van thought he appeared stronger in the thin mail, more robust. He did not look quite like a knight, but the simple armor looked nice on him.

More children wondered the halls than the previous morning whereas only a few came to Van's attention. So many parents must be eager to have their children become knights if many came by the dozens overnight. More potential allies or competition. Excitement reverberated through his bones.

He sat at the same table as he had yesterday, under the same stained glass windows at the side of the banquet hall. His breakfast had more substance than yesterday: slightly burnt eggs, a few sausage links, an apple, a banana, a handful of grapes, a few slices of bread baked freshly, and a mug of ivory juice. With training beginning soon, it was important to get the nutrition needed to endure whatever was to challenge him. A hearty meal would sustain him until the next one came around.

Claiming his favorite spot proved easier than anticipated with a mass of young pages swarming through the banquet hall. It was surprising no one else wanted to sit there.

"Well, we meet again, I see."

Van's eyes shot open. That familiarly chipper voice brought his mood to match it. Wally took his seat opposite him as he had before. Van smiled livelily, elated the kindly boy came back.

He expected him to dig in and scarf down every scrap of meat collected, but Wally refused to take even a nibble after sitting down. Though he found that odd, he unconsciously reached for a grape right as his new friend reached out and slapped it out of his hand. Van blinked before leering at him. "Don't give me that look," he said nonchalantly. "We're not allowed to eat until the Estrine family gets here, no excuses. To show respect, you know. I thought your parents told you that."

Waiting until the Estrines arrived? Van gave a silent groan under his lips. He became impatient when it came to food since his ninth birthday. It must have been a measure taken for the pages to learn patience if they had not already. Van asked Wally if that was the case. He just shrugged. "It could be that, or just something they came up with to mess with us. I wouldn't put it past them."

Is everything a joke to this kid?

Van did not know, but laughed at the thought. Everyone, even himself, seemed so tense and serious, and the lessons have yet to begin. Someone like him would come in handy in erasing that tension.

At the moment when Van was about to ask questions about his family—still curious about its size—the other pages went silent from those entering. Lord Estrine and various other armored men and well-dressed ladies walked in, carrying an illustrious aura of nobility.

The sight of Sir Charleston joining them made Van cringe. His false peach skin began to run pale, the bloody promise still fresh in his mind.

"Hey, are you all right, Van?"

Wally's voice provided a small sense of security. He could not relax, though. That man's threat left him shaking.

Unaware just how afraid Van was, Wally made a smile suited for a court jester. "Stay calm, all right? Everyone may treat the Estrines like these important big shots, but they're just a family of nobles. A lot of the pages here are nobles like you and me. They're just like you, so you don't have to act afraid of them, 'kay?"

He was right. Among the children there, he was no more than another page seeking knighthood. So long as he acted properly, Sir Charleston would be of no threat.

Wally became reassured when his new companion's tension melted away; Van could feel it.

The Estrine family took their place at the center of the banquet hall, up the few steps of the risen floor leading to the grand dining table large enough to seat them all. The servants brought out elegantly crafted cuisine for them. Van became jealous of the buffet provided for the noble family, having become so voracious in appetite. It took all his self-control to keep from drooling at the delectable scent steaming from the food.

Wally, however, could not keep such control over himself.

The Estrine family head stood atop the steps. He almost appeared of normal height standing at an elevation higher than the page's heads. Several of the young children had to keep their grins covered lest an inappropriate chuckle escaped their mouths. "Commoners, nobles, young dreamers, welcome to our chateau—my home, as well as yours for the next cycle of the seasons and possibly longer." He called out with the profound, booming voice that made his body appear even smaller by comparison. Upon hearing that voice, the pages were reminded of his position there and immediately respected him. "For many of you, this place is a familiar haven, as you have been our pages for some time now. I do see a number of new faces among you, a great many brimming with confidence. Forgive me for crushing that confidence, but I warn you that your time here will not be enjoyable. The work will be excruciating and the training exhausting. If time is used wisely, there will barely be a moment of rest within these walls. But, of course, knights do not have the luxury. You mustn't expect the training to be so simple either. Seeing as you are all here, you must understand that. If you carry true zeal and resolve, I do not doubt each and every one of you shall become exceptional warriors to the crown."

The pages seemed empowered by his speech, intimidating though it was.

Mere words did not impress Van very well. He had to be speaking falsely without any concern for who passed or failed. It did not matter. All he needed to believe was his own strength, not the words of others.

Those like Wally, however, were easily convinced. "See? What did I tell you? Lord Estrine is a nice guy. You can trust the knights here."

Trust: one thing he became completely uncertain of since learning who he was.

Wally decided to show Van around the chateau after breakfast. The previous day, he spent his time roaming the halls on each floor to see what he could learn about their new home. Among the many things shown to him, they came across a library on the upper levels of the chateau.

They decided to take a peek inside the monumentally spacious area and see what it had to offer.

The library was a labyrinth. They lost their way a few times searching for all the content the Estrine family had to offer. For everything to be academically sound, it was hard to believe there were over five hundred shelves packed with books thick as logs.

There were few books kept in the library about myths, as they were only to focus on their education. Although he knew none of these tomes would contain any of the stories from his childhood, Van had already taken great interest in a few selections.

Since they were already there, Wally took a gander at a history book telling of the Battle of Deamontal. His grandfather took part in that battle fifty years ago. Van would have asked more, but it seemed Wally had a few things to learn about himself. In the meantime, Van partook in something called Manèris Chantelle—what looked to be a book on etiquette or political affairs. It was written partially in another language, so he did not know. Part of the title had the author's name: Chantelle Cield'or. It meant Chantelle was a name, but what did Manèris mean?

It was best to speak to someone in their own language. At the time his mother taught him that, she was referring to how to speak to brigands, thieves, people of that like. But Van understood what she meant: people often misinterpreted each other because of their differences.

Knowing nothing about the words written irritated him terribly. He eventually gave up attempting to understand it and took to another book.

The time in the chateau's library felt wasted to Van, whereas the happy-go-lucky Wally managed to learn a few things. He might or might not have found the information about his grandfather he sought. His jolly behavior made it difficult to understand at first (or any) glance. That infectious attitude uplifted Van from his sour mood.

They wandered the halls in hopes of finding anything of interest after returning the books.

When on their way back to the boys' wing, Van and Wally stumbled upon a conflict between an abrasive female and a group of boys. A few from the gathering had already left in disgust from the girl's spirited ranting. No punches were thrown yet, but the threats she made suggested that would not be the case for long.

Stepping in for a closer look gave Van a surprise. He recognized the girl; it was the same redhead that tackled him the day before.

Taking an interest, Wally took a step forward. "Something up, fellas?" The back of the group had given a fraction of their attention to the new spectators. Van hoped to keep silent and observe the contained uproar from the sidelines so he could collect information; it was obvious Wally had not thought the same. As the uproar died down, Van took notice of a certain valsara from one of the taller young men, a tan boy with a somewhat muscular frame. He could tell this individual was a leader of sorts. Every boy there seemed to gather around him.

"This is nothing to worry about," the supposed leader said. "We are simply having a conversation with our new little friend here."

His speech was smooth, the proper language he used adding to his sincerity. He sounded convincing—perhaps too convincing. Van likely would not have noticed that if not for the flare of hostility he caught glimpse of in his valsara.

The redhead huffed assertively, her nostrils flaring. "I am *not* your friend!" She stormed past Van and Wally, not bothering to stay for more conversation.

Van's ears twitched at the sound of a tongue clicking from behind. Someone having shown disgust before, with reasons still evading him, hid among the crowd as everyone dispersed. The leader, however, stayed behind a moment more. Something about his smile was untrustworthy. Van had seen smiles like that before, on the huilo monkeys back home before they leaped at someone to steal something.

"I don't think I've seen your faces around here before. What are your names?"

"I'm Wallace Alivvrn of Illuascove."

"Vandelas."

It was rude not to include one's family name and place of origin when introducing one's self to another. It showed a sign of trust and respect, mainly among nobles. But he spoke in a kind enough tone to compensate for that.

"Kallant Ginnstom of Starscape," the proper boy said with a bow. "I look forward to learning the ways of the knight with you both."

With the next day about before either knew it, Van and Wally prepared themselves and went to the training grounds behind the chateau for their morning exercises.

After they worked through that, next would be mount handling, then archery, tactics, geography and nature, and finally etiquette and culture.

Worrying about what would come next did Van no good. *Save the effort for that when they come and worry about the now.*

Many of the pages have been divided into groups depending on their time spent learning under the Estrine family and estimated skill.

Leading the weapons training was Sir Charleston of Crownscape. He began by calling pages up one by one for them to announce themselves in front of the others. "If you are to learn with one another, we must learn about each other," the knight proclaimed.

Van had already learned the names of a few pages: Severic Valianc of Condoroost, Augustus Gloor of Tavern Spring, Portages Ferone of Pasturehill, Devere Transgres. Having already met Wally, he had little to learn from his name. When it came time for Van to introduce himself, he stepped forward. He held a composed demeanor even when standing before the stagnant stares of his fellow pages.

Then suddenly, he tensed up.

"State your name." Sir Charleston gave the slightest nudge in his forceful command.

Van abhorred his hesitance, but understood it. Everyone always looked at him differently when they knew he was related to Victoriah the Wolverine, and not always kindly.

They would catch on to who he was eventually.

Taking a breath, he kept his posture straight and exclaimed, "Vandelas Kronas of Southern Valley. It is a pleasure to know you all."

As expected, many, if not all, reacted with surprise upon hearing of his name. The pages either gave judgmental leers or gasps of surprise upon realizing he was the child of a champion.

It felt strange to stand back at attention with them knowing a few sets of eyes were still locked onto him. A name itself was a powerful thing.

Their uncomfortable valsara was palpable. Emotions such as those were easy to detect and interpret.

The first swordplay exercise of the day began after Sir Charleston divided the pages into pairs. He had them all take a dull sword from the barrels brought out, all except Van, who simply drew the one at his side.

Van dreaded taking his sword in hand. His form was no better, perhaps worse, than someone who never picked up a weapon. What really irked him, though, was being paired against Kallant Ginnstom.

The two clashed when Sir Charleston permitted them to begin. Van proved the quickest right away, lashing swiftly at his sparring partner. Kallant barely had the time to parry before the dull weapon hit on his face. Van relied on his quick feet and threw the enemy off balance before his movements became too much to control. Seconds after they began, he already struggled to maintain his stance. And soon after, Kallant took the opportunity, seeing how his foe's muscles moved, and swung across Van's chest, throwing him on his back.

The others stopped their practice after noticing that particular fight came to an end with Vandelas—the child of the monster knight—failing.

Van was humiliated. He gritted his teeth in anger, but realized the training session was not for nothing. That hostility, that frustration—he managed to confirm Kallant's true nature by sparring with him.

"Again!" Sir Charleston barked at Van. "A knight does not falter before the enemy. If you cannot overpower your enemy, then outwit them."

Kallant glared down at Van, his countenance snide and cruel. Those hard black eyes showed a mocking scorn that plainly said, "Come and play, little maggot!"

Even if he knew the results, even if he knew he would fall again, he refused to allow himself to stay down and admit defeat.

~ Fifth Chapter ~

Building a Unit

As expected, Van had failed to best anyone in swordplay. Aggression from his growing losses empowered him enough to keep trying, but it was never enough. His arms quaked from every static movement and jostled violently from every dynamic action.

It was the worst. Total humiliation.

Everyone expected him to be this terribly strong inhuman child because he was the son of the Victoriah the Wolverine—all unaware of his true bloodline and his real relations with her.

That sorry display of swordsmanship made him appear worse than unideal. It made him look like a fool.

But at the end of the exercise came an opportunity to redeem himself.

Sir Charleston guided all of the pages deeper into the wide grassy fields behind the Estrine Chateau to train them in how to handle horses. For generations, the Estrine family believed in having the youth interact with the mounts they would use by having the beasts come to them. Although not many believed animals capable of connecting with human beings, horses were considered an exception because of their ability to follow the commands of their rider.

Various breeds of majestic horses were released into the fields upon their arrival. They mainly frolicked about with one another for the most part, elated for the chance to run free once more.

A smile had forced its way over Van's face after witnessing such beauteous creatures look so happy. Had Sir Charleston not interrupted his happy thoughts, the smile might have been imprinted over his face.

"Your objective here is simple: convince of these horses to approach you and let you mount it. You have until sunset."

Pulling the horses away from their long-awaited run would be no simple task. Still, it was a challenge, and any knight worthy of a shield did not shy away from challenges.

By Sir Charleston's order, everyone immediately scattered to take a mount. They made haste, but Van approached the situation calmly, patiently, keeping his breathing tame and his mood relaxed. Animals, especially horses, were alert to what happened around them. As long as he kept himself composed, he would not frighten the horses off. He would have to concoct some plan, though, to catch one's interest, something different from what the other children were attempting. They only managed to startle them and drive them away.

I'm sure I can keep their attention once I take it, Van believed.

He did not have much of an opportunity to conceive a plan. There was a group of horses that had been evading the wilder pages not far from Van. They took notice of him when he stepped over a tall patch of grass. One horse in particular broke from the herd and headed his way. Its coat was a marvelous blend of black and dark gray fur akin to the dead of night. Those eyes—a gleam of hazel fascination—told Van something about it.

"You are a curious one, aren't you?"

It trotted closer, answering him with a snort. Van met the beautiful young creature halfway, reaching out his hand so it could give it a smell, then giving it a gentle but firm rub over its noses once it accepted him.

It gave a light nudge, asking him to continue. Curious. Affectionate. It might not be wise to choose the first one he approached, but the horse had already charmed him. While brushing its nose gently, Van had confirmed this one was a female, a mare. If she had not already been named, he had thought of an excellent one for her.

"Shall we meet up with your herd?"

The mare called out a loud neigh in agreement. Carefully, Van boarded the fair mare's back. The mount went into a sprint immediately upon her new rider gripping onto her short, dark mane.

Her stature appeared weak, but still the dark horse valiantly ran, catching up to her herd at astounding speed without concern for the extra weight. Her passenger felt the wind lash all over him in a thousand wisps. And he loved every second of it. Van loved the rush. This was the first time he had ever ridden a horse and felt the breathtaking forces of the wind. It was so fast, so free. It was the reason they loved to run.

"Page Kronas!"

Van did not wish for the magnificent rush to end, but he had been summoned by the training instructor. He realized that he had been calling him a few times without being heard. Although reluctant to pry the mare from her herd again, Van directed her toward Sir Charleston. He made sure to have her come to a slow, gentle stop when approaching the knight.

"My apologies, Sir Charleston. I could not hear you well through the wind."

"Understandable, given the speed your mount ran."

"Is there something wrong?"

"Nothing in particular," he responded with an oddly calm tone and the expected air of suspicion. "I am curious how you managed to bring your horse in so quickly. It is almost as if you could speak to it."

"I have a way with animals, sir. They seem to understand me well."

That was how he could best explain it. His peculiar connection with animals allowed him to communicate with them. The animals seemed to understand him word for word. And while he did not understand them in the same way, their feelings and intent always reached him.

Sir Charleston let him be on his way, giving the order to tend to his horse and challenge the others to races until given the call to return.

On the way to find his first opponent, he noticed Wally was one of the pages that had yet to lure in a horse. It did not feel right to leave him be after seeing him struggle. Van approached his humorous friend, having his mare run at a lesser speed so not to spook him or get his hopes up too high in case he did not notice him. Wally made with a brief greeting before resuming his task.

"Would you like any help?"

"No! No! It's okay. I should get one to me on my own. If you help, it won't be much of a success."

Van understood his argument. Even so, leaving him like that seemed wrong. Several pages have already brought in their horses and began racing one another.

He refused to go without finding some way to help him. Wally had been very kind to him. If Van could repay that kindness, even indirectly, then he would.

One of the young stallions to the rear of the running herd caught Van's eye. It ran at a pace more sluggish than the rest and seemed to stop a second every now and then to rest. It gnawed at the grass but remained dissatisfied with it alone.

He must be hungry.

There was an apple tree not too far from there, and they seemed the perfect shade of red deserving of a horse's appetite.

Smiling, Van looked down at his horse and stroked her mane. "Are you hungry, girl? Would you like me to get you an apple?"

He brought his mount over to the hill for a break, but she turned her head away from the apple he picked, not as hungry as the other horse. Fortunately, her head was at the right angle for him to drop the fruit and make it look like she ate it.

With that, Van let his new mare enjoy her run, leaving Wally to figure out how to lure in a horse with its appetite.

He boldly challenged the other pages to race, keeping a dignified speech for respect. Because of his terrible display of swordsmanship earlier, they blatantly laughed at him, believing they could easily best him yet again, especially with "that skinny filly" he rode.

A knight never refused a challenge—that ideal was the only reason they accepted at all.

His opponents directed him to certain points on the wild track for the starting line to the finish. They thought the race would be little more than a leisurely run for their horses. However, when the signal to start was given, the incompetent page and wimpy mount left their foes in the dust, demonstrating they were not to be trifled with. No horse matched their speed regardless of their breeding and growth.

He was nothing to fear to begin with; then suddenly, he was immeasurably capable. No one could figure out if they should consider him either an obstacle to avoid or a boy on his luck.

Looking back at the victory from his ninth race, Van noticed Wally had finally seized a mount. He took the vague advice he was given and lured the hungry horse with a few juicy apples.

He was glad for the cheerful jester. Now he could pay him back for besting him in the weapons lesson.

After more than half of the pages found their mount, Sir Charleston ordered everyone to return to him. He briefly explained that the horses they lured in would be the mounts for their training for as long as they remained pages under their care.

Van smiled fondly down at his new companion. Since she was not given a proper name, he proudly decided on one for her: Nightshade.

During the other lessons of the day, Van gave his best attempts to redeem himself for the mistakes made earlier.

Archery gave him the chance to demonstrate the accuracy he developed from seeing through snowstorms in the Sperov Mountains.

His eyes never had difficulty adjusting to suit his environment since death. Those new glacier-blue eyes gave him greater clarity of the world in extreme detail as well as adaptability to spot things from a distance.

The bow was one weapon he had no practice in. Despite how simple archers made it look, pulling the bow back took more strength and finesse than expected, and adjusting for better aim was all the more tricky. Yet all it took were a few instructions from Sir Charleston and a few attempts to manage some rather adequate shots.

Each time Van fired, the arrow darted closer to the target.

A few wandering eyes lost focus on their own targets seeing him progress quickly in a few simple shots. Whether he had training before or not was of little importance to any of them. Considering the distance of the targets placed, no one could have thought of landing a single bull's-eye, but he managed one on his tenth shot.

No one would admit it to be anything but a fleeting boon from Lady Sundralla. Luck, however, was as much an asset as anything.

If he managed to eventually prove as proficient with a sword, then Van would be content.

Hours of exercise having gone by, the pages earned a hearty meal to replenish their energy. Everyone looked forward to a nice feast after a series of exercises.

How disappointed they all were. The aghast expressions they shared made a few Estrine knights chuckle. But how was anyone supposed to react when they were being served a fixed portion of gruel instead of a delicious, filling meal like they had the other day? Miffed maybe and definitely baffled, but not much else.

Wally was not sure why they pulled such a joke, but he went along with it and advised Van to do the same. In the midst of the tangible melancholy in the air, Wally took his share of the bland food for the third time without anyone else the wiser. How, Van was unsure but chose not to get too involved.

So much of the swill sat before the jester it almost made Van lose his appetite. Almost. "We've got to eat something, I guess."

"Ah, don't be so picky," Wally retorted with a laugh. "A knight needs energy for every battle. We get energy from a good meal, and I want to keep all the energy I can."

Considering how much Van ate on a regular basis compared to the average preteen, he was not one to criticize another's eating habits.

"Gods! How can the two of you stomach so much of this slop?" a harsh voice sounded from behind them. It came from the girl standing punctually behind Wally with her tray in her thick hands. Her long red hair had been tied into an exceptionally long ponytail.

It was that girl, the one who crashed into him and clashed with Kallant and his entourage.

Without waiting for an invitation, the redhead sat herself next to Van. He saw no reason to send her away.

"How did you even get three bowls?"

Much of the girls who participated in the page training were quiet and stern, almost like the golems from stories of old. This one seemed like the children back at Russalin—outspoken with a certain flair of brashness.

Breaking focus from the jester, she then eyed the quiet page she sat beside, her spoon hanging from her mouth. Her eyes had this rough, craggy look with a subtle sparkle of emotion trying to hide out of sight. It was unusual yet intriguing.

Popping the spoon out from her mouth, she gave him a smile that boasted sheer moxie. "I don't think I properly introduced myself last time. My name is Rubella Ivanstronge of Cragfill." She held out a friendly hand much like the one Wally had given him. With many of the pages already against him, Van thought it smart to be cautious. Still, it would have been rude to leave her like that, so he met her halfway, giving a firm handshake.

"Rubella?" Wally muttered with his spoon jammed between his teeth. His mood dampened a little. "Aren't you that girl who likes to shoot arrows at people's heads?"

Her smile discarded, Rubella gritted her teeth, her blue eyes leering at the carefree boy who sat dumbfounded sucking on his spoon. "Shut up! I was aiming for the targets just like everyone else! And I don't need a sloppy ape like you criticizing my archery."

"Says the girl who criticized how much we boys eat."

"Wally, I don't think you should be starting a fight so early in the year," interrupted Van. "You could get in trouble with the Estrines."

His comment seemed to have driven Rubella's hostile temperament away momentarily. She was confused one moment but interested the next. "Peculiar," she muttered. "I thought the child of Victoriah the Wolverine would enjoy a good bout."

"You know of my mother?"

"Is there anyone who doesn't?" she asked into a chortle, holding back a snort. "Her accomplishments leave anyone who hears her name utterly breathless. She is strong, sharp, and can fight any enemy bare-handed. She's even a favorite of the good King Faustign himself. But ... you are her son, after all. Surely, she must tell you of the things she does while roaming the country, keeping the peace."

Van found himself grinning just like she was. "Yes. I always asked her to tell me about what she did whenever she returned home." He could go on for hours, even days on end, illustrating every battle and escapade exactly to the detail told to him. Were it not for the distractions of Wally chewing his food and utensil like a crazed animal, Van would have brought up the time she stormed an abandoned keep to flush out the brigands taking refuge there.

"Mm. Lady Victoriah is a marvelous knight. Someone worthy of praise. ...Hard to believe someone with such ineptitude handling a sword shares her blood."

And there it is, Van thought. He expected his poor swordsmanship to be mentioned at some point.

"Swordplay ... was never my forte, no matter how much I trained."

The humility and uncertainty in his words made her laugh. It was a rough sound with nary any feminine charm, but he could not think to call it unsavory. It brought a jolly grin back to his face.

"Come to think it," Rubella began again, stopping her laughter, "I never thought Lady Victoriah even had a child."

"Rumor never spread?"

"None that I heard of. And I hear a great deal from my family's grapevine."

"Meehee ... iee nush 'echash—"

Wally and Victoriah the Wolverine seemed to clash for focus between the three, and the young man's bad dining habits—to Rubella's disgust—dragged favor toward him. She looked his way, seeing him bring the bowl to his lips, unsatisfied with the small tastes from the spoon. "Attempt to swallow before you speak, ape."

He decided to take Rubella's advice, though it might have been for air instead of consideration. Despite the thick substance and pungent aroma, Wally downed his entire bowl of gruel without choking on it. "I was trying to say, 'Maybe it's because she wanted to keep you safe.'"

For a moment, Rubella sat with her mouth hung open, mockingly giving the impression she would imply, "What a foolish notion," yet she lost said composure quickly. "You have a point there. Lady Victoriah has many enemies, and I doubt they are very honorable. Some would be so bold as to target you to make her suffer."

As one had once before, Van thought ruefully. Although his thoughts were grim, he kept control over his countenance so as not to ruin the good mood.

"What made you come to that idea?" he asked his friend.

"The same thing happened to my eldest brother before he turned eight. He managed to live to tell the tale, but his right eye was gashed out by the assassin's dagger before help arrived."

Rubella gasped. "Is that true?"

"Yeah. If he didn't start learning to wield a sword when he was five, it would have been—"

Rather than listen to the story progress, Van tended to the cold thoughts bubbling in his mind. It was not so obvious in his eyes anymore, but his mother loved him. She did everything she could to give him a safe and happy life. Such knowledge, as unquestionable it should be, twisted in his mind as though it were a light refracting through a prism.

Why did he question something so absolute?

The two pages bickering beckoned him from his thoughts so he could see to another matter. Now Wally looked ready to leap for Rubella.

"Stop calling me ape!" was all Van heard upon his return.

"Both of you, please stop fighting," he demanded in his calmest tone. They listened to his reminder out of fear that the Estrine family would serve strict punishment for being disruptive. "We can't relax forever. We should take this time to regain our strength for the next lessons instead of wasting it." However reluctant they were, both of them calmed, unclenching their fists, and took to their gruel.

The next lessons required more mental acuity than muscular effort.

The pages gathered in a spacious study hall for an introduction into tactics and strategy after their meals. Rather than Sir Charleston, this lesson was led by a taller, hunched-over elderly gentleman who carried a sturdy cane fashioned from petrified wood. The children were expected to remain silent and punctual unless any of the Estrines ordered otherwise. For said reasons, everyone kept quiet in their seats while the elderly man stood motionless at the podium in the center of the room.

Several minutes passed with nary a word spoken. Their instructor had not so much as twitched. No one would risk stepping up and saying anything to get things started. They did not want to get in trouble.

Van had all but lost his patience. It amazed him how no one so much as groaned out of boredom waiting for the littlest of instructions. His eyes closed halfway through the wait, the silence becoming nauseatingly dull. If he had to remain idle, then he chose to use the time to develop his magic senses. He kept his eyes closes and breathing steady, focusing on the flow of energy around him.

Something in the valsara emanating from the elderly man left an odd impression on Van. He was much too calm. Some activity had to be happening with his spirit, otherwise, he would be presumed a specter.

Or—

Nothing was going to get done at this rate. Van stood and walked down the aisle toward the podium where the instructor stood.

Rubella reached a hand out and grabbed to his wrist, holding him back. "Van, what are you doing?" she whispered.

There was no need for him to shake free of her shackle grip. His icy cold skin shocked the nerves in her hands, urging her to release.

Even after approaching him, there was no reaction from the gentleman. The same blank expression covered by his thick mustache and eyebrows adorned his face, and his valsara did not stir.

I knew it.

"Excuse me, sir," spoke the quiet page.

His voice coaxed a prouder posture from the gentleman, his valsara suddenly lighting. The elderly man's hands, perched comfortably atop the old wood cane, began to tremble. It sounded like he was mumbling.

"Sir, are you all right?"

"Eh ... ah, yes. Perfectly well. I was in the middle of demonstrating the art of patience. Everyone, excellent work so far!" he announced. Upon laying his eyes on Van, though, he feigned disappointment. "You ... you need to learn more self-control. Go on now. Back to your seat."

Finally, an instruction from the instructor.

Van wasted no time making it back to his seat, though the scornful laughter of the other pages distracted him a tiny bit. They seemed to believe their instructor's words blindly, a trait he found most unusual yet remarkably common. Still, he paid them no heed. Let them think he was a buffoon with no common sense; it was not like they did not think that of him to begin with. Returning to his seat, he heard the man address himself to the pages as Lord Tamsilac K. Estrine of Everspeak.

"What in Ralias' name were you doing?" Wally whispered to Van, mentioning the god of war and prosperity. "You shouldn't be disrespectful to a veteran knight like that. It's almost like you thought he was asleep."

"He was," Van answered briefly.

Wally looked skeptical but came to believe him. "Wait. He w—"

Van held a finger to his mouth, demanding silence. Since the lesson was only beginning, he wanted to hear as much as he possibly could.

Out of everything, he wanted to learn about the unique geography of the kingdom. There was much that separated Vermalio from other countries, according to Lord Tamsilac, such as its various geological majesties both beautiful and harrowing. Any who were clueless to the "purities" of their region, as common Vermalians called them, wound up corpses before they were aware of it. And the country's weather phenomena were more often than not intense—be it sunny, rainy, windy, snowy, or otherwise.

Knights ventured wherever they were needed. It was prudent that they were prepared for anything that challenged them, even the will of the gods. Whatever disaster they faced, they were expected to overcome it.

When etiquette lessons came along, Van paid especially careful attention. They began by learning a little about Abioan, the language spoken in Ederea. He did not believe etiquette provided the most difficult challenge compared to the other lessons. Manners and good posture, he thought that was all it would take to impress.

Such arrogance.

For different cultures and nationalities, there was different etiquette to follow and different means of insulting others. Being too polite in the southern islands of Ederea made one appear arrogant.

Van's head throbbed as painfully as it had when someone bashed his skull during weapons training. It would take a lot of time for him to comprehend all of that information.

The same routine continued for the next week. All of the pages grew accustomed to their schedules quickly. Van abhorred the mundane routine. Had he not looked forward to learning new methods of swordplay or further developing his understanding of the country, his mood would have quickly declined.

Fortunately, with Wally's lively nature, he never had a dull moment amongst his new friends, especially when he and Rubella got into strangely entertaining arguments. He found Rubella rather witty.

The only changes made in the week were when the pages had time for themselves to choose which skills to sharpen. Both Wally and Rubella thought the same thing when they decided on what needed the most improvement: Van's swordsmanship.

Van, Wally, and Rubella had the training grounds to themselves. Every page had access to the space when lessons were not in progress and were permitted to use the practice weapons there. Not many pages chose to train as often, confident in their strength and abilities—perhaps from besting Victoriah the Wolverine's son. It only meant fewer distractions for the three while they practiced the swordsmanship Sir Charleston demonstrated on the pages—typically Van.

Wally had the best grasp on swordsmanship, but Rubella proved to be the better to test their friend's mettle. She was Van's sparring partner while Wally gave him instructions from the sidelines.

The girl was very strong and energetic. She only needed to make a few swings before knocking her opponent aside. Van did well to hold his own, but shortly after blocking a few attacks, his arms would tremble and his strength waned. His arms never held steady, and his wrists jostled.

At first, Van was confounded as to why his arms would not move as he directed, but then an epiphany hit. It was not resolve that he lacked, but control. His body defying that disciplined fashion with which he moved, fighting the control he made to attempt it.

No one could move through the motions perfectly when they first started, but anyone could see the difference between their inexperience and Van's inability. It was as though his very nature refused him to adapt to the stances he took.

Van found it difficult to resist charging at Rubella in the manner of a mad beast after the fifteenth time he had been knocked off his heels. Adding insult and injury, both of his comrades kept reminding him to keep his composure. But hearing those commands only stirred his fury even more, and the lack of control made him feel more amped for a fight.

They decided to rest for the time being, with no progress being made in the twentieth round.

Van refused to move off the ground afterward. He felt much too ashamed of himself for now following the simplest movements in swordplay. He could walk upright, act proper, fire arrows, ride a horse, and even balance books on his head, but he could not come close to maintaining decent form when bearing a sword.

Why can't I get this right?

Just as he was about to sink into depression, Rubella reached a hand down to her new comrade. Accepting it pulled Van out of his gloomy thoughts and onto his feet. "Thank you, Rubella."

"Don't mention it." Despite her many wins against him, she did not appear as boastful and brassy as she had when besting the other boys. She was either expressing sympathy or found no thrill in beating a weakling. She turned to put away the practice sword she borrowed, then faced Van once more. "You can call me Rubi, by the way. Rubella is much too formal for me."

He nodded, feeling much happier than his dry countenance dictated. Allowing him to address her that way meant she accepted him as one of her own. It was as much a comfort to him as it was to her.

Many pages came to dislike Van for being Victoriah the Wolverine's son and for his pitiful swordsmanship. But Wally offered kinship, and now Rubella offered compassion. He was not about to deny it.

Putting aside sword training for the day, they decided to move on to something else. Rubi demanded that she got to decide their next activity since Wally chose the first. Although that was not exactly true, neither argued; they were still stunned to see how she was in a fight. A broad grin over her face, she led them to the chateau.

While they were about to head inside, their attention drifted to something more interesting. Kallant and a couple more well-built, taller, meaner-looking pages—possibly fourth years—were pestering a few younger pages. They were a boy and a girl both with similar qualities in dirty gold locks, polished eyes, and innocent faces.

It was clear what was happening. The girl was shaking and the boy tried to act tough but looked ready to hurl.

He broke from his group and headed straight for them, not bothering to consider the choices Wally and Ruby planned on making, and not caring what Kallant wanted. Van was not a fool. He knew a bully when he saw one. "Page Ginnstom." Pages should not pick fights with one another, but he could not let the abuse go. He refused to. "What is the meaning of this?"

Kallant and his entourage glanced back at him once they heard his voice. The two thugs looked as gruesome as they were antagonizing the two small children. Kallant, however, made the attempt to hide his spite. From a pout to a cruel grin his smile shifted. "What is the meaning of that formal tone, Vandelas?" he asked nonchalantly. "We're all pages, aren't we? There is no reason we should address each other so coldly."

"I asked you a question."

"Such a scary kid. Must get that from his monster of a mother." Those words were more to entertain his cruel compatriots, who chortled dryly, than to insult Van or his family, though they certainly were not kind. "It's nothing to be so callous about, Vandelas. We were just having a little conversation with our little friends here."

"Liar!" the cowering boy blurted out. For a moment, he seemed to have regretted his choice, but he collected his courage.

Then the girl sharing his appearance spoke. "You demanded we pay you respects simply because we didn't bow or praise you when we passed."

"Respects?"

"This doesn't concern you, Vandelas," Kallant softly growled.

The crude boy suddenly lost the control he possessed moments before. Glancing backward, Van found it was because he noticed both of the pages tagging with Van approach and back him up. Ruby looked at the situation as seriously as her friend; Wally stood there almost looking blithe as always.

"You're right, it doesn't concern him. It concerns us!" the abrasive redhead barked. She flashed her teeth almost like an angry wildcat.

"It doesn't take a mage to see the hostility you were showing those two. Mind telling us what you planned on doing to them?" Wally sported a crooked leer much like a snake's, the same overconfident look he brought out during weapons training.

Kallant scoffed at their approach. "*To* them? You don't seem to understand. I was doing something *for* them. There is something they have neglected to learn here, you see."

"Is that right?" Time passing second by second, Van saw within this boy's valsara a greater disdain than he noted previously. All of Kallant's attention was now focused firmly on him. He did not mind provoking the thug. "Then perhaps you would be so kind as to teach us as well. What is this lesson, Page Ginnstom?"

A flare sparked from Kallant's valsara. The once faint flicker Van rarely noticed of others became an intense pulse rippling through him. It made him resemble a predator before it rushed out of hiding for a kill.

One of his lackeys tapped Kallant on the shoulder, taking his attention. Kallant glanced to the side and shared a hint of displeasure, but quickly masked it behind his smug countenance. "Perhaps another time." He and the burlier pages took their leave as quickly as they could without raising much suspicion, not wanting to be followed.

The look on his lackey's face gave Van all of the information he needed; someone was watching them, someone Kallant was afraid of. He was still there too. Van felt that same valsara behind him for some time, but because there was such a distance between them, it was impossible to tell who it belonged to. Looking back, he noticed it was an Estrine knight on patrol, curious over their gathering.

"Hey ... thanks for your help."

Van turned back to the two identical pages. The boy, the one who spoke up, tried acting like Van's help was unneeded or unwanted whereas the girl offered a smile, showing that gratitude in his place. It intrigued him how they looked so similar yet behaved so differently.

"What were they up to? Did they just want to scare you? Because I think they could have done better." Wally's comment made the boy laugh and, surprisingly, Rubi as well. Tensions between the two fell at his jocular words.

"That Kallant bum wanted us to address him like he was king after we passed each other," said the boy.

The girl continued in his place with a more respectful tone. "He could tell we are from the lower class."

His behavior came from differences in class? Van did not quite understand. At first, he believed them to be referring to the lessons they took from the Estrine family, but he quickly realized they spoke of the layers in the social system based on the differences between rags and riches. He learned about them before coming to the chateau, but it never made sense to him.

"The Ginnstom family are the nobles of the Starscape region. I heard from a few of the more experienced pages that is why he thinks he can act as though he can walk all over us. His ego is terrible. Just because we were born poor, he thinks he can bully us into worshipping him."

"Ah, I get it," said Wally. "He's the kind of page my brothers warned me about. Every time one of them was a page, they always complained about some boys that only knew how to pester others. You either did what they said, or they pummeled you for going against them."

"He's probably just one of those nobles that was raised poorly. They always demand a lot of attention," Rubi added. There was something to her voice that told Van she had some experience with such noble children.

"Whatever his reason, he shouldn' be botherin' me and my sister. If it weren' for those goons leechin' onto him, I'd—"

"You'd do nothing, Galvven," the girl interrupted harshly, though with the still gentle tone. "Kallant Ginnstom is a noble with training. We have only been here a week, and you can barely carry a sword."

The boy turned to the girl, grunting. "So what of it? We've survived scarier bunches than them when we were livin' in the slums. I bet even you could'a trounced him!"

"Was there something you two were in the middle of before this?"

Van felt the need to interrupt regardless of his desire to see where that was all going. He did not think Kallant would leave them be, and he did not want to know how poorly they would have handled him.

The girl looked back at him. "We were just heading to the library."

"And I was just tellin' her I didn—"

"Oh, perfect!" Rubi interrupted with an oddly big grin. "We were heading that way ourselves. Come on, we'll all go together. I will even help you study."

She guided the two inside before they could object. Even though the boy tried objecting, Rubi shoved him in the direction she was going and refused to listen. There would be no talking her out of it. Van and Wally shared a look of confusion before following her.

The two pages, while being guided, gave them their names: Galvven and Gallelia Erite.

When they got to the library, she told her friends she would be tutoring them on Ederean etiquette. As so it happened, she was quite knowledgeable of the country's culture. Her family had been for managing friendly relations with Ederea for the past few generations. She lived in a city bordering Ederea and learned plenty from the visits of diplomats and the occasional merchant hoping to do business.

Whether they needed it or not, Rubi made it clear she was going to instruct them in the linguistics and conduct of their neighbors' culture very thoroughly.

The twins tried going their own way after seeing how abrasively Rubi taught etiquette. She had none of that and made them sit down and pay close attention.

It was not so bad. She taught them with a calm demeanor and behaved peculiarly polite. Were anyone to say or act with even a hint of error, then they would see her fury. She lashed at them with a venomous tongue and approached them like she was on the attack, stopping just before she put a hand on them. Somehow, she continued to maintain an eloquent form of speech while doing so.

Galvven cringed so horribly from her verbal abuse. It looked like he would cry if he lost hold of himself.

Van felt a similar fear, though his tear ducts remained as dry as his sense of humor. And yet from this strict form of tutelage, he held a certain respect for her. This girl's passion for the culture of the people she came to befriend impressed him.

No one dared to oppose her ruling on their performance. Something in the back of their minds warned them they would come to regret it.

"From the top!" Rubi demanded after Van failed to answer how to address an elder figure. "Now, what do you say to an Ederean lady you greet for the first time?"

Most evenings before curfew, Van reflected on his day and briefly reviewed certain aspects he believed would be the trickiest things to remember. Studying certain tactics and repeating certain phrases from the challenging Ederean language was his primary focus.

Just like the previous nights, the adorable white fox who clung to him snuck into his bedchamber undetected for her time with him. Since he knew she would continue to visit regardless of the danger, Van went to the city one day after the lessons ended to purchase his furry friend a brush, which cost him his entire allowance. Snowflake saw no purpose in the strange tool considering she took grooming to herself and even told him so with a light growl, but she warmed over to the idea after realizing how the brush felt running across her fur. She loved it whenever Van took the time to hold her in his lap and brush her fur.

That night, Snowflake waited patiently for him on his bed, curled up into a puffy little ball.

Van was at his desk writing on a piece of parchment. Usually, he took to practicing his penmanship after a long day. But he realized he had yet to write to his parents since arriving at the Estrine Chateau. Two weeks had already passed. He thought it to be a good time to send something. He certainly had plenty to write about.

After giving his letter a little thought, he happily wrote:

Dear Mother and Father,

I'm sorry it took me so long to write. I'm having a wonderful time here. Maybe there are a few obstacles I need to see to, but it is not all bad here. I already made a few friends—one of them happens to be an admirer of Mother's. They are all helping me work through a few areas in my training that need improvement. It would be wonderful if you could meet them. I'm sure you would like them.

I miss you both, and I have been thinking of Russalin often. I promise
to make you both proud. Your efforts will not be wasted.
By this time next year, you will see how much I've grown.
Stay well.

In case his mother would not return home for some time, he wrote
another letter for her so both of his parents could hear from him as soon
as possible. And, as he promised, he even wrote a letter for Mini and the
rest of his friends. He wanted everyone to know he was well.

"I know they will worry no matter what I write," Van told Snowflake,
"but hopefully this will reassure them. You've seen how stressful my father
behaves. Just imagine what everyone else is like."

Snowflake gave her human friend a dreary glance, listening to him as
intently as possible, but yawned a moment afterward.

He was tired too. Both of them wanted to sleep, but Van did promise
Snowflake he would brush her.

After finishing the letters, he groomed Snowflake gently and
thoroughly. She tried remaining conscious while enjoying the comb tickle
through her fur, but the day caught up with her. Van kept brushing her a
while longer so it might soothe her into a comfortable slumber.

~ Sixth Chapter ~

Pride

With the days rolling by, Van found himself slowly adjusting to his new life. When not busy, Van visited Nightshade and took her for a run. She was always delighted to see him and get out of that filthy place. The stables were often in terrible shape. Every page was instructed to care for their mounts, but not everyone visited them more than once or twice a day to feed them and clean up a few spots in their stalls.

Van planned his days accordingly to be sure he had the chance to visit Nightshade at least four times a day—before breakfast, during mount training, after the lessons concluded for the day, and before supper. Their meetings were not long when he did not take her to run, but he always made sure to give her the attention she deserved and tended for her living space. He valued her as another member of his family.

One day, Snowflake came out from hiding while Van fed Nightshade. He could see that she felt lonely. When it came time for him to brush the mangled knots from Nightshade's mane, the fox pressed herself between them in an attempt to take back his focus. The mare did not appreciate the little thing scampering over her back. She tried to throw the fox off, knocking Van aside in the progress.

Perhaps she would come to regret it later, but Snowflake refused to let the horse have Van. Since then, she followed him to the stables to make sure she got her attention when no other humans were about. Once a night was no longer enough for the little fox.

Rather than be disappointed, Van felt flattered. His mother always said girls would fight over him. The thought of how she would react if she knew the first ones were beasts made him laugh.

The routine in the Estrine Chateau was rather fixed, but there was always something to make the days seem different.

On occasion, a knight would rob certain pages of their personal time and take them to a place that always eluded him. There were a few times he contributed to his training by following them from the shadows, curious as to where they were going. Alas, no matter how well he hid, Van always lost sight of them. How they all did it, he did not know. It was as if they were phantoms.

He never figured out where those pages went or why they were behaving so strangely.

Every few days, the etiquette lessons took place during luncheons for the pages to practice table manners. Remembering the correct utensils to use for certain dishes and how to hold them properly was not easy. The challenge for Van was keeping the perfect posture, sitting in a chair without any fault in his spine. Despite having no experience with such formal lessons, unlike most of the noble children, he proved a fast learner.

A few months passed. Van made a place for himself at the chateau.

Not many were kind to him, although it seemed only to be out of a twisted secondhand bitterness they held toward his parents. Perhaps their family held grudges against his own, but Van did not care.

What mattered to him were the friends he managed to make. Wally, Rubi, Gal, Lelia—they were all wonderful people he knew he could rely on. Putting aside things like family names and rumors, they came to like Van, even though he behaved a bit distant at times.

The same went for two other pages he met, a midnight-haired boy who kept to himself and a smoky-haired boy studying warfare.

Van came across Ccuivr, the morose loner, when he was riding Nightshade in the fields. Among many of the first-year pages, he excelled in armed combat. He paid little attention to strategy, but his instinct was rather keen, knowing what to do and when. Van heard from Gal that no one managed to make him so much as cringe.

And he grew bored of the sparse competition.

So one morning, Van decided to offer him some. The loner rode a young stallion much sprier and more erratic than the rest of its herd. Seeing the chance to get Nightshade some exercise as well, he proposed a race to entertain the page and tire out his horse.

Upon hearing the proposal, Ccuivr scoffed. Like everyone else, he was not impressed by Van's gangly mount. The very notion that Nightshade could keep up with his well-bred horse seemed improbable.

If anything, the only concern Ccuivr showed was for the stallion he rode. For only his mount's enjoyment, Ccuivr accepted the challenge.

The race was a simple one—start where the two old trees formed a natural arch, take three laps around the fields, and finish at the stables.

Both competitors started off strong, the stallion and mare dashing through the blades of overgrown grass at tremendous speed. Ccuivr proudly took the lead, almost bored with his chances for victory. It was that overconfidence that made him lower his guard. Despite Nightshade's stature, he soon realized she was lighter on her hooves than he expected after she swiped the lead in a few quick trots. How Ccuivr tried to push his mount to its limits to take it back!

One lap—he was three feet behind.

Two laps—he lost five more.

After the third passing lap, there was a seventeen-foot distance between the two.

Ccuivr failed to catch up with Van and Nightshade no matter how much he put his mount through. He looked to Van and black mare as he crossed the finish line behind them.

The failure irked him. He refused to admit defeat and demanded a rematch. Since Nightshade was still eager to run, Van accepted.

There was no need to worry about Nightshade. Her insatiable desire to feel the wind's embrace could keep going from dawn until dusk. It still amazed Van how much energy her frail body contained.

In the second race, Ccuivr and his mount both worked to maneuver themselves past Nightshade. Confidence in his abilities and his mount kept telling him Van's victory was only won by luck, but again he was passed and left in the dust. And as hard as it was to believe, from the looks of it, Nightshade did not tire in the least.

Again, he demanded a rematch.

Eventually, both Van and Ccuivr knew it was time to stop when the chateau bell alerted them that dinner would soon be ready. In the end, Ccuivr chose to consider the poor swordsman an equal, at least until he found a way to outrace him.

Van made a new friend and rival, and meet his admirably stubborn horse, Felltrot.

Stevene Inverg, the tactician trainee taking his second year as a page, often worked in the library studying the riddles of war. Van offered to help him study, believing that a second perspective would help them both.

He seemed wary of Van at first, but Stevene accepted the offer shortly after giving it some thought. They showed each other a few strategies, then exchanged thoughts on their effectiveness. From a few points, Stevene thought Van's explanations were rather contrived and arrogant. However, he came to understand his thinking and even wrapped those ideas around a few of his own.

After deciding to stop studying for the time being, the intellectual boy apologized for treating his new friend so coldly at first. He apparently heard the rumors spread about Van. Stevene valued the rumors he heard and followed them with caution since there were times when they came to be true. Whatever he heard, he confirmed it to be untrue, and came to like and respect Van.

Nothing more needed to be said.

Van came to understand his caution and the reason behind it the more time they spent together. Although not everyone possessed magic senses, there were some that were sensitive to the valsara of living beings. They were able to understand their feelings and intent, more or less, better than those who could not sense valsara at all. And he learned that Steven was one of those people.

As everyone came to know Van, they began to meet and befriend one another.

For someone that ostracized himself from others, Ccuivr took an interest in the fellow outcasts. He saw Gal and Lelia as something as a means of entertainment. There were rumors he never laughed before, but the twins confirmed it to be nothing more than that. He laughed at Lelia reminding Gal of his faults in his swordplay when he insisted on boasting of his skill. He almost seemed like an entirely different person with a small smile and a voice filled with laughter.

Wally and Stevene got along well. Since getting to know each other, they came to test the other's wit. But the two of them together made Rubi put her at wits' end. It bothered her enough being around Wally alone; having another smart aleck like him come into their faction made her want to tear her hair out, especially when the two of them began steering their japes at her. Unlike Wally, though, Stevene knew when he was about to push his luck and hushed up before Rubi turned feral.

Whenever Rubi's temper looked to reach its limit, Van either diverted their focus to something else or pried Rubi away from the group so she could vent her aggressions without harming the others.

Whenever she was in a foul mood, they would walk in the gardens and simply talk about whatever was on their minds. The environment respired a friendly atmosphere, valsara pleasantly flowing through the lush bushes and blooming flowers. It had quite the effect on Rubi's temper. But after she finished venting her frustrations, Van barely said a word. Not many things bothered him. Challenges regaled him. Puzzles intrigued him. Setbacks made the days more interesting. And with the daily get-togethers with his friends, Van felt content.

If something bothered him, he left it in the moment.

After another week of intense training, many of Van's faction found their studies becoming more problematic. They could not always go to the library. It closed its doors at an early hour before sunset. Studies ran so long that the curator insisted they leave before they were halfway through. A new space to keep working together was needed.

While going through this dilemma, Van and his friends ran into Lyn.

"Is something the matter, Young Master? You seem displeased."

She was very kind, always appearing when something troublesome came up. Even so, Van never liked relying on her more than he had to.

"Oh, no. It's nothing, L—"

"We were wondering if there was somewhere decent for us to study," Rubi cut him off. "Preferably where we can't be interrupted."

The maid put a finger to her lips, glancing at the ceiling with an expression most would see on another child.

It seemed to be a simple problem. Van did not think to bother the Estrines' servants about something so trivial, despite the lack of results.

"Ah! There is one place I believe will be to your liking. It's someplace near the fields, hidden from view."

"Can you please show us the way, miss'un?" Lelia asked.

Lyn bowed to the polite page and her company. "But of course, young lady. Please follow me."

Van said nothing and followed the others.

Wally noticed his friend's concern and chuckled. "Relax, Van. The servants here only want to help us pages."

"It seems like we're bothering her."

"Not at all!" chirped Lyn while she showed them the way. "I am glad to be of help to the pages here."

"It's their job to help us with our needs, right? It would be a waste not to ask when we need them," Rubi inclined.

"They have other duties to tend to. Asking them to put their work on hold for us makes it seem like we are interfering."

"Think about it like this," Stevene stated, "if we don't ask the servants for help, it would make them feel they are not useful. Wouldn't that be insulting?"

What he said made Van think.

Reacting to his silence, Lyn covered her mouth with her hand trying to hide a laugh. "This is quite a surprise. I have yet to see anyone make Vandelas fall silent." Truly, Van proved himself to be quite the stubborn mule. Before today, Lyn had never been able to convince the self-reliant young noble to call on her should he need anything. Perhaps now she could win an argument.

Guiding the pages outside of the chateau, she continued past the training grounds. Then she showed them to a large copse gathered to the northwest of the fields. The thick foliage barring the area off made finding a stable path difficult. But Lyn managed without any complications; she knew the way well.

The copse was something of a maze. So many of the trees' branches reached out to the sky that they formed a natural roof, shutting out the light. Eventually, Lyn brought them to an old shack in an enclosed clearing. Though it held an eerie impression, it looked sound enough and assured them it would be for their use alone. "I came across this old building when I was still new here. I could never figure out what it was doing here, and no one else seemed to know either."

Exactly what we need, Van thought.

"Maybe a murderer used to hide out here."

Lelia nudged her twin roughly. "Why would a murderer hide near the very place where the most skillful pages train and the mightiest military force in the kingdom exists?"

"It's exactly why a killer would hide here," Wally backed his little friend up. "Who would expect one to willingly hide so close to a place he can be easily found out and captured?"

Lyn could not conceal her glee as she had previously. "To have such imagination—that's good. Hold tight to them. A strong, sprawling mind is exactly what a knight needs to handle any situation."

While appearing caught up in the argument between the twins, Wally found himself intrigued by the stern, poised words Lyn used. Those exact words seemed to invoke an old memory, judging by his near-vacant expression. "I know I heard that saying somewhere before," he pondered. "You wouldn't happen to know Dougdin Alivvrn, would you?"

"Oh, the Marauding Knight!" Lyn stated. "Why yes, Young Master Wallace. I was well acquainted with your third eldest brother." No longer could she sustain her professional composure. Her entire demeanor changed; her body suddenly moved in a small sway and her face brightened. From Van's perspective, she appeared like she drank some of the aged northern wine he once served to the Estrine lords and ladies during one of the etiquette lessons. "I had just begun my training as a maid when we met. Sir Dougdin was beginning his fifth year as a page, and he was none too pleased that he took longer than his siblings to be chosen for a squire. He was certainly a hard worker, put all of his effort into earning the rite, but the Estrines kept pushing him to do better. Sir Dougdin went through such struggle time and again to prove he could excel the unruly expectations placed upon him. And the day he became squire to Sir Uerth, I could not have been happier for him."

"Yeah. That pretty much describes Din's time as a page. His letters home were mostly complaints."

For a brief moment, Van noticed a sudden frustration whelming in Lyn's valsara, which made her appear ready to strike at the boy. When it vanished a second later, though, he began to question whether or not he was imagining things.

"You sound a lot more cheerful after talking about the ape's older brother, Alicalyn," Rubi teased in a new provocative tone. "Could it be you fancied him?"

That jubilancy, unusual even for Lyn's cheerful behavior, had been broken by an equally abnormal nervousness she hoped to bury underneath her hands before anyone noticed. She kept her hands clasped together in a genteel gesture. The rich red blooming across her face gave away her answer. "It is true I held a ... certain infatuation toward the good Sir Dougdin." What remained of her ladylike composure fell apart as she spoke.

"Though I was well aware it interfered with his already sore confidence and future plans, I am ashamed to say I was glad he remained while I worked through my training. He was very kind and spoke with me often. Even with all of the pressure he put himself through, he always knew when I felt depressed or overworked and tried to ease my frustrations. He certainly knew how to treat a lady."

Stevene looked at Lyn with his typical skeptical expression. "Wouldn't it have been inappropriate for you and Sir Dougdin to be in such relations?"

"Yes, that is true. This place upholds a respectable training environment, meaning I am forbidden from fraternizing with anyone in such a manner. Even so, I couldn't help at least speaking to him on a friendly basis. My sentiments for him were kept concealed, so I believed it would not have mattered."

"And you came across this place while fraternizing with Wally's brother?" Ccuivr asked.

"Yes. He required a place to hide a family heirloom delivered to him for good luck. His roommates were rather envious he had it, you see."

Wally's eyes lit up. "Oh ho! Fíochmar?"

"Uh ... yes, I believe that is what he called it."

"What's a Fíochmar?" questioned Gal, hoping he pronounced it as his highborn friend had.

With a pleased grin and a dry chuckle under his breath, Wally responded, "It's my family's most treasured relic blade from the Old Age, said to have the soul of a gryphon embedded in the gemstone at its hilt."

A time of plentiful magic and when mythic creatures roamed the land, the Old Age was said to have been a dynamic part of history when anything could have happened. However, no one had any memory of what those mythic creatures were like or what happened during that time. Many believed the Old Age to be nothing more than a legend, an anomaly in time, existing only in children's stories and drunken hallucinations.

"It is said 'he who wields the majestic blade Fíochmar shall never lose heart in battle.'"

Delighted as she was to watch the children, Alicalyn knew she could not remain. "If there is nothing else, I should return. Oh, and I would give the hideaway a little sprucing up. It has been some time since it has been used." With that said, she returned to the chateau.

The children, while they were there, decided to visit the shack. A look inside brought them to consider Lyn's suggestion. The simplistic design and moldings appealed to them despite the grim gathered around them. The table and chairs left behind seemed like the shack's foundation—strong and enduring. Apart from the coats of dust and filth composed together from years of disuse, it seemed perfect.

Each of the pages contributed to cleaning a part of the shack. They all wanted a proper place to all gather when the library closed its doors. Sparing a little time to clean was a small price to pay.

It was a bit of a challenge, especially when it came to removing the hill of fire ants in the corner. Lelia kept making excuses so she would not have to go near it, her phobia of insects evident. Knights needed to conquer their fear, but seeing her flinch at the sight of a single ant, her valsara fluctuating furiously to distance herself from it, coaxed Van to help her with the task.

A few days after everything was neat and tidy, the faction finally took more time to work in peace.

This one evening, nearing the curfew hour, everyone was studying hard. Van and Stevene summarized a divide and conquer strategy and explaining the always precarious Wolverine stratagem—inspired by Victoriah Kronas herself. Rubi paid particular attention to every word Van uttered when speaking of his mother's combat strategy. It was a strategy often used with capture or rescue missions; the main faction would assault the enemy with their strongest men while other factions separated to secure the target.

Being too caught up in simplifying the strategy for Gal, he almost failed to keep a lookout of his surroundings. *Scutter! Skitter! Pomp! Scutter! Skitter! Pomp!* This nearly inaudible shuffling kept working its way toward them. *Scutter! Skitter! Pomp!*

The sound was too clear for it to come from the outside.

A look up, and Van saw there was an intruder, a snowfleece fox of small stature. Snowflake sat directly overhead of him. When the fox looked down and their eyes met, she lost her footing, falling from the support beam she crawled on and landing on Van's face.

His vision turned black one moment, white the next. Anything happening around Van passed by without his notice. The little fox did not weigh much, but the fall shocked him enough to fall back and bang his skull against the floor, putting him in a momentary daze.

A few normally easygoing valsara suddenly flared threateningly after she dropped in.

"Wait, stop!" Van sat up quickly before Gal and Ccuivr could come in close and harm the fox, wailing his arms ferociously to ward them away. "Everyone, calm down!" Those ready to go on the attack stood, wide-eyed, at his outburst.

Snowflake fled behind him, seeking his protection from the larger angry beasts that she thought were after her pelt. She trembled and let out light growls. Hoping to ease her worries, Van put a hand atop her scalp, gently scratching behind the ears.

"This isn't a wild animal. She is my friend."

His faction fell silent. They all knew well of his interest in animals, but they did not think he was keeping a pet.

Van explained how he came to encounter Snowflake and why she followed him so. The perilous climb across the Sperov Mountains for training, finding the poor kit injured and bleeding beneath the snow, rescuing her and nursing her back to health—he made sure to include it all while omitting any use of the Second Verse.

The twins tried to get a better look at the fox, but she crawled behind Van whenever thinking they could see her.

"Father believed she was with her family when they were attacked by predators. I was worried she wouldn't survive for a time."

Attempting to calm Snowflake, Van scratched her ears harder. Her stature became much less threatening when he scratched just the right spot, and her eyes drew halfway shut, showing her content.

Rubi tried calling the small fox to her, showing an abnormally smitten expression toward an adorable young animal. But Snowflake would not leave Van's side. Taken aback, she tried getting closer.

Pawr! Pawr! Snowflake barked her adorable warning shout at the redhead. It made Rubi flinch. *Pawr!* Van kept scratching behind the fox's ears to try and appease her when Rubi finally backed off.

"Hah, look at this! Big, bad Rubella is afraid of a little baby fox," Wally teased.

Although not an actual kit, Snowflake's diminutive size certainly gave the impression she was that young.

Van spoke up before another argument between the two could break out and frighten Snowflake even more. "She is not fond of humans. The little one even tried biting my father's nose off after she healed properly."

"And yet it followed you for two long years, and while it was still a baby no less," Stevene interrupted, still a bit skeptical.

"She learned to hunt on her own and survived whatever attacked her. Say what you will about her size, but Snowflake is a fierce little scrapper."

Everyone found the story about the little creature, and the little creature itself, very interesting. Even Ccuivr found himself intrigued by the meek-looking thing. Until everyone swore to keep Snowflake's presence a secret, Van refused to let anyone leave. It was a little difficult to convince a few, but everyone decided to keep the secret safe. No one was against it, not even the stickler Stevene.

"Put more muscle into your swings, Page Kronas!"

"Come on, come on! Try giving me an actual challenge."

Weapons training always brought a world of torment for Van. His inability to keep his arms stable when handling a sword brought Sir Charleston to harshly admonish him and Kallant to constantly provoke him. Were he more paranoid, he would assume the knight and page were conspiring to drive him mad. Whether or not it was true, it was working.

The delinquent always attacked using such excessive force just to taunt him. He wanted Van to go on the attack so he could strike him down.

If only he could swing a sword properly.

Any other weapon he handled, he could use as well as everyone else—spears, axes, bows. But whenever it came to swords...

Doing nothing would make him seem all the weaker, so Van endured everyone's scorn for looking a fumbling buffoon and did what he could to keep control of his arms.

His faction took every chance they could to intercept Kallant so he would not keep picking on him. While he appreciated their help, it was still humiliating for every page always bested him at swordplay.

The sting of defeat agitated him day after day throughout every lesson. It had gotten so bad that his dark mood would not fade. Not even a ride atop Nightshade, passing through the wisping winds, brightened his mood. He needed a change of pace, something to take his mind off all of the stress piled onto him.

Fortunately, something came up.

Lelia came to him as he returned from a ride and asked that he escort her into the city so she could visit her parents. One of the many rules they followed stated that pages must walk Brigadier's streets with at least one other person, be they page or knight. It puzzled him why she did not take her twin brother, but to repay her kindness, Van agreed to follow.

His mood uplifted when walking with Lelia, but that only lasted until they reached the chateau gates.

"Ho there!"

Van came to an irate halt at the gates hearing that irksome voice. He and Lelia turned to find Kallant and his faction approaching them.

"Fancy meeting you here, Vandelas."

Van sighed dryly under his breath. "Is there something you need?"

"Always so cold." That falsely casual tone was losing its deceptive charm. Instead of sounding the kindly gentleman he pretended to be, Van only heard a serpent's devilish hissing. "And here I came all this way to offer you a service. You've been having such trouble working with a sword. So I thought the boys and I could instruct you on how to properly wield one." His words were lost on Van. They were a twisted discord on the ears, the malevolence they carried clear as the bells. He could not be trusted. How others had yet to see that, he had no idea. "What say you? A little competition to show us our place?"

Though he wished he could be less polite toward Kallant, a knight had to be respectable even in undesirable situations. "You will have to find someone else to amuse you. I have a previous engagement to meet." That was as polite as he could be.

"What di—"

"Let's be on our way, Lelia."

Without a second thought, Van walked away from Kallant and his entourage with perfect composure. Those etiquette lessons came in handy. He appeared every bit the noble everyone expected him to be upon arrival.

Not wanting to be the next target for Kallant, Lelia stayed close to Van as they made their exit. They almost expected them to follow instead of standing there dumbfounded, but they did not complain when they knew they were gone.

"Van, do you know what you've just done?"

He knew. Van knew perfectly well what it meant to refuse a challenge presented to him. Proud knights staked their pride on proving their strength and capability to any who would oppose them. To refuse a challenge practically meant he admitted to being an inferior, but not only to himself. The pride of a knight belonged to its kingdom. A shamed knight put shame on the crown that they served.

But Van did not care about that. Training was one thing; proving one's skill and strength for the amusement of others was pointless. There was no purpose in fighting simply to fight.

Once they went into the city, they felt relieved at being in a friendlier atmosphere. The hustle and bustle exhibited great jubilancy from the citizens all pleased with their peaceful lives safe inside Brigadier's walls.

They had to go a fair distance from the chateau. Following the boardwalk to the marketplace, they took a turn at the giant tree around the center and went toward the southern district. Along the path, the buildings and streets became shabbier, in need of care. There were notably fewer soldiers patrolling the streets, but also fewer people out in the open. And when Lelia saw an inn near the end of the lane, she ran toward it.

The building appeared to be in rough condition, but not enough to cause concern. Upon entering the threshold, Van noticed the interior was not much different. The walls and floorboards had been patched together by a shoddy hand, and the space seemed fairly empty except for the dining hall cluttered with tables and chairs. A crisp smell of poultry lingered around the kitchen doors. It was homely, but also felt quite homey.

The innkeeper called to greet Lelia kindly and familiarly. She was a wide-boned woman with a firm girth and a smile as broad as her shoulders. Her personality filled the place with a welcoming air that made everything feel more pleasant.

Lelia waved at the woman before rushing up the stairs excitably. And Van followed suit after offering a kind "Good day, miss," to the innkeeper for politeness.

He found her knocking at the second door to the left of the staircase. "Ma! Pa! It's me!" The door opened as soon as Van caught up.

A woman with messy light bronze curls stood at the entryway with her dark blue eyes lit up. Her smile, while a bit tired, was aglow with a lovely maternal kindness. She stepped out to give her child a hug.

She held the door half open to let Lelia in, stopping only when she noticed Van. She seemed cautious for a moment. "Who have we here?"

"Vandelas Kronas, miss," he answered politely and with a small bow. "I am escorting Gallelia today."

Although a tad surprised upon hearing the family name, the woman smiled again. She opened the door completely, inviting both children inside. "So this is one of the friends you and Galvven tell me about. Very nice to meet you, young'un."

"Thank you, miss."

"You've been lookin' after my children, I hear."

Van gave a wry smile. "It's more like they've been looking after me." It certainly appeared that way as of late.

Lelia's mother had a laugh from his humble response. Her valsara flickered something akin to glee.

Everyone sat down at the little table by the window where a teakettle brewing hot steam waited for them. Fond of the view, Van took the seat next to Lelia by the window while her mother sat opposite of them.

Lelia looked to the teacups placed on the table, appearing to be counting them. No matter how she looked at it, there were only three. That seemed to upset her a little. "Ma, where is Pa at?" Her voice gave away how concerned she was. It was like she expected something terrible had occurred. Her mother's smile never yet left her, so it was safe to assume nothing was wrong.

"He finally found work. He's a stableman takin' care of horses for some rich fella."

Any doubt and concern Lelia had vanished. She could not have looked more delighted if she tried. "Really?"

"Yes. But this job leaves him busy much of the day. I don't think he'll be joinin' us."

Lelia shook her head. "As long as the two of you are okay."

"What about you two? Where's your brother at now?"

"He's busy himself. Got himself in trouble with Lord Tamsilac."

"A-ha! Still causin' trouble, that little one. Better get his act together if he knows what's good for him." Lelia's mother sounded serious, but she seemed to be enjoying herself. "Still, it means I get to meet your charming friend here."

For a time, Van sat silently while mother and daughter talked about everything in their lives. On Lelia's side, there was not much to talk about that Van did not already know; her mother, however, told of some things that caught his attention. Many things she said that sounded ordinary seemed extraordinary to the two of them.

Lelia looked to notice his confusion. Before she began talking about her friends, she explained what she and her mother were so elated about.

Her family was a poor one. Her father could never find work after his first three jobs ended with his employers' ruin. Word got around the city that he was cursed, and no one would hire him; some went as far as to lob stones at him to chase him away. Their mother tried to keep it from them, but they found out after they saw him chased out of a pub, the owner nearly bashing his head in with an ale bottle.

The twins did not act as though nothing was wrong. Instead, they worried for their family and tried to figure out how to help. Times were tough, and there were few opportunities available to two small children. But when they found out that poor families were given a dole if their child enlisted for knight training, they both became pages. Their parents only had to worry about looking after themselves while they trained to be of use to the kingdom.

Van did not know what to say, but he saw the twins in a new light. He only became a page for his own interests, unlike those two.

As much as they enjoyed their time, the pages could not stay for very long. They agreed to meet with their faction to study before the end of the day. So they left after Lelia gave her mother a kiss on the cheek. The mother saw them off, asking her daughter to look after her brother and Van to look after her daughter.

Brigadier's atmosphere seemed much livelier on the way back to the chateau. It might have been the clowns performing near the marketplace, but the people appeared more pleasant this time around.

It was fortunate Lelia knew the way through the excited crowds. Her guide kept getting distracted and losing his way.

"Good day, Page Kronas."

Recognizing his family name but not the voice calling it, Van turned around to see a soldier on patrol. He had a rugged bald head without one of the helms the others wore. Although his voice was clear as day, he thought of who it might belong to with the muffle of metal.

"Good day, Sir Gervall."

It was the same soldier his mother introduced Van to when he first arrived in the city.

He properly greeted the soldier with a bow when he realized his suspicion was correct, then introduced Lelia to him. They greeted one another the same proper way he had.

"Helping the little lady with her errands? You take after your father after all."

"It is simply a favor to a friend."

"And you sound like him too."

Van smiled and rolled his eyes.

"Little friends of yours, good sir?"

Behind the knight approached a tall man with trimmed silver hair and youthful black eyes. He wore beautifully forged, study-looking armor that made Sir Gervall's look like scrap metal in comparison. He had a calm, laidback demeanor that showed he was very comfortable with the lively atmosphere around him.

Sir Gervall straightened his spine when approached by his fellow knight. "My apologies, milord!" He spoke to the man promptly and tensely. "I thought you were still occupied with the people."

"Oh, don't fret, friend. They simply wanted to pass along their thanks to His Majesty." The knight looked to the pages with a kindly smile that grew brighter upon recognizing one of them. "Ah, young Gallelia. You're looking rather well."

Lelia looked rather stiff as she attempted to look proper, but she could not stop her hand from covering her mouth or color from spreading over her cheeks. "Lord Xanlir, you remember me?"

"But of course." The knight turned to Van, who stood there with an awestruck countenance when he heard that name. "Xanlir Estrine of Everspeak," he introduced himself to the speechless page.

Lord Xanlir, the renowned Champion of Duty, one of the Six Champions.

The names of the Six Champions were well-known throughout the kingdom. They were the elite knights recognized by the king for one of several traits: bravery, honor, compassion, strength, spirit, and duty. The six knights served their king by traversing different regions of Vermalio and ensuring the peace was kept. Should trouble arise anywhere, they were directed toward the chaos and worked to put a stop to it.

Lord Xanlir achieved and kept his title by upholding the values that made a great knight and inspiring others to nurture those values in themselves.

Van learned about the champions from one of them. Although many were reluctant to use it, Victoriah the Wolverine was known by another name: the Champion of Heart.

He bit the inside of his cheek, silently admonishing himself, for not giving the champion proper respect and returning the introduction with his own. "V-Vandelas Kronas of Southern Valley! It is an honor, sir."

"Ah, so this is the rumored son of the good Lady Victoriah! The honor is mine, young Vandelas."

The page felt his breath taken away when the champion bowed to him. It was such an honor, even if it was only to be polite. He hurried in returning the bow, not wanting to seem rude again.

"I was just returning home from a little expedition. There has been much unrest lately, it leaves even my poor mount exhausted. This gentleman was kind enough to escort me back to my family estate, but perhaps you two would be willing to take his place."

Lelia had no trouble with taking initiative. "Of course, Lord Xanlir!" Her answer was far brasher than any statement her friend had ever heard from her. It was almost like she had no control of her own lips. Pretending to clear her throat, she then addressed Lord Xanlir with more composure. "We would be delighted to be your escort."

The smile on Lord Xanlir's face brightened from the offer made by the little girl; Lelia's own smile grew in response. The great knight turned to Sir Gervall, keeping a dignified albeit gregarious expression. "My apologies again for taking you from your post."

"N-No! No, it was an honor to be of any help to you, Lord Xanlir."

The typically casual knight entrusted the children to their task, after giving another bow to Lord Xanlir, and went on his way.

The Champion of Duty was a rather loquacious sort. He enjoyed commenting on how strange it felt to be back in Brigadier, no matter how many times he returned, and speaking about the places he visited. Van did not have much to say. He did not wish to risk embarrassing himself. Thankfully, Lelia was happy to respond and entertain him. Her voice chirped pleasantly when she spoke to the champion, expressing a rare jubilance. While she wore a sweet countenance, her valsara shuddered in an abnormally quickened rate.

Van would have thought it was because she was nervous about being in a champion's presence, but she seemed to know him. How, he would have liked to know.

A crowd of people flocked around the renowned nobleman as they walked by. They all fawned over him, calling out his praise and trying to get noticed. He did not stop his march, but Lord Xanlir did respond, when he had not been speaking to Lelia, to the ecstatic people with waves and a glowing smile. He looked to enjoy the excessive attention given to him and being surrounded by smiling faces.

It all gave Van a headache, though.

Upon their return to the chateau, Lord Xanlir was greeted by an excessively loud bombardment of bugle horns erupting from every direction. Nearly every servant left their duties to meet the esteemed knight, and a few members of the Estrine family went to welcome back one of their own.

The windows on the upper levels were filled with pages coming to see what the commotion was about. It was only a matter of time until they gathered in the main hall in hopes of seeing one of the Six Champions.

It was not something Van hoped to stick around for.

The noise of the growing crowd distracted Lord Xanlir enough to not notice him slowly stepping away. Van escaped into the eastern halls, drowning out the noise with an expanding silence. Van kept moving until there was nothing more to be heard.

It was understandable why everyone was excited to see Lord Xanlir. No one so much as reacted when Victoriah visited, though.

While clearing his head of unpleasant thoughts, he wandered through the corridor where rows of paintings covered the left wall. Various eye-catching colors and hues drew in his attention, as had the mysterious quality in which they were used. Most of the paintings appeared to be portraits, commemorations of every member of the Estrine family all in the same scenery but at different periods in the year. He could feel the proud emotions each honorable man and woman held. Near the end of the line, he found a variety of the Estrines still instructing pages today and, of course, Lord Xanlir.

At the very end, his attention darted forward to the one at the very end. The subject was a child with burgundy hair and black eyes, younger than Van, younger than the twins even. His face definitely rang a bell, though he did not know why.

As he tried to assess who the subject could be, abrupt noises came echoing through the halls. Although it was nearly inaudible, something was definitely going on. It was not back in the direction he came, where the premature festivities were taking place, but in the opposite direction, where it was as silent and dreadful as a graveyard.

Curious, he walked down the hall following the faint noises. They became louder as he walked down the hall.

A chill ran through him as the sounds became clearer. There were four voices altogether. All of them sounded like grunting and groaning, but one of them was especially weak and difficult to hone in on.

Several thoughts rushed through his head when he began wondering what they were doing, but after confirming what those noises meant, he started running toward them. Someone was fighting. It began dying down shortly and was replaced with a disconcerting sound.

And with it came a painful cry that broke whatever peace Van had.

The next turn led him to a dead end where three burly young men stood laughing over something they found in the corner. The act they displayed irked him, but it became all the worse after fully realizing what had transpired. Kallant and his crooked cronies all ganged up on the small page curled into a corner.

Gal!

Something cracked inside Van at seeing the poor child covered in bruises and scrapes, his right eye swollen shut and blood dripping from his nose. His eyes had no trouble seeing every detail from his distance. The longer he stared at his little friend, taking in his wounds, the more something inside him kept chipping away into an empty void.

"Maybe now you'll go back to the gutter you crawled out of."

Kallant's comment broke Van from his daze and filled his mind with a frightening rage. His fists clenched tighter than a vise, and he began walking toward the concluded conflict, ready to start another.

"You should never have come here," Kallant continued.

Every word the thug uttered motioned Van to move faster, carrying more fury and hate into his stride.

"It's bad enough peasants like you think they can walk on the same ground as us, but to have the gall to talk back to me like we're equals! I blame that fallen noble you so idiotically follow. Someone like you, someone who doesn't take orders when given, doesn't belong here with the truly noble. You gutter-born trash are meant to follow us. To obey us! If you can't follow that simple, natural rule, then go back to the streets where you belong and take that wench of a sister with—"

Before he could declare any more, Kallant had been pulled aside by the shoulder with Van's icy hand clinging viciously to his chain mail and punched in the jaw by his frigid fist turned beet red from intense clenching.

The other two thugs never made a move. They stood petrified watching their leader get knocked to the stone floor, and looked at Van with fright, as though seeing him appear out of nowhere. How they had not noticed the *thud, thump* from his footsteps or the *swish, swang* of his chain mail was almost insulting, especially when each sound grew more intense with his rage.

Snapping back into focus, the thugs lunged themselves at him, fully intent on breaking him as badly as they had Gal. They were big, perhaps twice his size, but their movements were slow. Van took three intricate steps around the heavy limbs lying on the ground and let them ram into each other, then charged at them with full force.

They faltered but never fell. The furious child would not allow them time to recover and shoved them again, this time rushing his skull straight into the taller one's gut and his fist into the other one.

Listening to them squeal like dying pigs was bizarrely satisfying. He wanted to hear them cry as loudly as they made Gal.

An overbearing blow slamming into the back of his head shook him from the disturbing thought. The feeling his head might explode rattled him for but a moment, and quickly made way again for avid fury. He pulled his head back up, leering vilely at the wide-eyed ruffian.

Startled, he raised his arms again, hoping a second strike would be all it took to knock him down. Van kept eye contact with him as he quickly pulled back his fist and threw it right into his stomach. The chain mail branded his knuckles in marks that would soon disappear but did nothing to ward off his attack.

Down he fell like a monstrous oak, making a terrible thud upon hitting the floor.

With his back turned, Van left himself vulnerable to an assault from behind. Something smacked him clean across the head without warning. Turning around, he saw Kallant standing with a shaved sword.

Those were supposed to only be used for weapons training. How had he gotten his hands on one?

There was no time to think about that. Kallant was already rushing angrily at his attacker with his sword held at a low angle. His eyes showed an anger viler than Van's. Droplets of blood trickled from his throbbing nose whenever he made any sudden movement. He stopped for only a moment, surprised by the blood clot spattering everywhere.

"You unruly savage!"

Van watched the precise movements Kallant made, moving around the blunt instrument he swung madly. Though he was fast, he followed a near-constant rhythm that Van was able to interpret and dance around.

When he finally perfected the timing of Kallant's movements, Van caught the handle of the falling sword. Failing to comprehend what occurred, Kallant could not react when his opponent pulled in close and punched his nose again and again, until it bloated fatter than an eggplant.

It looked ready to pop if hit again.

Before it could happen, Van found his arms had been restrained. Kallant's goons had gotten up again and were holding him steady. They hurled him onto the floor, pinning him in place with their meaty palms.

Though he struggled, enough for the thugs to need both arms to hold him down, there was no chance for Van to escape. Kallant stood confidently over his prey after making sure he had been pinned down. With his nose inflated and those malicious piercing eyes peering down at him, he resembled an evil troll king from childhood stories.

"You've got more nerve than that gutter rat," hissed the infuriated troll. "I showed you *some* courtesy when you came here because you have a *shred* of nobility in you. But to strike at me as though you think me an equal..." The disgust rising in his voice, he spat at Van, staining his cheek with bloody saliva.

Van kept struggling with the thought of tearing those three apart; they misinterpreted it, thinking him afraid of getting hurt.

A foreboding sneer sprouted over Kallant's face.

Gripping the dull sword tightly, he raised it high so his next victim would get a good look, then hurled it at Van's face. Again and again and again he swung, growing more eager at seeing blood leak from Van's mouth. He savagely beat him with only the desire to see him squirm.

Even with his face becoming numb from the blistering pain, Van focused not on the agony he endured, but his burgeoning rage instead. All of his other senses began to weaken from the taste of his blood trickling across his tongue. The pungent flavor made him more hostile. Rational thought began to fade; he grew to want the taste of another's blood.

Upon Kallant swinging the sword for the fifteenth time, Van turned his head upon its approach and caught it in his teeth. He gripped his jaw to the old metal, keeping it wedged in place. Even as the thug struggled to break his weapon free of his jaws, Van only bit down harder. And when enough pressure was applied, a crack formed along the blade.

Kallant's hands began to tremble when the cracks became big enough for him to see, as though looking at something inhuman instead of the boy he enjoyed beating.

"What the devil are you boys doing?"

That booming voice was the only thing to make Kallant's emotions run cold. Sir Charleston stood at the corner of the hall, staring down the four pages gathered together.

The only look anyone had seen on the horribly strict instructor was his judgmental leer, but they clearly saw the rage Sir Charleston shot at them. The normally stagnant vein at the top of his forehead finally began to throb. "All of you, come with me this instant!"

Kallant immediately stood up, his thugs following suit. Van got up only to turn his back on them. None of them did anything for the brutally beaten boy lying in the corner, and it angered him to think they could just forget him. Had Sir Charleston not been there, Van would have continued the fight, ready to lacerate them bare-handed.

Struggling to hide that malicious desire, Van walked away from the knight and the ornery pages and crouched down beside Gal. He placed the hand without blood on it onto Gal's shoulder, shaking him lightly.

"Gal... Hey, Gal!"

There was no response.

His magic sight revealed Gal's valsara to be weak, but not enough for him to have lost consciousness. He had to have been playing possum, something Van confirmed when he found the courage to open an eye.

"Can you stand?"

Gal answered the question by doing so. His tongue had been slit: a common saying used to describe Russalin farmers who overworked themselves past the point of breathing. He managed, but his legs were about as stable as fallen tree branches.

Only when Gal managed to hold stand did Van follow the order given.

Sir Charleston brought the five pages to his quarters to question them. Strangely enough, the interrogation was carried out by splitting them into groups—Gal going first, then Kallant and his brood, and Van for last.

Usually when pages were being punished, the instructor would have all involved together so they would all hear each other's punishments, or so Van heard from the troublemaker in his faction.

The change in regulation likely had something to do with Van's secret. He would first hear what the others had to say, then weigh the evidence marked on them to decide what to do with the demon.

He struggled to keep from trembling while Kallant and his brood stood across from him. It would only feed their schadenfreude. Though he did not look their way, he still sensed the valsara crackling with spite. It was enough to make his skin crawl.

Even with their conflict ending as it had, Van had no regrets. They attacked his friend, so he paid them back. He felt no remorse whatsoever.

The massive doors leading to Sir Charleston's quarters opened. Gal made his exit to carry out his punishment for being involved. He moved slowly, limping every few steps. Kallant and his cronies silently laughed at their work while they stepped through the doors.

When they disappeared, Gal turned around and hurriedly walked over to Van. "Van ... I'm sorry you got dragged into this. You wouldn' be in trouble if I coulda taken 'em."

Gal liked to act big, like everything would go his way, but under the right circumstances, he was surprisingly humble.

Van tried to hide his own unrest from the guilt-ridden boy. "It was to protect you," he said with a smile. "I don't need an apology for that."

Granted the anxiety in his valsara, Van assumed his words would not make his friend feel less of the burden. Even so, Gal still smiled back at his friend.

"It would be best for you to leave before Sir Charleston dismisses Kallant. Go tend to your wounds."

Gal made himself scarce like he never got the limp. He was either a fast healer or wanted to look like he was.

Finally alone, Van allowed his repressed anxiety to show. He trembled violently enough for his chain mail to rattle. Not wanting to risk it being heard, he took deep breaths, white puffs of breath escaping him, and fought to slow the rampant beating at his chest.

His eyes eventually drew to the hand covered in now brittle crimson, and he came to ponder on how much blood he lost. He drew his left hand to his face and rubbed the spots struck by Kallant's stolen sword, eliciting a sharp exhale. Blotches of blood smeared onto his fingers, less than on the hand used to beat the bully.

It was his bare hand; he used a metal weapon. And that weapon cracked in between his teeth, none of which were dislodged from the excessive force used to keep it in place. It was unreal how easily he got out of that fight.

When he thought about the weapon, he looked down at his side. The practice sword his father gave him was left behind when he went into the city. Lord Estrine permitted him to use it for training but explicitly forbade him from leaving the chateau with it. He second-guessed how he thought the sword would have helped if he kept it with him. He was no match for anyone, let alone Kallant, in a sword fight.

The next sentence was delivered faster than the last. Kallant's brood left to tend to their punishments forthwith.

Van took one last breath, clouding the air before him, to ready himself for what might be his final punishment.

He hesitated to move. That heinous *click* from the unsheathing sword still echoed in his mind.

Upon entering Sir Charleston's quarters, he felt a haunting sensation smother him, as if he passed through the gates of the first hell.

As customary when presenting himself a senior noble, Van bowed to Sir Charleston before they began. It took everything he had to keep his body steady.

"Show your true self to me."

So this is how he wishes to take my life...

Disobeying him meant worsening his punishment—if possible. Van reached into his tunic's collar to grab the Shift Pendant dangling from his neck. Upon squeezing the stone, Van's skin and hair reverted back to their original hue, the unique red brands under his perpetually icy blue eyes appearing once again.

This form disgusted Sir Charleston. Despite those disapproving eyes, Van had to keep giving the knight perfect eye contact out of respect. The least he could do was demonstrate what he learned.

"We have gone through this before, have we not? Was I not clear about what would happen should you endanger anyone?"

"You were perfectly clear, sir."

"And yet you attacked three pages without a second thought. You disobeyed my warning, the warning of your superior, to act on your own whims in a blind rage—a shame perhaps not important to a Kindhrin, but one most intolerable for a Vermalian, and a knight no less."

"...Yes, sir."

"Have you nothing more to say for your actions?"

It did not take long for Van to assess Sir Charleston expected to see or hear something out of the ordinary, but Van could only make an assumption. His expression and valsara were equally stern and unreadable.

He did not know what to do, so he decided to clearly state what he believed should be said:

"I do not regret what I have done. Galvven became one of my own during the short time we have known each other. It became my responsibility to look after him. I acted in response to Page Ginnstom's behavior to unjustly attacking someone. Were Galvven just an ordinary commoner and Page Ginnstom a knight, his actions would be seen as inexcusable." Logical as his reasoning sounded, he still kept his true voice concealed. So to let it out, he took a deep breath and stared the knight down. "I cannot allow anyone to attack the people who need defending, not further cruelty!"

The knight made no reaction. He kept a cold expression etched onto his face that showed those words did nothing to move him. No words left his lips. Only when Sir Charleston put the quill in his hand down had Van known he made a decision.

~ Seventh Chapter ~

The Wayward Sword

Lady Sundralla's blessing shined upon Van when Sir Charleston gave his judgment. His punishment—originally an execution—had been reduced to cleaning the stables at the end of the lessons each day.

What made Sir Charleston change his mind was unclear. Thought of his decision lasted even as autumn gave way for the frigid winds of winter.

Tempestuous weather shrouded the capital. Heavy rain shot down at the earth, soon becoming sleet, and made way for gentle snowfall. The grass turned into tiny blades after being frozen over. The skies, always dark in this foreboding time of year, was bleak as the air became still. The howls and exhales from the dying winds often made the young and superstitious believe departed spirits came to haunt them.

None of the pages looked forward to their daily exercises in such morose conditions. Sadly, there was no choice of where or how they would train. Sir Charleston made that very clear. "There are no guarantees in war!" he promptly shouted to the pages as they trained. "However the elements decide to punish you, it is all the will of the gods themselves! You cannot defy it nor can you avoid it! You must endure every pain the world thrust upon you and march ever forward—that is the way of a Vermalian knight!"

That severe logic stuck to Van like bare skin to ice. There were turns of events in life no one could predetermine, as many blessings as perils.

"Mistakes mean death on the battlefield," another popular phrase Sir Charleston used when addressing those who slipped up in the exercises.

He was teaching them to be ready for anything and everything, no matter the circumstances. They did not respond very well to the simple exercises, though. Another approach was needed.

As the snow piled higher on the ground, established exercises that stimulated different situations in battle were established. The pages were separated into four different groups to do small mock battles with one another. The idea built confidence in those too timid to fight alone and gave a chance to put the tactics they learned into practice.

Each exercise offered a different situation for each team to face. There were times when certain sides were set up to fail, showing them the hard way how ineffective the strategies given to them were. Some were able to build up and improve their situations while others dithered.

Van felt a beat of excitement at the mention of a new training regimen. It meant something new he could apply his skills to. He was less enthusiastic, however, upon hearing the responses of the pages he had been paired with.

"That oaf? On our team?"

"He can't even hold on to a sword properly."

"Maybe we could trick him into going to the rear flank so he won't be in the way."

"Give him something besides a sword. Otherwise, he won't be of help."

Their words were hushed so Sir Charleston would not punish them for grousing, but they still reached Van's keen ears. Every insult riled his cold temper. He clenched his teeth together like a vise he was so furious, but he locked the fury away so his faction would not worry. A knight did not display emotion in the presence of his foe, after all.

Van had been practicing keeping a stagnant face since finding out how easily his expressions could be read.

The mock battles for him ended as they had during regular weapons training, with him shoved to the ground. Despite everything said about him, Van kept trying to find a way to wield his sword without looking like a fool. Nothing he did worked the way he wished.

No matter the humiliation he endured, he would not stop trying or allow surrender.

Regardless of how despondent the early morning exercises made him, the tension always melted away when he mounted Nightshade for riding practice afterward. The wind, a fickle phenomenon, treated Van fairly, brushing his body with a wicked flurry both refreshing and rough.

When joining with the wind, he and Nightshade were at their best. It gave them a rush of excitement when it came time to finally learn horseback combat. The extra weight in his arm from a weapon proved a considerable challenge, but like any warrior, Van learned to adapt.

Targets were set up for the pages to hit for each weapon suitable in mounted combat. They were ordered to have their mounts charge for every target at top speed, which made keeping an eye on the target difficult. Finding the point of aim became strenuous at best every time the horse jostled from the movement.

Seven pages fell from their mounts in failing to hit the target, one nearly facing a frightful trampling. Five more lost their balance, caught unprepared for when they did hit the target, and fell off. Ccuivr and Lelia were the only ones to clear the course without falling or missing the target. Whether it revolved around skill or luck, it did not matter to the others. They only wished to have some of it for themselves.

Van's grip over his emotions loosened significantly after witnessing Kallant's run. His mount kept a straight, steady path. The weapon in his hand was kept perfectly still. The target shattered from his pinpoint accuracy. He was an arrow tearing through the wind.

Van wanted that skill and control, the kind gained through experience; it was obvious Kallant had the time to learn.

Upon arriving at the Estrine Chateau, he received the chance for such experience. A never patient Vandelas found it hard to grasp that as of yet. He could believe in himself so soon.

Rider and mount stood together waiting impatiently for their turn. Although the horse was excited, Van knew from stroking her mane that she was also nervous. It was easy to see she feared the weapons everyone so proudly wielded. He drew his hand slowly along her head to soothe her. If circumstances were different, Van would not force her to go near the tools meant for training the young to kill, but she was being raised to help pages in their training, and quite possibly more if she showed promise. If she was to face such responsibilities, Nightshade would have to learn to deal with the weapons.

"It'll be okay. I won't let it hurt you." All the more reason for Van to keep the lance he held on mark, away from Nightshade's head.

He knew she was still scared, so Van allowed her to trot carefully at the start, easing her toward the target slowly.

"Pick up the pace!"

The spectators were oblivious to his gentle nature toward the timid animal. Sir Charleston's order only added to the hostilities of the others. His friends' vibrant voices, the only ones not conspiring to throw Van under their heels, reached him just as well.

He could not deny the pace was too slow. Even poor Nightshade found no joy running with fear, but could not find the courage to fight it.

"Nightshade, you won't be with the wind if you are afraid to run toward danger." Van hoped his words and presence would give her the courage she lacked. He understood his hyperactive mare's desires perfectly: to run as fast as she could for as long as she was able. "Keep dashing forward, and you will know more thrill than you ever have."

Nightshade Looked from the path to find his reassuring smile. She responded to Van's feelings by racing relentlessly through the field, her legs tearing apart the frozen grass. Even with the winds diverting Van's attention, he could still feel the valsara of everyone watching spike tremendously as Nightshade passed them.

Nightshade kept straight on the path her rider led her on, thrilled by the wind's caress while maintaining perfect focus on her goal, until a crunching crush caused her valsara to spike. Van hit the target, and held on to the reins for dear life when his horse lurched back on her hind legs at that frightening sound.

He maintained his own tranquility in order to calm Nightshade. Animals were extremely sensitive to the valsara of others. And valsara had a rather cryptic connection to emotion. If he kept calm, she would follow. So he held firmly onto the reins and stroked one hand down her neck until Nightshade finally decided to settle down.

He remained where he was until he was certain Nightshade had fully calmed down. He leaned in closer to her head, brushing her mane gently, his breathing in sync with hers.

As he eyed to target, Van tried to repress his irritation. The lance struck the upper left corner of the target seven notches from the mark.

"Page Kronas!"

That was their cue to move.

Van picked the reins back up and urged her in the direction of the other pages. "Come along now," he spoke in a hushed voice. "Let's rest up before we try running with a sword." It pained Van to force his mount to try another run with another weapon, especially when it was a sword. Nightshade did not hate it, though. A gleaming sparkle over her hazel eyes portrayed excitement. She had fun despite the fright she endured.

It would take a fair deal of time, but Van had confidence he could help her be brave.

Geography lessons came before the archery lesson, courtesy of the Estrine family's decision to move the lessons around. They were joined with cultural lessons every other day and led by the Estrine most knowledgeable of the subject.

None of the pages liked it but knew to keep their comments to themselves. Disciplinary work had been assigned to anyone who so much as groaned. Knights had to endure every order given to them by their superiors without a strand of insolence. Pages were expected to do as much also, as per Lord Estrine's philosophy for upbringing new warriors.

Van had no arguments about these changes, and neither had most of his faction. Ccuivr cared not what he did so long as he was kept busy.

Rubi looked forward to this time more than anyone else. Her knowledge of Ederean culture surpassed that of Lady Biancore D. Estrine, the woman responsible for teaching foreign relations. Lady Biancore prided herself on her knowledge of many foreign countries, but she failed to accurately describe the Land of the Golden Tides and slurred nearly every word of the Abioan language. The Estrine family expected perfection from their pages as everything taught to them was to be perfection. For the sake of accuracy, Lady Biancore often called on Rubi to give proper explanations and pronunciation.

But Ederea did not remain the topic forever. Other neighboring countries were discussed before the turn of the seasons.

As the days passed, Van noticed something unpleasant. Several countries were discussed in her speeches: Vermalio, Ederea to the east, Brungo to the northeast, Ptrena to the northwest. Even the countries conquered by the Abioan people in the past were discussed to further explain how Ederea currently functioned alongside the divided nations.

And yet the country the Kindhrin came from was never mentioned.

Why is it, Van thought, *that they don't tell anything about that country? Even if Vermalians hate the Kindhrin, they must know something about them.*

He went without answers for too long. He needed to hear something, anything, about them.

One day, after Lady Biancore concluded her lessons, Van walked directly up to the pedestal instead of following his friends to the next lesson. The proud, timeworn noblewoman was currently flipping through her thick tomes at a depressing pace.

"Pardon me, ma'am. May I ask for a moment of your time?"

Lady Biandore turned away from her books, surprised at first, but then showed a face that made him feel at home. "Ah, young Vandelas. To what do I owe this pleasant exchange?"

"I was curious to hear about a certain group you've yet to discuss, and I was hoping you could tell me about it."

Her smile became more sincere upon hearing such fine words. "A boy interested in cultures other than his own. It shows an appreciation for others—a fine quality for a future knight."

If only she knew.

"What were you hoping to discuss?"

"The Kindhrin."

Shock rippled through her once friendly countenance. Her bleak blue eyes were beaming with surprise, though she strived to conceal it. That emotion resonated from her valsara far too clearly for it to be fully hidden, even on the surface. "That is a rather ... fascinating topic indeed. Well, I cannot deny a curious youth. Let's see. The Kindhrin were a people rich in culture who—"

"Pardon the intrusion, Lady Biancore."

That falsely kind voice put a damper on Van's mood. Kallant was walking down the aisle closest to the exit with that insidious grin plastered onto his face. Other pages had also gathered at the doors, not bothering to leave yet, and waited for what was next to come.

"There is no need for you to concern yourself lecturing Vandelas here on Kindhrins. I myself am rather informed about that race. Please, allow me to educate him so that you may prepare for your next lecture."

Kallant? Knowledgeable about the Kindhrin?

Somehow, that did not settle quite right. But Van needed to know more of his people, even if it meant hearing of them from that thug's spiteful tongue.

Besides, Lady Biancore already gave her approval.

He followed Kallant outside only so they would not further bother to the kindly old lady, but he kept his wits about him. He could not trust him. He clearly wanted to go out of his way to hurt him.

The other pages who had not already left followed suit. There were too many for Kallant to lie in front of. Too many would see through him should he think to do so—too many to keep quiet should he cause mischief.

The thug stopped walking after they had gone a ways away from the lecture hall. The air was stagnant. The light from the windows shined away from them. If he wanted to fight, this would have been an ideal place.

"Why the sudden interest in Kindhrins, eh, Vandelas?" His casual voice seemed to be weakening. Although his words were still falsely kind, the malignant tone started to give way. The others did not seem too surprised by the change in demeanor. "You have been told the stories, haven't you? About Kindhrins being demonic incarnations?"

The description almost irked Van enough to show more disdain. "I know the stories, yes. The Kindhrin succumbed to greed and destroyed themselves. But I didn't bring them up to hear a story. Is it so hard to believe that I just want to know more?"

Kallant's smile grew wider as he spoke until appearing purely impish. Then he began to laugh something diabolical. Everyone else seemed to have similar reactions, chuckling and sighing while turning away as though they could not even look Van's way. Van's faction seemed to have similar reactions, though more out of pity.

"You want to know more about those monsters?"

"Do you or do you not know anything, Page Ginnstom?" It would be easier for Van to keep his resentment under control if he had not felt Kallant was wasting his time.

"I know more than I need to. My father crossed the Cascades with the king before they became tainted just to visit their dying country."

The Cascades was an expansive ocean to the south of Vermalio with the most beautiful water and the most delectable fish. Many rich nobles and successful merchants had homes in the southern cape so they could relish in the water's majestic beauty. There have even been artists that found inspiration simply from gazing at its waves. However, the tranquil beauty only resided within the shores. Past the horizon, it was a nightmarish abyss. Sailors have found it impossible to cross the Cascades due to the perpetual violent storms that spanned the southern sea, sinking ships and drowning hundreds of thousands of men turning to the seas for adventure and romance.

Hearing the Kindhrin homeland was beyond those waters boded ill fortune.

"Kindhrins were demons in human skin, nothing more. They lived like animals and only wrought disaster. And yet despite the sins they've committed, our glorious king was benevolent enough to attempt to put them on a prosperous path. When they rejected the help, they attacked us, running us to their borders. And if that wasn't enough, they even began slaughtering one another. The king had no choice but to call the soldiers back. What happened a year later? Their entire nation fell and their race perished. Not a single Kindhrin was left. Their evil tainted themselves, their future, and their land—something no Vermalian can forgive. So to learn about them means to learn about the evil they've sown."

Van was in shock. He did not know what to say.

"Is that true? They poisoned the land?"

"And killed people who only wanted to help them."

"I hate them! My father died because of those horrid Kindhrins!"

"I had no idea such evil creatures even existed."

"They're not creatures. They're monsters! Monsters—"

The pages' anger was riling one another up, their valsara as fire stoking fire until the rising flames became oppressive to be near. Such malignance. Van began receding further into his subconsciousness to hide from their terrifying words, to avoid lashing out in anger and fear, but that only broadened his perception of their hatred. Their bodies no longer had a normal shape to him. The entirety of their words morphed them into shadowy monsters, each with wicked irises, jagged smiles, sharp claws formed from their appendages. All of it flashed through his mind relentlessly.

It was almost as though they were becoming the demons they hated.

Take it in.

Those terrifying thoughts invited the collective voices of Pruina to join Van in his isolation. It was different from before. Memories of Pruina's realm reemerging in his mind, Van found the chill in his body taking a stronger grip. This chill felt familiar, like an embrace meant to shield Van from the pain that plagued him while still keeping in view what caused it. He felt Pruina's presence beside him this time, as if he had taken form and stood behind him, their backs pressed to the other.

No matter how murky my view of your reality is, I still see it. It never changes. Humankind scorns one another without thought of what possibilities may exist in the world around them other than the ones they cling to. They blind themselves and divide their world piece by piece, enforcing the ideals of their own and shunning the ones they oppose, unwilling to see the faults in themselves in place of others. This is how they are and always will be. This is human nature.

Van wanted to argue with the spirit. But something gnawing at his chest refused to contradict with Pruina. The proof was all around him. The voices outside his head echoed nothing more than the hatred they breathed. He could not turn away from it.

The anger of rejection—rejecting and being rejected together.

The hateful voices around Van eventually peeled through Pruina's protection. They riddled him with fear, putting a merciless grip around his throat until he felt he could not breathe.

He cringed when that pressure moved away only to clasp his shoulder. Panicked, he shot his terrified eyes back at the presence, ready to wield his power like any would a weapon in hand.

He slackened upon realizing it was Wally.

"You all right, Van?"

Wally's expression deeply contrasted with the abhorrent reading he detected from everyone's valsara. Then he realized the spiteful feeling had vanished. And there was no one else around. Just the two of them wandering a hall different from the one Kallant beckoned them to.

Had it all been some frightful dream? Van felt he had just awoken from an exhausting slumber. But how long had he zoned out for, and what had he done in that time? That was the immediate concern before Wally again broke the silence.

"I know everyone acted pretty rash earlier, losing their senses over hearing talk of the Kindhrin and all, but don't let it get to you."

How could he not when that very same disdain manifested, although weakly, in Wally himself upon mentioning the demonic race?

"They'll calm down and forget about the whole thing by morning at the earliest."

Van smiled for his friend's sake. "Perhaps I could do with a bit of rest. You remember how rambunctious Snowflake can be."

"I know you love that puffball, Van, but keep your priorities straight, okay? Training won't go as smoothly if you spend all your time pampering her."

"Yes. I will keep that in mind."

"Good. Now let's get moving. The evening gruel won't be there if we don't hurry!"

Van kept his composure while following his friend down the dark halls, but stayed behind a moment. To add to his lingering unease, he noticed how much time actually passed. The early afternoon broke way for dusk in the blink of an eye.

The lessons had just begun, yet it all ended in a blur. What more had everyone said while he blacked out? Unfortunately, he did not believe the answer would come, nor was he sure that he wanted it.

All of those negative emotions preyed on his mind for the rest of the day, leaving him uneasy walking among the others. The effort he put in with Sir Charleston with swordplay training after lessons took his mind off it, only lasting until the end of the session, however.

This was his second punishment for getting caught fighting with other pages. Sir Charleston took him to the training grounds every other day to personally instruct him in the art of swordplay.

Caution over Sir Charleston grew exponentially since that day.

Not until he found an environment free of hatred toward his race, free of any hatred whatsoever, could Van relax. Ironically, he found sanctuary in the stables, where he tended to his other punishment. Unlike humans, horses did not resent others for such ugly reasons. They were all still young too, pure and innocent. And whenever he was there, someone else decided to join them. His faithful snowfleece fox followed him while still remaining out of sight.

For a time, she relaxed atop his measured mount, making certain Van noticed her.

He had not the time for play, though. Paying for his behavior came first. Scrubbing up horse dung and brushing back the fur fallen off their nimble bodies provoked his keen sense of smell. The stench burned his nose. Placing these poor creatures in such squalid conditions was cruel. Unfortunately, the current stable hand was rather lax with enforcing the work required of the pages.

The work was disgusting, of course, but someone needed to do it.

"Hey, Snowflake."

The little fox sprung from the small mare's back and rushed over to the boy shoveling messy excrement. She perched herself atop a sturdy post to let him know he had her attention.

"Even though I'm Kindhrin ... you still love me, right?"

Her ears fell back, expressing her disappointment at those dry words. Further on Snowflake scampered to the nearest wooden platform for her to walk across. Van stopped cleaning a moment to watch her, curious. When climbing the closest available gate, she looked at him with those sparkly blue eyes. Then, as she closed in, the fox delicately licked Van's nose and nudged her forehead against his face.

Van smiled halfheartedly. "Thank you, Snowflake."

Stress from the day gave him a restless energy boost that ran cold quickly after his work was completed. The animals were all wide-eyed from watching the work he had done. The piles of dung put into a hefty burlap sack had been hauled outside.

Van had nothing more to do but did not feel like leaving the animals yet. He could tell they appreciated the cleanup, and he enjoyed the company.

Snowflake walked preciously up to Van like a little duchess, looking at him smugly, fearing nothing of her pet being drawn to another animal.

I never took Nightshade on her after-lessons run, have I?

The fox's possessive personality actually reminded him of that. He had never forgotten to care for his mount before, and it made him feel the need to repay that blunder.

Before taking his horse out for another run, Van decided it would be good to brush her first. He picked up the grooming brush provided to him and dragged it down her mangled mane. He needed to be gentle, otherwise risk startling the skittish Nightshade.

A soft patter and scratching at his shin stopped the brush in his hands. Looking down, he found Snowflake leaning her forepaws against his leg, giving him such a pleading gaze like when she was but a kit.

"Don't worry, Snowflake. I'm not using your brush. That is especially for you, remember?"

His smile and statement did not reassure her in the least. She would not let up on the adorable baby act.

Unable to resist her charm, he played along.

Van placed the horse brush down a moment, making sure Nightshade would not move too much, and reached for the attention hog of a fox. He scooped her up in his arms, then climbed aboard Nightshade's back. She stirred a little, assuming the run was about to start, and struggled a moment, then settled down. Van continued to brush Nightshade after he was sure Snowflake would not try to pounce. To keep her from being jealous, he stroked her back slowly.

"I just can't shake it... Why am I so hurt everyone hates the Kindhrin? I already knew it when Mother and Father told me... Why can't I shake this?"

Nightshade shook her head vigorously. Her wild movement threw Van's arm back when it was about to rest for another stroke. She turned to face him, putting a bright hazel eye into view, and murmured softly. Van felt their valsara resonate as they stared into each other's eyes. For a moment, he almost felt his true skin had been exposed to her.

Snowflake nudged Van's abdomen roughly, forcing his attention back to her again. He smiled, not just for the possessive fox and her adorable leer, but also for what he picked up from Nightshade.

"I didn't want to believe it, huh?" Van sighed and began to scratch behind Snowflake's big ears.

That was what he saw upon examining Nightshade's valsara, but her emotions seemed more ingrained than that. The poor mare had endured a lot of ridicule and scorn from human children.

Too scrawny. Fat jaws. Mule ears. Stubborn coward. Ugly.

She had been a mount for other pages before, and they were unpleasant. Not once had she been praised, and she was even beaten an unfair number of times with stones and branches.

Then she met Vandelas Kronas, this human child with this unusual valsara she had never seen even in the matured of his species. Doubts were held, but for reasons she failed to understand, she chose to trust him. The decision was definitely not a mistake. She had been given kindness, affection, compassion, even a name, one she felt proud to bear.

Upon that evening, Van's melancholy began to fade. So much time had passed since taking Nightshade out for a run that he failed to notice the moon silently stroking over the night sky. It was wonderfully pleasant. He had not seen such an expansive starry sky since leaving his village because of the curfew.

The nightly bells rang shortly after he returned Nightshade to the stables. He made hast back to the chateau's rear gate. Two more would resound, both five minutes apart. His poor ears still had not gotten used to the intensely loud frequency. All he could do was withstand it while moving through the halls.

No one was around to prove he had broken curfew, and he was only a foot from his door, but still Van dreaded Sir Charleston might come out of the blue and take his life. How would he do it? How much time would he take? Would he be fast and merciful? Slow and grueling?

Breaking a rule meant death; that was what Van foresaw. And yet Sir Charleston only stuck him with simple tasks meant to instill discipline. Was his warning nothing more than a simple threat?

No. That tone, those eyes, still fresh in Van's mind and lingering in his nightmares, expressed the same hostility of an angered beast willing to protect his territory at all costs.

His conflicted thoughts dictated he put more effort into finding the root of Sir Charleston's intentions, but curiosity took priority of Van's focus upon spotting a letter on his desk. Four months passed with nothing for him. He wondered who sent it. He pulled off the thin string wrapped around the letter and began reading it. As he read the midsection, his expression slipped into a vague frown. The exhaustion from the day finally caught up to him around the final sentence.

Dropping the letter to the floor, Van walked semiconsciously to the window and opened the tall lower shutters, letting the night air in. It was hazy, and the sensation was meager at best, but Van felt the night breeze he remembered so fondly, a refreshingly crisp breeze that reminded him of home. He missed it. It reached him only so far before being disrupted by a thin barrier of frozen air.

Minutes passed, and he sat there, head resting on his crossed arms, looking up at the moon with longing. Something about its luminance sank deeply into his dreary mind. He could not bring himself to look away.

His lethargic concentration was broken, however, by Snowflake sticking her puffy face before his. She was just a glutton for attention.

She seemed to be trying to cheer him up, snuggling up to his face. She could sense his fatigue plainly.

"Do you think we can skip brushing for tonight? I just want to lie here for now."

Normally, such words would offend her, seeing as he spent so much time tending to the horse. Even so, instead of griping like a spoiled little princess, Snowflake continued to cuddle him. When the fox finally decided to relax, she dug under Van's limp arm and rested beneath it.

They took to each other's comfort, gazing at the glorious pearl in the treasured sky. Try as he might to comprehend it, he could not figure out why he found the moon so captivating since those blithe days he spent stargazing. That glow added a sparkle to Snowflake's eyes. They were a pair of glimmering gems Van had only seen on rings.

Spending time in a bustling city made him yearn for life in the countryside. He missed his home and his family. They were in his dreams as he drifted off into peaceful slumber.

A restful night's sleep gave Van plenty of energy to take on the next day. It made him all the more ferocious when it came time for the additional training with Sir Charleston.

The results were the same as always, but something was different that day.

Overhearing Sir Charleston speak with other members of his family about his incompetence, Van finally understood why the stern knight enforced the extra sessions. He meant to push the page to the breaking point from failure after endless failure, after enough of which he would be begging to return home.

The training was a form of torture in itself. Van understood that, but he did not show that or hesitate in their personal sparring sessions. All he did was charge at Sir Charleston with everything he had and endure the punishment for failing to outdo him.

Sir Charleston was more so relentless than usual. The tenacity he saw in Van to stand no matter how many times he had been thrown down brought him to put even more pressure on the page. He scowled at him every time their eyes met when he got back on his feet.

Van met that hostility with a cold, unwavering stare every time he retook his stance. He was dead set on becoming a knight. The only way Sir Charleston or anyone could stop him would be to strike him down. He would not stop it—that was what he decided.

"As harsh with your students as ever, eh, brother?"

A calm voice called from the chateau's back entrance when Sir Charleston knocked Van down for the hundredth time that day.

Opening his eyes again, Van saw the Estrine family's pride and joy, the Champion of Duty, Lord Xanlir, making his way toward them.

"Witnessing your little session could make one think you wish to slaughter him."

Sir Charleston openly scoffed at his sibling. "I have told you before,

Little Brother, that a sword will not remain suitable for battle unless sharpened properly. If we are to make a warrior of this boy, he must be tempered for battle."

"This boy is as much a weapon as the hounds we use," said the champion as he patted the kneeling Van on his shoulder. "And they bite back when they feel threatened. Some respect must be given to him, or he may lose respect for you."

Van stood back up. "With all due respect, Lord Xanlir, Sir Charleston's training will make me stronger. That alone is respect enough for me." He kept his expression and voice rigid as he addressed the champion.

A little kindness would have been appreciated, but he meant what he said. Whether the knight liked it or not, Van was getting stronger. The beatings he received only toughened his body.

Lord Xanlir strained to hold back a laugh. "I am having trouble telling if this child is too frightened to give an honest answer or truly feels that way. You have quite a strange one here, Charlie."

"I have been aware of that since we met. The boy can't even keep his arms still when holding a sword."

Van dared not say another word. He tried to retain his composure while retrieving his sword—it pained him to even pick it up.

Lord Xanlir set his eyes onto him. It took a moment for Van to notice those eyes held no criticism, but instead curiosity. "In that case, why don't you leave young Vandelas to me? Perhaps I can help keep him steady."

"I will warn you now not to expect anything."

Sir Charleston slid his sheathed sword back into his metal strap at his back. He walked away without so much as a glance in the page's direction, leaving the rest to the champion.

Lord Xanlir patted Van on the head. "Don't take it personally. Charlie was raised like the rest of our family—under a firm, intolerant hand. Wrongful actions earn strict punishment; proper ones earn nothing. It is the only way he knows."

Van grew used to it and expected no less from Sir Charleston. That was the way things were. Arguing about it would be meaningless.

"Now, why don't we see what we can do for that arm of yours, hm?"

Van hesitated a moment. Lord Xanlir was different from Sir Charleston. He had to be a better warrior to be given one of the most prestigious titles a knight could have.

As his brother had, Lord Xanlir took the sheathed sword strapped to his back in hand. Van took a step backward. Something changed in that moment, and it made him shudder.

He sensed a notable change in Lord Xanlir's valsara. Although he mainly exuded a kind presence, a malignant pressure suddenly spiked from his sword arm.

What was this pressure? It was not just disconcerting, but also dangerous. Even though the sword was kept in its scabbard, Van feared getting run through. It almost seemed like he looked at the page like an actual enemy.

"Come now, Vandelas! Show me what you can do."

A simple exercise it might have been, but unless Van took it seriously, he might not react the way he wished in a real fight.

Steeling himself, stopping any thought of the Champion of Duty being an ally, Van rushed swiftly at Lord Xanlir, aiming his blunt blade at his chest.

As expected, Lord Xanlir expertly parried Van's preemptive strike. One swing was all it took to throw the boy off balance and into the plush snow.

"Come on now! Don't hold back!" Something about Lord Xanlir's encouragement riled Van's adrenaline, bringing him to take a stronger grip on his sword.

Van charged again. Lord Xanlir observed his movements carefully. Those legs of his had no trouble maneuvering through the snow. Endurance was not an issue. He stood again after being knocked down without fretting over bruises.

"Perhaps my brother knows what he is doing," Van heard the champion say under his breath.

Then his valsara flared.

There was no time to react. Lord Xanlir's rushed up to the poor page, tearing through the snow, and knocked him aside with an unrelenting swipe of the sword.

As Van worked to shake off the pain and stand again, his muscles became still upon seeing Lord Xanlir draw his sword. The champion came in close and thrust his sword past Van's head.

He continued the assault while Van evaded. Not once had Lord Xanlir's attacks made contact. From what the page could put together in the rush of adrenaline, the attacks served to keep him on edge. He was using a similar, albeit deadlier, teaching method to Sir Charleston's.

It was not enough. The sword in his hands still wavered.

Dissatisfied, Lord Xanlir forced his hand, swinging the sword relentlessly closer. No hits connected, but each swing closed in on him, cutting off the inches of the space he had left to escape. The force put into those swings alone made Van feel that he was already getting cut.

As the blade drew ever closer, Van detected an overwhelming murderous intent imbued into it. The same sense of peril he felt before getting killed by that barbarian two years ago overcame him.

Lord Xanlir closed in again, readying a swing that would cut at an area far too close for comfort. Every hair on Van's body stood on end, his body screaming at him to move.

The dreadful sensation froze him for but a moment. All further resistance failed. No more thought came with his actions. A foreign instinct assumed control of his body, releasing the left hand's grasp of the sword, leaving the right alone to bear its weight. He then took hold of the scabbard strapped to his side and drew it along Lord Xanlir's swing.

He pivoted into a small spin, dragging his feet through the loosened snow, and swung his dull sword at Lord Xanlir's clavicle, only to miss by a hair's length.

Both master and student put the session on hold a moment to grasp what just happened. Lord Xanlir needed time to assess that unorthodox movement. The instructors made up of his family would never have taught, or even have knowledge of, such a technique.

Van was just as conflicted. He barely realized what he did. It was unusual, but not disturbing. That felt breathtaking. A rush of wind brushed across his body as it had when riding atop Nightshade. The spin felt invigorating, like the wind had joined in his steps.

"How did you do that?"

Lying to one of the Six Champions would be pointless and very uncouth for a page. He caught his breath before answering. "I ... I don't know. All of a sudden, I just felt—" He paused a moment, finding his thoughts unable to form coherent words well. "I moved to the way you threw your sword at me and ... and that happened." That was the best way he could express the vibration he felt pass through his body.

It was impossible to understand how Lord Xanlir felt. Both his expression and his valsara were unsettled. He looked upon Van with skepticism, then arched his eyebrow, depicting intrigue.

"Again," he ordered. "Come at me with that technique."

Any other Estrine would have hounded him for using such unrefined swordsmanship. But he obeyed. Whatever Lord Xanlir had in mind, he was Van's current instructor.

Van took charge this time, holding the scabbard before him with the sword to the side. Lord Xanlir was ready to strike back faster than Van could swing, but the rhythm his body followed gave him away. Instead of blocking with his blade, he used the scabbard and swept the attack away, leaving an opening to strike. Van aimed for the abdomen, but it proved much too obvious. Lord Xanlir leaped back to dodge, skidding across the snow.

As Van made one final attempt, moving with his sword in a low blow, Lord Xanlir took advantage of his exposed flank and thrust his boot forcefully into it when he slowed down. No escape could be taken when the champion swiftly held his sword to the page's neck.

Just when I finally found a way to use a sword...

After taking a deep breath, Lord Xanlir took the sword from Van's throat, offering an open hand in its place.

Van's body was sore in several places from the bruises inflicted by the champion and his older brother. It was a workout he felt proud to withstand. He leaned up to grasp Lord Xanlir's hand with the hand that held onto the scabbard.

"Never before have my eyes beheld such a wily fighting style. Put some more effort into perfecting it, and my brother will favor you yet."

Lord Xanlir's words were sincere, though a little overwhelming. It would be a lie to say it had not been his mind once before. Impressing a knight like Sir Charleston certainly defined achievement in some form.

His body felt like it would crumble at any moment, but the praise from Lord Xanlir excited Van enough to forget about it.

"Lord Xanlir, sir ... will you permit me another try?"

The man admired his enthusiasm, something that showed from his broadened smile and enthusiastic laugh. He could not refuse what was asked of him.

Further training brought his enigmatic swordsmanship to new levels. His faction was amazed and astonished by what he could now do. Those willing to oppose the uncanny fighting style squared off against Van through the best of their abilities. His capable companions had more luck attempting to fell a tree with a thin branch than toppling Van now that he found his way to fight.

None of them could match his new skills.

Ccuivr and Rubi, the most stalwart of the bunch, constantly demanded rematches so they could best his new swordsmanship. Neither allowed it to end. Rubi staked her pride on the strength tucked in her fair muscles and kept fighting back, unwilling to walk away defeated. Ccuivr found the challenge invigorating and the sputters of snow brushed against his face refreshing; he wanted the thrill of turning his losses into a win.

Then came the chilling day at the dead of winter when the snow turned to ice, and the ice into raw iron. The sky itself froze into an eerily charming gray. Even within the walls of the Estrine Chateau, the frigid temperature crept through every crack, leaving even the spaces close to the fires uncomfortable.

And naturally, the pages were ordered to endure the extreme weather for the sake of training. Many wondered during the morning exercises how they would handle their training without getting caught in the snow. Everyone contemplated how they might possibly endure the frigid temperature when they were not permitted to wear anything above their uniforms. They were not even allowed to shiver.

That day, for the first time, everyone saw Van as a boy of iron will. He stood still with controlled breath waiting for his instructions without a complaint. Even Kallant's faction could not help admire it.

The extreme chill had no effect on his reforged frozen body. The weather, to him, was pleasant and tolerable, the cold snaps of wind refreshing breezes. For the first time in a long while, he did not have to worry about his breaths of white air being seen.

Sir Charleston left the children alone to fight off the freeze, and his return brought them with a sense of relief—as well as a growing hatred they forced themselves to hide.

"I trust you all remained patient in my absence," said the knight upon his return, as if they had a choice. He threatened everyone with spear repetitions in their smallclothes if they moved from their spot. There would be no hiding their tracks since every step left cracks, not footprints, in the snow. "Times like these, when the gods choose to temper the souls of mortal man, offer us the opportunity to prove how strong our resolve truly is." Sir Charleston's voice carried well across the stagnant air and the beds of snow.

Something about him seemed different. Adults knew how to contain their excitement, and the steely Sir Charleston was no exception. He maintained his demeanor well, but there was an unmistakable excitement in his valsara that Van could not help notice. And with it, a tinge of unease and, oddly enough, discomfort.

"If you all wish to be knights of Vermalio, you must demonstrate unbreakable spirit through trials that test the body and the mind. This hostile weather adds only meager weight to your bodies, while your spirits are unforgivingly taxed. To see whether any of you have what it takes to be the spears and shields of our fair kingdom, we are today visited by a knight who will appraise your skills and push your wills, your muscles, your very bones to their limits. Should you survive this session, you may well have what it takes to cripple the Renegade insurgents infesting our homes. And if not, well, it will not surprise me. My pages, you are about to be honored with the formidable pres—"

"Calm down already, Charlie! You sound like you're warning of a monster approaching."

A woman's rough voice interrupted Sir Charleston's startling speech. For a moment, Van thought he was hallucinating. There was a voice he recognized that nearly matched it, but this one sounded so harsh and foreboding compared to his warm, comforting memory. That voice belonged to an overwhelming force within a tall, slender suit of stunning silver armor crossing the hardened snow. A woman with a dark mane donned the armor. She came to a halt before the children and struck the ground with her favored broadsword, her hands atop its pommel. Her cold hazel eyes gazed upon the children, her fearsome presence spreading into their muddled minds.

Rubi was the only one to feel the same excitement Van had. Everyone else trembled from fear in place of the cold air.

Sir Charleston gave a rare smile, then cleared his throat. "Presenting Lady Victoriah Kronas, the renowned Champion of Heart. Otherwise known as Victoriah the Wolverine."

~ Eighth Chapter ~

Sharpening Fangs

The wicked winter winds that enjoyed teasing the pages were nothing compared to the choking tension exuded by Victoriah the Wolverine.

Van felt as though he was staring down an actual beast. His mother was always sweet and kind to him, the hostility and frustration he saw from her always directed toward someone else. But now that she projected her powerful presence his way, he almost feared getting trampled by her.

He knew to remain silent. Before anything else, he is a page, which made her Lady Victoriah to him for the time being, not his mother.

Victoriah set eyes on the pages at attention before her. Each one froze solid when they felt her eyes trail over them and looked ready to crumble to their knees. "So these are the pages you're training now, huh?" she asked nonchalantly. Not once had her eyes rested on Van, leaving him with a shred of relief but also vexing insecurity. "I can't say I'm impressed. You usually have scars on at least a few of them." Her words were used as much to scare the pages as they were to tease the knight who trained them. The glance she offered Sir Charleston was snide. "What's the matter, Charlie? Don't tell me you've gone soft now."

The pages were speechless at the way Victoriah treated their instructor. They had never seen him tolerate such disrespectful talk from even members of his own family, and yet when it came from her, he made no retort.

With only a few words and her strong demeanor, she made it perfectly clear who was in charge now.

"It is all for the better that you are here to demonstrate effective combat techniques then," Sir Charleston replied, calmly. He spoke with respect to the knight who vastly outranked him, but not with restraint. "Now will be your chance to give them scars."

Suddenly, the pages began hoping their disingenuous prayers for a new combat instructor had not been heard by any of the gods.

That sinister smirk drawn across Victoriah's face spoke ill omens. It did not take a mage to know what went on in her mind, though Van hoped his contradicting doubts were closer to the truth.

"Opportunity is a wonderful thing indeed."

It seemed the majority knew this twisted side of Victoriah better than her own son.

"Before we get to that, though, I need to know what I'm working with. Have them show me what they're capable of."

A soft muttering under Sir Charleston's breath distracted Victoriah.

The champion turned her head and shot him a feral leer. "You have something to say, Charlie?" she asked aloud.

He continued to speak in a hushed tone low enough for the pages not to hear it over the gentle breaths of wind, but those near-silent words reached Van's keen ears. "There is something I believe you should see before anything else. We have had concerns regarding certain pages' abilities to respond to our teachings."

It was obvious who he was talking about.

"They should have thought twice about enlisting then," Victoriah harshly retorted. "Show me how much trouble these concerned runts are."

Sir Charleston nodded and turned back toward the pages.

"Page Ginnstom, Page Kronas, step forward!"

Both pages stepped forward and performed the proper salute, pounding their clenched fists over their hearts. Taken aback though she was that her child had been called, Victoriah kept it well hidden from anyone who did not appraise her too carefully.

"Show Lady Victoriah what you have learned."

Kallant nodded and took the blunt sword he was earlier given in hand, facing his opponent with a wry grin. He felt he understood why he had been ordered to do this: to humiliate Victoriah the Wolverine for having such an incompetent son.

Of all the pages to call, he picked the one who took the most joy out of his failures. The outcome was evident even before Van took his sword in hand, and it made him grip the handle tighter in frustration.

He could not allow defeat, not in front of her.

Van and Kallant crossed their swords, their gazes locked firmly onto each other. Kallant taunted his foe with his expression alone, looking upon his foe like a sad pup that he enjoyed kicking. The emotionless stare on Van's face only made his grin broaden.

A wave from Sir Charleston's hand let them know to begin.

They drew their weapons back and immediately began to swing at each other. Upon their meeting again, the one to be pushed back, overwhelmed by his opponent's strength, was Kallant.

Since he was so insecure about his swordsmanship, Van always remained on the defensive when he sparred and watched how his opponents moved, hoping to spot an opening and take advantage of it before his arms stopped moving the way he wanted. But now, instead, he was throwing himself at Kallant, clenching the muscles in his arms and guiding all of his strength through his sword.

No one had ever seen him take the offensive, but they understood why he chose to. Even the thickest mind could comprehend he wished to prove himself before his mother.

Kallant was no slouch. Of the pages, he was one of the better sword fighters. He adjusted his grip on the sword upon lurching backward from his foe and met the attacks accordingly. When finally seeing Van's arm spasm, his wicked grin forming again, he swept his sword aside and thrust the tip of his weapon into his chest.

Van tumbled into the snow with the loud *slosh*. He picked up his head only to smack it back into the indention he made. That determined advance only earned him a few more seconds on his feet. He could not win. He lost, in front of his mother.

Pathetic...

He refused to pick himself up. He could imagine her looking down at him, the disappointment on her face.

"As expected." And then there was Sir Charleston, who only ever looked upon him with disappointment. "Now, Page Kronas, again!"

"Charlie, what are—"

"Show us what you've been practicing with my brother."

Van darted his eyes wide open in disbelief. He was talking about the swordsmanship he learned when training with Lord Xanlir. It was hard to believe, though. Lord Xanlir had shown the instructor the progress they had made once, and he did not find it to be positive. Abiding by Vermalian-style swordplay was crucial, and what Van picked up certainly did not follow the traditional methods.

Whatever his reasoning, he gave Van an order, and he was obliged to follow. Van got back on his feet and held his sword in his right hand, drawing the scabbard at his side and holding it close.

The grin Kallant wore twisted heinously as he laughed at his foe. The stance Van had taken was flawed with plenty of openings to strike.

When they were instructed to cross their swords again, Van's slew cleanly through the air and clashed fiercely with Kallant's. The impact caused the swords to resound a soft hum. The sound carried across the snow, reaching the onlookers, stunning them as much as Kallant.

He only changed how he held his sword, but looked as though he was a different fighter. He stood tall and proud, ready for his foe. His icy stare bore into Kallant, almost threatening to freeze him solid.

At Sir Charleston's signal, both pages drew their swords back and began. Again, Van hurled his sword at Kallant. When parried, he moved in the direction his sword had been guided and watched as the enemy's blunt blade fell his way. The weapon's voice was coarse, and its wielder's rhythm obvious.

The scabbard Van held drew up to meet the enemy weapon, following its wielder's momentum, and blocked the attack, then dragged it along the weapon, throwing Kallant off balance.

Were Kallant not quick on his feet, Van would have run his sword at his side. He was a wily one, but Van was not giving up.

He was not sure if it was the way he held his sword or that he finally matched Kallant, but he felt truly invigorated. He wanted to keep going, to move with the rhythm of battle and the air twisting with his nimble steps.

Not wanting to drag this out further, Kallant moved in swiftly and aimed for his chest. Van disoriented Kallant by swiping away his sword with the scabbard, but Kallant used his loss of balance to slide away through the thick snow before being hit by the sword.

He thought he had an opening. He thought he put Van back in his place as he pushed himself off the ground. But Van was ready for him. Where Kallant's blade fell, Van used his scabbard to sweep it aside, dragging the bully forward, causing him to falter to the left, then swung his sword at Kallant's exposed back.

It was over. Everyone to the sidelines was breathless at what unfolded before them. No one, not even Van's own faction, could believe the astonishing progress he made simply by switching techniques.

Sir Charleston kept his composure as he stepped up to the teetering page. "Page Ginnstom, if that sword wasn't blunt, you would be dead."

The page growled under his breath.

For a moment, Van stood in awe himself. The instructor said those exact same words on him often. For once, they were directed toward another. He had trouble figuring out how to process his feelings. All he recognized was a flood of vigor purging his body of ache and fatigue.

Sir Charleston turned back to the champion. "There you have it."

Victoriah stood awestruck like the pages, but not as skeptical. She seemed pleased, thrilled even. Van did not want to look away from her yet. He never saw her that way before. Such a radiance came off her that it was almost overwhelming. He reacted timidly, if not distant, unable to say anything. Van and Kallant were returning to their places along the other pages when suddenly—

"Hey, Van."

He stopped at Victoriah's call.

She could not be hoping for mother-son quality time now, not when both of them were expected to act professionally. Ignoring her would only get him into trouble with Sir Charleston and disappoint Victoriah. He was not certain whether or not to address her as his mother even though everyone knew of their relationship. Words failed him, so he simply turned around, granting her his full attention.

There was a smile upon Victoriah's face, one of a more devious nature than Van knew. Even with the practice he had using his magic sight, her valsara was one of those he had a hard time reading. "That's quite the technique you showed off. I'm guessing Charlie here never taught you to move like that."

Van merely nodded. Not being able to say what went through his mind gnawed at him like a mite.

"I've never seen a knight move that way before, or anyone for that matter. You took care of that Ginnstom runt pretty easily too."

A wave of hostility rose behind Van. Eyes were on him, scornful ones, though he could not determine how many. Only a few looked upon him without any grief; they must have been his faction.

All of the negative energy from behind quickly fizzled and was smothered in face of the growing presence easily mistaken for a mighty beast's. Putting focus back onto his mother showed her taking the sheathed sword of hers firmly in hand.

"Looks like you'll be the first one getting his scars."

Time started to slow around Van as fear seeped in. For a moment, he thought—or rather, hoped—he had misheard her.

"What do you say? Are you up for a challenge?"

Refusing outright came to mind immediately, but Van did not do it. He could not bear the thought of fighting his mother—or the beast possessing her spirit—even under the pretense of an exercise. But how soon he forgot that the one who spoke to him was not his mother, but the Champion of Heart overseeing today's exercises. It was not a question she gave him, but an order.

An enemy and a challenge presented themselves before him. Responding to them, Van retook his unique stance once more.

Suddenly, all of the resentment behind him froze. It was only for a moment, then rose a tremendous spike of excitement. For one reason or another, they anticipated the clash between the Wolverine and her spawn.

Adrenaline still coursed through him from the round with Kallant. His hands trembled slightly from excitement, though any who saw it would naturally think it fear. A transparent vapor not easily seen in the cold air wafted from his body from firmly gripping the sword and scabbard.

Victoriah flashed a wicked grin as her hand took a similar grip of her weapon. "That's what I like to see. Ready, little man?" she asked without giving the time for an answer. She rushed forth with incredible speed, tearing through the snow, and was upon Van before he knew it. He barely managed to intercept her weapon with both sword and scabbard before it hit his skull. Blocking the timbering attack did not entirely protect him, though; the impact rattled his bones.

She kept pushing down, the force bringing her victim to sink deeper into the snow. Van quaked under her might. If he stayed put, Victoriah would flatten him. His predicament seemed to be working for him, though, the snow around him loosening the more he sank. After shifting his feet to flatten some of the snow, Van jostled to the side and slipped outside of the Wolverine's swing. The sword's thick scabbard dug into the snow with a loud *bong*.

Van darted straight for her exposed left side the moment he had the chance. It did not take long for him to realize assuming he had an opening was a mistake. Victoriah pivoted and brought her sword to meet his in a clean swipe. Van tumbled backward, barely able to keep on his feet.

The grin worn by the Wolverine taunted him and his failed attempt of attack, and she further assailed him with ferocious lashes of her sword. Merely jumping around her attacks did not accomplish anything, but remaining an easy target only led him closer to defeat.

How could a mere child hope to stand against the fearsome champion?

Her strength was unsurpassed. She possessed an instinct that made her a monster in battle. Even when she held back, toying with her prey, it took everything Van had just to keep from getting hit. His technique worked well against those his own size, but a tall powerhouse like Victoriah could not be fought off so easily.

Victoriah was relentless. Each strike she brought at him caused his legs to tremble. Slowly, they began to ache, and moving to block became more and more straining.

Pain shot up his legs and along his arms as he danced around another swing of her sword. The longer the fight dragged on, the more he feared one of them falling off. A thought crossed Van's mind as he began favoring his left side. At first, he thought to dismiss it; there was no way it could work. But it was the only idea he got outside of evading her attacks until he dropped.

He could not win, that much he knew. But he refused to let the battle end without putting up some struggle. He had to show her what he was made of.

Throwing caution to the wind, Van charged at Victoriah. She held up her sword to block his attack—exactly what he wanted. He threw his scabbard and blade against her weapon in a rapid flurry, striking wherever it waved. At each strike, pain shifted to and tore at the leg opposite of the arm he threw. He focused not on that, but instead of the rhythm of his foe, determining how steady her sword was and when she would move to attack.

The vapor emitting from his worn body became less transparent the more effort he gave. While those at a distance were unaware, the knight he fought recognize his fatigue and, as her widening grin showed, thought to test how he would fight with it.

She swung down, scarcely missing him by a sidestep, then drew her sword horizontally to swat him. Following her momentum, Van ducked down and slid through the snow, then picked himself back up to strike at her sword again. He wasted no time in moving into a brief spin, bringing his blade to the guard of her sword, and with all his strength pried the proud Victoriah the Wolverine's weapon from her grip.

He leaped back before she could retaliate, breathing heavily from the intense exertion.

Everyone was in disarray. The pages could not help whisper among them their disbelief. Sir Charleston stood in place with his mouth agape. Not even Van believed he managed to disarm her.

For the moment, Victoriah could not help but stare. Out of everyone else there, she seemed to be the only one expressing a form of delight. It was written all over her valsara, just as resentment and ... another ugly emotion he failed to identify were in everyone else's.

Victoriah narrowed her brows and smirked. "What're you waiting for?" she asked impatiently. "You still haven't come close to landing a hit. Come on, give me all you've got!"

Van was surprised she still wanted to continue. Even without her weapon or a shield in hand, he would not make any sudden moves. His opponent was Victoriah the Wolverine, a force not to be taken lightly.

So as not to disappoint his mother, he steeled himself and rushed at her. He readied his sword, swinging up and along his side. Deep down, he hoped he had not the energy to swing too hard, but held nothing back.

Just as he guided his sword to swing across her, his arm suddenly came to a halt. He looked to Victoriah and saw she caught his blade by its flat edges in one hand before the shaven end could touch her palm.

The last thing Van saw before a faded blur of what he assumed was the dull sky and bare trees was Victoriah's unfamiliar vile grin. Everything became hazy after hitting the ground. He struggled to move, but the pain at the back of his skull spread the more he continued to do so.

"And that's your first lesson, runts: if you don't have a weapon on hand, make yourself into one."

The words he heard etched into his mind before it gave out, everything turning black.

Waking only agitated the pain burrowing into his head. His eyes had yet to open, and already his sight spun, twisted. Consciousness slowly returning, the pain reminded Van of the seizures back when he still trained to control the Second Verse.

"So are we just going to wait for him to wake up?" A voice—embittered and tired—distracted him from the pain.

"You know you don't have to. Go somewhere else if you're going to have that kind of attitude!" another cheeky voice sneered at the other.

"You can tell him that, but he won't go." That lax voice was unmistakable. "They've spent the most time training together. He's worried he'll have to find a new sparring partner."

Out of habit, Van tried to identify the owners of the voices through his magic senses before attempting to open his eyes again. The way they sounded made it easy to identify them; he already knew them to be Wally, Rubi, and Ccuivr. But a magic sense, be it from sight or feeling, was better for determining where they were precisely.

His tired, distorted focus could not interpret much of what they said. He ignored a dead quarrel between the two boys, putting his focus on his layout of wherever he had been taken; there was no chill like there had been outside.

Van had been placed in this small room, at its lower eastern corner. The others scattered themselves throughout the room. Rubi, her silhouette a blended shade of magenta and gray, was nearest to him. This silhouette of light violet, belonging to Ccuivr, had secluded himself in the corner opposite to Van. Wally stood parallel to Ccuivr, his valsara a light blue radiance with specs of bog green.

"Why didn't you say anything when I asked you what you were doing with Van?"

"It wasn't your business to ask. Why didn't you ask him instead?"

"It wouldn't be as fun getting it out of him. He would have given me a straightforward answer. You're closed off most of the time, so it was more entertaining trying to get it from you."

They must have been discussing when Ccuivr and Van began practicing swordplay together. For a time, those two sparred against one another in seclusion without help from the others. It only mattered that Van had someone to practice with while he learned how to use a sword.

Although he would not admit it, Ccuivr was having too much fun the entire time to want anyone to join in and interfere.

"He is starting to irk me," Ccuivr groaned.

Stress accumulated over Ccuivr, and that spread over to Rubi.

"Wait until he starts playing jokes, and you'll know how I feel."

It was about time Van woke up completely before the three of them began to fight.

As he struggled to open his eyes, his vision somehow became more distraught, and that pain at the back of his head pulsated the more light that leaked through his eyelids. It was tempting to use his ice to freeze the pain over, but he knew better. Readjusting to the light was painful, and the irritating sounds around him occasionally made it more irksome.

Several arguments had been slung Van felt ready to speak without getting a migraine. Glancing slightly to the left, he saw Ccuivr looked ready to go for Wally's throat.

"Would you two please shut up?" Van groaned. "How am I supposed to sleep with you barking like rabid dogs?" He sat up as they quieted down. Looking ahead, he saw Rubi sitting at the foot of the bed he lay on. There seemed to be only one chair, and Wally took it.

It took him a few minutes, but Van managed to figure out he had been taken to a medical ward.

"I think you've had enough sleep, buddy," said Wally.

"How did I got here? Wasn't I sparring against Mother?"

"Yes, you were. And may I say, that was the craziest thing I've ever seen you do!"

No one argued with him. Van glanced away from him, trying to hide his embarrassment. He knew he could not have won, but he had to try. His mother would have been disappointed otherwise.

"For once, I agree with the ape," Rubi stated, though sounding a bit reluctant and sickened. "She was ruthless—to her own son no less. She could have killed you!" While she sounded frightened, there was no denying was still dazzled by that ruthlessness all the same.

Raised by Victoriah, Van could see why she was impressed by it nonetheless. "If that were true, she wouldn't have left her sword in its scabbard." Usually, he left the sarcasm and jests to Wally, but he thought to let the others know he was okay in some way.

"She was holding back, probably more so because you're her own," Ccuivr stated. "Maybe nothing would have happened to you were it not for that rock you hit your crown on."

"Rock?"

"You conked your noggin on it and passed out." Putting it so simply made it sound less severe and more amusing. "And it wasn't just a little bump either. Lady Victoriah threw you so hard, you shattered it. So she had me and Ccuivr bring you here. Of course, we could have left you in the snow, but—"

"Then we would have been the next ones to give her a warm-up."

It did not sound like Ccuivr was kidding, nor it did sound far from the truth.

"How long have I been under?"

"Since this morning. The sun's already making its way out of the sky now."

"Lady Victoriah had us keep an eye on you while you got your beauty sleep, though I can't say I know why Rubi decided to come."

The rowdy redhead did not take too kindly to Wally's words. She looked ready to bash his head in. "I couldn't likely leave Van here with the baron of buffoonery keeping watch over him."

"Now do I seem so devious a person as to lark with someone when they're asleep?"

No one needed answer. Whenever he acted innocent with that crooked smile across his face, there was never a doubt the jester was up to something.

Poor Gal learned that the hard way the previous month when Wally decided to rig a contraption that dropped a load of apples—that he somehow swiped from under the servants' noses—onto his head when he was about to wake up after dozing off under an old tree. At least he got to him before Sir Charleston did for wasting time.

Someone entered the room before anything else could be said. It was one of the maids assigned to medical detail.

Now that Van was awake, his friends excused themselves. No doubt they missed most of the day's lessons to keep an eye on him. They would either be marching toward punishment work or reporting to the other instructors for remedial assignments.

Thought of what he would have to do for shirking his work while he was under came to Van's mind. While he wanted to find out as quickly as possible, the maid intervened before he stood. "Forgive me, Young Master, but I was told you are to remain here for the time being," she insisted. "Please keep to the bed. I'll fetch you a wet cloth."

He saw no reason to disobey and remained where he was.

The maid returned to him after retrieving a small rag from the bucket she brought in, applying the moist rag against his bruise. "Hold still, please." Van cringed involuntarily, struggling to follow the maid's instructions. He felt a small crack in his head that he thought might break open if treated too roughly. "Is it too cold?"

Reassuring her only took a simple "No." The damp press agitated his injury, but there was no hope that would stop soon.

"You must be hungry. Would you like me to get you anything to eat?"

"No, thank you ... but can you find something in the library for me? A book titled *Foreign Outlands*?"

"Of course. Hold this for me, please."

She left to fulfill his request as soon as he held the rag in place. If he was going to be recovering there for a while, he would rather quench his hunger for knowledge instead of for food—for the time being.

About two weeks ago, Van discovered this absorbing read about lands across the sea while probing the library for material regarding war tactics. Much of the book contained details of landscape and weather patterns cataloged by a travelling chronicler, but there were occasional chapters—sometimes just paragraphs—on the culture of the natives. For the facts he never learned from Lady Biancore, Van relied on the book. It was thick and riddled with fine detail. The shortest chapter he read was about seventy-five long, incredibly condensed pages.

One section discussed the homeland of the Kindhrin: Harah Krid.

Whenever Van had any free time to himself, no friends or training or studies whatsoever, he went to the library and read as much as possible. And he learned a great deal about his homeland.

Harah Krid was a barren land consisting mostly of a vast golden desert. The days and nights both were grueling, the sun scorching the land by day only for everything to turn frigid at night. Barely any foliage grew on the patches of tough rock and seas of loose sand. The animals that adapted to the environment were ferocious, driven by survival instinct to take what they needed. The air was always dry and evaporated any sources of precious, life-revitalizing water. Yet even in that lifeless land, there were sanctions where life thrived called oases: large springs of the purest water drawn from the deepest depths of the earth, giving plants an opportunity to grow and people a safe place to rest and rehydrate. Those were the easiest places to survive in. Many of the Kindhrin populace, however, lived in places without direct access to an oasis and survived well across the desert. Born and raised in the country, they were accustomed to the extreme heat and found methods to stay cool and hydrated.

As Victoriah once told him, the Kindhrin adored music. Nearly every section of the book involving their race mentioned music in some form. The arts were important symbols of freedom and true living among the Kindhrin, and riveting stories were told by those who created them.

One page told of a song called *Freelance Goddess*, which was inspired by a woman who roamed the deserts guiding those lost in its gilded expanse. A bard who found his way to a budding settlement told the tale of this mysterious beauty that reeled him back from the hereafter. She graced his soul with an angel's smile and told him of a haven where he could regain his strength. She guided him down a path that nearly killed him again, but the poor soul found himself among his brethren once more. The bard turned to thank the maiden, only to find nothing but the sands that nearly claimed him. He told everyone of his encounter. To his surprise, the man who brought him water claimed to have had the same experience, and so had the woman tending to laundry, and even the new family with their children at play. Everyone claimed that the enigmatic maiden brought them to the same place, sparing them from death. In ten years' time, a city formed in place of the settlement and was named after their savior, Cryzt Mikil—from the Kindhrin tongue meaning *sand maiden.*

That story was followed by a description of the city tied to it. The capital of Cryzt Mikil, like the majority of the country, was dominated by the sweltering desert heat. Tall buildings stood around the main palace at the edge of the city, where the royalty have made their home. Most of Cryzt Mikil was built atop tall hills and sudden pits, making for difficult walks. The streets were wide for recreational purposed, so dances could be performed to the music they loved to play.

Although the Kindhrin favored the capital for its many conveniences and the comfortable houses, no one remained in the same place. Every forty days or so, the citizens left Cryzt Mikil to traverse the desert; the writer theorized it to be an unspoken tradition to test their tenacity. Even the royal family made the journey and offered their palace to a select number of people, but they returned immediately after the next month, whereas the other Kindhrin continued venturing to several other towns until visiting them all, then returned to Cryzt Mikil to continue the cycle.

Why the Kindhrin would completely abandon their homes—and many of their belongings—and offer them to complete strangers baffled Van, but he found those findings fascinating all the same.

He failed to see why everyone thought so terribly of them. But judging by the occasional patches of faded ink and the torn-up pages and cover, the book was rather old, perhaps even aged a century. So much could have changed in that time, like the hearts of people.

The incomplete history left him wanting to know more.

The injury he sustained made his mind spin with every move he made for the next week. Even the slightest twitch distorted his vision and frightened away all thought. Thankfully, there was no permanent damage to the skull and no complications with his mind. But for that remaining week, Van was dismissed from weapons training, and someone else was assigned to tend to Nightshade's feeding and exercise.

Waiting to recover felt incredibly dull, with only the company of his faction to lift his spirits. All his efforts have been directed toward maintaining focus during intellectual and etiquette classes, where action resulted in the world churning faintly in his eyes.

The time spent with his friends diminished his boredom, but unfortunately, that had its drawbacks too. Fights still broke out between Wally and Rubi, inevitable as it was. The twins were not so friendly toward each other that week either. As impetuous as the faction might have been, it was beginning to get out of hand. They barked at each other nonstop. They almost made it impossible to keep his head together.

With the order to postpone his weapons training, half of his day was left with nothing but time to study strategy and ethics. While it was not untrue that he needed the extra effort, skipping his daily exercises left him with a flat fatigue.

The nights were not so simple either, what with Snowflake begging for attention. She did not make as much noise as human children, though, and was relatively easier to understand. The first few nights of brushing her fur were torture on his aching head. Snowflake understood he was in pain, thus leading her to cling to him more. While appreciating the sentiment and plush fur stroking against him, the sensations sent to his mind only further agitated his condition.

After he recovered significantly, Van decided to visit the stables while the other pages were training. He missed his curious mount and thought clearing his head with some fresh air would do him good.

At times, he wished there was someone at the chateau with the ability to use healing magic. Rare were the people who possessed knowledge of the mystic arts, as Lord Tamsilac explained during a lesson near the year's beginning; in his prime, many people once brandished magic in many forms. Since the last generation, the number of known people who could use magic had severely deteriorated, just as there were more people to use it before Lord Tamsilac's time. "Mages are slowly becoming extinct," the tactics instructor stated. A rather surreal way to address the matter, but it got everyone's attention.

Sometimes, Van was unsure whether to believe if what Lord Tamsilac said was true. After all, he—a mere village child—attained a great power capable of forming, sculpting, and controlling ice. If it was true, though, would something happen to the Second Verse?

The thought stuck to him along the path to the stables and chipped off when he saw his lovely mare. The horse was already in disarray when he got there, batting her hooves against the stall door, standing thrilled on her hind legs. Van was happy to see her too, and would have sooner if he did not know his injury would only suffer from her raucous energy.

Nightshade was not as hostile toward humans as Snowflake, but still adhered caution around the other children. The thought of Kallant or any of his cronies even touching her made Van grit his teeth. He needed to make certain she was doing all right.

Her vigor and vivacity proved she was still fine.

"I have not been away for that long. You must've really missed me."

She neighed something that sounded like a scream of laughter. *Was there ever a doubt?* that seemed to imply.

Lessons were put on hold four days after Van sustained his injury in observance of a traditional celebration, the Flame Festival. This time of year, when winter had taken to its coldest days, had been celebrated for many generations. Originally, it was created to commemorate the successful reign of the kingdom's founder, but as time snuffed out his rule and that of his offspring, it became known as a time to stay warm in such chilling times. The festivities were held in every village and city across the country so that everyone could celebrate while fending off the cold.

This time of year was known for when the winds brought their heaviest snows and deathliest chills. Simply remaining indoors was no longer enough to keep warm.

Van made a full recovery by the start of the seven-day festival. With the festivities beginning, no one wanted to spar with him. Everyone either left for the city to partake in the merriment or began their search for presents before the peak of the festival. He spent much of his time alone in the chateau's empty fields, reconditioning his muscles.

Concern over finding a present for his friends never crossed his mind. He had already gotten them ahead of time—a dagger for Ccuivr, a ball weighed with sand for Rubi, a spyglass for Stevene, a humorous book he failed to follow for Wally, and a pair of matching bracelets for the twins. What he planned to get for his parents, though, Van had no idea. He thought of this shimmering dagger Victoriah would have loved when getting Ccuivr's gift, but the small blade was much too expensive.

Although it went against tradition, he planned to ask his mother what she would want from him.

The attractions prepared in the streets of Brigadier did not appeal to him. For one reason or another, he found them to be tedious. He went regardless only to appease the twins' and Rubi's persistence.

Nearing the end of the festival, everyone gathered at the heart of the city to laugh and sing and dance around a massive bonfire.

Everyone came out to enjoy the event, even the Vermalian royal family. A tall man garbed in dignified red and saffron robes, holding onto a scepter and crowned with a vermilion metal circlet, had the honors of setting the massive pile of wood ablaze. That man was King Faustign L. S. Vermalio. His face's rugged edges and glistening brown hair charmed the people, and his brilliant red eyes glimmered with kindness. Selenee, his wife and queen, stood comfortably beside him atop a secured bridge where they watched their people be merry and relished in the marvelous roar of the flames.

Word of a prince in the royal family reached Van's ears before, but he saw only those two.

Not many guards surrounded the king or his family, but they were not entirely defenseless. A keen eye could detect snipers and suspicious characters lurking in the shadows. There was no malevolent intent in their valsara, so they had to be guards sent to keep watch for anything that would disturb the merriment.

It was easy to see why the final day of the Flame Festival was so popular. The bonfire drew people from every corner of the city together. The joyous music played by the bards liberated them of their focus and fatigue, bringing out their spontaneous sides. Even those who typically did not get along behaved pleasantly in this joyous occasion.

Van could not help be drawn into the revelries himself. Joining his friends in this peculiarly peppy song lifted this frustration he held onto for two long weeks. He felt as light on his feet moving to the rhythm of the merry music as he had with weapons in his hands. His faction danced rowdily with him. Rubi enjoyed throwing him around every few steps, then shoving him forcefully toward new dance partners. Ccuivr and Stevene did not dance much, but even they could not escape the pull of the music.

The moon had risen to its apex in the starlit sky. Its glow added a beauteous glow to the flames. A strong spiritual energy radiated from them.

It all overwhelmed Van after a while. Dancing around the flames exhausted him. It hurt to breathe, and the energy he wasted and had drained left him about ready to collapse. Somehow, he managed to slip away from the dance circle and hide in a nearby alley. Snow still lingered at its corners, and the walls shielded him from the heat. He chose to rest there until he could feel his body again.

"What are you doing back here?" His mother stood at the edge of the alley where the light of the flames brought a lovely glimmer to those compassionate eyes he recognized. "I would have thought you had the energy to outlast your rowdy dance partner."

What would Rubi think if she knew her idol called her "rowdy?" Van did not think it would offend her much since she nearly strangled Wally for calling her Lady Ivanstronge. Compared to that, Victoriah's words would probably pass as praise.

"I don't want to go near the fire anymore," her son responded after letting out one last exasperated, chilled breath.

"Too hot for you?"

"Do you remember that drought in Russalin five years ago? It kind of reminds me of that."

Victoriah looked a little concerned for a moment but tried to keep her smile. "Do you think it is because of your body?"

The thought had crossed his mind before. Since death, his body could no longer feel heat. Getting close to the flames affected him in different albeit grueling ways; the feeling of heat had been replaced with this anguishing force pressing over his frozen body. It was trying enough learning to keep from inadvertently freezing anything. Coming to deal with that new sensation was all the more insufferable.

"I can't go near the fire again." The poor boy worried he would melt if exposed to it any longer.

His mother kept quiet a moment to find a way to make him feel better. It gave her son the chance to breathe a little longer.

"I've been meaning to ask you about that technique of yours. What you used on me, it was incredible." Victoriah stepped into the alley with her son. "How did you learn to fight like that?"

Van was not sure how to answer. Color rushed to his cheeks listening to your praise. He could feel her smiling down at him as he turned away, embarrassed. "I'm ... not sure. I was taking extra lessons with Sir Charleston and Lord Xanlir. For some reason, my body refused to adapt to the traditional swordplay, so they tried to help me adjust, and while I was training... It felt so natural, like I was doing it for a long time."

The more he talked about it, the stranger it sounded. The way he spoke sounded so reserved and abashed. Even he would have doubted his own words had he not experienced what happened.

He glanced back at his mother hoping she did not think he was telling some tall tale. "It sounds unusual, huh?"

The smile across her face reassured him otherwise. "Not too unusual, I'd say. Combat allows movement to become instinct over time. Some people's bodies just move in certain ways—ways that set them apart from everyone else. You found your way earlier than the others, that's all."

It was hard to believe she received her own training from the Estrine family. Every instructor demanded complete conformity to their teachings, for their guidance to be followed without question or thought, convinced that the children they teach did not know better. Was it her time as a champion that allowed her to grow so lax, the people's praise and horror stories convincing her she could do as she pleased? Victoriah the Wolverine was confident in herself, and for good reason. But it was not her strength and skill alone that earned her the title of a champion. She knew more about the ways of battle than many.

"That fighting style of yours is something else. When you moved, it almost looked like you were dancing. To think you learned how to move like that while practicing with Charlie. It's so ironic, it's funny. ...Why were you practicing with him anyway?"

Van swallowed hard. It occurred to him she already knew but wanted to hear it directly from him. The words of others could so easily become twisted, enough to tell a different story entirely. Lying would only infuriate her. Suddenly, the pressure of the flames did not seem so bad.

"It was my punishment. Sir Charleston assigned me to clean the stables, then had me practice swordplay with him ... after I was caught fighting with another page when they were beating up Gal."

Saying anything beyond that was difficult. A lump formed in his throat that cut off much of his breath. It was the first time Van had broken a rule—aside from hiding Snowflake.

Now that he told Victoriah, he expected punishment from her too. But instead, she smiled proudly and took her child into her arms for a comforting hug. Her embrace felt much too kind for him to wonder why she was not admonishing him.

"A knight protects the weak. You did your part well."

Victoriah was not the type of knight to follow every single rule. She understood the intent behind his actions and judged him based on that. Knights got into as many fights as pages, sometimes over things more trivial than children's antics; that much she knew.

She finally let go of him. "Oh yeah." She reached behind her, then presented to him with a smooth-looking gray brick. It was very glossy, something like marble. "I bought you something."

Tilting his head, Van saw a few leather straps attached to it. He held out his hand to accept it When he did, though, it nearly made him fall forward. The weight was more than immense for such a small thing.

"W-What is this thing?"

"Your present, for the Flame Festival. I thought you'd like something to help condition your muscles, so I bought you a whole bunch of those weights. They can be strapped to your arms and legs so you can get a workout throughout the day."

That was very thoughtful of her. The exercises done for pages in the Estrine Chateau could not be done throughout the day, which meant he did not get results as fast as he desired. Any method he could take to get stronger he would gladly accept. Unless a knight was strong, they could not protect themselves, let alone their people.

Such a nice gift. And yet Van looked conflicted to receive it.

"...Should I have gotten you something else?"

The boy flinched when he realized his worry showed. His mother's words did more than surprise him. They almost scared him.

She never behaved that way when giving gifts to her husband. Once, Jerrell was so surprised at his wife's thoughtfulness that he was stunned. Victoriah thought he hated it, sneered, and grabbed his collar, shaking him while saying, "You're going to take it and love it, meathead!"

"No! I like it, really! This is an incredible gift. But ... I couldn't find anything nice for you."

"You sweet boy! Don't you worry about that," said the tender mother as she patted her son's head. "I can't carry much on me when I travel anyway."

It was the same response she gave him every Flame Festival. They were kind words meant to reassure him, but Van always felt guilty. That did not change this year either, especially since he got his friends something. He once tried carving her a lucky charm, but it was too bulky for her to carry, so it was left in her home, safe with him.

"You haven't been using your power lately, have you?"

"No! Of course not!" Van hushed himself, realizing how loud he was, and spoke the rest in a hushed voice. "I've been careful to keep it a secret, so I never used it once."

She frowned at his answer. "That won't do. You still have to practice, or you'll lose your grip on it," she suggested in a playful manner. Then she smiled and added, "I know of a place secluded enough for you to practice. What say we go there and spar some more?"

The idea seemed nice, but something caught Van's attention. Mentioning his Second Verse and sparring, she must have meant for him to use it against her. A part of him wanted to protest, but another part— the one that remembered his defeat against her—welcomed it.

"Don't worry. I promise not to throw you on a rock this time."

Van laughed.

It would take too much time to find his friends and let them know of his plans. There was a chance they were not aware he left the dance anyway.

He followed his mother, a smile on his face. How long had it been since they had quality time together? He had long forgotten.

It was the perfect opportunity to make up for lost time—the perfect present a child could give their parent.

~ Ninth Chapter ~

To the Wilderness

Victoriah guided Van to the lush copse behind the Estrine Chateau. The trees' cover promised no one would be aware of what went on there.

Victoriah meant what she said about Van using his Second Verse. Not only would it be good practice for him, but she rarely had the opportunity to fight with someone with mystic powers. It would be entertaining for her.

Of course, she needed to be sure he still utilized the same skill he had when last she saw him.

Van began by freezing the air and sculpting ice into certain shapes. He started out small by making a ring around the area—the borders of their training ground. Moonlight gleamed through the tree leaves and refracted off the ice, giving it an ethereal sheen of nightly colors.

His mother grinned while watching him. She could tell his focus had improved greatly since coming to the Estrine Chateau. But how much? Along the line, she asked Van if he could mold the ice without making direct contact with anything. The challenge intrigued him. It took all of his mental strength to make those walls sturdy. If he could accomplish that, there would be a number of things he could do.

He knew this would be substantially more difficult, and took a moment to prepare. He closed his eyes and put an image of the world around him in his mind. With each breath, he saw more and more. Faint traces of unseen things began appearing—the breaths of the wind, the dormant life in the trees, the power emanating from him. After finding the tiniest water droplets suspended in the air, he knew where to begin.

He sent waves of his energy throughout the area within the ice ring, creating what he called an area of influence. Manifesting and directing his power was a simple matter after two years. He could feel everything in the area of influence, as if it were all in his grasp.

The problem was making the water droplets freeze and bend to his will. The concentration he used when crafting a sphere by hand was not enough. He strained his mind trying to give shape to his thoughts. Eventually, something began to form in the air, but he could not figure out where. He tried to build upon it.

It was working. He felt something clustering nearby. He actually thought it would work. Then suddenly, the ice cracked and shattered.

Van figured out where the sphere appeared when specs of frost fell atop his head. His mother made a meager attempt to suppress her laughter while her child shook off the chilled powder. While embarrassing, it also left him slightly refreshed.

It became clear his concentration still needed work. He needed to shatter his limits to become stronger. And to do that, Victoriah decided to add a little pressure. She told him to stop what he was doing so they could begin sparring.

Before taking his weapon in hand, he went to the tree where Victoriah left the weights she gave Van—the lightest ones, apparently. Van strapped the weights around his legs and arms with the leather wrapping they came with.

Victoriah had been sitting patiently in the snow, waiting for him to finish. She watched Van ready himself with a wry smile, her expression provocative. They sparred together only once, but she quickly learned when to show herself as his mother and when to be an instructor for him.

When the weights were secure, Van drew the scabbard at his side, then took the sword it housed into his right hand. The weights pushed against him more as he took his stance. Holding it for a few seconds strained his arms. A moment longer, he ached.

And Victoriah only sat there to further pester Van, her gaze and grin implying, "How much longer can you go, huh?" She thought to keep it going a little longer, returning to her feet rather slowly. She took her time stretching and lazily taking her sheathed sword in hand.

When she finally took her stance, Van felt his arms were about ready to give out on him.

"Are you going to make the first strike, or are you waiting for me?"

Van knew he did not stand a chance. He hesitated a moment but shook off that cowardice like a wet dog drying out his fur. Winning was not the objective; it was training. And though he knew she wanted him to use the Second Verse, he wanted to try without it first.

Making the first move had its advantages as well as disadvantages, but he knew he did not want her taking it. So Van charged first, taking the opportunity, for whatever it was worth. He swung strongly, but hesitated when Victoriah held up her right hand. She took a firm hold of the sword and threw him flat on his back. This time, he was only stunned for a second. The snow cushioned his fall.

Judging by the way she tossed him around, Victoriah must have been fairly familiar with that technique; her hands had such a soft feel too.

Paralysis melting away, Van got back on his feet using his scabbard for support. The hefty weights made moving off of the plush snow as difficult as it was uncomfortable.

Once again, he charged, hoping to clash with a sword this time, but only saw his dull blade get caught in Victoriah's hand again and met another brutal impact with the snow.

"You know, maybe I don't need my sword this time. I can just keep tenderizing you like I do with wild game."

Growr!

A growl passing his lips, Van got back up ready for more.

"Here's a lesson you missed out on, love," she said when Van went in for a third attempt. Her small movements dictated she thought to keep teasing him by flinging him into the snow, but the rhythm in her valsara quickly changed, spiking, as she instead swung her safeguarded sword directly into his chest. The unexpected swing hurled him against a tall, frozen oak. "Learn to adapt to *any* and *every* situation before it kills you!"

Van knew his mother's strength, but he was still getting used to enduring it in this manner. The weights were not the reason his body protested against sudden movement anymore. That strong arm of Victoriah's left his chest throbbing in pain. Van thought a few pieces of his chain mail fell out of place from the impact. Either that or his ribs.

Lying against the tree would not make him any stronger. With that in mind, Van forced himself to power through the pain and stumble to his feet. "I'm starting to see why you never took a squire."

He pondered on whether jesting while he was in pain was a good idea until he caught her chortling. "Well, knowing I can easily break a kid is one reason," replied Victoriah the Wolverine. "But if I got a squire to teach, I'd find it harder to come back home to you and your father."

The sentiment was touching. Before becoming a page, Van always ran to her for a hug whenever she came home.

Very fond memories they were, but the adrenaline coursing through his body made him overlook them. It would not allow him to rest yet. He stood again, hunched over for a moment, then adjusted his stance.

"Think you can take another blow?"

Actions meant far more than words. Sluggish as Van's movements were, Victoriah could easily determine him repeating the same action out of impulse. She looked amused, but also dissatisfied. The Wolverine held out her sword once more, ready to strike at a moment's notice.

A grin borne across his face, Van kept running forward until Victoriah began her swing, where he ducked down and skidded across the snow. From there, he dug his scabbard into her shin guard, pulling hard enough to topple her into the snow bed.

Van picked himself back up as Victoriah pushed herself out of the snow. Victoriah looked as baffled by Van's action as he was. Thought and strategy did not guide his response so much as the timed spike in his opponent's valsara, which he reacted to promptly. Van felt a little foolish. They were having a sword fight. He was expected to take a win using his swordsmanship, not a stunt made by impulse.

But the raucous laughter she let out drove off his doubts. She looked to her son with a proud smile. "Looks like you won't need to be told to act unpredictably." She pushed herself up a little more so she did lie in the snow she plowed. "Nice work pulling me down to your level."

"Thank you, Mother."

The boy leaned in to help his mother off the ground.

"All right... Now try using your power again."

Van took a moment to breathe, then nodded and closed his eyes to prepare. It did not take long for him to form his area of influence and sense the water suspended in the air.

"Movements from your body can manipulate the flow of energy in our plane. Try pretending to grab hold of whatever you see."

Van nodded and attempted to follow with his mother's instructions when his focus had parted, the pain taking root into his raised arms. It felt as though the weights were expanding, threatening to crush him, now that he had expended some energy.

Sshaaaa!

The vapor permeating from his body further thickened, blurring out what it moved over.

"Work with the pain, Van. Make your body work for you if it won't."

There was little else to do. Stopping because he was a little sore was not an option. If he was going to make use of his power in the future, he had to use it quickly and expertly like a weapon at his disposal.

He gathered the power inside him while slowly spreading his arms far apart. Rather than focusing on the pain and hindering his progress, he listened to the whistle of the winter wind being carried over the snow and through the trees. It relaxed him a little, allowing his power to steadily cluster the droplets together. The sound of frost building excited him, but he kept his thoughts from running amok. He took a deep breath, exhaled white breath, breathing steadily until his limbs and mind could not take anymore, then fell limply back, letting the snow embrace him.

Van let his breathing become frantic, his lungs aching so much they felt ready to pop. Amassing the energy for his Second Verse while he was already fatigued took its toll. The rush of power flowed through his body before suddenly coming to a painful, excruciating halt. He suddenly became aware of the dozens of his long, branchy blood vessels. Even after two years of adapting to the cold, there were these new phases of sensation Van came across when he least expected it, letting him find a cold that made him shudder, as well as new capabilities for his Second Verse. This new one felt as irksome as that crushed rock to the head, if not more.

If magic was anything like the Second Verse, then magic was far more strenuous than most hopeful people would believe.

"Hey, Van." Obscured as her voice was from his position, he heard his mother. "Look at this."

Letting out a groan, Van struggled to push his head off the ground. He did not even want to think about moving. The thought of it made his head spin. The woman's footsteps sinking into the thick layers of snow let him know she was coming to him.

"Guess the weights I got you are a bit too hefty, huh?"

Van did not want to say so. Tiny and thin as they were, the size of a small tile, the density of each piece was ludicrous. He might not be able to lift one of the heavier weights until his seventeenth year.

Victoriah took a knee beside her son. Glancing her way, Van noticed something round and shiny resting in her palm. His glacial eyes glimmered at the sight of the crystalline sphere resting in her hand. Calling it glarious while it reflected the beauteous moonlight did not seem to do it justice.

"Did I really—?" gasped the breathless child. "I made this?" He doubted it was so. The shape of the sphere was so finely crafted, without a single flat edge seen, the ice clear like glass.

Seeing such a glimmer in Van's eyes coerced a familiarly pleasant smile from his mother. Deciding to rest, Victoriah scooted next to him and laid her back against the powdered snow. "I'm glad I had you try again. Otherwise, you would never have made this treasure."

"But I'm in worse shape than before we started. How could I have made *that*?"

"A strong body is the foundation for a strong mind. Because you used some energy toward something you appreciate, it was easier for you to hone that Second Verse of yours."

Her words did not make much sense to him, but Van felt too tired to argue. "The way you put it almost makes you sound like a mage. Where did you hear these things?"

Victoriah had a little laugh before answering. "Didn't I tell you? Your father once had magic himself."

Van nearly jumped from the snow. That was certainly news to him.

His surprised reaction amused Victoriah. "Yeah. That meathead trained to be a mage before coming to the chateau."

"What kind of magic did he use?"

"The best thing I've seen in my younger days: a magic called Gendae. He used it to sharpen and restore old weapons. All he had to do was touch them, and they were as good as new."

From her description, Van could imagine what the spells he cast were like. Perhaps not the most extravagant and eye-catching display, but it still fascinated him how he envisioned the worn blades were restored. To someone as a knight, that was a power of tremendous value. The inability to use a weapon sometimes proved fatal.

"His parents insisted he continued to master his power, but he had his heart set on the path paved with blood." Startling though her words were, it made Jerrell sound all the more tenacious. "He was a real help back when we were pages—fixed the sword my great-uncle gave me after some arses snapped it in two."

"Why doesn't he use it now?"

If he had not heard about it for so long, it must have been a touchy topic. And the dull wavelength Victoriah's valsara gave off, resonating a strong depression or grief, made him all the more curious.

Victoriah sighed. "You heard about magic disappearing from the world, right?" she spoke with an ominous tone. "It's not a truth a lot of people like to face. Charms and weapons carrying magic that are affected lose their power. But ... people blessed with these gifts go through a much more ... severe backlash." The strain in her voice echoed her discomfort. Talking about it agitated a wound she had not touched in some time. "Mages are deeply tied to their magic in body and soul. Any affliction to their power weighs on them as heavily as physical pain. Worst-case scenario, the mages lose their lives along with their power.

"Your father was one of the few favored by Lady Sundralla. He endured the anguish of having his power siphoned from him and barely survived. And even though he did, he was a shell of his former self. It took months of rehabilitation before Jerrell was his old self again. He couldn't so much as lift a finger, let alone a sword. For a time, he became the dreariest boy I've ever met. Those sparkling eyes I grew so fond of lost their luster... Every time we sparred against each other, my victories grew much less engaging... As did he.

"He wouldn't snap out of it, even after I slapped him silly."

Try as he could to see how all those things transpired, he could not believe it happened. Victoriah saw the victim through his tortured time; Jerrell experienced every harrowing sensation and the emptiness it left in its place. They probably did not want to believe that happened either.

The story made it perfectly clear as to why Jerrell never spoke of his lost power. An experience like that must have left a terrible scar.

Victoriah turned to her son with the unease and anguish from that time still in her eyes, and graced him with a gentle smile. "Your father might have changed in that time, but he changed a lot over the years, and no matter what, he's still him."

Van returned her smile and nodded. He chose not to dig any deeper than he had. He understood perfectly how such experiences were hard to accept, even as time went on.

Nary a word had been said between the parent and child. They spent the majority of their rest with their backs against the snow, eyes gazing upon the twilight sky.

They valued their time together more than anything else. Even laying comfortably in the snow and simply enjoying the refreshing silver earth and sky, doing nothing but being together, was a moment irreplaceable to them. A part of Van wished they could always stay together like that.

He nearly fell asleep by the time Victoriah stood, and pulled him up with her, to continue their session.

The rest of winter passed without much strife. Victoriah remained in Brigadier for another half week, claiming to have become interested in the current crop of pages. There was business to attend to at the palace, but afterwards, she took the opportunity to train her son. Rather than attempt to better him in Vermalian swordplay, they sparred to see how much potential she could pull out of his unique swordsmanship.

Despite her wishes, she could not remain with her son forever. It was the Champion of Heart's role to ensure the well-being of the kingdom was being upheld. She was responsible for more than just her own family.

She never could remain in one place for too long.

It was a cold morning, the sun had yet to rise, the blistering air waking the children before the bell, when she left. She departed long before anyone could see her, before she lost the will to leave her son again.

Unaffected by the whispers of winter, Van had awoken to the light of the rising sun along with the usual ruckus made by Snowflake, who stayed behind to enjoy his company in slumber. She made for an exit through the open window before Lyn arrived to wake him.

The kindly maid began tending to him regularly ever since she found him wounded from the fight with Kallant. She worried for him so after seeing the bruises on his face and tended to them with care. Van did not understand why his injuries upset her so much. Pages got in fights regularly, even when it was not permitted. But seeing the ones given to him made Lyn turn red with fury.

Although it made him a bit uncomfortable, Van did not reject her help. It was nice having her around as often as she was.

He closed the window immediately upon his fox's escape. The air in the room was comfortable for him, but would make anyone else recoil; Lyn greeted him every morning with her arms wrapped around herself.

Before he began his morning routine, Van noticed a letter was left atop his desk. Just like the one before, it was from Victoriah. He spared no time in reading it.

I'm sorry I didn't say goodbye in person. You weren't too fond of that bauble you made, were you? Because I took it with me. I don't know why, but it is still the same as the night you made it. If you don't believe me, you may get the chance to see for yourself when you return to Russalin. Until then, stay strong and look after your friends. They are your family for as long as you are there, perhaps even longer.

Best of luck, love.

-Mother

A laugh escaped him after finishing the letter. Her worry, her maternal concern, expressed itself heavily in the extra application of ink where it seemed important. It was nice that she mentioned his friends too. It was a shame he had to destroy the letter when he finished reading.

But before that, he noticed a fold in the parchment. His mother had a tendency to hide postscripts in the letters she sent. A brief note was written beneath the fold.

Come the first light of spring, you'll be leaving the chateau for a favorite activity of mine. Don't let Charlie find out I told you about it. He'd give me a hard time if he knew I gave you notice.

Curiosity began to bud, but it did little more. All she informed him of was that he would be doing something different in the springtime. As far as he knew, there was nothing to keep secret. He would find out what it was soon enough.

Flowers soon sprouted through the melting snow, nourished by it. The birds returned from their yearly migration to the southern lands and familiarized themselves with the area once more.

Spring had returned. Many of the pages were overjoyed to see the bright sunlight slowly return to the morning.

His own faction also showed signs of change. The twins were much friendlier with each other again, nary an argument between them. Ccuivr almost seemed serene, but that could have been because of the exotic tea someone gave him for the Flame Festival. Even Rubi's smile lasted past the comments Wally provoked her with. Wally, however, seemed the same as ever. His valsara glimmered the same unnatural joy as ever.

Van did not quite understand why everyone behaved so chipper. He wanted to share in that feeling, but he did not feel any different than usual. But that did not make his time with his friends any less enjoyable.

It took a few more days of patience to discover the Estrine family had planned hunting trips for the pages. Sir Charleston explained everything before forcing Van to help him demonstrate a new maneuver—one that focused on using a shield as a weapon instead of for just protection. Half of the senior knights would take half of the pages to different regions for a week; the other half would depart for theirs upon their return.

For as sore as he was being a demonstration dummy for Sir Charleston, it excited Van to think of where he would go.

The only thing that left him a uneasy was the ominous warning given by Lord Tamsilac. "Whatever you are told, never go hunting by your lonesome. There are many dangers in our kingdom, and they are all the more frightening when faced alone. And the worst is that accursed adolescent assassin... Heed my words lest you become hunted yourselves!"

How anyone could forget such a dramatic warning was befuddling. The frantic way the elderly knight spoke intrigued Van, so he asked his faction if they knew what he spoke of.

From what Stevene had collected from a fourth-year colleague, this adolescent assassin was a serial killer known for targeting children, and mainly favored pages.

Perhaps going on a hunting trip might not have been the best course of action. But regardless of who or what that assassin was, those who trained the pages could not delay their progress. For the sake of their futures, the pages had to be prepared for the present.

Van learned he would join the first party of pages journeying to the dense forest out east named the Wayward Wood. They left immediately midday, leaving very little time to prepare. And unfortunately, his faction was split in two for the time being. Only Wally, Lelia, and Stevene would be joining him. Rubi and Ccuivr were being sent to a lake in the south while Gal would be waiting for his trip upon their return.

Although the twins often bickered, they enjoyed having each other around, and hearing they would be separated disheartened them both.

The pages were all dismissed immediately after the news was given so they could pack a few precious belongings or necessities.

Van took his chance to pack the weight set he could lift. While he did so, Lyn barged in and frantically gave him some helpful advice, rather hastily at that. Apparently, she was waiting for this outing, worrying herself sick over what would happen to him.

"Your chain mail can be easily cleaned by a river using a smooth rock, not a rough one. And be sure to brush it gently."

"Be careful not to touch poison oak, but if you do, just look for an aloe plant and rub it against any area exposed to it."

"Keep everything important on hand. They can easily be misplaced if you are not careful."

"Remember not to wander off on your own. It can be easy to lose your way in a forest."

"No matter what, you must not approach anyone you do not know. Gods forbid it, but there may be brigands or slavers or—"

All of her fretting made Van worry for her own well-being. He wondered how much oxygen reached her lungs with each additional warning and her raised voice.

"Lyn, don't worry so much. I will return in the same condition I'm in now. Trust me, nothing will happen."

The words of a child usually did not amount to anything, something Van easily understood when he saw the reaction in Lyn's valsara. Her smile tried to mislead him, saying she was confidence he was right, but her spirit crackled and wavered trying to hide her angst.

I suppose I'll just have to back up my words, Van thought.

And so, Van's group set off after roll call. Sir Charleston counted heads to see if anyone would remain behind, but he—Van admitted, to his relief—gave command over them to another. Lord Xanlir decided to involve himself with the pages this year and ended up looking after Van's group. Someone of his stature had to be as strict and imposing as his brother. Fortunately, everyone arrived before the midday bell rang, so no one had to see an ugly side to the Champion of Duty.

The group travelled by horse-drawn wagons steered by Estrine knights. Lord Xanlir took point atop his crimson war stallion, giving the pages aboard his wagon a bumpy ride. Even while they were on the move, at incredibly fast speeds no less, with a few getting ill from the raucous ride, he had the pages on lookout the entire way.

"Knights must be vigilant no matter where we are. Fine as our kingdom is, it is not without threats, and they linger everywhere, even in these open fields, waiting to pounce upon the opportune victims. It will one day fall to you to snuff them out before they bring harm to others."

Those who did not suspect Lord Xanlir and Sir Charleston of being siblings had after hearing him talk. They sounded so different—Lord Xanlir being a glib, persuasive voice, Sir Charleston a harsh one that demanded obedience. But they showed the same devotion to their roles.

In three days' time, they arrived before a forest lush with sharp pines and thick foliage that sheltered the forest creatures. The dirt path faded toward the Wayward Wood. Lord Xanlir attempted to navigate them through the cloister of nature, but only managed to take them in the wrong direction. Had Lelia not shown him the compass she held onto, he might have taken them through the other side of the forest.

The setback cost them time. The sun began to set before they found a spot to make camp. Before the cover of darkness could drape over the sky, Lord Xanlir decided to make do with what the clearing they found.

"All right, pages! Set up the tents while I survey the area! Vandelas, be a good lad and dig a trench for the boys behind those bushes. Gallelia, be a lamb and dig one for the girls over there."

He went on his way to accomplish his own task. The other knights who transported them had departed for the nearest village upon dropping them off at the forest entrance, so the pages were looking after themselves. Everyone remained docile and obedient until moments after Lord Xanlir was out of sight. Then many of the pages began wandering around, partaking in random activities Van paid no attention to. Getting involved would only implicate him, so he shrugged off the noise and kept to digging.

"What are you doing?" Stevene did not seem to think the same way. "If you don't get to work, you'll get it from Lord Xanlir."

"Lord Xanlir?" Kallant spoke. "That man is a joke."

Now Van could not help but peek through the bushes and see what was happening. Kallant and his thugs were loafing about at the lone wagon.

"I never understood why the Estrines had him going around the country instead of training pages like the rest of his family. Until I met him, that is. He couldn't even lead his mount here." Kallant paused to pat the resting stallion's hide. "I'm surprised no one fell off in that ride. He is unfocused, easily distracted. That man cannot be trusted to lead us."

The insults Kallant hurled at Lord Xanlir made Van's blood come close to a boiling. Having spent much time training with the champion in place of Sir Charleston, Van had grown to greatly admire him. He felt obligated to pounce at Kallant and wring his neck.

Except that he saw someone better suited for the job. Lord Xanlir must not have gone far because he returned at a comfortable pace, looking rather content until seeing the pages lollygagging and hearing Kallant's ugly words. He stood rather leisurely against a tree while listening in on them. There was still something left unsaid, and judging by the inquisitive yet sharp stare of his, he wanted to find out what it was.

"Why should I have to listen to an embarrassment who was only made a knight so his own family could keep him away?"

And with those choice words said, Lord Xanlir decided to take action. He looked rather carefree as he skulked toward the loafers. It piqued Van's curiosity to see why he had not yet let his rage known.

By the time Kallant realized Lord Xanlir stood behind him, it was already too late. "I believe I gave you children instructions to follow." The champion's voice still rang calmly, revealing no plausible threat.

Dazed and tongue-tied, Kallant tried thinking of a way to respond that would not ruin him.

Lord Xanlir sighed. "A shame to hear your parents do not approve of the stature I built for myself. You may have shown better judgment otherwise." The arm on his hip drooped, bending back a bit. Before they could react, he flicked the three pages at their foreheads with enough force to knock them off their feet. It was bewildering to see such a cheeky method actually threw enough force to put them on the ground. "There will be times where you won't always approve of your commanding officer. I can tell by looking at you that you may even hold murderous intent toward them. Yet regardless of your feelings toward your superior, you are expected to carry out any and all orders he or she will give, for their decisions affect more than just their position. If they cannot be properly carried out, then the soldiers beneath them prove themselves expendable."

With the turn of his voice from jolly to dark, all of the pages learned to respect Lord Xanlir whether for his title, his composure, or for fear of what he would do if they shirked their work.

"Reflect on that while you spend the cold night there."

Those who have not been working, focus derailed by the pages' humiliation, immediately returned to their tasks, not wishing to be the next to endure Lord Xanlir's spite.

He made his way around the camp like how Sir Charleston observed them during training exercises, slowly and with a critical stare. He then stopped at the bush concealing Van. "Oh, and Vandelas, when you finish digging that trench, come see me. I'd like to get a workout in before bed."

It was difficult to tell whether or not Kallant was in the better position. Despite how much Van's swordsmanship improved, Lord Xanlir learned of its flaws and took advantage of them.

Lying comfortably on the grass, gazing at the moon and stars, was certainly more comfortable than taking another beating from Lord Xanlir.

Falling asleep and waking up with the mild injuries inflicted by him was almost as irksome as listening to the chateau bell's thunderous ringing.

The usual morning exercises were performed before Lord Xanlir gave instructions on how they would be hunting.

Stevene whispered to his companions that bows might be involved since Sir Charleston had them sharpen their skills in archery before they left. Neither Van nor Lelia doubted their intelligent friend.

As predicted, Lord Xanlir explained to the pages that they would use bows and arrows for the hunt.

Their excitement began to pick up; seeing as many of the children never went on a hunt before, they reveled in the chance to claim their first pelt. "Remember: we are here for meat, not fur. Save the chance for bonding with your fathers." Those words killed nearly everyone's spirits, but they hid their disappointment and groans to avoid getting scolded.

Lord Xanlir quickly taught them how to set up a snare, leaving out no details. Since he also said what they caught would be what they ate, everyone made sure to pay attention.

The pages checked to make sure they had a fair supply of arrows and rope before splitting up. Their instructions were to set up snares and search the forest for small animals, then lead them toward the snares with the arrows, where, with any luck, they would be captured.

Although not a part of Lord Xanlir's instructions, with Lord Tamsilac's warning still fresh in their minds, everyone formed teams as small as two to as large as five before beginning the hunt.

Wally went along with a few others he made laugh while Van, Stevene, and Lelia remained together. They offered a lone boy to join their hunt so that he would not have to be by himself.

To everyone's surprise, that boy was Prince Aeron K. G. Vermalio. It was hard to believe at first. Why would the others not want to benefit from befriending the prince? It mattered very little to Van for him to put much thought into it. They had other things to think about.

Since Kallant and his brood went north, Van's group decided to turn south and find prey that had not been spooked off.

Stevene suggested that Prince Aeron take the lead so he could gain experience as a leader. A rather humble sort, the prince replied by claiming he would prefer not to be addressed by his royal title. As curious as that was, they obliged so long as he did a good job. While Aeron took charge, Stevene arranged a plan he assured them would "nab them fair prizes for the fire," as he put it. After briefly surveying the area, he discovered a few food sources the local fauna would love. The arched path they found was the perfect place for setting their traps. Van and Lelia collected and laid the bait while the aspiring tactician and future king remained behind to set up this pattern of traps elegant in its simplicity.

Aeron and Stevene pointed out where the traps had been set to their other teammates. That did not offer much help, though. No matter which direction they turned, it all looked the same—just dirt and leaves. Little clues gave way, like the leaves bulging out in the form of a ring. The only visible ones were the traps close to their feet. The rest blended in well with the surroundings.

The excitement of the hunt was getting to everyone. Van could not keep still. Lelia clenched her bow close like a toy. Stevene flashed this foolish grin. Aeron began dancing like an idiot, happy enough to scream. Luckily, he held back before scaring anything off.

"Look there!" the prince called them quietly.

Something had crawled from the bushes just inches before the traps' at the southern perimeter. Its small stature and fluffy body told them it was a small mammal. It looked rather rabbit-like from afar until it became obvious the tail was long like its ears.

"It's a fox!"

Oh no!

It was Snowflake. There were a few things the pages talked about while they were setting up the traps; Van's pet was not one of them. All Aeron knew was the creature had a rare pelt color corresponding with the region and that its meat would be appetizing.

"Small though it may be, but it'll last us the night."

Even in that hushed tone, those words did not sound any less like a warning shriek from the witch god of death. Aeron already drew his bow and was readying to take an arrow from his quiver, and spun it in his hand like a wheel. He was obviously well trained in archery. If he fired even one arrow, it would spell the poor fox's doom.

If Van interfered, it would only arouse suspicion. His thoughts raged with great anguish, but there was no time to think.

Panicked, Van drew his own arrow and readied it the moment Aeron fired. No aim. No calculation. No thought at all. He let loose the arrow immediately so it could catch up with Aeron's. Both flew with the wind, each trying to land their distinct targets.

The moment Snowflake picked up her head to see danger looming in, Van's arrow narrowly snapped Aeron's and pierced the ground before her.

She was stunned for a moment, but seeing the angry child gave Snowflake the motivation to flee.

"What did you do?" Aeron snarled at Van. "I almost had it!"

"I-I'm sorry. I guess ... I wanted to try my hand at it too." Van did not have to pretend to look guilty. From where the poor fox looked, she must have thought he was the one who threatened her life.

"Forget it," the prince groaned. "I think I can still catch it if I—"

"Careful!" Stevene stopped Aeron in his tracks with an outstretched arm. "You almost stepped in a snare!"

"I did? Well, where should I go?"

By the time he figured that out, Snowflake would have already fled far from danger—and from Van.

~ Tenth Chapter ~

Hunting Instinct

The guilt Van felt for scaring off Snowflake plagued him during the hunt. Even it if was to protect her, it made his chest knot up.

His melancholy was evident to those who knew him. Lelia and Stevene snapped him out of it by tapping his shoulder and asking if he found anything when they saw him lose composure.

Unbeknownst to Van's relationships, Aeron assumed his grief was due to losing the white fox along with the other prey they failed to bag. The prince dignified him with a sincere apology, believing he reacted too harshly. Van respected the attempt to maintain camaraderie and apologized to meet the prince halfway. Hiding his guilt became easier from that point; he could not allow his own issues to meddle in their task.

It was not easy learning to hide his emotions. The failure he experienced in training and the scorn he received from others nearly made him lose control time and again. None of that came without something in return, though. He learned to endure pain in many forms. And from enduring it, he came to learn how to surpass it.

But when it came to the pain of those he cared for, he was not prepared.

He buried his guilt beneath the intensity of the hunt. Growling stomachs became the only issue soon enough. Since only those who caught anything were allowed to eat, they used everything they knew to draw out prey. That misdirection trick, using arrows to lead animals into snares, would not work for everyone.

Giving in to hunger, Van had been occasionally picking these small purple berries from bushes he passed by.

Hours have passed, and still they had no luck. The snares managed to snag a few stray squirrels, but they slipped out before getting captured. They began to think the animals were teasing them.

Van tried listening for any signs of animals. All that passed his ears was the brush of air teasing the tree's leaves and the lovey songs of the birds echoing through the forest air.

Stevene groaned. "The sun is going to set soon, and we haven't caught a thing yet!"

"What kind of failure am I?" brooded Aeron. "My father caught a wolf on his first hunt, and we couldn't even catch the puniest of foxes."

Van let that comment pass, understanding his stress.

"I'd thought of everything we can do: expanding our trapping vicinity, burying every hole for escape, masking our scent with—"

"*Please* don't say any more!" Lelia shrieked.

"We have nothing to show for our efforts. If we go back to Lord Xanlir empty-handed, we'll be laughingstocks!"

Lelia sighed. "Most first-year pages are beginners at this, Page Vermalio. He wouldn't think less of us for not finding anything."

Stevene took a deep breath to calm down. "She's right, Aeron." Admitting failure did not come easy for him. "You should not let your father's success make expectations for your own."

"Who are you kidding? You're just as upset about this as I am."

"Dwelling on it will do us no good."

"You were just panicking about how we haven't caught a thing!"

"Can I just—"

Neither of the bickering boys listened to Lelia, and soon she joined in the argument. Thinking back to how the children were in Russalin, when they behaved like that, they were beyond hope. Gentle words would not sway them while they argued, leaving only one viable method Van could think of—courtesy of his mother.

He never thought of intimidating others so they might see things his way and never considered the need to resort to such, but his friends looked ready to nock their arrows for the one agitating them the most.

How does Mother do it?

Furrowed brows. Strong demeanor. Fists clenched. Eyes focused straight.

Correcting his appearance was simple, but he needed something more, something that would make the most stubborn of people listen to him. The loud arguing made his suppressed frustrations fester and threaten to overwhelm him. All the better for him to use.

He took one step forward. Hesitation gripped him for a moment, but he tore its shaky yet forceful clamps off for a second step, and felt ready to conquer upon the third. "Enough!"

His howl startled them enough to stop arguing. Lelia and Stevene stared at him wide-eyed, speechless. They had never heard him raise his voice so loud, and could not help but feel unnerved by his outburst.

"Your bickering will frighten off whatever is left. If any of you want to catch anything, then shut up and listen to what's around us, or we really will be going back with nothing!"

It actually worked. Those three went dead silent. Having been close enough to see the cracks in his glacial gaze, they remained frozen and did as he demanded.

With that settled, Van took a few steps away from everyone to heighten his concentration. He closed his eyes, shutting off one sense to better grasp the environment with the others. What the others decided to do was beyond him, though he knew they remained in the same spot since their valsara's glow radiated where they stood. The life energy of the plants and trees then manifested behind them. The valsara of plant life was not as clear in his eyes, but still vibrant.

He waited patiently for signs of change. A soft rustling disturbed the image in his mind before long, and from it came a voice. Stevene, Lelia, and Aeron remained silent, unmoved by the disturbance. For a moment, Van thought some pages stumbled into their hunting ground, but when he learned what the voice expressed, he knew it was not human.

They would overreact if given the news directly, so Van quietly brushed a finger over his mouth, bidding them to remain hushed. The most excitable action taken was Lelia looking over her shoulder to where he looked. A wall of foliage in the way, the sound had to be coming from the other side.

"Stevene, come with me. Aeron, take Lelia and circle around that opening in the bushes."

Everyone took action, forgoing any hesitation, moving slowly and quietly. They crouched behind the bushes, peering around the corner to spot whatever it was Van overheard. A lone hare sat comfortably in the open, taking an interest in the bait it found. It was too busy munching on fibrous tree bark to notice them.

Hares were faster than any man. And their ears were keen. If they made one false move, it would take notice and flee.

How to ensure it would not escape...?

Aeron's hasty attempt to bag prey earlier gave Van an idea. Firing an arrow with his proficiency was risky, but the archer prodigy could not accomplish the task where he stood, and the hare would not remain there for very long. And Stevene's arrows scarcely met their marks, much to his chagrin. Hoping his actions would go unnoticed, Van promptly nocked an arrow. He took a second to aim for the hare before letting it fly.

It missed, landing an inch apart from the hare, which dashed in the opposite direction the arrow came from.

Van knew his shot would not hit, but knowing the arrow struck so close to its target tortured him. He gritted his teeth imagining the scorn the others would show for being the one to scare off their prey.

The imminent shame he felt distracted him from spotting the little hare getting snared. It dangled from the air with all four paws restrained painfully.

Everyone rushed toward the poor hare, unable to contain their excitement. Finally, their first catch had been made, and they could return to Lord Xanlir with their heads held high.

"Nice shot, Van!" Stevene patted him on the back.

"Splendid shot, Vandelas!" said the prince.

"Wonderful job!" added Lelia with a bright smile.

Their words all felt so reassuring. After hearing their praise in lieu of the derisive scorn he feared, Van could not admit to never noticing the trap when he shot the arrow. He just smiled and laughed awkwardly.

The excitement passing, everyone put their focus back onto the hare struggling for escape. Aeron cut the rope, holding enough of it at length so the little thing did not bite him.

No one made another move past that, though.

Someone had to put the creature out of its misery, but no one would step up to do it. Those big, twinkling eyes made the children see the hare as another living creature instead of food. Prince Aeron tried putting it to Stevene and Lelia before long, saying he could not with the prey in hand. Neither of them budged. Stevene tried to put focus off him, accusing the prince of being too weak to kill the rodent. Having never killed a thing before, Lelia held her hands up in refusal.

Next was Van, who heard the animal's cries clearer than anyone else. He could not look any more confident than the others hearing its terrified squeaks. No response was given when he was asked to do it.

The others began to argue again, all the while the hare dangled in its bindings. The little animal cried out louder as it swung. With each frightened sound it made, Van heard it panic over something other than itself. He counted each cry as one for a family member—a mate and seventeen younglings.

They could not let it go, and the building delay was cruel to the little hare. So Van made the choice.

He drew the dirk strapped to his hip as Aeron and Stevene looked ready to fight again. He struck fast, thrusting the blade into the hare.

First taking the lead when things looked hopeless, then being the one to repress his conscience and end their prey, the pages continued to be left in awe of Van. He even surprised himself; ignoring the pleas to be freed to return to its family was difficult.

For a moment, he thought he would need to reassure himself by thinking the baby hares had another to look after them, yet the images of other predators—pages—seeking them out came to pass. Then he came to realize the inevitable kills they, as knights, would make in the future.

"Aeron, the next one is yours. Even a king must know how to kill."

Van was not making jokes. If a boy who could communicate with animals could do it, then the same should be said for them.

The prince made no objections. He seemed to regret not doing it himself. "Let's check the other traps and return to camp."

Since they were so lucky to get one catch, the others questioned the odds of finding another, but that one catch gave them the motivation to keep searching. Great Gaia did not offer much save the extra hare to their snares, which the prince slayed as promised. He tried offering a merciful end, swift and painless.

Everyone returned to camp bit upset as they found themselves the last to arrive. A large fire had been made. The pages gathered around it, their hands pressed against its warm, comforting glow, some hanging freshly skinned animals over the flames.

As he earlier declared, Lord Xanlir forbade those who failed to bag any game from sharing in the spoils of the hunt. Some pages felt sorry for their companions and were bold enough to sneak them a few scraps so they did not go hungry; that earned them a firm whack at the wrists from Lord Xanlir. He stated that hunger would further motivate them to capture prey the next day.

Going about his own business, Van sat away from the fire while enjoying some of the hare his friends skinned and charred. With the fire being so crowded, his faction—Wally included—joined him.

The long day's work left Van craving more meat. But to stay in favor with Lord Xanlir and not get another mark on the wrist, he withheld from eating the dried leftovers they rationed. His ravenous hunger demanded more, though. Luckily, he still had some of those berries he collected earlier. Those juicy little beads were not very filling but had a tart flavor.

"Whoa!"

Wally slapped at the berry between Van's fingers before he got the chance to pop it into his mouth.

Being addressed like a misbehaving mule only added to the frustration of being denied food, the vein at his forehead throbbing.

"You do *not* want to eat those berries."

Van leered at his impish friend, his head half-cocked upon noticing his concern. "Why not? I've been snacking on them all day." He dropped the rest of his berries after hearing Stevene choke, and looked over to him.

"Van, those are midnight vipers," Stevene cried. "They're poisonous! Have just one, and you're dead in less than a day."

Dead in less than a day? From just one berry?

Van instinctively clenched his neck, waiting for the end to come. Dozens of those little droplets were senselessly dropped down his throat since midday.

Any minute Van would begin hyperventilating and break out in uncontrollable sweating, then suffer from hot flashes, until finally collapsing and meeting a slow, agonizing death—as per the frightfully specific symptoms given by Stevene, who lost his fool of an uncle the same way.

Knowing he snacked on them all day made him realize something crucial. Having eaten so many, the symptoms should have taken effect by now, yet he felt nothing out of the ordinary. His body was as cold as ever, his muscles weighed only from fatigue, and he still had some energy left. And the animals he saw eating them before they ran away seemed perfectly fine as well. Were they really poisonous?

Lelia reported this to Lord Xanlir shortly after finding out. The other pages wore grave concern on their faces knowing that one of their own would be dying. The knight approached, ready to make his diagnosis.

After carefully inspecting for all of the symptoms, Lord Xanlir eventually looked at Van's pulse and froze in astonishment. It seemed like it was a miracle he still drew breath.

Anger at his foolishness vanished, leaving a mild color of caution in his valsara. Lord Xanlir had on the straightest face while he dug into his pack for some medicine. "So this won't be left up to Lady Sundralla's hasty hand, take this vial with some water, and *never* eat another of those berries again."

"Yes, milord."

It was a little disappointing. For poisonous berries, they were surprisingly scrumptious.

After the pages had their fill and stored their rations for later, they were ordered into their tents for some rest. A few pages were selected to watch over the campsite until dawn while the others slept, and they would be allowed to sleep through the morning. Lord Xanlir claimed it to be an exercise of perseverance before returning to the wagon; hearing it come from him almost made it sound like he was merely trying to get out of it himself.

Van and Stevene volunteered to keep watch. The hungry page felt he should stay awake until the poison dissipated from his body, even if it would not kill him. The other wanted to train himself to be more observant for the next hunt.

Stevene invited his friend to join him by the fire, but Van politely declined, saying he should patrol the area. Being near flames still exhausted him. He kept nearby, though, noticing how irritated Stevene felt never noticing one of his own pick poisonous berries.

Walking around the clearing left his mind free to ponder on different things: home, the southern crops, how tasty pumpkins looked while they were still puny, how Brute used to use them for his tiny catapult, the way Mini always scolded him for hitting sheep, and so on.

Eventually, thought moved to memories of Snowflake, and thus the most recent one. The fear he saw speckled in those big blue eyes flashed in his head again and again.

Van needed to sit down. Seeing as the fire had gone low at last, he decided to accept a spot next to Stevene.

"Stevene."

"Hm?"

"I wanted to thank you."

Stevene glanced his way. "What do you mean?"

"I know you tricked the prince. There was no snare under his foot."

He grinned. "So you noticed."

"I saw there wasn't rope anywhere near us."

"Well—" Stevene stretched his arms over his head "—you're fond of that fox, so I had to do something." His arms fell like old cloth upon relaxing. He halted the right arm and brought its hand up to rub his eyes. "Just wish it wouldn't follow you around everywhere."

"I can't say I know how she does it. No matter where I go, she always finds me. She's just been attached to me ever since I found her."

"I'll say this much: for a beast, Snowflake is pretty smart."

Knowing Stevene's dislike for the clingy fox, Van wondered what would be the point in asking him if he thought Snowflake was upset at him. But his thoughts left his lips before he realized it.

They both remained silent, staring at the fire until either felt it appropriate to speak up. One of them loved animals enough to think them as people; the other found them only suitable for labor or food. In that area, they could not see eye to eye.

But they were also comrades who respected each other. And that seemed to be enough to show compassion. "If it is as smart as we think it to be, then your pet will understand."

Three days of running around through the forest half-cocked left the pages exhausted and hungry. They often returned to camp with nothing in hand, forced to endure meals without anything to eat.

Since the areas they searched were not providing much and the weather appeared favorable, the pages were instructed to spread out to farther reaches of the forest. Meat was the necessity, but everyone began bringing back anything that looked edible so they could move the next day. Lord Xanlir did not oppose that; gathering was a skill as favorable as hunting.

Lelia caught the most attention when she hauled back an armful of amber gourds. She brought her find to Lord Xanlir to see what he thought. Curiosity turned into excitement as the champion looked upon the fat fruits, a spot of drool almost escaping his lips. Apparently, those gourds were a favorite of his. The lone twin smirked upon taking notice of that.

He charmingly asked to sample one of the smaller ones, to which Lelia claimed she would have loved to share, but sadly, Lord Xanlir had not found any himself. The move was a sly one, and Lord Xanlir's grin showed that he respected it. A child-like persona overshadowed the Champion of Duty's dignified character; he made a deal to abolish the rule forbidding pages from sharing food with those who have found none in exchange for a share of her haul.

It was safe to say Lelia had a bright future in handling negotiations if she could take advantage of Lord Xanlir.

Everyone broke into groups in hopes of finding more patches of the amber gourds. A few asked Lelia where she had found them, but she conveniently forgot where she picked the worshipped fruits.

With stomachs full and spirits high, the pages all scattered to reaches they dared not tread previously.

The groups dividing even further into pairs, Wally and Van stayed with each other as they ventured to the northern areas. Growing up in a castle left Wally without knowledge of where fruits and vegetables grew, so he relied on his partner, a fallen noble from Southern Valley, to find the amber gourds. Since he got a hold of one the night before, Van had a vague idea of where they might grow. The slick texture of the thick shell suggested that particular gourd thrived in areas with plenty of water and, judging by the shell's dark hue, shade.

They began their search near a little creek. A bed of petite white flowers bloomed close to the small waterfall formed along a ledge. Animals of all sizes likely gathered there. The boys built a few snares close to the water before continuing their search for the amber gourds in case their efforts proved fruitless.

The trees grew thicker and closer together the farther they went, the leaves blocking out much of the sunlight. The air was still moist along an emerald path.

Along the path that shifted from day to night, the environment came to slowly change. Van thought it best to turn back, but Wally did not listen, claiming he could practically smell a garden of amber gourds nearby. As the environment became darker, there was an uncomfortable feeling that came with it, a disturbing atmosphere that slowly closed in around them. It was as though there were predators lurking in the shadows, watching their every move, biding their time until the two morsels could no longer escape. And yet Van only sensed the valsara of himself, his friend, and the harmless plant life.

They ran out of rope a while ago, using it as a means to find their way back to camp as well as bag prey. Van mentioned this but was ignored as he was before.

Even though they were alone, he got this unsettling feeling that if they wandered too far into the dark, they might never leave it again.

Soon, every corner of the murky forest looked the same. The grass, bushes, trees—it all blended together. Even with the dark cutting off more and more of the path, Wally still would not concede to turning back.

His sanguinity never frightened Van until now.

He could not stay quiet any longer. Fear began to overcome him. They should not be there. "We need to go back," Van insisted. "We've found nothing this far in, and I know we went farther than we're supposed to."

Wally slowed until coming to a stop. He did not look prepared to argue, his shoulders sagging upon a sigh. Upon turning back, he looking Van straight in the eye, but flinched when he did. He never noticed how his eyes gave off this faint glow in the dark.

Attempting to hide his shock, Wally put back on his usual happy-go-lucky expression. "Come on, Van. Did you see the look on Lord Xanlir's face when Lelia brought him those gourds? We bring back some of those overripened fruits, and they'll show us the respect we deserve."

"They wouldn't admit it, but I know they respect you, Wally. No one can manipulate people as well as you, in or out of a fight."

That response startled Wally more than his friend's glowing eyes. He could not reply. For the first time, he could not counter the words hurled at him, and there were not many to intercept.

Van expected some light taunting, normally used on Rubi and Ccuivr, or maybe a bargain, a tool very effective on Gal. Instead, Wally just cracked a crooked smile and uneasily said, "Do you remember the path we took? I may have ... gotten us lost."

It seemed he expected Van to be upset with him. Van, however, lost his frustration in face of that sympathetic plea for help. Whether agitating an adversary or soothing an angry ally, Wally knew exactly how to deter someone's focus and make them move as he needed.

It was a quality that always impressed Van.

He led them back the way they came, keeping a careful watch of their surroundings. Although their surroundings were dark and misleading, he managed to find a way onto the path without much difficulty.

The disturbing atmosphere he felt kept bothering him. He adhered to caution as they moved, the tension ever thickening. Van had his doubts before, but now he was certain they were being followed. And yet he saw and heard nothing. If it was simply an animal, he would normally hear a voice, something mumbled or groaned at least.

That was what he dreaded most—the silence.

"Wally," Van whispered low enough for no one else to hear, "draw your sword, now."

"Why?"

Expecting an argument, Van turned back, looking Wally squarely in the eye to make him understand their dreadful position. Though he expressed confusion, Wally did what was asked of him.

Van whispered a silent thanks to Lord Tamsilac. He doubted that Wally would have listened were it not for his long lectures on the vital importance of communication and cooperation in battle.

Upon grasping the scabbard at his side, Van's eyes drew open wide. A twig had snapped from above. He glanced toward a westward tree's branches, where a human silhouette perched itself. It held an axe that gleamed brightly enough from the moonlight to warn him it would be thrown at Wally.

Impulse drove him to throw a swift kick at the oblivious boy's abdomen, shoving him away before the axe hit. Van was glad he forgot to strap the weights on that morning, otherwise they would have kept him from pulling his leg back before the axe struck bone.

The hurler could no longer hide. It leaped from the tree, launching itself through the air like a wraith. Both boys leaped away from each other, taking notice the daggers held in their assailant's hands.

Not much could be interpreted about the assailant's identity; its torso had been draped in an old cloak, their face concealed beneath some thick wrapping. The impressive stature revealed it to be a male, but nothing more than that.

His presence, brought so close, horrified Van. It reminded him of the barbarian that struck him down two years ago.

The wrapping that masked him did not cover a set of crimson eyes shimmering with a terrifying bloodlust. Before his movements could be followed, Van dug up as much dirt as he could into his palm, then flung it directly into the man's face. He covered his concealed face much too late.

"Wally, run!"

Van did not bother waiting for a response before he rushed past the man and hoped Wally followed. He ran down the path fast enough to feel the air brutally hitting his face.

Carrying around those weights day in and day out brought Van's endurance and running speed to levels that almost made him forget a murderer was behind him.

He worried Wally might not be able to keep up, but was soon reassured otherwise. That jester closed the distance faster than worry could plague his thoughts. Never before had Van seen Wally run so briskly. It made him ponder on how he trained himself.

"I guess I owe you for kicking me out of the way, huh?" Even in times of peril he never refrained from making the occasional joke. In a way, though, that was good. It might keep him from panicking.

They kept running, making sharp turns, in hopes of losing their assailant, before stopping to rest. Both of them drained their lungs of air in making their desperate escape. They lay exhausted against a thick tree, perishing the thought of movement apart from slumping against the rugged trunk.

Wally tried speaking in between heavy breaths. "I never ... knew ... you could run ... so fast—"

Van withheld from saying anything until finally catching his breath. In taking one long breath, he felt awash with cool relief. "Me neither. The winds never treated me so fairly when I'm not riding Nightshade."

"Who do you suppose that guy was? Upset anyone recently?"

"No... I leave that to you."

Wally's laugh sounded rather disheartening when he was tired. "I'll have to think about the adults I've offended later. Maybe it was another ploy at my life, like when I was four."

"Tell me about that when we're safe."

Wally nodded and pressed against the tree to help him stand.

Van followed his lead, but then froze after standing. When his eyes fell shut, he noticed something odd. With his magic sight, he saw a thin layer of unusual energy enveloping everything around them. Although he wanted to dismiss it as a mental relapse, he soon thought otherwise. He could sense the energy circling them. Looking up at the tree they rested under made him see it had grown in eerily familiar directions.

Van turned to Wally. "Do you notice something familiar about this place? It looks exactly the same as where we were attacked."

For a moment, he looked to think Van paranoid, but after taking a look around, Wally's expression showed he saw it too. And his eyes became as wide as hen eggs when looking in Van's direction again.

Footsteps were heard from behind. Van turned back to find the danger they thought had left behind slowly march toward them in a macabre momentum.

"How did he find us!?"

"We never escaped," Van dreadfully stated, no longer doubtful. "We were caught in his trap before he even threw the axe. This entire time, we've been led astray by this man's power. What we thought we saw and felt was nothing more than what he wanted us to perceive, an illusion he conjured to deceive and tire us. We ran in circles without realizing it." He did not want to believe in his own words but saw no other explanation. The magic he sensed kept him from seeing past a certain proximity of their surroundings.

This man fooled them into lowering their guard only to rise from peril once more. It was a ploy to rob them of hope before claiming their lives.

"In other words, we're trapped until he kills us," Wally mumbled.

"...Or until we kill him."

The assailant plunged his cloaked right arm through his left sleeve, pulling out a long, fiendish scythe. To hide four deadly weapons on his person and never make a sound—it was like they were being pursued by the witch god of death.

"Van, keep him busy."

The sound of Wally retiring his sword to its scabbard was immediately followed by his startled hand drawing for an arrow nesting in his quiver. He took his bow in hand and nocked an arrow.

It was a smart idea. While one of them engaged the assailant, the other would look for the perfect opening to finish him off. Luckily, Wally was one of the better archers in their faction, and with his swordsmanship, Van was the best one to take him on.

Arming himself with the sharp sword he was given and its scabbard, Van charged at the man, who suddenly became still as the dead. He spun and swiped for the chest, only to be blocked by the assailant flaunting his weapon's snath. His attack was parried, the following unbalance leaving Van open for the scythe to fall down at him. He anticipated where the blade would fall, gripped his scabbard, and threw it to intercept the blow and compromise his foe's balance.

Wise to the openings at the side, Van then threw his sword for the enemy's right hip. The assailant met that blow, spinning his weapon and guarding with the snath again. A third attempt at rebounding his enemy's force back at him only led to the same result. No matter where either of them aimed, they repulsed one another in moves that almost seemed rhythmic.

Block, repulse, and strike. Block, repulse, strike. Block, repulse, strike. The cycle continued in a deadly dance that both performers refused to break on their end.

It aggravated Van to think there was someone who could match his movements so effectively. Even two of the Six Champions had to be wary of how he moved. His blood boiled just looking at the man who resisted him. How was he doing it? How did he read and move to his rhythm?

A *twang* from Wally's bow sounded.

The arrow flew for the assailant's torso and looked like it would meet its mark. But in the instant when he repulsed Van, he skillfully swung at the arrow, cutting it in two a foot from its mark. That left him open for another strike Van gladly took. His reactions sharp, the assailant drew in his scythe, this time blocking with the blade instead of the snath.

And from there, their dance continued. Van felt a strong desire to sink his weapon into the assailant's flesh. Each time their blades met, he felt the same desire from the assailant. It was not malice—not exactly. They both took pride in their skill, their ability to keep up the dance. They felt each other's bewilderment, adrenaline, and desire to understand how they matched each other's rhythm. But there was also something else, something the assailant tried to repress.

Another arrow fired from Wally's bow.

The assailant again anticipated where it would hit and swung, then swiftly moved to block Van's attack. That time, the arrow came within six inches of him before being snapped in two. Van and Wally's joined efforts were wearing the assailant down.

When Wally fired his third arrow—only two inches more did it need to pierce its target's skull—the assailant decided he had enough. Pure malice now exuding from him, he met Van's strike by sliding forward and swinging the scythe horizontally. While he managed to block the attack, Van could not endure the force applied to it and was thrown hard against a sturdy oak. Disoriented, he crumbled against its trunk.

Open your eyes! he demanded of himself. *You'll be killed!*

The malignant valsara looming over him flared, but its owner did not go for him. The frantic sound of a bowstring began playing in repetition. Van fought his fatigue and caught a glimpse of Wally firing a flurry of arrows at their assailant, who cut back any that flew too close.

Wally could not fight him alone.

Try as he might, Van could not stand without a jolt of pain shooting up his back. He could not move his body higher than a few feet off the ground before toppling back down, gasping a thick white breath. As he looked on, he saw Wally's fate: split where the axe could not land, then his limbs, head, and torso all minced in sheer bloodlust.

He refused to allow it to happen.

Ignoring the sword in his grasp, Van pounded his hand to the ground, unleashing his ethereal power. A wave of razor-tipped ice rose from where he struck, reaching to heights almost meeting the trees tops to form a mighty wall between the assailant and Wally, who fell on his rump.

Van saw his skin revert back to its natural russet hue as he forced himself to stand again. "Not a step closer to him," he growled, letting out another puff of icy breath. "Or I'll freeze you to the core!"

He managed to lift his head enough to shoot a fierce glare, adding weight to his threat. The assailant looked to him and trembled, the scythe he held rattling. Van dared not lose his composure; he was uncertain he had the focus to do that again.

The assailant did not look away from Van. Seeing one of the demons the Vermalian people feared appear before him must have been a tremendous shock. He even dropped his weapon, which dissipated into a breath of black mist, and began backing away.

For a moment, Van thought he was imagining things. Had fear numbed his focus? Was that why he no longer sensed malice from the enemy?

Something else caught the assailant's focus, something in Wally's direction. Reacting to it, he took a bizarre sphere hidden in his sleeve and spiked it to the ground. A sharp spark of light ignited, blinding the boys he attacked.

His vision obstructed again, Van could not track where or how the assailant moved. A ringing filled his ears as he was blinded. His senses soon returned to normal, and confusion remained in the place of fear.

Where did he go?

The assailant had completely disappeared without a trace, and his magic was beginning to fade. The dangerous atmosphere slowly vanished.

The threat finally passing, Van wanted to topple over and let himself pass out. He looked over to Wally, who still sat behind a wall that was no longer there. The Second Verse reacted to his instability and shattered the ice he sculpted, leaving only tiny, dissipating specks of frost.

Their eyes met for a moment. Wally's were wide with bewilderment. Van could not bear to look directly at him. He felt exposed, vulnerable, for he was not yet out of danger. He saw him. He saw his true colors.

His eyes glanced along the thinning veil of magic. They saw the tears in the illusion and the world returning to normal. Someone else was coming. He did not know who.

And it did not matter. Too many have seen him in his true form already. He struggled to make a quick escape, toppling over and falling through the bushes. The injury he sustained kept him from going far.

Van remained perfectly silent behind the bushes, not allowing himself to so much as breathe. The vapor he perspired thinned as a result. No one would be able to see it behind the shroud of darkness.

"Wallace, are you all right?"

That voice belonged to one of the last people he wanted to see him exposed: Lord Xanlir. Van put more effort into masking his presence and struggled to remain calm.

But it was already too late. Wally had already seen him. No matter what he did, it was the end.

"Yeah ... just shaken up, that's all."

"Come. We must get back to camp immediately."

"No, I can't!" Wally suddenly shouted. "Van—"

Consumed by fear, Van slowly curled up into a ball. It was an old reflex. In his younger years, whenever he feared the monsters from his nightmares would harm him, he hid under the blankets on his bed. Now he hid from the people he admired, fearing they would kill him without a second thought.

The slight pause Wally withheld tortured him.

"Van ... Van and I got separated. I need to find him! That lunatic will murder him if I don't!"

All of the thoughts rushing through Van's mind came to a halt. Those words were not of hatred passed down to him. It was a lie molded out of deep concern.

"You saw him?"

Lord Xanlir had seen him?

"Just ran off in that direction!"

"Perhaps I can catch him. Search for Vandelas on your way back to camp. Don't stop for anything else."

Clanking metal and hefty stomps sounded in the opposite direction Lord Xanlir came from. He ran down the path in search of the man who might not be there anymore.

Van was immobilized by confusion and anxiety. He trembled uncontrollably, unsure of what to do. But survival instinct gave him a firm kick, and he struggled to move again. The movement caused the vapor to thicken again, giving away his exhaustion.

Patmp! Patmp! Patmp!

Rustle! Patmp! Rustle!

He went still again upon hearing footsteps rush his way. A lump formed in his throat when the bushes rustled. Wally's dirt-covered face popped through the leaves. He pushed his way through the foliage to sit beside Van.

How should he respond? What should he say? Having lost his disguise, he also lost the confidence he felt in the company of his faction.

"You all right? That guy rough you up too badly?"

Van dared not say anything.

"Come on, Van. Speak up. I don't know if your skull is bleeding if you don't tell me."

Hearing something so disturbing made him reach for his head and pat it down his skull to check for any cracks or leaks. It was unnecessary. No blood doused his skin.

That rascally laughter of Wally's was never so upsetting before now. As soon as it stopped, Van wondered what went through Wally's mind.

"Okay, Van, sing. What just happened? Why do you suddenly look ... like this?"

Van calmed himself as much as he could. His secret was out now. It would be pointless to hide anything from him.

Before all else, Van made it clear the dark skin he wore was his real form, not some trick. When asked what he meant, he explained what he was, how someone like him came to be the son of a Vermalian couple, how he concealed himself that entire time. He lingered on the origin of his power and what effects it had on him since interest was shown in it. From it, among other things, led to the decision to become a knight.

He spoke everything clearly so not to leave any doubt in Wally. It was hard to say whether or not he would believe it; Van, himself, had difficulty accepting the truth of his lineage when he was first told.

After everything had been explained, Wally sat still for some time, appearing deep in thought. He assessed everything he had been told, looking to weigh them carefully. Then he looked to Van with an arched brow. "You mean to tell me you've been holding back in weapons training to hide the fog you sweat?"

The breath Van exhaled had been caught in his throat. So many things he said were a world apart from what Wally focused on. Frustration flooded through Van thinking how ridiculous Wally seemed until in boiled over, and he glared at him, crossed. "Is that really what bothers you right now? Gods! How can you be this calm? I just told you I'm not a Vermalian. I'm a Kindhrin!"

"Why does that matter any?" He was not kidding. Wally's words carried a seriousness Van rarely heard him use. "Kindhrin? Vermalian? The color of your skin and those prints on your face don't change one important thing: you are Vandelas Kronas, my best friend. And that's all I need to understand."

Those words left him utterly stupefied. Wally had recognized their relationship as a strong one, that they were true friends, all along. All the while, Van lived in fear with his secret, only seeing him and the rest as mere associates with similar dreams.

He could not believe what it took for him to realize that. Fear had utterly faded. He felt assured, safe, in the presence of his friend again.

"If you want to tell me something that'll make me feel less hysterical, tell me why you were hiding that you can use magic!"

In his moment of turmoil, Van realized he did not mention what happened when he used his Second Verse. He pulled out the Shift Pendant hidden beneath his tunic to check if it would reset his disguise yet. "The Second Verse negates the magic in my Shift Pendent. If I use it, it stops working." The crimson glow it usually radiated was still faint.

Wally watched the little pink flicker the charm had with fascination. It held his attention for a moment, then he looked back up at Van with a sad face expressing ruth. "You were really killed?"

"I can show you the scar later if you'd like."

"Yikes! If the others knew about this, they'd lose their minds."

"They can't. You can't tell the others about this. No one can know that I'm a Kindhrin, or—"

"Say no more, Van," Wally interrupted, sounding more like his usual self. "No way I'm letting anyone take you to the Guillotine Rocks."

Van felt reassured to hear that. It took him long enough, but he finally saw Wally as his friend, someone he could truly rely on.

He finally thought they were past the awkwardness, but then Wally became a bit antsy. "Listen ... I— *We* all said some things about your people, things you don't deserve to be told. So, since I'm the only one who knows, I need to let you know—"

Van smiled. "There's no need, Wally. My people have done a lot of terrible things to sate their greed. It is only natural yours should be so hateful toward them. I'm just relieved I grew on a different path."

Those words were enough to put Wally at ease. His smile let Van know he was glad that he did not hate him for it. "We should probably head back to camp. Is that gem of yours ready yet?"

The Shift Pendant regained its former glow and its concealing power. Simply gripping the stone caused the changes to affect Van's form once more—white hair bled back to shimmering blonde, russet skin paling until turning a light peach, the blood-red brands fading. Compared to the instant change earlier, the activation of the charm was almost enchanting.

The sight made Wally whistle. "That's some magic trick."

Van managed to stand again with Wally's help. His arm had been taken around his friend's shoulders for support. Try as he might, Van could not ignore the rupturing pain at the peak of his spine.

"Whoever he was, he's a tough one. I've rarely ever seen you take a beating and not get up afterward."

"Given he was twice my size and had an unholy weapon as tall as him," Van grumbled, "I think he had the advantage."

And he doubted that he was going all out. It was not just that he toyed with them. When engaged, the assailant could have disrupted Van's dance, as he had when he threw him into the tree, whenever he wanted. He had the strength; it vastly outmatched Van's.

So why didn't he?

He could not focus on it too clearly in the heat of battle, but in the deadly dance, he sensed the enemy's desire to kill wane. Thinking back, he realized that could have started as early as when he took his sword and scabbard in hand.

"You still know the way back, right?"

"Yes. I'll direct you, just don't drop me."

"Wouldn't think of it."

Rather than focus on the enigma that was their assailant or the pain in his back, Van fed Wally the directions he needed. He needed a reminder every few moments, as the forest was dark and difficult to navigate. Fortunately, Van's eyes were perfectly adjusted to their surroundings.

They made for perfect prey moving as slow as they were. Human children had little chance of surviving against the likes of coyotes or bears or wild cats. Even though Van could speak to them, they likely would not care for anything he said. If all else failed, he would use the Second Verse again. Nothing was going to take his friend away from him.

"Hey, Wally ... why are you always so nice to me?"

Wally looked his way for a moment, then turned back the path. "That's a weird thing to ask." True as it was, he knew well that Van would not let up until he got his answer. "Have you heard the phrase noblesse oblige?"

"I can't say I have."

"It means someone who is born into a position of wealth, power, and prestige is obliged to prove they are worthy of it. My mother taught that to me and my siblings when we were very young, hoping that it would inspire us to help those who need it. My brothers did not take to it well, but she enchanted me with the tales of noblemen who lived their lives following that principle. I wanted to be like those great men. So when I became a page, I decided to start my trial on becoming a true noble with you."

"With me?"

"I knew when I saw you that you needed a friend the most. Maybe it was because of this secret you are keeping or because you've never been to the capital before, but I knew you felt more anxious than anyone else."

An excellent observation. Though Van tried to deny it, being judged by the senior knights and other pages was incredibly strenuous.

"All the more reason to make you feel welcome," Wally finished with a smile bright enough to almost light their way.

Van laughed. "If you are all about helping others, then why play so many pranks?"

Now Wally laughed, feeling more energetic after hearing his friend was doing well enough to make jokes. "I prefer to think of my antics as a way to keep everyone sharp. After all, a knight should be aware of danger as well as—well, as you, I'd say."

While that reasoning had some logic, it sounded like a half-truth. He enjoyed causing his own mischief in addition to the good he did—a little weakness of his. But Van could overlook that as well as he had before this night. Everyone, noble or not, had their own little weaknesses they could not get rid of easily.

"Thank you, Wally. For everything."

A unique child both just and mischievous, there was no one else like him. Van could not have been happier to have met him.

~ Eleventh Chapter ~

Surprises

It was the adolescent assassin. The man who attacked Wally and Van was none other than the assassin Lord Tamsilac warned them about.

At first, Wally only joked about it in a rough attempt to keep Van's mind off his injury, but they found it to be so upon their return to camp. Most of the pages had gathered back there by the time they returned. No one could relax, not with the three horrendously lacerated corpses laid near the low-lit campfire. They had all been left with hideous gashes all over their bodies, their eyes frozen open in terror.

Van and Wally nearly had the same looks themselves, the same fear etched into them.

Saddening as it was to see three fellow pages slaughtered, Van saw it as a blessing that none of them were of his own.

At the edge of camp, Stevene was with Prince Aeron keeping a sharp eye out for anything suspicious.

Concerned for the smallest member of the faction, Van fought through his pain to search for Lelia.

And he was looking in all the wrong places. Wally came up to him after his fifth lap around camp with the lone twin in tow, supporting her while she softly sobbed. Her eyes were red from how much she cried and her nose dripped a string of mucus. She tried to behave stably in the company of her friends.

Wally left her with Van, heading back to the dying fire where the corpses lay. He needed to see if he recognized them.

The two sat down on the tree stump Lord Xanlir always used when instructing the pages. If the assassin did return, she would be safest there. Poor Lelia still trembled in an effort to fight back her tears. A knot tightened in Van's chest. Her fear, her pain, her guilt—it was more than explicit in her valsara. He hid a clenching fist from her eyes as he tried, in his most gentle voice, to console her.

The poor girl merely nodded or shook her head at anything Van asked since she was too rattled to speak. When she did, she sounded so different. It was a surprise indeed to hear her speak in the loose accent many common folk used; she always tried to keep her tone steady and her words perfectly annunciated. The linguistic practice she committed to heart unraveled from fear's touch.

But it was not fear that brought her to tears. She gravely spoke of two of the three at the fire. They were gathering with her when it happened. Lelia fought bravely but was no match for the assassin. She would have been in their place had they not protected her. And were it not for Lord Xanlir's heroic entrance, she would have joined them in their ascent to the Elysium.

"D-Do ya think I'm a weaklin', Van?" she asked in a sniffle.

Van patted her head—a force of habit he normally did to soothe Snowflake. "I have no reason to." Were Wally to have been felled earlier, Van would likely have gone through the same grief. He managed to protect his friend, but she could not. He could only imagine how gut-wrenching it felt to watch someone that could have been saved slip away.

She blamed herself for their deaths. Had they fought for themselves, one of them would have been saved by Lord Xanlir instead. She did not accept being told that was not true, and she could not forgive herself for her own weakness.

It pained Van to see her like that. He had to take her mind off that crushing feeling, if only for a short time.

It was a long shot, but she always lit up whenever she talked about him. Lord Xanlir. She knew him familiarly. When asked how, Lelia admitted it had something to do with how she typically spoke. Her countenance grew less strained as she spoke about her life before the chateau. It was difficult, to say the least. With her father's unfathomable bad luck and her mother growing ill from stress, fatigue, and feeble rations, the Erite family struggled to survive in the city. They thought of taking to life in the countryside and help work off the land, but they did not have the lev to afford such a journey.

Then one day, while Lelia was begging for money, she met him, the only stranger who stopped to hear her pleas. He showed her sympathy and, along with the gift of a gold lev piece, gave her and her brother the chance to become pages so they might one day serve the realm. It was a chance to better their lives and their parents'.

The twins were made pages, and their parents were gifted a fair purse of lev, enough to survive for weeks on, because of Lord Xanlir.

"We wasn' fed by the silva' spoon or strong like the others, but he still said we could do great things. If it weren' for His Lordship's kindness, we would not have lasted another month." She was starting to calm down and take control of her speech more. "I'm indebted to him for giving our family another chance."

Lord Xanlir was a great man. To instill hope in a family that nearly lost everything made it clear why he was made the Champion of Duty. It was little wonder why Lelia was so taken with him.

Van understood Lelia better after hearing her story. She devoted herself entirely to those who helped her—a loyal and passionate soul who wished to repay that kindness in full, and then some.

While she hung her head in deep thought, Van looked to the sky and thought on the immeasurable kindnesses his parents had done for him.

They took him in as their own, raised and loved him, taught him all they knew, gave him the means to walk among other people. He perfectly understood why Lelia wanted to give back.

"I couldn't do anything..."

Looking back down at her, Van saw Lelia stopped shaking in fear but fumed with frustration.

"I wasn't strong enough to do anything. If I stay like this, I'll let everyone down." She looked up to him with determination in her eyes. "Van, when we get back to the chateau, will you help me train? I need you to help me get stronger."

A smile drew over his face. He did not think he could muster one at a time like this, but he did. "Of course, my friend."

After that, a genuine smile finally returned to Lelia's face. Such a charming smile.

Should he ever see the adolescent assassin again, Van swore to kill him for taking it away.

Lord Xanlir led the pages out of the Wayward Wood upon his return. They made way for the village the other knights rested at. The slain were wrapped in blankets and carried in the wagon while the pages travelled on foot.

No one could rest after the experience they had. The shroud of night made them dread the return of the assassin and the light of day prolonged their need for sleep. Those who managed slumber could only keep it for some time—their dreams now breeding grounds for fear.

Van kept his senses sharp throughout the long nights. He thought he would be exhausted, but he never let it show. He made do with brief momentary respites and woke up immediately at the slightest sound.

Nature itself was at ease. There was nothing to cause alarm for the pages or the wildlife. Very few animals came out into the open apart from a few bold deer eager to graze.

It was rather cathartic to just watch the animals again instead of hunting them.

As he kept watch one night, Van noticed some movement in the distance. His senses did not warn of danger, but he could not ignore it. Before he stood to take a look, he saw a lovely white tail pop from the tall grass momentarily. He smiled, pleased to see the snowfleece fox still following him.

She kept her distance and remained hidden until they returned to Brigadier. Unable to wait for the cover of night, she excitably made way to the window of Van's bedchamber and clawed at it for him to let her in. She leaped into his arms the first chance she got.

Van held the small thing in his arms and pet her head. "I'm sorry for scaring you back at the forest. I didn't want them to hurt you."

Snowflake pressed her head against his hand, asking for more. She seemed to understand but focused mainly on getting more affection. He was happy to grant her wish.

He brought his hand lower to stroke her back and scratch her uncomfortable itches. As he petted her, he came to realize her back stretched about half an inch longer than it had before. And her skull fitted better into his hand too. She grew a little.

"And to think Father said you'd never grow."

She bit his hand playfully, having little interest in the man he mentioned.

Van laughed, not bothered by the little incisors pinching him. "He'll be surprised when he sees you again."

After he played with the energetic Snowflake, Van went to the stables to see his faithful mount.

Some pages were practicing swordplay behind the chateau. Wally was among them. Van stopped a moment to watch as he noticed how fiercely he fought. It was unlike him; he typically enjoyed playing with and taunting his adversaries whenever he found he had the advantage. The encounter with the assassin left him yearning for strength.

Everyone who saw those corpses, let alone the assassin, shared the same sentiment, Van included. But he also felt the need to see those he almost lost that night.

Nightshade was elated to see him return safely, nearly skipping high enough to jump her confines. She did not calm down until he went in close enough to pet her snout. The cold touch of the boy she took to always made her feel refreshed and calm, but whenever he stopped, it left her ready for a run.

Before undoing the latch on Nightshade's stable, Van noticed Snowflake had followed him. The little thing stared sternly at her human pet to admonish him. It always irritated her whenever he focused on the horse instead of her.

The preparations were made quickly. He grabbed Nightshade's saddle and slid it onto her back, pulling the straps tight, and checked the saddlebags for any holes or tears. Rather than head out immediately, he looked to the little fox kept nudging her head against his arm for attention, then reached out to pick her up and placed her in the left saddlebag.

Snowflake was not eager to be part of a ride-along; the frightful look in her eyes made it very clear. But she also did not want to leave him alone with the mare either. For that reason, she did not resist. She kept to the bag despite how she detested the constant shaking during the ride.

Van rode into the fields atop his hyperactive mount, feeling the mischievous winds lash at him more liberally than before. Nightshade had been waiting so impatiently to run with her rider again. She was not the only one excited; Van laughed and hollered pure elation throughout the run. He was so thrilled to experience the breakneck speed again. Lap after lap, she dashed past the Estrine Chateau, circling the fields and tearing apart the patches of grass with her thin yet sturdy legs.

After her thrilling run, Nightshade broke from the flattened track and paced herself up a small hill. Van slipped off Nightshade and walked to the apple tree atop the hill. He leaned against it for a moment, then scaled it for the fruits hanging from the branches.

Snowflake crawled out of the bag she hid in, slinking her forepaws out before falling onto the ground. All four of her stubby legs had shaken much worse than the branch supporting Van. She likely would have scampered to join him if she had not collapsed from trembling so much.

Eager to get down for some rest, Van gathering a couple of apples and leaped down. He offered the apple in his left hand to Nightshade before partaking in the other.

He sat down on the blades of grass wisping in the breeze. The clouds looked comforting hung in the azure skies above. They relaxed him enough to recline backward and lie down. Before taking a bite out of the heavenly red fruit, Van offered it to Snowflake. The most she did was sniff its red shell and nip into it enough for thin drops of its juice to dribble out.

While snacking on the apple, Van began to wonder what Snowflake did to sustain herself. He could not help be curious at how such a small creature managed to take care of herself.

Thought soon shifted to the elusive adolescent assassin. There was little to go by regarding him aside from the offhand rumors. One of them speculated that the man worked for the Renegades hoping to overthrow the reigning monarchy. The seemingly random assassinations were thought to be an attempt to slowly weaken the kingdom's strength for the coming future. Such a rumor might have been true in some aspects, but since clashing blades with the assassin, Van came to doubt it. Why, he did not know. Something deep inside him contended that the man was not all that he seemed, although whatever he was seemed to be part of a bigger mystery.

Spending time under the entrancing clouds and thinking of what they looked like brought all other thought to a gentle halt. The first few puffs looked like animals. Eventually, he only saw morsels that made his mouth water. Then the shapes all changed into something alarming: a pack of wild dogs chasing something without form. When he blinked to make sure he was not seeing things, the thin clouds painting the cryptic image disappeared before he got a good look at what the prey was.

Then there was a horse— No, Nightshade had just put her face in front of Van's. Her large nostrils covered him with her breath and her big tongue tickled Van's cheek, making him laugh. When he thought he could get up, Snowflake pushed her way up to him to take his attention.

Van fought to pull away from his animal companions' affection and stood quickly. He took the horse's reins after he stopped laughing. "Come along. Let's get you back to your friends."

The sun began its descent as Van returned to the chateau. The dimming daylight peered through the open doors and windows, its thin rays crawling across the halls.

Van thought it prudent to meet with Lyn. She would doubtlessly be worrying herself sick if word of the assassin already reached her. How she fretted before he left—he felt guilty for not looking for her sooner.

The halls remained mostly empty, as they had been since he returned. The pages who were not training outside rested in their bedchambers. Many of them became despondent when they heard the remaining hunting trips had been postponed. They looked forward to leaving the city to explore new environments, to challenge and conquer the wildlife.

The corridor leading to the boy's wing was especially quiet, more so than it had been earlier. A light brush of wind whistled faintly against Van's ear. It would have been calming had he not been distracted.

Something was different. Everything was in place, neat, clean, and tended to. Nothing had been where it should not. And yet there still lingered this unusual feeling of dread in the air.

Van often felt such a sensation when danger loomed, but this feeling was not as strong and much less alarming. It was faint, so he thought to ignore it, but as he went on, it became harder to do so. The dread was all but palpable when he ascended the stairs, its touch pricking the inside of his skull, forcing him to remain alert.

He kept calm and breathed steadily so as not to let his unease show. For a moment, he suspected Kallant and his brood were on the prowl in search of someone to torment. No one was in the hall with him, and as he passed the maids' chambers, the dread lingered behind him.

What am I being told?

He turned around and went up to the door to the maids' chambers, softly rapping it with the back of his hand.

A tall brunette answered. The weary expression she wore unnerved

Van, but she masked it with a kindly smile upon noticing him. "Good day, Young Master. How may I be of service?"

The woman's tone hid a frightful unease. It was rather contagious, but instead of showing his, Van kept it concealed.

"If I may, I am looking for Ms. Ferosite."

The maid's mask broke and her concerning expression resurfaced. She could not hide her unease after hearing that. "I am afraid she has grown rather ill."

Van could no more easily hide his concern than the maid. His first instinct was to push past her and see what became of Lyn, but he restrained himself. "May I please see her?"

Believing him to be genuinely worried, the maid held the door open and stepped aside to invite him in. "Please keep your voice low."

The servants lived with comfortable accommodations. The furniture in the maids' chambers was placed in an efficient manner, leaving room for people to cross them. A few bookshelves, stocked to the brim with reading materials and bric-a-brac, stood against the wall near a resting area. The beds were all neatly made and in full view, except for this one that was completely shrouded by the cleanest night-blue sheets arranged into canopy curtains. The brunette escorted Van directly toward that spot, mindful of the others on break.

He took a deep breath, bracing for whatever awaited behind the sheets before the maid carefully made a small opening. The sight was not as gruesome as his imagination led Van to believe, but it was still frightening. There lay Lyn, sweating violently and breathing hoarsely. She seemed to be breaking out in a fever while suffering from a nightmare. It could not be just that, though, not since that feeling of dread led to her.

"The poor dear has been bedridden since late yesterday afternoon."

"What happened to her?"

"The doctors and priests say she suffers from a magic deficiency." The maid tried to keep her voice low and controlled despite the strain behind it. Perhaps they were close. "For the past few days, she complained about her Praecur magic being unresponsive. I thought it unusual since she rarely mentions it as is. Then she began behaving lethargically, and just yesterday, for the first time, she was the last to wake for her daily duties. Then someone found her unconscious in the halls ... and she was like this ever since."

Although he would not be rude and admit to it, Van lost interest in everything the brunette said. The minute details were of no importance. Experiencing magic deficiency boded a cruel omen.

The excruciating pain of a mage losing their magic was equivalent to the body's nerves being severed by a rigid blade. Scantly anyone survived such torture, and those who did became a shell of their former selves. No matter the result, Lyn would never be the same.

"All we can do is pray the gods have mercy on her."

The silent Van could not stand to hear another word. He simply allowed the brunette to escort him back to the door, thanked her for her time, and walked back to his bedchamber, attempting to appear as composed as possible.

Upon entering his room, Van slid against the door shut behind him until he sat curled up into a ball on the ground. He honestly felt he could cry, but no tears whelmed. Lyn had gone out of her way to tend to him beyond the care of a servant. Her attentiveness could not have been from duty alone. Whenever he felt things were going roughly, Lyn would always ask if he was okay and talk to him, and she even held him. She tended his wounds whenever someone bullied him and commended him for behaving civilly. Van never had siblings, but he believed her compassion resembled that of a loving older sister.

He did not want her to die. He could not bear the thought. Waiting for death or a lifeless existence for her tormented him.

It was unacceptable. Something needed to be done. But what could he do? No one looked for a way to cure her ailment. Everyone only watched and waited and eased her suffering in any possible way. He could not rely on anyone to save Lyn.

Nroaw. Nroo.

Furtive as ever, Snowflake had arrived without his notice. Her powdered little face, big jewellike eyes and all, stared at him with her head atilt. She knew something was wrong.

Not wanting to neglect her, Van opened his arms and straightened his legs enough for Snowflake to crawl into his lap. She did not curl up like she always had, and instead glanced up at her pet in hopes she could find out what bothered him so.

Death was a universal matter, something animals understood as much as humans. The fox understood more than what little Van could utter. Snowflake rubbed her head against his chest hoping to ease his anxieties. She lost family long ago and related well to the pressure of loved ones in jeopardy. She never encountered Lyn before, but she knew she made her pet happy and her impending doom haunted him.

You must feel so helpless, her actions implied with sympathy.

Talk of the situation was getting him nowhere. Solutions were what he wanted, not pity. But where to begin?

Even if he spent the night combing through the entirety of the Estrine Chateau's articles on magic, he would not get anywhere—not to mention the harsh punishment for skipping curfew. And he did not expect to understand whatever he might possibly find. Magic was a spiritual phenomenon as well as physical, a logic that still bewildered him despite his understanding of the Second Verse.

As he aimlessly pondered what steps he could take, an epiphany had struck. There was likely nothing to be gained from it, but he could not just do nothing. If it could save Lyn, he had to take the chance.

Van picked Snowflake up in his arms while he stood. "Let's turn in early tonight. I think we could use the rest."

That was not enough to convince Snowflake to think he was feeling better, but she did not protest. After all, it was another chance to keep him close for the whole night.

He placed Snowflake on the bed, letting her rest in the blankets while he removed the chain mail that clung to him all day. Every strap of his thin armor had been placed on top of the dresser as per the norm. He watched Snowflake vacate the blankets as he walked back to the bed.

Lying back down against the soft comfort of a bed felt so different compared to the hard earth.

Van stared blankly at the ceiling as he silently questioned his plan. Sensing his anxiety worsening from doubt, Snowflake snuck up to him and brushed herself against his face. Her plush pelt soothed his weary mind enough to let go of uncertainty and ease him into slumber.

* * *

So sudden. A minute didn't even pass, and yet I'm in this place.

I still can't believe it worked. Focusing on the image of this plane seems to have been enough. The silver landscape looks as barren and frigid as the last time I was here. Every glacier, every crevasse brings back a piece of the confusion and horror I felt after I died. Everything looks the same, except for that odd rippling rainbow in the bleak sky.

Now ... where is Pruina?

It has been so long since I was last here. Finding Pruina may not be simple. There is so much about where I wound up that I do not recognize. Where to start? I may as well be staring into a murky pond...

Pond... Water! Yes, that's it! Pruina never strayed far from the water surrounding this land. If I take to the edge of this island, I should find him there.

These frigid winds are so aggressive. Ignoring how they bite into me is not easy; they keep pushing back. If I lose my way or become too distracted, I might fall out of this dreamscape into a deeper slumber.

There is no way I'm going to be tossed out so easily, not with what is at stake. You are not getting rid of me, Pruina!

It's strange how I find these imaginary paths at every turn. It's like someone prepared them. I wonder what for. Well, I suppose even an elemental must pass the eternity it has somehow.

There! Water! The sea stretches out so vast that it looks to blend with the sky, as if they are one. But that shimmering light above—its reflection does not imitate it well.

It is quite the sight, but Pruina is still nowhere to be found. Time is running out. I cannot afford to search this whole place. ...What now?

Just like a Kindhrin to not know when to stay in one place.

And how like the spirit to give me a fright out of the blue.

Pruina still takes to the form of that frostbitten, pale version of my disguise. Curious as I am as to why he will not present himself in another way, that is not the reason I am here.

This is the first time anyone has dove into my realm of their own volition. Had you stayed put, I would have come to greet you like a good host.

"Really?"

This realm and I are one and the same, mortal child. Everything that transpires here comes to my knowledge as it happens. Now, what is it that you want from me?

This needs to go well. Just stay stalwart and let him know what you need. "You are knowledgeable of magic, yes?"

...He looks almost disturbed.

In the past, I have revived a great many mages. Their wisdom was relinquished unto me after their second passing. So, yes, I suppose you could say that.

"Then maybe you could help me. I need to know a way to cure someone suffering from magic deficiency."

Why look at me like I'm mad?

...A cure for magic deficiency is impossible to attain. For there to be a cure, there must be an illness to originate from.

"What do you mean?"

Magic cannot be destroyed by any natural cause regardless of the plane in which it thrives. A deficiency of magic is neither disease nor infection. For someone to suffer a deficiency, something must be draining them of their magic. The only way for one to survive being leeched of their power would be to eliminate the source of their suffering before their bodies become husks.

If it were that simple, it would have been dealt with a long time ago. Mages have been dying from magic deficiency for ages. Whatever it is that's causing this has to be tucked away in a place too secluded or dangerous for anyone to find it.

...Then does that mean I can't save her?

"Are you saying there is no other way it can be done?"

This silence is torture. And carried by the stagnant air, it is all the more deafening. He must be trying to think of a way to give a smug response. But the way he has his frozen arm against his waist, his normal fingers scratching the forehead, he looks to be in deep thought. Could it be he really does not know?

Well ... if your problem lies in saving a mortal life, all you must do is contain their magic before it is entirely drained away, fashion something that will cradle it and remain with the afflicted. A trifling matter, I know, but simple enough for one such as yourself to accomplish.

If the problem lies in saving a mortal life?

If that bit of wisdom suffices your needs, then I suggest you return to your plane. The concept of time there is considered of great importance, if I remember correctly.

Wait, what is he— Gah! He always finds some way to make me jump. I did not expect him to turn into a cloud of fog from walking into me. There he goes, disappearing across the frigid waters.

The concept of time being important. What did he mean by that? And why would he bring that up when I still have no idea how to save Lyn? How am I supposed to contain something that can't be touched!?

...What? A bark? Since when did animals live here? The winds splitting at the icy mountains were the only other voices I've ever heard here. But this... It sounds like—

*   *   *

By the time Van realized that barking he heard came from his fox, he awoke back into his bedchamber half aware of the changes that occurred the few hours he had been asleep. A faint rubicund light burned through the window, alerting him to what Pruina meant.

Morning had already arrived.

Pawr! Pawr!

Snowflake's barking was quieter and more frequent than it had been in Pruina's realm. She sounded like she came from directly above him instead of outside from the windowsill where she hid. She skulked farther out the window until making for a hesitant escape.

When he sat up, Van noticed his skin reverted back to its dark shade. Dizzy and barely conscious, he could not figure out what she was so alarmed over. A rhythmic sound came from the hall, getting closer by the second. Someone was coming!

"Excuse me, Young Master Vandelas?"

They were already at the door! Without a moment to waste, Van reached for the Shift Pendant, reactivating its magic so that he appeared a normal Vermalian just as the door crept open.

"Ah, good. You are already awake."

It was the same maid that showed him to the ailing Lyn yesterday. A brief glance outside the window, while he checked to see if Snowflake managed to escape undetected, showed him it was a little early for the bells to have rung yet.

He turned back to the maid and tried to act like he had not just woken up. "Is something the matter?"

"I came to deliver a clean uniform." She walked over to the dresser to collect the clothes from yesterday, slinging them over her arm, and put a new, neatly folded set in its place. "Since Alicalyn is indisposed, I have been issued to cover her work while she recovers. I like to tend to my duties starting early. It seemed appropriate to let you know so as not to cause a disturbance."

Van could not help rubbing his eyes, his hands balled up like paws. "Oh. Thank you, Miss—"

"Gretchen Silvise." She performed the customary curtsy servants normally present to their masters and guests of the manor: crossing her right ankle past her left leg, taking ends of her dress with a delicate clutch, and lowering herself to a bow. "I look forward to serving you, Young Master. Alicalyn spoke of you often of late."

Until she mentioned Lyn, Van did not believe her gracious words to be true. While he wanted to know more of what she said to her cohorts, he needed to continue the morning as he always had.

"Oh! I knew I forgot something. Please excuse me a moment." Gretchen left quickly after performing another curtsy. It seemed she had forgotten the bucket of water to fill his tub tucked in the corner.

The sudden need for energy and awareness finally gone, Van flopped against the bed and sighed. "That was *too* close..."

The pages who returned with Lord Xanlir continued their normal regimens that morning on. With several of their typical instructors still away on hunting trips, they were directed to join the lessons led by those who remained, whether they were official instructors or merely taking their place.

Van was chastised by the stone-faced man who led weapons training as often as he had been by Sir Charleston. Impressive as his unique techniques were, he was expected to perform Vermalian-style swordplay during practice, and at a better degree than he could. His wild flailing made him a source of amusement for the other pages and contempt for the knight.

That knight was harsh like any Estrine, but not nearly as imposing. The drivel that came out of him was nothing but hot air. It made it easy to just take his orders and get on with the routine humiliation.

Upon everyone returning from the hunt, the pages were notified of a change to their regimen. They all attended a seminar on strategy and tactics first thing in the morning, then were briefed on geography. Before they were excused for lunch, they were advised to be ready to be on their feet for the remainder of the day.

What the Estrine family could have planned for them was debated among Van's faction throughout the meal. The exercises have been getting more strenuous as of late, but they lasted as long as they always had; the instructors used their time in a very strict yet efficient manner, careful not to waste the hours. To plan something that would take up what remained of the day, not to mention use an entire morning they could have spent taking care of it to prepare, it had to be important.

They came to similar conclusions—they would be weary, sore, and cursing the Estrines by the end of it.

When asked what he thought about it, Wally only shrugged and kept eating. Although a simple (and messy) response, it was not one his friends expected. He always had something to say about everything, especially when it was peculiar and unexpected. Even when he ate, it did not let it keep him from putting his thoughts in. No one believed he was not bothered by curiosity.

Except for Van, who took his indifference for how he saw it and remembered how many sibling knights he had. "You know." He could have stayed quiet and let the charade continue, but he liked it when his faction was lively.

The sudden awareness on Wally's face let the others know he was right. The impish grin he flashed at Van let him know how impressed he was that he noticed. But he remained adamant in his refusal to say anything, which made Rubi grit her teeth.

"You'll see soon enough," Stevene intervened. "Trust me, you'll be glad he's keeping it a surprise."

He had not spoken his thoughts on the matter, having engrossed himself in a book while he ate. But it made sense that he knew. Stevene was the only second-year among them.

The twins begged for someone to tell them. Rubi tried tricking Wally into saying it by claiming he did not really know. Ccuivr butted heads with Stevene. They received no answer until finally presenting themselves to the Estrine family in the fields.

No horses stood ready for a run. No weapons were piled into barrels or hung on racks. From what they could see, nothing had been prepared for the event.

It was easy to distinguish the first-year pages from those with more experience; they were the only ones bewildered by this. They knew not to whisper any questions or complaints among themselves, mostly from knowing what such disruptions earned them, but also by following the other pages' lead. Van's faction looked to Stevene, who stood silently at attention yet with excitement in his eyes.

"Pages!" Lord Estrine bellowed, his booming voice reaching every last page. "I commend you all for the efforts you have made these passing seasons in the pursuit of knighthood. Vermalio's future shines bright, bright as the sun that rises over the horizon. That is because we have you, our committed youth, vying for the opportunity to be the spears and shields that allow the kingdom and its people to grow and prosper. We, the knights of the kingdom, the forces that stand to protect those who need protecting, the arms that rise to quash those that threaten our peace, are the rays of light that shine upon Vermalio. And what of you? Are you worthy of being part of this light?"

Those fierce words enraptured the pages enough to almost break out in an uproar. Many were not sure whether he was truly asking a question or being rhetorical, but either way, they voiced their excitement in spirited calls and rowdy cheers. He really knew how to work a crowd.

"Well then, let's see! You are here now to test the skills you have honed in simulated warfare combat."

Here? In this empty field? Van pondered.

"For this enactment, every one of you will be divided into two 'armies' and do battle with the other. And *this* will be your battlefield."

Lord Estrine pulled out from his pocket and presented the smallest shard of glass. Much of the pages' excitement fizzled out when they realized he was being serious.

How was a virtual battalion of pages supposed to do battle atop a piece of glass?

Not as ignorant to the Estrine family's knowledge, Van looked at the clear shard with his magic sight and found an immense amount of energy condensed inside.

Not willing to keep the pages in suspense for long, Lord Estrine flung the magic charm into the air. Light gathered into the glossy stone as it soared toward the sun until a brilliant flash engulfed the fields entirely and blinded everyone. With one of his crystalline eyes peering through the piercing light, Van witnessed the magic terraforming everything in its borders—the grass receding, trees spurting forth, water flowing from the depths of the earth, ridges and hills building upon themselves, stone and wood collaborating to form structures.

The pages were completely astonished when they opened their eyes. A lush, dense forest and a pristine lake now lay where there was once an empty field, stretched out to where the tall grass formed a border, and were suddenly cut off where they met.

"You will treat this as an actual war where the victors claim the life of the enemy leader. One side will be stationed in the forest, the other in by the lake. Bravv Ginnstom of Starscape will lead one army. Wallace Alivvrn of Illuascove shall take command of the other. Now, decide who you will follow."

Their decisions were made rather quickly, many of them in favor of Bravv. His army quickly grew around him. They did little more than stand in place, but it was all that was needed to shake Wally's confidence.

The arrangement was cruel from the very start. Bravv was a fourth-year with much skill and experience, a figure many were familiar with and recognized as the more favorable ally. In contrast, few recognized Wally as anything more than a jester—one they doubted would be more than a foot soldier.

Things looked bleak for the attention-seeking clown. But despite Bravv's numbers escalating to oppressive levels, Van refused to leave his friend to fend for himself. His choice was made from the very beginning.

The twins followed Van's lead, loyal to him and Wally. Although she hesitated at first, Rubi preferred to side with her natural enemy over a Ginnstom.

Some of those who had yet to decide looked to those willing to fight for a lost cause.

Stevene and Ccuivr joined their faction after seeing where the situation led. While they did not think they could win, they thought of joining the lesser army as the better chance to show how much they could give.

The unity between those seven began to sway the choices of the mercenaries for hire. It was difficult to know who they would join. That changed when Prince Aeron chose to ally himself with Wally's forces. His decision turned the tables, coaxing those who were ready to bow to the

Ginnstoms to resist.

Wally's army was outnumbered at least five to one. Despite the support he received, victory did not appear any closer. But no one changed their minds.

Their decisions were made. The lines were drawn. War had begun.

~ Twelfth Chapter ~

All-Out War

The pages marched to their designated territories—Wally's army to the forest, Bravv's army to the lake. There, they readily made use of the available foundations for their military bases.

At the heart of the forest stood a humble hovel before a deep, foreboding crag. It was a tight fit, but the entirety of the Wally's army managed to squeeze inside. Inside was a stockpile of weapons, enough for each page to be armed.

Like the weapons they trained with, those were blunt, without any sharp edges, but, as explained to the first-years by the experienced pages, they carried as much power as whole weapons. Those weapons were enchanted to ensure the pages treated their enactment as an actual war. When hit in the right way, the afflicted were put into a comatose state for the duration of the enactment.

It frightened some of the first-years, but that fear would only push them to win.

The ringing of the chateau's bell signaled for the enactment to begin.

Wally's army could not afford a direct assault. Their defeat would be certain. Realizing that, Stevene and several others suggested lying in wait for the enemy to breach their territory so they could ambush them. In agreement with them, Wally deployed several parties of least six pages, all taking different routes headed in the direction of the lake.

The party Van joined marched along the two hills surrounding an open path. Albeit a replica, the forest reflected the tranquility of a true one. A few birds perched themselves along the trees, unaware that they were mere images. The midday sun gleamed through the verdant leaves. Quiet wafts of air carrying the spring heat brushed gently against the skin.

The enemy must have invaded the forest by now. They outnumbered them five to one at least. If they were not careful, they would fall before long.

Van and his party familiarized themselves with the area and awaited the enemy. With the map left at their base, Stevene predicted the range each enemy platoon would spread out, enough for them to intercept any incoming attack. So long as they followed the plan, they would be able to protect their territory with minimal losses.

Patrolling the area took a lot out of everyone. They decided to conserve energy before the enemy arrived.

Focusing his senses on the changes in his surroundings allowed Van to see what the others could not. He gazed at the simulated milieu around him, curious as to how the magic maintaining it flowed. Every tree, stone, and speck of dirt contained a concentration of magic a tenth the size of their shells. Through past observations, Van learned that magic tended to flow in one constant direction. But the magic that manifested a pure physical form shifted every few seconds—from circulating to expanding and receding to a brief spiral. It functioned differently than the few spells he had seen.

He also took note of the simulations' abnormalities with his natural sight. Not every tree branch held a fully solid image and was diaphanous, the sunlight slipping through. Sometimes, he felt the wind brush in directions that conflicted with the environment. To make certain the magic was not distorting his senses, he held his hand an inch apart from a tree barely blocking the sun—the breeze blew through it. Then he pressed his palm against it. Its surface remained as solid as a real tree while having a surface as rough as stone.

"Are you sure we shouldn't be on the attack yet?"

The page acting as their commander looked to the page who spoke. "We stick to the plan. We'll move out after ambushing a few parties that come our way." The party leader, a fourth-year, spoke strictly and sternly. He knew he was in charge and was not afraid to act on his authority.

Recognizing that, the other page badgered him no further.

His impatience was understandable. They faced a mighty enemy that had more at its disposal—troops, land, weapons, morale. Leveling their numbers and taking some advantage was the only thing that would put their bothered minds at ease. A plan would not offer much, as plans, from what they learned, often went awry, but it was all they had. It was best to act on it for as long as they could.

But as they waited to put it into action, they were beset by bothersome thoughts. What were they plotting? What would happen when they attacked? How many would fall?

As those questions went through Van's mind, more formed without him realizing it. How far would their struggle serve? How close would they get to the end? How much longer until a blade could be swung?

The wait was the worst, and that thinking did little to kept time from eating away at his patience.

Fortunately, it came to an end before too long. Footsteps beat against the ground not far from their position. The invasion had begun.

The commander directed everyone to conceal themselves along the hills and wait for the enemy to reach the point of no return. They masked their presence behind the greenery. The archers held their bows at the ready, arrows to be let loose at a second's notice.

Hushed voices emerged from the path as an enemy party came within view. Despite their numbers, they knew not to underestimate the resisting army, although Van did hear one call his side "a dying band of Renegades."

Arrows had yet to fly, and the atmosphere was still calm. Yet the tension was so thick it was likely someone would choke on it. The first to do so would likely spell doom for them and their allies.

"Watch out for that tall one with the thick forehead."

The third-year who questioned their commander earlier spoke to Van with barely a whisper. Van tensed up when he spoke but calmed down when he saw the invaders never noticed them. Not wanting to dismiss his advice, Van looked to the tallest enemy that kept to the rear, the one with black hair and slanted eyes.

He nodded in reply.

The enemy party, still unaware of those watching them, soon came down the middle of the path, walking into the line of fire. The archers took aim at the most vulnerable and let their arrows loose. Four arrows were fired and three ghastly cries were heard before bodies fell.

Van rushed out of hiding while the invaders were still off guard. He sprinted into action immediately upon descending the hill and struck down one, two, three enemies with waves of his sword. When hit by the blunt edges, the enchantment imbued to them activated and disrupted the flow of their valsara. They fell to the ground, appearing dead.

His allies joined the charge and took targets of their own. Seven enemies now lay still on the ground; six still stood strong, ready for battle.

The page Van was warned of rushed at him from the side, his sword raised high. Van pivoted and parried with his scabbard, making the enemy dance to his rhythm.

His foe was surprised by the force that dragged him, but he managed to keep his balance, and attacked once more. Van swept the blade aside again, flicking it away, then spun into a quick turn to drive his sword into his foe's ribs. The attack left its mark. A faint, pale crimson spark briefly flared along his chest. As it disappeared, his weapon slipped from his grasp and he fell backward.

Another enemy page became livid at seeing Van eliminate her teammate and ducked away from his allies to take revenge. He retook his stance for the next foe he faced. But before he could continue his dance, an archer shot another arrow at the back of her head. Again, the same spark appeared at the spot the ovoid arrow hit, and the page toppled to the ground. She remained where she was, motionless.

When he looked to his allies, Van saw that the clash was already over. The enemy was routed. Glad as he was that they won, it almost disappointed him that it was so brief. He was looking forward to putting the techniques he was previously prohibited from using into practice.

The page who fought beside Van walked his way when he was certain none of their foes would get back up. Despite his experience, he still could not entirely tell whether or not the enchantments did their work. "You really weren't just showing off back at the base."

Van only returned those words with a bewildered grimace. He did not believe he ever showed off.

As he thought back to when the enactment began, he understood why he might have left that impression. Van had just chosen a sword and noticed it was lighter than the one he usually carried. He wanted to be certain it was not his imagination, so he drew and waved it around where no one stood. It was as he anticipated; the weapon was much lighter, making his movements faster than normal. Having realized that, he determined that the old practice sword he used to train with was weighted. His father had given him more than a good luck charm.

He was so focused on that at the time that he remained oblivious to the scorn of those around him.

Putting that aside, Van approached their fallen foes and looked them over. They appeared perfectly well, but when looked at closely with his magic sight, he saw the magic at work. Eerie sparks of energy lingered on the exact spots they were hit. He then looked down at his weapon, then the fallen arrows the archers were picking up. The enchantment on them was an interesting one. It stuck to the afflicted like paint and kept their minds bound, shutting off certain bodily functions.

He would have been tempted to check their pulses had he not heard them breathe faintly.

Although it appeared to be of no imminent threat, Van felt skeptical.

Those disturbed gazes the victims shared bothered him.

With the first enemy party disposed of, Van and his allies made ready for the next one. They picked up the "corpses" and carried them out of sight.

All the while, Van could not help look at their enemies' frozen expressions of pain and fear. He wondered what they felt, if anything at all, and how soon it would be before he found out for himself. He tried to focus on victory, to remind himself they were not the ones that he wanted to help. It was the only way to repress his compassion.

More enemies invaded the forest soon after the first wave, and they fell just as their comrades had. Although they vastly outnumbered Wally's forces, they were completely unprepared for the ambushes set upon them.

Van's party took out a number of enemies to protect their territory. Unfortunately, victory did not come without sacrifice. Their commander had been hit hard. The eerie light that came from the enchantment lingered at his hip. It visibly flickered and spread along his side, the phenomenon mimicking the ooze of blood. When he tried to move, he pressed a hand to his hip and limped.

They tried to patch up the wound with medical supplies they had on hand, which were branded by a similar enchantment, like they would a real injury. The magic stopped spreading as a result, but it still kept him from moving properly.

He could not continue. He was a liability. Rather than slow his allies down and risk the enactment, the commander decided to return to the base and act as a shield for their general. And, much to everyone's surprise, he gave control of the party to Van.

Rather than argue and waste time, as well as his ally's energy, Van accepted the task and watched the former commander go.

Fighting in the enactment was overwhelming enough, but to be handed that responsibility and trust, Van felt he was going to be crushed. He never thought of himself as a leader.

He could not afford to focus on that or the judgmental stares boring into the back of his head. His friend was given a far heavier burden. He needed to carry on so as not to disappoint him.

"So what's our next move?" the third-year asked him.

"We routed plenty of the enemy forces already. Now may be a good time to advance toward the lake. If we can get there without trouble, we'll be in position for the rest of the plan."

That response coaxed a smile from the third-year. It seemed favorable to the other pages as well. They had been lying in wait and ambushing their enemy for a long while now. It made them impatient.

Van's party marched along the quickest route between the dense botanical fortress and the open fields. Fewer enemies met them on the way and were taken care of the same way they had been for the past few hours. His allies were not keen on continuing the ambushes, but they followed Van's command.

Toward the edge of the forest, more enemies were lying in wait. They formed a veritable blockade and remained ever observant for anyone coming and going. Had Van not spotted them first, they would have seen his party and rushed in to crush them.

Taking the main path was no longer an option. They had to find an alternate path without alerting the enemy. Seeing no other way, Van led them through the thicket away from the blockade. Crawling through the vines, branches, and bushes proved troublesome and drained the party of their energy. The sun's rays glared down at them through the roof of leaves, its heat wearing them down even more.

They had to advance silently, but once they went a fair distance from the blockade, they began using their weapons to cut through the foliage. It surprised Van to know they could. While he followed his comrades, he noticed the magic that gave the plants form was weaker than the enchantment on the swords, and thus gave way to the more powerful force.

It was fascinating how the images created from the same spell differed in density. Imperfect as it was, the spell had to be incredibly complex to support the many aspects of the simulated environment.

Upon passing the thicket, once they realized the coast was clear, Van and his party marched out to the forest border. The grass suddenly grew taller and with a brighter shade where the two territories met. The towering trees also became transparent, their bodies fading at the other side of the border as though they were never there. If it were possible to look at everything from the air, it would be like someone had torn two different paintings in half and put them with the opposite one.

While it was stimulating to see, they had not the time to take it in. Van's party advanced through the fields, remaining cautious and ready for anything. Would the enemy hide their numbers in the sea of green or send them directly at invaders in full force?

Not wanting to be kept in suspense, they climbed up a tall hill with a gradual slope outside the enemy base. They paced themselves so they would not leap headfirst into a horde of enemies.

Nothing sounded from the other side. Either the plan had not progressed so far yet or they went to the wrong location.

As the party kept hiking, Van began to question the holes in their plan. After the parties arrived around the enemy base and receive the signal, they were to begin the attack.

What was the signal supposed to be, though? Where would they have to look? Why could Stevene and the other studious pages not have explained everything back at the hovel?

Van hoped the answers would come as events played through. He grew tired not knowing halfway up the hill. Turning back now would only compromise the plan, however porous it was.

Stevene, you never took me for a fool before. Don't start now.

As he thought that, Van remembered the aspiring tactician never took chances when his intellect was put to the question. He had to have thought of something, something he knew would work.

A vague riddling sensation gnawed at him the farther they climbed. Van stopped immediately before crossing over the peak, startled and wary. There was a commotion over the ridge, a loud one. Quarreling comrades perhaps? How arrogant they were to fight among themselves when there was an enemy to overthrow.

As fun as it would be to jump out and surprise them, they knew not to risk alerting the enemy. They stayed low and silent, careful not to be seen or heard.

A strong, hostile envy possessed Van's party when they got a look at the enemy territory. At the center of the valley, south of the great lake, stood a grand stronghold capable of taking in the entire army, both active and incapacitated. Soldiers stood armed patrolling the entire area. There was no way to proceed without being wiped out.

So the Estrines did put victory in Ginnstom's favor.

It was only hours before dusk. The enemy would be making another move soon, and it would be fierce and devastating. Whatever they were waiting for, it needed to be put into motion soon.

"And we continue to wait," complained the third-year page.

"Would you rather we take them on alone?"

Van felt no differently than his impatient comrade. Were he still the same energetic, naïve boy he was a couple of years ago, he would have charged right in with the confidence that they would win and come out unscathed. Experiencing pain, fear, and death helped to bury that naivete.

Perhaps he could do with some training in the Sperov Mountains.

While waiting for the plan to continue, Van reminisced about his time in the perilous mountain range. An abundance of exhilarating experiences had been made there every day, even the first days spent trudging through the snow and over steep cliffs.

A week after they reached the first mountain pass, Jerrell taught his son the basics of swordplay using petrified branches.

Snowflake watched the humans while swaddled in Van's coat. She often protested the pummeling the large man gave her savior, barking angrily from her resting spot and attempting to stand, the thick coat around her restraining her movements. It took a while for Van to convince her to allow the training to continue without argument.

Strong gust often plowed layers of snow into the air, mixing it with the crystal powder falling to the ground.

Their training sessions lasted for long periods of time, and Van was always able to keep going. Whereas he thrived, the retired knight shivered violently. It was moments like that where Van remembered he was not an ordinary human anymore—and he still had yet to fully process that he was a Kindhrin at the time.

The cold was vicious and the winds fierce. But Jerrell kept going regardless, if only to keep his blood from freezing.

They took their positions again atop the paved mountain rock and began the next round quickly.

No thick layers of clothing restricted Van's movements, unlike Jerrell, who could not react as quickly. That still posed no threat to the retired knight. He met every swing and punished the boy for leaving himself open.

When asked if Van had enough, the boy bore his teeth and charged again. The spirit he displayed amused Jerrell, riling him up to keep the fight going. His strikes gradually became rougher on the child. The man sometimes fretted over landing an attack his son could not endure, but his torn muscles lost the strength that would do so long ago. He did not need to hold much back.

Van's grasp on swordsmanship was just as deplorable at the time.

Swing. Miss. Fall.

Swing. Miss. Fall.

The cycle only broke when the Second Verse began to act on its own and harden the snow around his ankles, hardening it into ice.

Whenever he had the chance, Jerrell taught Van a few tricks to maintain his power. Twenty-seven days did not amount to much. The level of concentration he developed at that point only allowed him to keep from freezing things unconsciously—unless he lost focus. Maintaining that control subconsciously did not happen for another month.

It took Van considerable effort to break out of the frigid shackles and resume their training.

Each counter pushed his body skidding across the frozen rock. He always went running back, ready for another swing. Each strike pushed him farther. Both father and son soon became careless. They realized that when Van finally refused to get back up.

He dared not flinch from where he kneeled. One look down left him petrified. The small ledge scarcely supporting his weight loomed over a deep, ravenous crevasse below. At such heights, it appeared as a gaping abyss breaching the layers of earth into the bowels of the first hell. The cold air formed a thick haze around him, intensifying the terror he felt as he looked down into the emptiness.

Once the surface chipped, cracked, and crumbled, Van would plummet into the depths, just like the branch he watched sink into the abyss.

He could not bring himself to move. He was petrified by fear. His thoughts came to a halt when he saw the cracks at his knees.

Jerrell ran to save him but fell over himself, the scar at his leg acting up. Snowflake struggled to stand but could barely move a muscle. None of them could move and quickly became bound by despair.

The scar around Van's torso throbbed painfully. Dying once was traumatic enough. To die again so soon, the future being ripped from him again, snuffed out his hope. He could not even cry out for help.

Jerrell tried to draw his attention, but the winds drowned out his voice. He desperately crawled closer, somewhat resembling a dying man, which terrified his son even more. It was a nightmare to think they would all die there together.

But his despair fractured when Jerrell's voice broke through the wind.

Fear had blinded Van to his abilities, but upon hearing his father, he pressed his hands against the ledge and concentrated his power. No ice formed at first, even though he was not holding anything back. He acted on desperation, fear still choking him and restraining the Second Verse.

He did not want the last thing he saw to be his father looking at him so desperately. He closed his eyes, channeling his breathing to a slow, stable rhythm. His valsara ceased fluctuating erratically. When next his eyes drifted open, he saw his hand spreading ice over the cracks. As a safety measure, he tried directing another wave under the plateau to maintain support, but the rushed work instead further tore at the ice underneath.

Soon, he lost his nerve and ran off the ledge when he witnessed a stone drop into the abyss. He kept running as the ice crumbled until finding himself in his father's secure embrace.

There were no tears. He just breathed heavily, letting out all of his fright and exhaustion through the long white breaths. Again and again Jerrell apologized, trying to ease his son's grief and his own guilt.

From that experience, though, Jerrell learned to make sure they kept away from cliffs and unstable ground when training Van. And Van learned that his power failed him when crippled by fear.

Looking back now, the memory was almost refreshing.

Unfortunately, it had been spoiled by a sudden surge of magic energy and a massive *ka-bang* following suit.

Van leaped to his feet and turned to the open field as another explosion resounded. Down below, the enemy pages were scattering in a panic. He scanned the entire area but found no remains of what could have made those harrowing sounds.

Another blast erupted. Pieces of the stronghold were scattered violently through the air. Its tower stood with a chunk of it missing. A bizarrely strong updraft came from out of nowhere, striding up the hill with great force.

In standing against the winds' mighty brush, Van felt they were not spells from the charm. His magic senses detected magic building up extravagantly at several pinpoint locations. In seconds, they expanded a hundredfold, rending everything in its vicinity to shreds. Each speck of energy flew from one point of origin at the far northeastern hill overlooking the stronghold. It was far, out of sight for most, but Van saw the source to be of a human child. Another party of pages arrived, and considering they were letting magic loose against the stronghold, they sided with Wally.

That has to be the signal!

Many ran far in attempt to escape the monstrous gales chipping away at the stronghold. Anyone caught in the razing blast, tossed about like rag dolls, lost the strength and will to fight.

One party took advantage of the chaos and made their advance into enemy territory—Van's party. They could not restrain themselves after seeing the enemy army fall to pieces and rushed in ready for battle, leaving their leader in their dust. "Wait!" Van intended to wait for the aspiring mage to cease his barrage before advancing. He called out to them, but they would not listen. His voice fell on ears deafened by impatience and disrespect. Fools though they were, he could not leave them on their own.

Van attempted to follow, but he found it increasingly difficult to move from where he was. The blasts ringing in his ears and stirring the winds and the continuous screams made his limbs tremble and his mind waver. Before long, his heartbeat pounded against his chest so violently, it became painful to endure. The grass and pollen rent from the earth scattered to the wind, making it difficult to see anything ahead.

Then he began to see things—disturbing things. The flying foliage made his eyes water. Then the next moment, the skies began to darken and fierce flames came to burn, spreading all around. And the screams he heard became bloodcurdling.

Every moment spent enduring the wailing screams and watching the flames grow tormented him. His breathing became erratic. The air around him became frigid. Everything was becoming too much for him to bear, his mind on the verge of collapse.

But the hallucinations faded after the winds died down and the grass fell back to the ground. His anxiety diminished but had not entirely disappeared. What was that? What had he seen? Something like that had never happened to him before.

For all the questions that formed, he could not focus on them. There was still a battle to fight.

With his body no longer weighed in place, Van rushed down the hill in hopes of catching up with the others.

The air seemed heavier after being churned so savagely. The winds beat weakly around the battered field, then became still and carried well the silence. Nothing felt quite the same. This broken atmosphere, where emptiness remained in place of the clamor, left a weight on the spirit.

Van assumed that was what the end of a battle crudely resembled, albeit without the foul odor of death.

The emptiness was off-putting, not to mention suspicious.

The enemy parties fled in various directions. From the way they moved, like roaches exposed to light, none of them could have gone very far, and there was no decent place to hide. Van did not believe everyone was blown away by the winds.

It looked like he was alone, but he knew otherwise. The Estrine family taught them how to respond to the most adverse situations. What mattered most was keeping calm, and even if there were some who lost heart, the experienced and stubborn would undoubtedly lie in wait and surprise the invading army.

Whatever his party planned on doing, nothing good would come from it. They rushed into enemy territory without a plan or thought of how to breach the base unscathed. He did not need to think about it much to realize the simple truth: their recklessness would cost them.

Regardless of their feelings of the matter, Van was the one in charge and knew their safety was a priority he could not neglect.

He caught sight of them before long. None of them were as fast as him. Thoughts of frustration began to fume as he considered how he would chew them out.

Unfortunately, it was already too late.

Several enemy pages hid themselves in the grass not mowed down by the monstrous winds, and leaped out when they saw the chance to attack. They were in the open long enough for the hapless lambs to get a faint look at their faces before being put to the slaughter.

The third-year who once followed Van was the only one left baring his fangs in the struggle. Enemy soldiers one after the next tried keeping him in place, and only succeeded in slowing him down. Putting to use the wooden shield on his left arm allowed him to endure attacks from the front, but they kept going at him from behind and the sides.

Although an insubordinate soldier, seeing him in danger ushered Van to race into action. The enemies were not aware of his presence. Taking advantage of their focus on his former partner, he closed the gap as quickly as he could. Those Van set his sights on noticed him too late.

He stepped in to swipe one, carving the spell into his back, and used that momentum to keep moving and move onto the next, but faster.

Van turned quickly to his next target, smacking her at the back of her head with his scabbard. Three charged at him from the sides and front when she fell. He moved quickly to block the sword at his left with the scabbard, then spun to throw the wielder off balance, repulse the axe-wielder at his right, and intercept the frontward attacker's strike with a swift kick to the wrist. It was a difficult rhythm to move with, but he managed well.

His cadent fighting style left his foes stunned. They remained motionless, unsure of how to approach such unpredictable moves. They watched him carefully, but could not keep him from reuniting with his ally. He danced around the one who tried cut him down.

"Unless you want to end up like them, you'll follow my lead!" Van's order was stern, direct, and unmistakably belligerent.

He did not take his eyes off the enemies, but he felt that the third-year was looking down at their fallen comrades while everyone thought of their next moves.

Neither side would take the first step out of fear of falling victim to the enchantment next. They stared each other down, still as death, not willing to let more than breath move them. A few had sweat running down their brows and along their arms. The heavy tension in the air made their shake, causing their weapons to rattle lightly. The first to move would sway the scales shouldering victory and defeat—in which direction, neither side knew.

Unable to keep still any longer, the enemy pages came down on Van and his reluctant ally with all of the vigor and determination they held.

Van stood his ground, waiting for the right moment before drawing his sword and scabbard at the two who blindly threw their swords straight for him, following their rhythm and unbalancing them. The third-year at his side intercepted the enemy who tried to strike Van while he spun. Van bashed one of his enemies with his scabbard and slew his sword across the other, returning to the one getting back up to jab their shoulder with a thrust of the sword.

The rhythm he and his ally danced to gave Van a sense of security.

But the rhythm of battle could change erratically at any moment.

The last enemy standing was quicker and more observant than the others. He pulled back, evading the quick draw of Van's blade, and leaped back in to throw his sword at Van's left upper arm.

Upon impact, his whole arm went numb. A pulsating pain the size of the dull weapon and an unruly, icy sensation seared down his arm in floods. All other feeling faded.

The shock from the impact shot off Van's awareness. He failed to muster the will to move.

The third-year came to his rescue just as the enemy prepared the final blow. He ran his sword across the enemy's back and shoved him to the ground. When he was certain the enchantment left the enemy motionless, he let himself heave from the exhaustion, then turned to Van.

"Are you all right?"

No, he wanted to say. Obviously, no one would feel well after getting cut. "I'll survive..."

Terrible though the pain was, he fought through it. That one strike was not enough for the enchantment to put him into the death-like state.

Van looked down to his arm. With his magic sight, he saw how the magic clung to his valsara and attacked his nerves. It simulated numbness and blood loss, and also added a daunting weight to his arm that made it feel like it would fall off.

Treating it there would hinder whatever progress they already made. The enactment was coming to its conclusion. If having to fall to the spell meant making a difference before then, Van preferred using the time left to make it a favorable one.

"We need to infiltrate the enemy base," Van said as he got back to his feet.

The third-year made no arguments. He likely understood that going back now was not an option. "Can you fight with your arm like that?" Although he could not see the flow of magic, he plainly saw Van clinging to his arm for some time.

So not to cause further concern, he released his arm, letting the magic spread slowly. "I'll manage."

He would have to if they hoped to win. They still needed more time. If worse came to worse, he could use his arm as a meat shield.

Van went through the fields with the third-year in tow. He put his focus on their surroundings rather than on the pain in his arm.

The storm had all but cleared the fields. Only the instable breeze fighting to retake its natural wavelength broke the forlorn silence. The paths seemed peaceful, the magic-crafted grass reflecting the gentle golden light of the sun. Trouble seemed a realm away.

Even as they neared the stronghold's gate, victory began to seem much closer. All of the watchtowers had been wrecked and no one stood at the gates left open wide.

Van did not get any closer to the gates. The enemy base could not have been so carelessly unguarded. It was much too convenient. Even with the disturbance made, there had to be places inside perfect for weathering small disasters.

Just when Van was beginning to think himself paranoid, he heard a faint *clank* grate against the rock walls. It was a trap. And there was no way to avoid it either. The only entrances were limited to the open gate and the hidden breach in their wall; if the enemy found out about that, it would compromise the plan.

They may need more time.

Sound began to stir from behind the welcoming gate. The two bold pages prepared for an army to charge out and trample them. Seeing one enemy alone stroll leisurely into the open aggravated them both. It was all too tempting to charge at Kallant while he stood there alone and vulnerable, but they knew better than to fall for his taunting. He wanted them to come in closer for his comrades to jump out and crush them.

"Don't have the brass to face me?"

They did not budge. They would not encourage him, much to Kallant's chagrin.

He sighed dryly and looked at them with disdain. "Very well then. If you won't come to me..." A snap of the fingers, and several enemy soldiers amassed at the gates, each of them carrying a surplus of weapons.

There was no way an injured Van and his exhausted ally alone could manage a victory against such ample numbers. But they would not turn away even knowing that. They did not waver or look away from the enemy. If there really was no chance for victory, they would lose with dignity—and take down as many as they could with them.

Kallant, wearing a snide grin, was ready to order his subordinates to swarm the invaders when he was interrupted by a loud *gong! Gong! Gong!* The chateau bell alarmed Bravv's forces into dropping the weapons in hand. Rather than focus on the bell, Van turned upward to the flag waving valiantly atop the enemy stronghold. He saw it set to an eerie flame until turning to ashes.

Now that grin drew across Van's face. Wally's army had won.

~ Thirteenth Chapter ~

For What It Is Worth

Or so it appeared. Right at the moment when Bravv Ginnstom had been immobilized by the enchanted weapons, so had Wally.

With both army leaders defeated, the senior knights decided to determine the victor based on each army's performance.

The enchantment lifted once the bell rang, waking everyone from their comatose states. The pages were awake and aware but groggy and aching where the magic lingered for so long. They all gathered together before the chateau as the spell faded, the simulated environment dissipating into thousands of specks of flickering blue light. Both sides waited patiently while the Estrine family debated on which army showed the best results.

Everyone was unbearably anxious waiting to hear how they did. Hiding their nervousness behind strong expressions proved almost as challenging as the enactment. Both sides thought they had done very well for themselves in fighting the enemy as they would a threat to their lives.

Those siding with Wally never thought they would get as far as defeating Bravv or so severely leveling the playing field. With so few on their side, they were satisfied knowing they managed to best so many with what they had.

Van kept a stern face while the others panicked in silence. He worked for victory and nothing else. To witness his group break apart, abandoning him like they did, it made the progress ere then meaningless. The only good that came out of their effort was managing to distract their enemies long enough for their plan to be put into action.

Everyone nearly stopped breathing when Lord Estrine approached them with their decision.

That night, a loud party was held in the banquet hall to celebrate the winners. The Estrine family put plenty of preparation into presenting their students with the most delectable food. Succulent mutton, arrangements of juicy fruit, gourmet dishes fit for royalty—all of it had been spread out at every table. Such tantalizing food had been scarce since the first few days of hospitality in the chateau.

Wally nearly cried at the sight of the spread.

The most tasteful music was played to complement the food, a feast for the senses. The serene notes from the violins and piano moved with each other in perfect harmony. The melody gradually became more upbeat, the bards working to suit the mood of the room.

If Van had not been stuffing his face, he would have been drawn in by the wondrously lively music.

The banquet hall seemed dead regardless. Not many of the pages felt like reveling. Those that made up Bravv's army had been broken by Lord Estrine announcing that their enemy's performance trumped their legion.

Teamwork and dedication to their causes put them on a par with each other, but what won them the Estrine family's favor was the intricate plan put together and executed by Wally and his supporters.

The parties Wally deployed to protect his territory served to keep the invaders' attention. While they drove them back, Ccuivr led a party past the conflict and infiltrated Bravv's base. The enemy general spread his forces so thin that he gave Ccuivr's party a path that led right to him, indirect as it was.

While Van felt a little jealous that Wally had not chosen him to carry out that attack, he knew his choice to be the right one when he came in contact with Kallant. The thug had become obsessed with trying to best Van's unconventional swordsmanship since suffering defeat against him last winter. He sought him out, pestered him and his faction, and constantly tried goading him into fights just to get another chance. Van never used it during weapons training since Sir Charleston instructed him to practice Vermalian swordplay. The enactment was the perfect opportunity to avenge his defeat, and he likely would have had it not ended when it did.

It made Van wonder what he would do next.

It seemed cruel for the losing side to be forced to eat gruel while such good food sat within reach. It served as motivation, according to the Estrine family, for them to take victory the next year. A few of them tried to end their torture and swipe some of the feast; they only made it all the worse when they were caught. Those who refused to comply were forced to serve the knights who visited to watch the enactment and were not allowed another scrap of food for the rest of the night.

Van and his faction sat at their table. Accompanying them were a few pages who fought with them, even the third-year that abandoned Van, who introduced himself as Quintin Hildegolde of Rippling Wilderness.

Van still begrudged his party's decision to act on their own, but he chose to forgive Quintin and allow him to stay if he told them about his region. Rippling Valley sounded like a pleasant place.

"Man, you would not believe how painful it was getting killed like that!" Wally's comment ended the other discussions at the table. The many others who felt that same pain offered firm nods in agreement. "I may not get magic, but I know I don't want to go through that again."

"For once, I agree with you," added Rubi. "I couldn't feel my leg after it was hit. It's like it was not even there, but the pain still was."

The same thing applied to Van when his arm had been hacked at. He could barely move it, let alone hold his scabbard.

Stevene sighed. "A little tap to the forehead got me. It felt like it had been split in two."

Everyone shared their experiences of being struck down by the enchantment. Their words expressed the strife they felt after the magic ensnared their bodies and silenced their minds. First they were hit, then a vile sensation purged them of thought and perception. All was quiet until the sounding bell ripped away the darkness enshrouding them.

For Van, though, the enchantment was not the most frightening thing he experienced. It was those hallucinations.

Those haunting screams. The malignant flames. The skies darkening with clouds of smoke. Everything looked so real. It terrified him. Whatever it was, he hoped never to see it again.

"Had my party not acted so gallantly to shield me, I may have gone through the same pain." Even Prince Aeron could barely hold his own, it seemed. "Though none of us actually died, I still feel I owe them."

"I hear you. Lelia had my back the whole time and got taken down because I got careless."

"Do not say things you do not mean. It will come to haunt you."

Gal went silent after his sister's blunt comment. The others stared at him with mild inquiry, hoping he would slip up and say what it was Lelia scolded him for. He played the innocent boy, laughing like a fool.

"Besides, I don't think I could take anything from you after watching you cry like a baby."

The boy's face lit up a vibrant red. "Stop patronizin' me! It really looked like you were dead!"

Everyone laughed. Van could not restrain a small chortle seeing Gal act a bit hysterical. Reacting to everything so seriously made him a means of entertainment, as Ccuivr's unversed and unexpected laughter denoted.

Had the chefs not prepared such fantastic food, Gal would have left in a huff, but instead he stayed put, pouting while stuffing his face.

Van suggested Gal try the ivory juice to soothe his unsteady temper.

No one understood why he took to the bitter beverage so well. It tasted of bland old fruit and herbs and left a tart aftertaste. It was mainly a drink the elderly had if tea was unavailable. Van always liked the pungent flavor, though. Fatigue and aches washed away when so much as a drop trickled over his tongue. Having the rest flow down his throat brought him more energy than he often needed.

It was mostly out of politeness that Gal took his offer. He finished the last of his water before reaching for the pitcher of ivory juice.

Stevene advised him against drowning his frustrations in something so tart. Gal did not listen, not caring for what the jerk who called him an "adorable boy" had to say.

He filled his cup halfway so as not to waste any in case the taste did not agree with him, then set the pitcher down and chugged it all down.

Wally and Stevene leaned away from the boy, worried how excessively he would react to the bitter flavor. To their amazement, and perhaps disappointment, he did nothing rash. He even smiled and refilled his cup to the brim.

"You actually like that bilge water?" asked Ccuivr.

Gal downed the glass, setting it down in a gasp. "Yeah. Tastes kinda like the stuff my parents drank."

Curious, Lelia decided to have a cup herself.

This time, the two clowns leaned in to be sure they would have a look at how the more mature twin would react. Would she keep herself composed in straining to hide a sour expression? Or would she let her inner thoughts be heard in the most outrageous volumes?

None of that happened. Lelia wore the same smile as her brother, yet with a charm befitting her feminine mien. "Yummy!"

Quintin blinked. "Huh. Maybe it's something for hayseeds."

The ham slab he was about to savor slid out of his teeth and fell onto the floor when Rubi and Ccuivr—nearly in synch—jabbed their elbows into his ribs. They leered at the haughty boy resentfully.

The timing informed Van that the word could only be an unfriendly term for peasants.

"Careful now, Rubella. Don't go breaking our new friend here like you did the last one," teased Wally.

Before Rubi could go off at Wally, she watched him sink his teeth into the third slice of ham to pass down his wide throat. She hated his repulsive eating habits. It still amazed her how much meat wound up on his face instead of down his gullet. She failed to understand how he could look so composed in the etiquette lessons and never put that effort into everyday life. It always put her in a bad mood.

"Want me to break your arm like I did Ccuivr?"

The once morose page stopped the fork between his teeth when he heard her. "Wasn't that an accident?"

From what Ccuivr told Van, he and Rubi were sparring when it happened, inspired by the bout between Van and Victoriah. They held nothing back, respecting each other's strength. At one point, Rubi had the advantage; the next, it was Ccuivr. And just when it seemed Ccuivr was about to take the win, Rubi suddenly attempted to mimic Van's technique and used her whole body's force to slam the sword into his arm.

She had no control of where her arm flew, as Rubi later confessed to Van, along with her insistence that he did not tell anyone else.

"Want to go at it again and find out?"

Van did not feel it wise to point out Rubi nearly broke her arm when she tried to show him how she intimidated the technique. If Wally heard and laughed at her clumsy mistake, she would chew him out for it instead.

Regardless, Wally did not seem afraid. Had the need to protect himself against her arise, he was confident in his abilities to fend her off. Like the wily Ccuivr, Wally was agile and reflexive whether defending or going on the offensive.

But putting Rubi's skill into question was downright foolish. Quick to anger and impulsive as she was, her intuition and responsiveness were impeccable. Looking at her when she fought made it easy to see she was well on her way to following in her role model's image.

And if the others were to go at one another, it would definitely be a spectacle worth watching.

With how much time Stevene spent learning strategies and tactics, he was easily the most cunning among them. The fear of the future served as an excellent motivator to keep his mind sharp. Not every soldier survived their first battle, and he wanted to be sure he would.

Ccuivr was a natural fighter, though competitive to a fault. He picked fights with pages bigger and stronger than him and, more often than not, came out on top. Many of the knights attending the banquet mentioned the promise he showed.

Small as they were, the twins had also made great progress. Gal's enthusiasm toward everything he did and the teasing he endured inspirited him to fight and train with passion. Lelia often got knocked down in training, but after the trauma she endured, she found the will to always get back up for more.

The seven children had come far since they began their training. If they continued on the courses they took, they would one day make great knights.

While pondering on what knight might want him for a squire, Van's focus turned to Wally, who left his seat for a fifth helping of anything he could find. His ravenous hunger was nothing new, but his movements across the hall struck Van as rather odd. He ventured to twenty-seven different tables, snatching up enough food to fill his plate. Along the way, he stopped for a short banter with each table he crossed. It looked to be he was making snide comments to those who lost the enactment. It was rather unlike him to taunt those who did not provoke him.

And then, it happened again.

Right when it seemed Wally said something excitable, by the wave of an arm, some food slid away from the platters toward the pages playing with their gruel. They all furtively took the food as Wally went to the next table.

Van never noticed that his good friend did that earlier. The knights seemed busy in their own repartee to notice as well, thankfully.

The glutton returned carrying his own weight in food on the small plate in his hands. His faction began to question if he could finish off all that food while their new companions wondered if he was really human, eating as much as he did.

Van took a quick sip of ivory juice before confronting him. "Wally, you shouldn't be doing this."

"Why not? It's a banquet. We can't let this food go to waste."

"Someone has to worry for your health, ape," Rubi snapped. "It may as well be someone unfortunate enough to be your best friend."

"I mean you shouldn't be swiping food for the Ginnstom pages. You know they aren't allowed to eat any of it."

Van's observation disturbed the culprit as well as the rest of the pages within earshot. Stevene rocked in his seat from nearly choking on water.

Apart from the sudden widening eyes, Wally kept calm, easing back in his seat. "You've got good eyes there, Van. You didn't steal them from an owl, did you?"

"Wally!"

"Take it easy! Take it easy!" he said gently. "Those pages worked as hard as we did in that little 'war.'" Casually as he put it, he started to sound as serious as an Estrine. "If it went up to deciding the victor through battle, I'd be okay with it, but the Estrine family making the choice kind of makes our win feel ... uninspiring."

"I'm certain they evaluated us based on our strategic choices," interrupted Stevene.

"The only one who decides who wins and loses battles is Lord Ralias." Wally's family worshipped the god of war and prosperity, and his words showed how devoted they were to him. "And as great as the Estrine family is, they're no gods."

"Nor were we real armies in a real war," stated Lelia.

"Don't take that leap again, Wally."

"You worry too much, Van. I haven't been caught yet."

"Didn't he just catch you?" Rubi said with a shrewd smirk.

For once, she managed to puzzle Wally enough for him to lose his rein on the topic. He could not even come up with a fitting remark.

One more push from Van managed to convince Wally to slip away from the hunter's snare with his tail still attached. He began stuffing himself again until he heard Quintin comment on his impish nature. With a wide grin and a snicker, Wally started to regale him with a few of the practical jokes he pulled.

While he listened to his friend's stories, Van noticed that Sir Charleston excused himself from his family's table. He had been picking at his food and indulging in the pleasant exchanges between his friends, but when he saw Sir Charleston on the move, he scarfed down the last of the food on his plate.

He could not stick around. This was the chance he was waiting for.

"You leaving already, Van?"

He turned from his thoughts when Rubi spoke up and looked to her, seeing her eye him curiously.

"You can't be full already!" Wally laughed. "I've seen you eat more than I do on occasion."

Quintin blinked. "Is that even possible?"

"We don' get a feast very often," Gal added. "Sit down and enjoy it with us."

They did not need to concern themselves, especially when it could jeopardize his secret if they did. He gave his friends a small, reassuring smile. "There is something I need to do, so this will be it for me. I'll see you all in the morning."

He left them to their food before they could ask any more questions.

It seemed he left at the right time. As Van followed Sir Charleston's tracks, he heard a depressed page ask one of the Estrines if so much raucous noise was appropriate for a formal celebration.

"Those that return from war often revel more senselessly than this," he overheard the Estrine state. "Just be glad none of us allow Lord Estrine to drink, or there wouldn't be anything left to celebrate."

The halls became silent after he left the banquet hall. The echoing voices and music soon faded, leaving only the faintest of noises to interrupt the silence. Van tuned out the sound of his boots clopping against the floor and his chain mail swaying in a rhythmic *sheen, sheen*. He needed to focus on where he was going.

He lost sight of his target before leaving the banquet hall. Finding one man in a vast mansion was a challenge, but one made easier with the trail he left behind. It smelled bitter, much like ivory juice but mustier, and it lingered. Were he to close his eyes, he would be able to picture a trail in which the odor hung in the air.

The odor wafted against his nose the more he followed it. As he did, it began to remind him of a time when he last noticed that scent.

It was four years ago (or maybe longer) when he was under the same roof as his parents, enjoying his mother's irresistible cooking. The day went by quickly he was having so much fun with his friends. It was especially notable since he sprained his leg. His mother made him buttery biscuits as a treat to complement the ivory juice he drank. His family was together, smiling, laughing, enjoying their company. Then after the second serving of lamb, Jerrell poured himself and his wife the very thing that made him recollect the memory.

To be drinking in front of Lord Estrine seemed rude, but it was Sir Charleston, after all. Everyone knew he was cold. But Van saw it as the knight trying to remind his father of restraint through struggle.

If he were only concerned with himself alone, he would never have become a knight.

The halls looked the same in every direction as when Van found Sir Charleston's quarters. The smell crept through the doors leading inside.

Van ignored his nose wrinkling to the liquor's lingering pungency and knocked on the doors with the back of his knuckle.

"Enter!"

He opened one of the doors and closed it quickly, causing as little disturbance for the knight as possible. He would need to be quick and concise in order to get what he was after.

Sir Charleston stood at the wall-spread window, allowing the moonlight to glisten over the parchment in his hands. Upon glancing at his doors, he tucked the document into the shadows.

"Page Kronas?" He sounded surprised. "What is it?"

"I have an important question to ask of you, sir."

Sir Charleston remained silent. His valsara flickered with disapproval.

Looking back to make certain the door had been closed, Van gave a little more thought to what he might say. He turned back to Sir Charleston with wavering hesitation, but then hushed his doubts and fears. This man was the only Estrine who knew of his secret, and the only one who could help him.

He reached into his tunic, grabbed the Shift Pendant, then brought it into full view, causing the spell to break, the Vermalian disguise stripped away. "Do you know how my father came across this charm?"

Sir Charleston said nothing as he appraised Van. His gaze became more intolerant and hostile when the Kindhrin showed himself.

The hate in his eyes petrified the Kindhrin child. It was difficult to discern whether he was thinking of a response or how to keep from running him through. But Van looked Sir Charleston in those piercing red eyes and forced his muscles to keep from shaking. He could not let him know he was afraid. If he was going to get what he was after, then he had to remain resolute.

The knight could clearly see through his calm charade. But it did not seem to matter. "That stone around your neck was not something he came across. It is not something naturally found, you see. It is a charm, and thus must be forged by human hand. Your father, possessing no magic himself, likely sought out an alchemist to craft it for him."

What he said piqued Van's curiosity. Sir Charleston was well acquainted with Victoriah and Jerrell, and though he did not know how well, it was enough for him to keep their secret. And from how he spoke, he sounded like he knew more. Perhaps he knew of Jerrell's lost Gendae magic and left knowledge of it unsaid out of respect for him, or perhaps he was merely informed of how they kept Van hidden for so long. Either way, he was giving an answer.

"To make a magic charm takes little more than a scrap of aurichalcum. The stone itself absorbs and retains magic. For the desired effect, it must be imbued with something to invoke it—in this case, a pint of your father's blood for you to adopt his likeness."

An entire pint!?

Hearing so much blood had been accumulated to enhance a gem the size of a man's thumb made Van's heart stop a moment.

"Now tell me *exactly* why you need information of this nature."

Van blinked as he attempted to focus again. He was not certain how Sir Charleston would react if he knew the truth. But if he were to lie, the conversation would not end well. But perhaps a fear that had crossed his mind before would suffice, something he experienced before.

"I thought knowledge of this may help me forge a new pendant in the event something happens to this one."

Sir Charleston's stern expression and the intensity of his valsara had not changed to suggest suspicion. He remained silent to further appraise the page, cautious of treachery. His eyes narrowed. "Something like that is far too valuable to lose, boy. If you are without it for even a moment, anyone who sees you will put you to death." He let those words sink in, along with the malice laced in them. "That said, your Second Verse does not possess the potential to replicate the power for a Shift Pendant. At the most, I theorize it would— No, even I don't know what that would do. My knowledge of magic is limited. The expert of the family is my younger sister, Abeel, and you are *forbidden* to speak of this to her."

"Yes, sir."

"Now that you have what you need, get out of my sight."

"Yes, sir."

Van tucked the Shift Pendant back into his tunic, reassuming his false peach skin, then proceeded for the door.

A journey did not come to an end after something obstructed the path. Van was in need of a detour if he hoped to reach his goal. If he could not rely on the magic of others, he needed to force the Second Verse to work for him the way he needed.

He made use of his limited time in the fields. Scavenging through the tall grass proved fruitless, but after noticing a tiny flicker of light, he began looking along the ground near the weapons shack. On his knees he dug at the dirt like an eager dog searching his lost bone. He stopped only to pull away from the glass shard he found.

One disappointment did not diminish his spirit. He was determined to find the aurichalcum he needed at whatever cost. So he kept digging, hoping that somehow, someway he would come upon the stone.

It was surprising how easily his hands moved through the dirt. He dug through it like it was powdery snow. He was so focused on the task at hand that he did not notice how well he tore through it.

Nothing. He dug deeper and faster, clinging to that strand of hope he refused to let go of. The soil was harder the deeper he went. It felt like ripping through stone. Blood soon trickled down his fingers.

Exhaustion began to overcome him. He came to a stop, on all fours and hanging his head, until the strength in his arms gave out and he collapsed. Where had all of his energy gone? Now that he started thinking that, it made him wonder where it came from in the first place.

I need to keep going.

He took a deep breath and suddenly felt revitalized. Cold air travelled down his throat, purging fatigue from his muscles.

And yet tension and frustration from finding only specks of dirt and blood between his fingernails made his temper flare. He felt more at ease enduring a beating in sword training. Vexed, Van raised a clenched fist high and viciously bashed it into the ground.

Something lodged itself between his fingers upon impact. It had a texture that felt smooth at various edges yet rigid. When he lifted his hand, he found another reflective surface wedged into the dirt. He carefully picked away the dirt around it.

A gem! It was a clear white gem. And it shone beautifully like the tip of a dagger.

It did not take long to realize the glimmer came from the moon looming high above. Pulled by its glow, he stood tall and stared at the glorious crescent. He looked to the moon for minutes without turning away, but the trance broke when he realized how high the moon had risen.

It was already curfew!

He ran back to the chateau in a panic, holding his chain mail in place with the hand securing the gem so he would not alert the guards. Severe punishments were carried out for those who skipped curfew, the worst

Van could imagine. Anyone caught wandering the grounds after curfew was denied breakfast the next day. Worse than that, those pages were to sit patiently with the others while they ate.

Van could barely get by on gruel and water. Losing a meal would be torture.

When he turned the corner to the boys' hall, several of the pages were still returning to their bedchambers, all wearing dreary expressions. Van let out a sigh of relief and joined the others.

Sleep had not been on his mind that night, despite the fatigue. After getting what he was after, Van was much too excited for even a moment's rest. He sat cross-legged on the floor in the middle of his room, staring at the gem and pondering how he could infuse it with his power.

Touch a surface, and it froze solid. Focus on a distant space, and ice clustered. That was basically all Van knew about how to use his Second Verse.

From that tip of the iceberg of his power's capabilities, there was nothing on how to transfer the energy. But he could not waste the night wondering how to act, and simply took action.

Centering his focus toward the gem between his outstretched hands, Van closed his eyes. He envisioned where the flow of power should bend. All he saw was the vibrant cerulean valsara that shaped from his hands.

Minutes passed, and nothing happened. Van had not the courage to open his eyes and find the gem still unchanged. He worried it would only cause his focus to waver.

Just be patient. Be patient and focus.

The silence was unpleasant. It made the fatigue coursing through his body unsettling. Although there was this sudden pressure pressed atop his lap and a patting at his stomach.

A tad perplexed, Van opened his right eye to find a certain snowfleece fox leaning against him, begging for attention. He smiled sympathetically. "Sorry, Snowflake," he said while lifting a hand to pet her plush head, "I can't cuddle right now. There's something I need to do."

Snowflake kept her head pressed against his hand for as long as possible before it was taken away. Displeasure flickered in her eyes when she looked up at him. *Something more important than paying attention to me?* it implied.

Van placed his focus back to the gem. Snowflake's valsara, now visible to him, burned like fire a moment, then simmered when she understood. Life and death, the universal matter.

But she did not leave him be for even a moment. Instead, she curled up in his lap, intent on watching over him while he worked. Her comfort gave Van the support to hold on a bit longer.

His focus was balanced between the gem in the void and his own life energy running through his fingers. It became difficult to focus on directing his valsara. It flared every now and then, resetting back to its original flow. If the transfer had any possibility of working, Van would need to tame that wild instability.

I need to create this charm. I have to!

Those were the only things to cross his mind during the process.

He began thinking all of the effort was in vain, only to shake off that feeling so as not to worry Snowflake. The last thing he needed was pity, especially with what was at stake.

He felt frustrated again, cynically spiteful toward himself for not getting the results he needed. Erratic thoughts, following the unstable emotions plaguing him, began to disrupt his focus and put further strain on him. Then they settled and took rein of those emotions, directing them toward a more productive direction.

I have to create this charm. ...I will create it!

Thoughts transfigured into power. His valsara became steady in accordance with his will, flowing to a single fixed point. His energy ran from him into the triangle his hands formed, slowly enshrouding the gem.

Finally, he could begin creating the charm.

His burgeoning excitement ended up draining the last of his energy. His eyes drooped open, showing the world at a different angle. Everything fell to its side. Snowflake scampered back to his bleak face, her wet nose prodding it before she muffled him with her fur.

Van smiled. "Yes, you're right. That'll do for the night."

When he sat up, his head spinning, Van saw the proof that his effort was worth something. His skin reverted back to its natural russet shade. But the gem remained unchanged in appearance or property.

After fetching and placing it safely into the bedside drawer, Van flopped onto his bed and, after making sure the Shift Pendant reactivated, drifted off to sleep.

Van's efforts to create the charm continued day in and day out without any change.

Every day after the lessons, he took every opportunity possible to step away and return to his bedchamber. He continued his fruitless efforts in solitude. His struggles allowed him to learn how to better transfer his energy without tiring himself so quickly. But the main issue was with the white gem. It would not retain anything he gave it.

To ease his wary mind, he crossed the maids' chambers on his way back to his own so he could check on Lyn's condition. Sensing valsara through walls was difficult and he did not offer a complete feel, but it was enough to know he could not remain idle. Time was running out.

After so many failed attempts, Van became impatient and hasty. His concentration thus fell askew, adversely affecting his progress and draining him mentally. The more he tired himself out, the more restless it made him.

He was deep in a trance one late afternoon, fixated on the gem between his hands, and ushering his energy to flow into the gem. He settled his mind so his valsara would flow uncompromised until able to guide it. It ran along him and directly into the gem without interference, as it had before. But as it also had before, most of the energy dispersed upon release from his body instead of being drawn into the gem.

Letting frustration overwhelm him only muddled the flow of his valsara. He strived to maintain a calm mind and continued.

A knocking at the door then startled him, causing his power to run rampant. A small burst of frigid air froze the wall in several places. The timing could not be any more problematic. He had been using the Second Verse for so long that the Shift Pendant would be useless for some time.

"Hey Van, you in there?"

That voice, to Van's relief, belonged to Wally. A heavy, dreary sigh escaped him while he turned to the door. "Come in, but don't open the door all the way." There was only his valsara on the other side; no one else followed. He would not have given the invitation otherwise.

Just in case, when the door creaked open, he scooted into the shadows.

Wally did as his friend asked, opening the door wide enough for him to slide through, then shutting it quickly. Upon turning around, he flinched and looked his way wide-eyed.

Begrudgingly, Van offered a little smile. "Are you still not used to my Kindhrin skin?"

"It's not that. I'm worried your pet will bite."

Snowflake hid in the shadows near Van upon the knock at the door. She was staring at the intruder with hostility.

"She won't do anything so long as you don't take anything ... I think."

The clingy snowfleece fox always behaved unpredictably when it came to other humans. He was not entirely sure what she would do.

"How comforting..."

"Is there a reason why you're here?"

"Can't a guy visit his best buddy just for the fun of it?"

As normal a reply as that would be, an abnormal tension resonated in his pale golden valsara. Van's blank stare showed Wally how serious he was at the moment.

The jester chuckled a little, then spoke his mind. "Okay, okay. I'll come clean. We're all starting to worry about you."

"Worry?"

"Yeah, couldn't you tell? You've been acting strange lately. Your mind's always elsewhere and you're shrugging us off. We try to talk to you, but you barely notice. And you nearly bit Gal's little head off just because he tried to stop you from going once."

Did that ... really happen?

Saying he could not remember such a thing sounded like an excuse for rude behavior. If he were to be honest, though, he did not remember any of that.

"I don't mind having someone quick to anger around, but you're even starting to scare Rubi."

That girl did not scare easily. For him to unnerve her, Van had to have been utterly coarse.

"What's gotten into you, Van?"

The damage could be mended later. For now, Van needed to keep from making the fractures in his best friend's trust worse.

He reached over to the white gem and showed it to Wally. "I've been trying to imbue my Second Verse into this aurichalcum." Handing the gem to Wally, he turned back to find Snowflake, out in the open again and growling malignantly. Van hushed her before she dared go on the attack, then turned back to Wally. "I've spent days trying but never got any closer to making a charm. I guess I've been rather unruly after all the work I put into it."

"Why do you need a charm?"

"Alicalyn is bedridden from magic deficiency."

Wally shook off any lingering animosity for his friend at the news. His eyes shot open, wide and panicked.

"I don't want to chance her dying, so I've been looking into ways to cure her. I've given it some thought, and a charm made from my Second Verse may be what I need."

"How'd you think of that?"

"Before I died, my Shift Pendant functioned on its own power. But when I became a Nascitte, something was different about it. My Second Verse allows me to see the flow of magic, and looking at my Shift Pendant, I found its magic somehow mixed and shared energy with my power.

"When I first started using the Second Verse, the Shift Pendant stopped working because of its interference. It took hours to recharge before I could use it again. And every time that happened, I saw a small strand of the magic being absorbed into my valsara. After a while, I started to see the magic put back into the pendant before it was fully recharged. I don't know if I completely understand this, but I think my power is somehow collecting small traces of magic from the Shift Pendant to use later on.

"If that's really what happens, then I can use that to save Lyn. A charm infused with the Second Verse could safely store Lyn's magic away before the deficiency kills her. Maybe ... it can save her."

His understanding of the Second Verse's nature was nothing short of conjecture. The plan made from it was poor and not well contrived, and he did not like staking Lyn's life on maybes alone, but it was better than waiting for her preordained demise.

Wally must have believed that as well. He would not talk him out of keeping a good woman from dying. He was much too kind and followed his noblesse oblige principle devoutly. This was in Van's power. He could give to someone who might not be able to save herself.

The jocular page began scratching the back of his scalp, his expression as worn out as it was confused. "Magic is just as complicated as I thought it," he stated. "Still, I don't think you should keep at it, at least not with this."

"What do you mean?"

He cracked a crooked smile. "This isn't aurichalcum, mate!"

Van could not muster a single word whereas his good friend kept laughing so ridiculously it looked like his head would deflate from oxygen loss. All he did in the confusion was stare at Wally impatiently, waiting for an answer.

"Sorry! Sorry, Van, but how could you confuse this with aurichalcum? This looks like a gem you'd see on a vow ring."

Van's mind snapped then and there. Not aurichalcum, but something put into rings for well-off lovers.

"Hm ... wait right here. I'll be back."

Wally quickly left with the white gem in hand.

The shock of learning his efforts were completely wasted made exhaustion overwhelm him. He fell on his back and stared at the ceiling with his eyes spread wide, stupefied at how his ignorance betrayed him yet again. It should have crossed his mind the moment he found the useless stone that he never even knew what aurichalcum was. He assumed he was on the right track and leaped at the apparent chance.

Why didn't he give it any thought first? Why did it slip his mind that he knew absolutely nothing about aurichalcum?

Snowflake scampered over to his side. She gave him a look of empathy, not wanting him to have any distraught thoughts riling him more. She tried comforting him with the caress of her plush white pelt.

Van took a deep breath, letting his muscles relax, and exhaled a puff of white air. He finally calmed down for the first time in over a week, taking the moment to think.

There was another knock at the door, undoubtedly Wally's.

Van sat back up as his friend reentered with as much caution as he had the first time.

Wally crouched down to the floor, meeting his friend at eye level. "You need aurichalcum, right? Will this do?" Beside the white gem in his hand was a black metal ring crowned by an amber prism.

"W-Where did you get that?"

"The ring was a gift from my mother—for good luck. But since I've got more luck than lip ..." While holding the white gem between with his ring and pinky fingers, Wally adeptly slid the ring down his hand, catching it in his index finger while holding it in place with the thumb. Van watched with amazement as he took hold of the aurichalcum with his other hand and pulled hard enough to pop it off of the black prongs. What befuddled him more than that was the boy handing him the precious stone.

All Van needed to do to create the charm was take it, but—

"I ... I can't accept this."

"Don't worry about it. I'm confident enough to say I am the luckiest page in the chateau. How else could I survive the year without that crazed Rubella skinning me alive?"

"That's not what I meant. This is from your mother, right?"

"If she asks, I'll trick her into thinking the ring had this gem instead. Trust me, it'll work. I love her to death, but she's not the sharpest woman in the kingdom." He lodged the gem he got in exchange into the black ring's grasping prongs. "A fair trade, don't you think?"

"But—"

"Look, Van, forget about where I got this for just a little while and think of the bigger picture: Alicalyn is dying! If it takes this little pebble to make sure she can live, then it's worth me telling one little lie, don't you think?"

The lie was not what Van was concerned with. Although Wally said he did not need it, it was still a present from his mother, and he dreaded the idea of taking it. Van considered his Shift Pendant his most valuable treasure long before knowing how necessary it was because it was a present from his father. It was why he always remembered to put it on.

Had Wally not been so insistent, he would not have taken it. But he was right. A life was at stake, and there could be no hesitation.

His bright smile gleaming, Wally stood again. He wanted to sit on Van's desk chair, but alerted by Snowflake's angry barking, he instead chose another section on the floor to sit at.

"All righty then, show me how you work your magic."

Fully intended to oblige, Van closed his eyes and formed his hands into a triangle arch above the aurichalcum. This time, he would not fail.

It worked. It actually worked!

Van finally managed to create a charm imbued with his power. And how glorious it was! The amber gem glowed a dim light, reacting to the energy of the Second Verse as it flowed from his body into it. As more of it inundated the aurichalcum given to him, the gem's glow began to resemble his valsara until taking in all it could and released a burst of bright cerulean light. The procedure was a complete success.

Van walked with Wally quietly down the hallway brushed in shimmering moonlight. He held the aurichalcum turned a tremendous crystal blue in his hand.

They kept a sharp lookout the entire way. Curfew had long passed, and the only feet meant to be treading the halls were servants doing some last-minute work and soldiers on the prowl. At the very least, it meant there was time to visit the maids before they all fell asleep.

Upon reaching the hallway's end, Wally hid himself where light would not reach.

Van made sure his spine was aligned straight before taking a free hand to the door, a force of habit he found rather difficult to break. His knock was answered immediately by Gretchen, the maid that had been tending to him in Lyn's place. She rubbed her eyes drearily, probably readying for sleep herself.

"Young Master Vandelas?"

He made his claim fast before she could comment on how late it was. "Forgive the intrusion at this late hour, but this is important. Please let me see Alicalyn."

"Look now—"

"I have something I need to give her."

Van showed her the closed hand that held the charm.

Strife contorted the weary maid's countenance as she agonized over what to do. Pages were not allowed into the servants' chambers to begin with unless being fitted for a uniform. Being concerned with that, she had to be worried he would get spotted by patrolling knights, which must have been why she made way for him to enter so quickly.

"Be quick about it, then return to your room."

It did not take very long.

From his previous visit, Van knew to check the bed shielded from light and barred away from the eyes of others. He strode past the other maids asleep in their beds quietly.

When parting the drapes concealing Lyn, he saw she weakly tossed and turned in her sleep, writhing from the intense pain. Her condition was worsening. Her forehead burned, her skin turned pale, sweat was rolling down every bit of skin. What light rasps she let out sounded like she was giving her last breaths again and again.

Van could not bear to watch but found it difficult to move. His magic sight revealed to him what the others could not see. Several spaces where her sweet, rosy valsara used to flow freely had been erased, leaving only splotches of inky darkness in its place.

Unable to allow it to go on, Van stepped into the drapes, leaving Gretchen to hold them open. He held out the charm, which Wally helped make into a necklace by tying a worn string around it. Its glow was the thing fending off the vile shadows threatening to consume Lyn. He gave a silent prayer to no one, and upon tying the necklace's string around Lyn's neck, he felt a sense of relief.

He wanted to see fast results despite knowing it to be an impossibility. But he found hope upon spotting the empty voids inside Lyn illuminate the cerulean light. It felt as though dawn had finally parted after a long, ominous dark.

He had done his part. Hopefully, it was enough. Hopefully, she would rest easier.

After bowing his head to the slumbering woman out of respect, he approached Gretchen again, thanked her kindly for her cooperation, and showed himself out, carrying the same composure he had upon entering.

He could not, however, hold himself up after closing the door behind him. It took every shred of willpower he could harness to pull that ruse so no other would fuss over him.

That did not stop Wally from leaving the cover of the shadows for him. "Hey Van, how are you feeling?"

"Exhausted..." he sighed. "Making that charm took a lot out of me."

The process exerted more energy from Van than he utilized before. Crafting ice was so much easier than sapping the power itself from him. Even though he learned how to control his valsara's flow more effectively, it was still a challenge guiding it exactly where it needed to be.

Though he had lost the strength in his limbs, seeing the radiant glow given off by the transformed aurichalcum gave him a reason to remain resolute for a few moments more.

Wally crouched down to Van's side, grabbing his arm and throwing it over his shoulder so they could stand together. "Come on. Let's get you back to your mangy roommate. I know she'll be mad if you stay out too late partying with me."

Van chuckled and followed his friend.

~ Fourteenth Chapter ~

Home Again

The rest of spring passed without incident. The pages had grown used to everything the Estrine family threw at them, and though the training did not get easier, they learned to expect what would come and how to handle difficult situations.

The training and education were arduous during the last few weeks. Perhaps it served as a fair warning for what was to come. Whatever the case, getting through it all meant they were growing as pages, into suitable potential squires.

Most training regimens ended when the days grew excruciatingly hot and spring made way for summer. The noble children prepared to return home and reconnect with their families. The lowborn who relied on the Estrine family entirely, however, remained to continue training.

Van worried whether it would be possible for him to continue his training after the trouble he caused. Sir Charleston, the sole knight aware of what he was, accompanied him on the ride back to his village.

Why he would want to travel to Southern Valley was beyond Van.

Perhaps he planned to personally inform his parents that he would not be welcome back into his home.

A paranoid thought, even for Van, but it would not leave him. It was true that he barely brought trouble to the family compared to other children. But Sir Charleston had a particular disdain for him. There was no guarantee he would be safe.

"What is going through your mind?"

The coach they rode together in had been silent for the most part. All they heard for much of the way were the wooden wheels grinding against their old axles and rolling over the dirt road.

Van felt it prudent not to make eye contact with the knight, but he could not help glancing at him every now and then.

Before departing, Van's faction got together to see each other. They all behaved excitably as they told each other the things they would share with their loved ones back home. Between Wally and Rubi, it was a competition to see who could make the other look worse. The merriment ended when everyone saw Sir Charleston boarding Van's coach.

Then talk turned to a more unpleasant subject.

The twins noticed Rubi acting uncharacteristically jittery. Everyone tried getting her to say what was on her mind. She protested that it was just last night's rancid portions still clawing at her stomach. Her lie only fooled them until they saw her twirling her hair with her finger.

Then came a ludicrous statement from Wally about the girl's maturing body. The fiery redhead ran her fist true into his gut, gagging the fool before he could finish.

Ever the curious one, Stevene asked if it had anything to do with the rumor about Sir Charleston and Lady Victoriah's past relationships.

A rumor and nothing more. That was all it could have been.

But much to Van's discomfort, that very comment was what stilled Rubi's hand. Ccuivr heard the same rumor, it seemed. Perhaps Van and Stevene would not mind scaring him with a petty joke, but that was not something Rubi would do.

Even so, Van found it difficult to believe.

The doubt he held on to and the trust he had in his friends sparked an uneasy conflict within him. Having been ignorant about many things before, Van could not be certain what to believe and what to dismiss.

He thought deeply about it during the ride home, not a word leaving his lips. The longer he spent without answers, the more it ate at him.

And, naturally, the attention Sir Charleston got from his nervous company did not sit well with him.

Asking the knight directly would not improve their situation, though. So rather than answer with the truth, Van again used another grievance to throw him astray. "You do not like me, right? Because I am Kindhrin?"

Sir Charleston seemed crossed with him for a brief moment, but nonetheless held an air of curiosity. His expression fractured when his right eyebrow rose slightly. "You know the truth. Why bother asking?"

It might not have been precisely what was on his mind, but he had thought about that often. It never ceased to frighten him how much contempt Sir Charleston held for him. All for what he was, not for anything he did or aspired to do.

"You and my parents have known each other for a long time, right? Whatever relationship you have, I don't want to be the one to ruin it. Maybe I wasn't born into their family, Sir Charleston, but ... Mother and Father care for me as they would a child they had together. I know you will not stop hating me since I am a Kindhrin. So..."

That was as far as he went. Try as he might, Van never could think of what to say beyond that. What could he have said? There was only so much that could be done to lead a lifelong impression astray.

Sir Charleston stared the child down with sharp discernment.

Van made sure to keep a straight face until the knight gave his answer.

For as much as Sir Charleston frightened him, he did not need him to stop. It mattered not whether or not the knight took a liking to him. He was a teacher, Van a mere student. Their relationship was only a means to suit each other's ends. They had their roles to play, and they would not falter from them.

The stern knight scowled for a moment and brought his hand up the bridge of his nose, pinching the space between his brows. "Hate is not something so easy to surrender, child." That might have been all he needed to say to convey his message. And yet the man's hand lingered where it was, tensing up every few moments. His closed eyes squeezed together, his head tilting downward slightly. "What I know of your kind compels me to feel that way. I do not regret it nor do I have the need to believe otherwise. For all I know, your tainted blood could awaken and lead you to seek the destruction of the land you now call home."

Van looked away from his mentor and hung his head. It hurt to be seen in that light. He loved his home. Although not how he once saw it, the realization of his true heritage and the scorn of the Vermalians now all too real, he loved the country he was raised in. It was the land where his family, his friends, everything he knew and cared about was.

Never could he understand why the Kindhrin destroyed Harah Krid.

"Do you know why I teach pages?"

Van looked back to Sir Charleston. "Family tradition?"

"Nothing so frivolous." Sir Charleston lifted his head again to look Van squarely in the eye. "I abhor children. Training them, even with a heavy hand, is no pleasure for me. Were I so inclined, I would find an excuse to leave the chateau and serve the kingdom another way.

"My family matters to me, not our traditions. I remain in Brigadier to protect them from the Renegades."

The Estrine family had gone over the topic of the Renegades in many lectures. The insurgents have been scheming to usurp the current monarchy for over a decade. Those captured alive were bold enough to call themselves revolutionaries working to remove a false king. Many good people lost their loved ones to their destructive, spontaneous revolts.

And Sir Charleston was afraid he would suffer the same loss.

Van believed he understood the message and felt all the more nervous being in the same space as him.

"There are pages who share that sentiment—you included."

The boy was taken aback by what he added.

Sir Charleston finally let his hand slip from his face. "I haven't forgotten. And I have been keeping a careful watch over you. Let it be said that I do not condone you picking fights with pages, but ... I am impressed with what you have done for your friends."

Van orchestrated to throw Sir Charleston off his trail, not be thrown off himself. He always looked at him with the harshest discontent, and now he actually offered him praise.

"...Sir?"

"Everyone has different experiences that affect who they are. I have focused so much on what you are that I neglected to remember who you had for parents. You certainly inherited their protectiveness." For a moment, Sir Charleston had a look of nostalgia. In the corner of his eye was a flicker of soberness.

It was hard for Van to believe what he heard and saw. He thought he was hallucinating. Needing further reassurance, he switched to his magic sight. Sir Charleston's valsara, while calm and steady, occasionally rippled at the center of his being. He was not telling the whole truth, although who he was denying remained uncertain.

Aware that his stare would give away his actions before long, he reverted to his regular vision.

Sir Charleston showed that he knew what the boy thought through a gruff sigh. "You've proven where your loyalty lies, Vandelas. You fight for your own, and thus, you fight for Vermalio. So long as that remains unchanged, we will not have any trouble. Understood?"

Van could scarcely hold back from gagging on the air he breathed in, but he took a breath and answered, "Yes, sir."

"Excellent."

The remainder of the ride was as quiet as when they left the city. For the first time, he felt safe in the company of the stern knight, enough to occupy himself with the moving scenery. It was the perfect distraction from the only other thing that made his muscles weak: the smoldering summer sun. Keeping watch for familiar landmarks kept his mind relaxed.

At times, Van became curious of Snowflake's whereabouts. How did she always follow him so elusively? He never saw her trail him once.

When night rolled in and the horses rested, Sir Charleston, on occasion, spoke to Van while the coachman was collecting water. Van answered Sir Charleston promptly for politeness's sake. The only thing that interested the knight was the Second Verse. He asked some unusual questions, and they brought Van to think about any changes in him, anything unusual.

Everything was normal as far as he knew. It was not a lie either. He had simply overlooked how his nose could now track the faintest of smells and that his hands worked wonders for digging or keeping a fearsome grip. It never dawned on him how or why he suddenly learned the unique swordsmanship everyone criticized either.

The only changes he noticed were how the injuries he received healed more quickly than they used to.

After going over that, they had a discussion about what the Second Verse truly was. There were points where they argued, but out of everything, they agreed it was something more than magic. They did not discuss further than that.

When night came, Sir Charleston offered himself and the boy to keep watch for threats lurking in the dark. Van had no objections—not that he had the right to refuse.

The arrival of a calm summer night quieted their restless souls. The glittering stars and a waxing crescent moon decorated the black sky, gleaming like a treasure trove that would forever remain outside the reach of man. And the grass, grown long from being untouched by human hands, danced to the gentle blow of the wind.

With the nights always peaceful and serene, Van took the time to enjoy the scenery.

One night, he rested comfortably against a tall, sturdy tree while on lookout. Sir Charleston had advised him to rest since he believed they were safe for the night, but Van could not bring himself to sleep. His mind was still fret with worry over his little fox.

Snowflake had been tracking him like a bloodhound since they met and always kept close, even when in hiding. Her wandering about on her own frightened Van sometimes. She could not possibly blend in with the greenery in the plains, and hiding from and evading predators could not be a simple task with her little body.

Van tried to reassure himself that she was safe, but could never convince himself.

With it being so dark, it would not be easy to see her. All he could do was hope nothing took her away and sleep.

A village became a rare sight during their travels. When Van caught view of Russalin, he could barely contain his excitement. He tried to keep it together the best he could to show an air of dignity suitable for a knight. Keeping still for a long period of time racked his patience, and waiting in the sunbeam peering through the window made it all the more unbearable. Remembering how healthy their chauffer's mount was helped him cope. At the very least, it kept at a quick pace.

It was not until the coach passed the first building at the village gate that he was allowed to step outside and roam freely. He was so happy to be home again that he practically flew past the coach doors.

Russalin was lively, as to be expected. The streets were littered with children at play, rambunctious and energetic. Women hung laundry outside their open windows while keeping watch over their young. Those not tending to the fields roamed the plaza, gathering around stalls for business and the latest gossip. Everyone was happy as could be.

Theirs was the prominent farming village in the region, abundant in its population and crop production. Everyone was like family to each other.

While crossing the plaza, Van eyed the dress shop. A woman had just stepped out the door with a bright smile from purchasing a beauteous pearl-colored dress, followed by a girl waving goodbye. As she stepped outside, the girl's focus shifted their way, and while it seemed to have been on the tall, suave knight, she lit up and approached Van instead.

"Welcome back!"

Van blinked. He was unaware he knew a girl taller than him. Then it hit him; her endearing blue eyes and quirky voice were unmistakable.

"Mini? Is that really you?"

Without a doubt. It became clear when she gave him her signature scowl and puffed cheeks. "Don't tell me you forgot about me already? It's only been a year."

"Sorry! Sorry! It's just that you changed so much. I never saw you with your hair down before."

Mini always used to wear her hair in two stubby pigtails. Her milky brown hair was now straight and long, held down by a silky kerchief complementing its luster.

It shocked Van that he had to look up to notice that.

"Have you gotten taller?"

Mini's smile sprouted all the way to her red cheeks. Even with her newfound grace, she still radiated a delightful child-like charm. Obviously pleased by the response, she took a step back and spun, letting her wavy dress ripple and flutter. "I've blossomed, wouldn't you say?"

"Definitely. I don't think I can call you Mini anymore."

"Oh no, you still can. I don't mind."

Sir Charleston interrupted them, loudly clearing his throat. Apparently, it was time to keep moving.

"I'm going ahead. Do not take long." He did not leave time for a reply before walking away, leaving the two children to themselves.

Why did he not order me to follow?

He always smacked the pages upside their heads whenever they got distracted. It was very uncharacteristic of him to let Van's blunder pass.

Mini questioned why the knight who healed him years back returned, but she lost interest in him quickly. It had been a long time since she saw her friend. She wanted to get reacquainted.

They kept the conversation going inside the dress shop after being interrupted by the proprietress calling Mini back inside.

Since the last winter, Mini's mother enlisted her daughter as her apprentice so she may one day continue the tailoring business she worked tirelessly to build. Her training started by learning how to stitch tears in fabric. She did no more until showing she could do it without revealing any patchwork. Mini complained about how it seemed to be going nowhere because all she had been allowed to mend were doilies.

Van sympathized with her frustrations, feeling his repetitive training also took a great deal of time and stress. But the times spent practicing one maneuver gave him a better understanding of how to use it.

Mini grew about as quickly after making so many attempts. After doilies, she started mending scarves and helping her mother make shirts. All things considered, she seemed to be doing well for herself.

But she did not want to discuss her apprenticeship. She instead hit Van with a bombardment of questions about his page training. The letters she received were considerate, but not very informative.

To begin, he regaled her with stories about his training, leaving out nothing he remembered. He discussed how strict weapons training was, how he struggled to speak Abioan and how harsh Rubi was on him whenever he mispronounced a syllable or used a word incorrectly.

Mini asked about the girl he mentioned. She listened attentively when he spoke of his other friends, although she seemed particularly interested in Rubi. Van did not mind very much. He enjoyed telling her about the friends he made; it was likely the closest she would get to meeting them.

The entire faction entertained her. True to his comedic companion, Van told her of the kind of person Wally was until she nearly choked on her laughter. Mention of fights, from verbal and from training, with Rubi nearly made her pass out.

Mentioning combat brought Mini to ask what sort of fights he had gotten into. He did not wish to speak of that, but he knew well Mini would not let him off without at least one story. If he wanted to avoid the subject, at least for the time being, he needed to think of a way to throw her off.

"I've told enough about me for now. How are Brute and Davern? Are they doing well?"

It worked like a charm. Mini fell silent. She looked terribly surprised, almost aghast, and so had her mother.

Suddenly, the happy little dress shop turned atypically despondent, almost miserable. A quick glance at their once tranquil valsara now rippling with dread alerted Van that something was wrong.

Mini swallowed before speaking and looked away from Van. "Well ... Brute became an apprentice to a visiting blacksmith from Grand Cliffs."

Now he was certain something was wrong. Her valsara rippled more when she swallowed, and she looked to be forcing her mood to change, only to worsen it. She was hiding something, and it had something to do with the boy she neglected to speak of.

When he looked to her mother, he knew it would not be kept hidden for long.

The woman stepped out from behind her counter and walked slowly to the children. "This may come as a shock, Vandelas, but please try to stay calm." She took a moment to regain composure, then smoothly explained their sudden pause. "Last winter, the Lyone family had been struck with Daezal's Vice. Although the father survived," she paused again, unable to keep from shaking her head, "Davern was not strong enough, and his mother ... lost her strength while tending to them. The poor things... They never made it to see spring."

The vigor Van held for his return faded.

The illness well-known in the southern regions as Daezal's Vice was a common cause for death. Once infected, the victim suffered from violent migraines, then stumbled over their legs in sudden weakness and could barely move. Before long, they suffered from a grueling fever that led to death unless treated with care.

Van always knew Davern was not very strong. He was always a frail one even when they first met.

No one wanted to play with him because he was skinny and pale. Davern always spent his time outside alone. He seemed so out of place. When first laying eyes on him, Van snuck away from his father so he could say hello. The lonely boy behaved skeptically at first, but the two quickly warmed up to one another. They were both able to make their first friend because of each other.

Everyone always saw Davern as a strange boy who enjoyed harvesting knowledge more than playing war, but Van admired his thirst for knowledge. He was always amazed by how much he learned.

And to learn that the bright boy had left their world...

"Van ... are you okay?" asked Mini.

Who would be okay after hearing people they once held dear had been plucked out of their lives? He did not want to hear any more.

"It's ... terrible to hear that happened to him, but there's nothing that can be done about it. Except hope his spirit has reached the Elysium."

He tried concealing his true feelings from Mini, but lying to her was difficult. She looked at him with such sympathy in her eyes. Those eyes could see right through him. They always have, and that would not change.

"I should go home. See you later."

Van hastily made for the door. He kept up that pace even after going outside, hoping to put as much distance between him and the sad truth bearing down on him as possible.

His body began to fume a thin vapor upon crossing the plaza. The anguish he held in made the pressure all the more unbearable.

He kept moving without concern for the voices around him. He heard some words directed at him, but said gave no response and kept walking.

Van managed to control himself well until climbing the hill outside the village, where the vapor brewed thick enough for a dirk to tear through. Taking refuge from the heat under a large oak, Van allowed his true feelings to surface without any eyes on him. Sorrow creased over his face, his eyes turning red, appearing ready to overflow. No tears formed despite his sadness. The cold vapor began sticking to his skin and clothes. Had he not learned such control over the Second Verse, it would have frozen him.

Expressing such emotion in public was always frowned upon. It was important for everyone, regardless of class, to maintain an air of dignity until they found themselves alone or in the company of loved ones. Even sadness over deceased loved ones was meant to be concealed from prying eyes.

His mind ran amok. He thought he would react much more dynamically to the news of his first friend's painful passing. Tears were expected, howls of anguish, pounding the earth in a fury he could not contain. But Van only huddled himself against a tree. Again and again he asked himself why he did not do anything more over hearing Davern was gone.

Perhaps it might have been worse had he seen the dead body with his own eyes.

No... I don't want that...

Van snapped out of his grief, flinching when he heard something come his way. It was the sound of the ground shifting under shoes of thin material. A shadow loomed over him by the time he looked up. He tried to keep his face straight, but he could not help looking surprised.

It was his mother.

She must have been expecting something of a rare occasion because the woman had shed her heavy armor for a lovely dark violet dress. Van had never seen her in any feminine clothes before, and had been taken aback by the sight of her.

"Van, are you okay?"

Van was still fixated on Victoriah's inclination to wear something besides armor. He wanted to tell her what was wrong, but all that passed his lips was a broken whimper.

Victoriah crouched down to her son and gave him a sympathetic look. "You heard about Davern, huh?"

Van only nodded.

Victoriah leaned in and wrapped her arms around her child. She held him gently, her arms brushing along him slowly, a hand caressing the back of his head and bringing him closer.

It felt strange to be in her embrace without metal plating pressing against him. The soft dress almost made it feel like he was hugging someone else, but those familiarly firm muscles reassured him it was her. Her steady heartbeat soothed him. Although he no longer felt her warmth, that embrace still comforted him.

He did not want her to pull away when she did.

"Come on, let's go home. I got a nice, fat chicken waiting for us."

Van nodded and followed his mother. Grief gnawed at his insides so incessantly it made his already empty stomach snarl like a coyote. If anything, he could bury his sorrow in her heavenly food.

It had been so long since he crossed that path, Van almost forgot how it was shaped. The dirt path that dug into the grassy road led up the hill toward the steep crest, where his home, the humble little cottage, sat. He remembered how when he was younger that he thought it had been made by a giant snake slithering across the cliffs.

The trees of the forest began to stand tall around them, gracing them with a comforting shade, the higher they climbed. Allowing his eyes to wander, Van noticed a small troop of huilo monkeys going wild on the branches. At first, they seemed to be having fun, but a closer look showed they were at conflict with one another. He recalled their love for sweet fruits and assumed it was over that.

The smallest monkey hopping frantically from branch to branch near the big-jawed one reminded Van of how Davern and Brute used to argue. Their disagreements would start small before escalating. Then Brute would resort to chasing the frail boy until wrapping an arm around his neck and slowly choking him just enough so he may speak. Either he would keep going until Davern would admit to being wrong or, when she still resided in the village, Mari would tackle him and force him to release the boy.

Suddenly, Van did not feel as troubled. But the memory of his friends only reminded him that making more would not happen.

A familiar outrageous neighing at the top of the hill caught Van's attention. With a smile, he rushed up the hill to say hello to Timberhoof.

The massive warhorse was as delighted to see the human child as he was to see him. Van eagerly reached for the snout Timberhoof lowered to meet him. His fur was smoother than he remembered. His mistress had to have been grooming him more thoroughly lately—a good thing considering she always left dirt in the horse's mane.

"How have you been, big fella? Has Mother been treating you well?"

Timberhoof snorted hard enough to bury the human child's face in a spatter of mucus. Trying to refrain from holding it against the horse, Van wiped his face clean, then noticed a rather fatigued look in his eyes.

She was pushing him again.

Van smiled, then reached out to scratch down his mane until stopping from a small jolt of pain shooting up his leg. Below him sat the little fox he spent many a night worrying over.

It was a wonderful relief to know another of his friends had not perished without his knowing.

He crouched down to Snowflake's level and scooped her up in his arms, holding her near and playfully ruffling her plush fur. Snowflake returned his affections with a lick to his cheek.

As he petted her, the earthy air reaching his nostrils had been cut off by the succulent aroma of roasted poultry.

Van left the stables, bringing Snowflake with him, and made way for the front door to his loving home. He went inside to find Jerrell sitting patiently at the table and Victoriah stocking it with a plethora of food. Lying on a platter at the center of it all was the plump chicken he smelled from outside. Its scent was not the only appealing aspect; the crisp orange skin soaked in its own grease looked tantalizingly juicy, and the way the meat tore so easily when Victoriah served it made his mouth water.

"Don't be shy, love. Come on in and enjoy!"

Victoriah's invitation beckoned him like a siren's song to a drunken seafarer. He carried the fox inside and joined his family, sitting opposite his father. Upon putting Snowflake on the floor, Van helped himself to the potatoes and corncob on his plate while waiting for a slice of the chicken. It had been so long since he enjoyed his mother's cooking. He barely stopped a moment to breathe in the flavors that excited him so.

Half of his plate had been cleaned by the time he realized his table manners were less than acceptable. Pausing with a strip of chicken still in his teeth, he looked up to see his mother laughing heartily like a stout old man and his father staring at him with a grin. He pried the chicken loose, setting the fork holding it on his plate, and swallowed. "I apologize for my uncouth behavior. The food is delicious."

His manners only made Victoriah laugh harder. "Don't start acting like Charlie now, Van. No need to act so stiff here."

With that said, Victoriah turned her attention to the snowfleece fox hiding behind her son. It was hard to tell whether she was bothered by the new creature in her territory or sizing it up, testing it to see what it would do. Snowflake stared back at the human woman, trying to show she was not afraid of the dominant force in her pet's family. Jerrell looked between the two of them, curious to see who would look away first.

Van just kept eating. It would do him no good to start thinking those two would not get along.

"The same goes for you too." Victoriah reached for the chicken, tearing off a flimsy piece, then tossed it on the floor in direction of the fox. She was making an offering for Snowflake to show she was welcome. The situation seemed a bit reversed, but intriguing nonetheless.

Snowflake did not know what to make of the woman's offering, having never been served food that way. She stepped up to the scrap, sniffing it. Reluctant at first, though quite peckish, she accepted it.

She seemed to like the taste. Snowflake looked back up at Victoriah with different eyes than from before. She did not like the woman yet, but any suspicion and disdain toward her vanished.

Van stopped eating, left in awe. For once, Snowflake was willingly approaching another human being without baring claws or fangs. She slowly stepped closer to Victoriah, looking up at her, adhering to caution and curiosity both. She stopped at the foot of Victoriah's chair. Carefully, she gently scratched against the chair leg.

Victoriah looked down into the fox's pleading eyes, unmoved by the irresistible charm of their round sapphire allure. "You liked that, huh? All right then." She took a lumpy piece set to the side of the chicken and bent down to hand it to Snowflake this time. "Help yourself to the heart."

Slowly, Snowflake leaned in toward the heart for another sample smell, then snatched it and swiftly ran back behind Van's chair.

It seemed Victoriah took a liking to Snowflake. She always saved the hearts for herself. She never let anyone else have it. She even fought Jerrell for it on occasion.

"So that's the angry little fox you told me about, eh?" Victoriah leaned toward her husband and nudged him rowdily. Jerrell always complained over how aggressive Snowflake was toward him, even when he only intended to help her.

Van nodded before devouring the last of the chicken on his plate. "She follows me wherever I go, even if it means she has to hide from others."

Jerrell bore a dry smile. "Even if you threw her out, I doubt that would keep her away. The little devil always found us no matter where we climbed in the Sperov Mountains."

"I always thought the first girl that claimed Van would be human, but it doesn't look like this one will let you go."

Victoriah's little jab did not pass her son as remotely entertaining. At the very least, it did not look like the Wolverine minded the extra mouth to feed.

"You can keep the fox since she likes you so much, Van, but you'll have to take good care of her. Keep her fed, groomed, and make sure to clean up after her."

"In other words, treat her better than your mother does Timberhoof," Jerrell chided.

Van could not help laughing, but stopped himself after catching the Wolverine's gaze shifting callously toward his father. He had trouble anticipating whether she would whack him with her unfinished chicken leg or scold him. When Van raised his cup to take a quick swig of ivory juice, he heard a gagging sound from across the table, meaning she got to her feet and reached an arm over Jerrell's neck for a choke hold. Upon lowering the cup, he found that was exactly what happened.

The married couple had teased and quarreled with each other so many times that it was easy to see how they would react.

"You want to go another round after what I did to you yesterday?" stated Victoriah with a wicked smile.

It was always frightening to hear she still treated her crippled husband so roughly.

"Oh! By the way, Van," Victoriah spoke after releasing Jerrell, "how'd you like to go on a hunting trip?"

Van withheld from taking a bite of his second serving of chicken.

"You really want me to come with you?"

"Of course! Think about it—the three of us on the prowl, searching for the strongest prey, our prizes roasting over a roaring fire under the magical night sky. It'll be a lot of fun."

She always had a way with words. Everything she said excited him.

"I'm sorry. Did you say the *three* of us?"

Victoriah turned back to her husband, her arms folded. "Yes, I did. You've been stuck in this village ever since you got back from the Sperov Mountains, just wasting away. Crippled or not, you need to keep in shape, so you're coming with us even if I have to drag you alongside Timberhoof. Besides, it's been ages since we've all been together. It'll be good bonding time before I'm supposed to ride again."

Even as those two quarreled, no matter how angry or sarcastic either of them was, they always had a hint of love and care in their words. Victoriah still smiled, showing all of her beautiful teeth and the color in her face; Jerrell still remained calm and comfortable whether seeing his wife's joy or temper.

Happy their relationship still stood strong, Van partook in the rest of his dinner, eager for more food and time with his wonderful parents.

That night, Van slept much more peacefully than he had in months. Without the angst that came with worrying over Snowflake, fear of being found out as a Kindhrin, and dreading the morning bell, sleep came easily.

But halfway through the night, he had an awful nightmare; he was being chased by a pack of shapeless beasts. He could not escape them even after slipping away and finding cover. Their howling followed him, filling his head, driving him mad. Every thought had been chased away, leaving only fear in its place. Before he could find out what would become of him, everything faded.

When Van awoke, his head throbbed from an inexplicable pain. Barely any light peered inside, but it still strained his eyes terribly. His muscles ached. His head spun from trying to lift it so much as an inch off the pillow. When he finally sat up, he felt his gut was about to cave in.

He could not let the pain bother him. Today was the day he and his parents would leave for an exciting outing, and he refused to miss it.

He took slow, deep breaths to numb the pain.

Snowflake crawled over to Van from the head of the bed, her eyes speckled with concern. Van, to prove he was well, took one last breath and reached out to scratch the fox's fluffy scalp.

After pacifying her, Van took his hand back and pushed himself off the bed. He needed to be slow because of the tearing sensation rending his stomach, but he eventually relaxed and went into the hall.

It seemed unusual for Snowflake to follow him instead of leaving before someone else saw her. Having her by his side made Van feel more at home.

That joy slowly melted into confusion.

Something about the air seemed different. He felt very comfortable with it; that was not right. Normally, around this time of year, the air was much too warm for Van to be completely comfortable. But now the air felt cool, refreshing.

Upon reaching the end of the hall, he came to an abrupt halt. In front of him was a gaping hole where the front door used to be, jagged ice clustered around it. Victoriah and Jerrell were struggling to remove the ice, chipping away at the surface; Jerrell worked at it with an old sword, Victoriah with a thick axe. No matter how they hurled their weapons, they left nothing more than scratches on the surface and chipped away naught but shavings.

And as he looked around the room, he noticed shards of ice had been scattered all around. A few chairs were broken and the dining table was punctured. The family portrait had been torn, a piece separating baby Van from his beloved parents. The enchantment imbued on the paint went haywire; it was supposed to depict the baby as Vermalian whenever someone other than the family entered their home, but now the magic flickered erratically, causing him to have pale peach skin on one side of his face and russet on the other. The colorless stone on the frame that supported the enchantment was only chipped—perhaps it could be fixed.

"This isn't working," Jerrell grunted. "We'll never get this cleared before the sun fully rises. The villagers will see—"

"Forget about them. I'm more worried about Van."

Victoriah's words perplexed him. Skeptical, Van looked back at the ice with his magic sight. At first, he only felt the cold carried from the ice by a brush of wind, but then his eyes widened in disbelief. The ice contained concentrated traces of his valsara.

Even with the proof in front of him, he could not believe it. He had no memory of using the Second Verse since returning home. What's more, it had been used in a malicious manner.

"I ... did this?"

His parents jumped when they heard his overwhelmed voice. They turned around, surprised to see he was awake and among them.

"You don't remember?" Jerrell asked.

Victoriah walked up to her son. She kneeled down to him, ignoring Snowflake's growling, grasping her hands at his shoulders. "Van, what happened last night?" It seemed she still wanted to confirm it herself.

"Last night? I was asleep all night ... wasn't I?" His memories conflicted with what he now knew, making him anxious and afraid. "What happened? Where did the door go!? Why is everything—"

"Easy! Easy, Van. Calm down now." Victoriah tried pacifying him with a gentle tone. She pulled him closer and took a hand from his shoulder to tenderly stroke the back of his head. "You woke up last night when someone visited. It was Charlie."

"S-Sir Charleston...?"

"He came by for a little talk about your power. And you came out here, agitated and confused. You kept saying these crazy things I couldn't understand; it's like you thought he was trying to attack me. Then you attacked him, hurling ice and threatening to freeze him.

"We tried to get you to stop. We even tried pinning you down, but..."

Van could not believe his ears. Denying it did not seem possible at this point. The evidence clearly showed that a skirmish took place, and it was just as obvious that he was the instigator.

His actions frightened him. For as callous as the man was toward him, Van never once thought about attacking Sir Charleston. He did not hate him nor did he wish him harm, even with his animosity for the Kindhrin. But now Van began to question how well he knew himself and what he denied as he looked at the destruction he caused.

"Charlie knocked you out before anything else could happen."

If he was the one to do it, it meant he was okay. That helped Van calm down, and he tried to focus only on that, not what it would eventually lead to.

"He said it had something to do with your Second Verse. I honestly don't see it, but I trust his word."

Van was as perplexed as his mother. Of the many things his Second Verse affected, his volition and memory were not of them, so he thought.

"Maybe your control slipped since you haven't been using your power often. If that's all, then we just need to have you train a little more... The hunting trip is a perfect opportunity for that."

"We're still going...?" he asked with a voice riddled with guilt.

"As soon as we fix everything here." Victoriah patted her son's head, then turned to her husband. "Jerrell, dear, can you go see how much lumber we got left?"

Jerrell left behind his sword, giving a sigh of relief, and exited through the opening where the door once was. It looked like the extra effort was straining his arm.

"Let's take care of the ice. Then we can start rebuilding."

Victoriah stood back up and took her axe back in hand. Another swing bored the weapon into the ice, a crack about an inch wide forming.

Van did not move from the hallway, still bothered by what had transpired. Whether it was his power taking control or a drowsy Van abusing it, he still endangered a man who did no wrong, and he knew of only one thing that could make him act that way.

"Mother ... you said Sir Charleston was an old friend once... What sort of relationship did you two have?"

Victoriah stopped her axe mid-swing upon hearing that question. She looked back to her son, an eyebrow raised, looking like she was half upset. Then she inhaled, chuckled a little, and shook her head with a wry smile. "That's what Charlie meant by rumors. Oh boy. Come over here and I'll tell you everything."

He did as he was told, eager to hear what she might say. She talked while she worked, swinging the axe where she thought it would leave a mark. "Back when I was a page, your father was not the only one who took an interest in me. For whatever reason, Charlie found me 'a refreshing beauty' and 'a gem rarer than the strongest aurichalcum'—yeah, those were his words. He sure was a sweet talker back then. I rejected his feelings because, even though I didn't acknowledge it at the time, I was already smitten with your father.

"But Charlie wouldn't accept that and often challenged him to all sorts of duels when we became squires. They were already in the middle of a swordfight when I found out about it from my meister knight. I watched them for a bit for laughs, but it became boring fast, so I joined the fight and slaughtered the both of them."

Van was not sure he wanted to interrupt after seeing how enthusiastic Victoriah got mentioning a slaughter.

"A lot of girls dream of men fighting over them. Me, I found it insulting those two thought I couldn't choose for myself."

Van could not help but say, "And you still chose Father."

Victoriah nodded before driving the axe into the crack she made. "Charlie is a sweet guy, but way too protective. A guy like him would not approve of his wife being a knight. Besides, I always feel comfortable with your father. He can take the way I speak without feeling insulted, knows how to make me laugh, and can keep up with me when we tussle."

Suddenly, Van began to feel he was the kingdom's biggest fool for doubting the connection his parents had.

"Charlie got over me and found another woman to love. If he hadn't, I'd have lost all respect for him. So believe me when I say whatever rumor you heard is a load of pigswill."

It had to be the truth. His mother hated pathetic people and did not take to them lightly if proven a problem.

His mind clear once more, Van looked to the ice he so maliciously sculpted. Again, he closed his eyes to focus on the energy stored inside. The *clang, clang* constantly resonating from Victoriah's axe proved no distraction. The ice seemed different from when looking upon it with magic sight. At certain angles, there seemed to be trails where the power ran the strongest, which, while peculiar, gave him an idea.

Van raised his arms, examined the flow once again, then tightly clenched his hands. As he had, his influence immediately reached over to the cluster and, in response, the cluster broke loose from the cabin's structure, shattering into thousands of glittery specks.

When opening his eyes again, breaking the magic sight, he saw the ice was gone, and all that remained was the gaping hole.

His mother stood there, staring blankly at the nothing left behind. Her shock was more intense than when she heard her child question her loyalty to her husband. Victoriah held on to it when looking down at her son. Van smiled, and while a tad uneasy from the sudden demonstration of power, so did she.

~ Fifteenth Chapter ~

Growing Stronger

Autumn returned to Vermalio after a long summer. The farmers of Russalin gathered the last harvest of the year—a sign that it was time again for Van to return to Brigadier.

He could not relax during the journey back. It felt like he was being sent to his death. There was no chance that Sir Charleston would forgive the attempt on his life. It was clear what went through his mind to Jerrell, who rode the coach with him. He wanted to reassure his son that he was safe; if Sir Charleston intended to kill him, he would not have taken his eyes off of him, even if it meant provoking the fierce Wolverine. And his parents would not send him back if there was the risk of him doing so.

Regardless of his feelings, an apology was in order. The moment he returned to the Estrine Chateau, Van made for Sir Charleston's quarters.

Approaching the massive doors to his quarters made his blood run cold. His courage gradually slipped away the closer he got to them. But he had already gone that far. He knew the air needed to be cleared without any further delays, and forced his knuckle against the door.

"Enter!"

Van pushed the door open and made his way inside.

Sir Charleston's eyes were set on him quickly. His silence and that malicious gaze boded terribly for Van, who so foolishly marched into the lion's den. It was only his patience, waiting for the Kindhrin to reveal his true skin as he had when they were alone, that kept him quiet.

Van did not reach for the Shift Pendant until forcing his hand to stop trembling. He was afraid to reveal himself now, but the conversation would not begin unless he did what was expected of him.

The knight did not look any less hostile when he saw the spell fade around the Kindhrin child. "What business do you have with me?"

It was best to get to the point before losing his nerve. Pressing his arms firm against his sides, Van bent his spine into a perfect bow. "Sir Charleston, I humbly beg your forgiveness. My actions against you were inexcusable." He stayed that way for many minutes, awaiting his response without moving an inch out of the bow.

He began to shake after holding it for so long. Sir Charleston had yet to say anything, only watching his reactions. He needed to hold on until the knight decided on what to do.

It seemed like Sir Charleston was ignoring him when the sound of a quill pen dragging against parchment reached his ear.

"After the lessons end on nights of the full moon, you are to return to your bedchamber and remain there until morning. No exceptions!"

Van stood straight again, a gasp escaping him. "Um ... pardon my asking, sir, but ... why only the nights of the full moon?"

The enmity emitting from Sir Charleston partially diminished as he stopped writing his letter. Hostility still lingered in his stare, but it wavered. Somehow, he seemed less malicious, more disturbed. "You really aren't aware, are you?"

Van's mute confusion confirmed his suspicions quickly.

Sir Charleston let out a brusque sigh and set down his quill, then motioned the boy to approach. As Van stepped closer, he leaned forward, resting his chin onto his linked hands. "I've been investigating the nature of your Second Verse for some time. And what I noticed about you has led me to believe you rely on abilities not of normal man... It almost seems fitting to thank you. Your attack on me that night allowed me to prove my theory. Your eyes told me everything I needed to know—you've become a beast enslaved by your instincts."

What he said frightened Van. Those words burned his ears and pricked at his chest. The need to run jolted through his legs, but he remained in place. "Sir Charleston, you told my mother the Second Verse had something to do with what happened. What did you mean? How could my power make me act like that?"

"Your power did nothing to you." He paused to look upon the disbelief on Van's face. "The term 'Second Verse' relates to both your power and your state of existence. Before you were killed, you existed as an ordinary human being. But upon revival, you became something else. Nascitte are revived with their bodies, and at times, their minds, reformed to ensure survival. The process is different for each one, and from what I have seen, yours involves adopting the attributes of beasts, particularly when the full moon is out, as it was that night."

Many believed that an animal's instincts were heightened when under the light of the full moon. Stories have spread far and wide of how beasts of burden disobeyed and even threatened their owners under its influence. It was the very reason why churchmen often blindfolded their mounts during the nights when the full moon shone.

While he did not threaten his own, Van did remember being told how he targeted Sir Charleston in particular. Because he thought that he was threatening his family, that he was taking away his mother. He had become impulsive, enough for rational thought to lag and drastically affect decision making.

"Regardless of your intent, I cannot risk you endangering anyone due to your lack of control. You may even harm your own faction without realizing it if given the motivation."

Ignorance kept Van from realizing many truths. And for it to delude him from his own behavior, he agreed it would be dangerous for him to be around others when he could impulsively maim anything without conscience. Until he learned control, he needed to keep his distance.

"Is that all?"

"Y-Yes, sir."

"Then be on your way."

"Sir!" Van responded with a salute.

He reactivated his Shift Pendant and exited Sir Charleston's study forthwith. He left with as many questions as answers.

No one had disturbed the few belongings he brought along and set aside to speak with the stern knight properly. It only went to show how few pages arrived before training officially began. Still, Van knew it was wise to deliver them to his room before taking to the banquet hall.

He was assigned to the same room as last year, so he knew where to go. The halls had a more pleasant air than usual. Much of the facility never seemed friendly, with many of the pages always keeping their distance or teasing him about how much time he spent in the stables. The paths were committed to memory by using those upsetting times as landmarks and connecting them.

From Sir Charleston's quarters, where he went for a few reasons, there was a left turn to the stairs. Taking them to the second floor, it was a straight path with many of the servants' bedchambers on both sides of the hall. At the end of the path was another flight of stairs connecting to the ground level. Afterwards, it was only a matter of walking across the foyer, up the next flight of stairs, and turning right upon reaching the second floor to reach the boys' wing.

He arrived in the foyer after he finished mentally reciting the directions. The halls were quiet and tranquil until the sound of collective footsteps penetrated the silence. A little startled, Van hid behind the corner, from which he saw a gathering of children marching down the hall opposite him. Very few pages were about when he arrived, and not as many associated with one another unless they were close. Seeing so many group together piqued his curiosity and, soon after, his suspicion. They all moved quickly, as though aiming to avoid detection.

Curious, Van left his things and decided to pursue them.

He followed the group closely while keeping a fair distance. It was easy to do so since he had yet to reclaim his chain mail. A few pages tried to speak, and he listened in very carefully to find out about what, but they were silenced immediately. But by who? It was difficult to see the front of the group, and whoever urged them to remain quiet kept their voice so low even Van had trouble hearing it.

They had all gone deep into the chateau's eastern corridors, but they could not go much farther. Everyone made a turn leading to a dead end. Very few went down the far eastern halls of the chateau. Even servants rarely went to that section since there were not many significant rooms there aside from storage. It was the perfect space to hide a shared secret.

Van slunk along the wall, remaining hidden behind the corner. Minutes went by without anything being said. They had to be very wary of the chance of anyone passing by. The silence extended to a point where it became unusual. When Van peered over the corner to see what was happening, he found nothing. Nary a soul.

He leaped out from behind the wall to inspect the corridor. It made no sense. They all marched toward a dead end with no turns into other halls or stairs to climb. The sound of footsteps stopped when they reached the end. And yet they were gone, vanished into thin air.

The more he thought about it, the more his head spun. Confusion warped his mind as he reached the end of the hall until becoming a migraine, a menacing, painful bolt digging into the crevasses in his brain. He nearly doubled over it hurt so much.

By the time it faded, his concentration had abandoned him. Where he was going and what he was doing had slipped his mind. His thoughts blurred until he took a few steps back and thought things through.

That's right... I was bringing my things to my bedchamber.

He turned back the way he came without a second thought or recollection of how he got so far from the lower western halls.

No one crossed his path while he retraced his steps. It was to be expected since barely any pages came to the chateau so soon.

Having the boys' wing all to himself, Van breathed in the soft air it always had before the afternoon, when everyone went every which way. It was relaxing to hear only the gentle wind moving faintly through the hall, sweeping the dust off open windowsills. The walls carried those sounds beautifully, creating a tune that was almost musical.

Relaxing as it was, Van could not ignore his arms aching from carrying the bearskin satchel holding his weights. He needed to set them down before his arms snapped. Once he arrived at his bedchamber, he set the satchel down, a tired grunt passing his lips. He almost regretted not accepting his father's help to see him inside and bring the weights to his room when he had the chance, but he did not want him agitating his scars.

Having taken a moment to rest his muscles, he reached into his pocket for the key. Feeling skin where metal should have rested brought his patience to an end. There was a hole in his pocket, a small one but apparently wide enough for the key to slip through.

Van gritted his teeth he was so frustrated, struggling to avoid letting out a howl that would carry for the next mile.

"Is there something you require, Young Master?"

All of Van's tension melted away upon hearing that voice. That voice, that sweet tone could only belong to one person. When turning around to identify her, he lost the composure he strived to keep.

It was Lyn.

The young woman was as prim and peppy as she had been before slipping into a coma, drained of her magic. Her blue eyes carried a dazzling luster strongly contrasting that she had been fatally ill months earlier.

Along with the three sets of page uniforms slung over her left arm, Lyn pulled out a key matching the one he lost.

Knowing they were still in the hall, Van withheld his excitement and stood aside. Lyn slid the key into the keyhole and pushed the door open.

When they entered and shut the door behind them, Van let his excitement show again, ambushing Lyn with a bear hug. After setting his uniforms atop the dresser, she returned that affection.

"You're well again?" asked the boy, his eyes aglitter.

She nodded. "I am."

"You're not still groggy? It's not hard to walk?"

Lyn reached a hand out and stroked the boy's scalp. Her touch soothed Van into silence.

It was most unbecoming for a maid to lay a hand on a noble, fallen or otherwise, in such a manner. For Van to address a servant so familiarly was also frowned upon, but he did not reject the rapport between them. He liked Lyn and her wonderfully kind nature.

When she thought his tension was gone and they let each other go, Lyn slipped a hand around her collar. There was a light *click, click* of metal coming from her blouse. She took out a silver lavaliere hung around her neck, and on it hung the glowing blue aurichalcum Van had given her. She had given it a lovely chain in place of the worn string.

"I endured a great deal of pain while I was being stripped of my magic. No matter how much time passed or how much I hurt, it would not go away. Every moment, I was frightened death would come to claim me. And then ..." She grasped the protective charm like she would someone's hand. "It all vanished, fast as the summer rain."

It brought Van great relief to know the charm he worked so hard to create protected her from further anguish.

"I do not remember ever wearing jewelry before the day I fell ill. You gave this to me, didn't you?"

Van nodded.

"I did not understand why the pain faded when it happened. I feared it was an omen that my time had finally come. But when I woke up to find this on me, I knew it had to have been what saved me.

"Thank you for working so hard to make this for me."

Those final words sent a frightful chill up Van's spine. He masked his discomfort quickly and tried to appear confused instead.

"What are you talking about? I didn't make it. I found it in a mage's workshop when I strolled through the city. When he said it could cure you, I had to get it." His words were somewhat rushed and barely convincing, but it was all Van could muster after being so caught off guard.

Lyn looked a bit confused, then snapped out of it. "Oh, excuse me. That was a slip of the tongue—embarrassing, truly."

It was the first time her words failed to reassure him.

The maid crouched down to Van's level and patted his head gently. "But you know, pages are forbidden from making deals with the charm brokers in Brigadier. Many have been accused of using such items to cheat in training." She drew her hand away from Van's head and instead used it to cup his shoulder. "But you did it to help me, and for that, I am forever grateful. Let's keep this our little secret, okay?"

Van nodded again. "Thank you, Lyn."

"You're more than welcome. Well..." The maid stood tall again. "I have other duties I must tend to, so if you'll excuse me, Young Master."

Van watched Lyn go with a smile on his face, expressing joy for her health and letting her know her kindness was much appreciated. But when he was alone, just him and his thoughts, he slumped against the sill of his bed, letting out a groggy sigh, a white breath passing his lips.

He was still taken aback by what Lyn had said to him. The way she chose to express herself was all too alarming. It was no slip of the tongue. Thanking him for making the charm she now wore stated she knew he possessed some sort of power. She said it with confidence, as if she did not need proof to know what to believe.

If Lyn was aware of his power, what else had she discovered? That he could communicate with animals? That he had been harboring one since he first arrived? Or worst yet...

The subject strained his mind terribly, as well as his stomach. He was safe for now, so the matter would wait until after lunch. Maybe then he could wrap his head around how to think and what to do.

A cloud of delightful aromas wafted from the banquet hall, beckoning Van to follow and partake in what was offered. Inside was spread after spread of gourmet food presented at the edge of the room.

It was the same as last year; delectable food was served to the pages to lure the new into a sense of comfort before showing them what donkey feed they would be eating for the rest of their stay. Van never understood why the Estrine family played such a cruel joke, but he was not inclined to ask. Getting a few words in was not worth a month of serving the Estrine family during dinner and only dining on stale bread and water afterward.

Luckily, the food always sat well with him.

Everyone always took the opportunity while the buffets were there, stuffing their gullets until moving became irksome. His appetite having grown over the summer, Van had to restrain himself to keep a presentable appearance while walking to the buffet.

It was favorable for the pages to act as upstanding members of the royal court everywhere eyes may follow. The knights expected absolute perfection, and not just in combat training. Whenever an Estrine noticed a slight upset in a page's posture, manners, language, even hygiene, they put the pages through an entire seminar to better themselves in areas they lacked in until it left them sore.

"A mistake is not the last thing you want to make," the Estrines said.

During the summer, Van realized how vital that discipline was. His mother used those same words on their hunting trip across the southern plateau, after he was nearly battered to death by an angry bear. He got between it and a bush of midnight vipers without realizing it, and the bear—and her cubs—were not happy about that.

Van was not certain what nearly killed him that day—the bear's humongous paws or his mother crushing him in her viselike arms in trying to get him to cough up the poisonous berries.

"Glad to see you've come back to us, mate."

Wally greeted his friend as he walked over to the table. His friendly disposition could not be concealed, unlike his face, which had been eclipsed by a mound of food.

It was good to see a friend he grew as close to as the one who departed.

"I take it the Estrines aren't bothered by you being here anymore?" Wally asked, sitting across his friend. The outgoing lad jammed a slab of mutton into his jaws the moment he stopped talking, wanting to make use of his mouth one way or the other.

"I'm never too sure, but since I am here, it can only be assumed."

Wally shrugged. "So long as you're Victoriah the Wolverine's runt, you'll get sour stares from basically everyone here."

He was not wrong. Things would not likely be different from the previous year. Whether it was scorn from parents passed down to their children or begrudged pages envious that they did not have one of the Six Champions to teach them, Van was victim to the resentment of many. It was something he learned to deal with in silence.

But it was still vexing all the same. Stabbing a ham slice brutally with a fork, Van tore away at the meat. After sliding the thick meat down his throat, he reached for his mug of ivory juice, chugging it down until breathless. All their negativity only fueled Van's ambition.

"It's no different from the criticisms every page, you and me included, has about the Estrines when their backs are turned."

Wally's eye twitched involuntarily at the response, then he snickered. "What exactly did you hear me say?" He was ready for a good laugh.

"Quite a bit. From your comment on Lord Estrine having 'a voice as deafening as a screaming whale' to what you said last spring: 'Ol' Charlie is so uptight I'm betting even his mount would like to ram its hoof up his—" Van grunted when interrupted by something rapping against his ankle, his teeth clenched tight.

That was normally when Ccuivr would cut Wally off by smacking him across the head.

Realizing it was a swift kick from under the table, Van glared at Wally and the impish grin he flashed.

"You don't want to be saying anything I would."

The frustration in Van's stare lessened when he caught on that Wally was only looking out for him. His japes and teasing were so commonplace with others, he always wondered why he held back with him.

A familiar fragrance tickled at his nose.

"No, no! Let him keep going." Placing her plate next to Van's, Rubi sat down beside him cross-legged, a fishbone hanging from her lips. "I kind of want to hear him say it."

"What'd he do to you, grisly? I thought you liked the guy."

"Who are you calling grisly?"

"What, you can call me ape and I'm just to take it? You always did remind me of an angry bear, like the one my father put on his mantle."

Rubi scoffed, unimpressed. "I would have thought a fool like you would have come up with something more inspired."

"I did, but I'll save those for when I can get you the angriest. Maybe I'll be lucky enough to see your face turn as red as your hair."

Van could not help but crack a smile. The little arguments and brawls those two had used to make him nervous, but seeing them go at it again made him happy. After all, it was their way of getting along. Perhaps it did not start that way, but, deny it though they would, they grew fond each other.

"I didn't think either of you would have arrived so soon." He chose to speak when the two began eating instead of hurling insults.

Rubi set down the bright tropical fruit she smacked between her teeth, wiping the juice dripping at the edges of her mouth with a free hand. Judging by the satisfied pant, it must have been particularly sweet.

Wally finished off his meat before speaking. "My father was displeased with the review he was given, so he sent me back early. And I'm to remain here next summer so I can 'learn to be of proper use,' like he said."

The relationship Wally had with his family was, as per the norm, unfortunately strained. For someone who spent his time pulling practical jokes and teasing the weak-witted, Wally actually progressed fairly well.

A few of the senior knights even favored him over many of the other first-years—when he was not fooling around. His older brothers must have been greatly renowned knights for his parents to put so much pressure on their youngest male.

Even though his voice remained perfectly nonchalant, his valsara shivered. He held a powerful animosity against his father, who was never pleased with his efforts.

Rubi whipped her face and looked over to Van. "I actually requested to arrive early so I could see you."

The boys had fallen silent at hearing Rubi's comment.

Van was surprised that he would be the object of her focus. "Really? Why is that?"

"Isn't it obvious? I can't make myself known to Victoriah the Wolverine if her son outshines me," she said with a laugh. "I've been practicing my own technique over the summer, and I could not wait to try it out on you."

What she said came across as flattery to Van. Rubi had been so fixated on the possibility of becoming Victoriah the Wolverine's squire ever since she met him. That she wanted to outshine him meant she worried the champion would pick him instead.

When thinking about who would prepare him for knighthood, Van often thought she might consider getting a squire when he became ready to be one. It was rather presumptive; she had once told him she had no interest in mentoring anyone. But it was fun to think about.

Being squire to the Champion of Heart would be an incredible opportunity. However, heavy-handed and unrelenting as she was, Victoriah was still his mother. She coddled him all his life. Even though she began handling him a bit rougher, Van found it hard to believe she would be entirely comfortable leading him into life-and-death situations.

As far as he was concerned, it would not be the worst thing for Rubi to be her squire instead of him. She would likely be a better fit.

Keeping a calm demeanor, Van picked up a baked potato from his plate. He ate it like he would an apple. "I'll gladly take you on after we've eaten. We can put more energy into it that way."

Rubi grinned and took to her food, rather enthusiastically.

Wally was already scarfing down everything on his plate. Nothing could stop his appetite.

Somewhere along the line, though Van was not certain how, those two competed to see who could clear their plate first. It did not make sense considering Rubi's was only covered the surface whereas Wally's food scaled up to his neck, but Wally cleared through an entire layer whenever Rubi finished a portion.

Strangely, Van could not take his eyes off the two. He ate his meal at his own pace, intrigued by what might happen when they had a winner.

Once the three had their fill, they headed for the training grounds, ready and eager to challenge each other's grit. After a summer of wrestling with the scariest animal alive, Van felt confident he could take them on.

But Wally and Rubi got into another argument as they neared the training grounds; they both wanted to be the ones to face his wild swordsmanship first. When they got there, they decided to compete for that as well.

It was enjoyable to watch them go at each other. They put so much more energy into their attacks when they competed against each other, more so than when they faced the others.

The weapon Wally chose to confront his friends was a glaive. Rubi chose an axe. Van kept his father's old practice sword and its scabbard at the hip, ready for his dance with the winner.

"Oh, I am going to enjoy this! I've been itching to throw you on your arse since I saw your ugly mug again."

Wally yawned, portraying disinterest in Rubi's taunting. His silence and smug look irked Rubi, coaxing a fierce leer from her. Their eyes locked, the competitive drive in them flaring. They wielded their weapons in a violent manner, as they would against real threats.

Wary of the other's abilities, they waited for their foe to make the first move. They were fully aware of the skills they possessed and cautious of how much impact they could leave.

Van's gaze shifted between Wally and Rubi, wondering which would move first.

Rubi was very strong. Van once saw her lift an entire barrel filled with the Estrines' dull weaponry and carry it all the way to the stables in repetitions. One strike from her would be enough to knock someone her size off their feet.

Wally was one of the spriest pages in the chateau. He moved quicker than many. The main reason he survived being targeted by the many he pulled pranks on was he could outrun and outsmart any of them. When applied to combat, those traits kept him out of his enemy's reach and put him in close when he needed to.

Unable to resist anymore, Rubi charged headstrong at Wally with her axe held to her side. She shocked both her opponent and their spectator by closing the gap between her and Wally in a quick stride.

Wally deftly raised the pole of his glaive before his face, which protected it from Rubi's strong uppercut. He then made his counterattack, shoving his opponent away and thrusting the glaive's dull blade at her. She moved out of the way and attempted to circle Wally, but he followed her with a wave of the glaive, forcing her to move back.

Their reflexes have gotten sharper. And Rubi was learning to use her lithe body to her advantage.

As the battle continued, it became easier for Van to track and predict their movements. He steadily lost interest after he figured out what they were doing five steps ahead of them, and his mind began to wander.

As it did, he began reminiscing about his time hunting with his parents.

When they first arrived in the expansive southern plateau, there were so many animals, predator and prey alike, on the prowl. Graceful deer leaping through the glades, cunning coyotes lurking, observant raptorial birds soaring through the air, powerful bears idly marching through the lush greenery—it made Van think of a community similar to the city.

He was so excited to bag some prey, but his parents insisted on setting up camp somewhere secluded beforehand. Excited as he was, he followed his parents' lead and helped find a suitable spot. Anyplace with a cave or trampled foliage would not do, as they would likely have been home to territorial animals. Eventually, they found a very appealing spot behind a hill too steep even for coyotes to scale with some foliage to shield them from view. They decided to stop there and rest.

Victoriah surveyed the perimeter while her husband and child gathered firewood and set up a tent. She did not come back for a while.

While waiting with his father, Van took an interest in the birds that flew overhead. Many of them were small and spry, and they danced beautifully in the air.

His mother took her time inspecting the area and familiarizing herself with the movements of the local fauna. She wanted to be prepared. Contrary to the unflattering rumors about her, Victoriah the Wolverine knew how to use her head. A knight tracking enemy troops or escaped criminals was no different from a hunter tracking its prey.

They spent the first day recuperating their energy and showing Van how the animals moved. It bored him at first, but when Victoriah explained how thrilling it would be when he stalked the animals, the prey unaware of their presence, and pounced once the opportunity was upon him, his eyes lit up.

Seeing how energetically the deer danced around the landscape made Van so excited that he could barely sleep the night away. His parents expected as much and tried to tire him out with a little sparring. If nothing else, his mother's brutal attacks and his father's controlled precision tired him out before the moon fully peaked in the sky.

At dawn, Van awoke with the energy of a hopeful pup. He pestered his parents to wake up, shaking them vigorously until they joined him in the world of the living, as he had in his earlier years.

He was all too eager to begin the hunt and show his parents what he could do. Victoriah and Jerrell managed to keep him calm by imparting a few pearls of wisdom they learned. That only kept him steady for so long.

Despite his excitement, when he stepped outside of the campsite and out in the open, he managed to remain perfectly silent and mask his presence. No jittery movements. No impulsive firing of the arrow. Just silent breathing and waiting for precisely the right moment to shoot either a vital artery or a vulnerable limb.

One shot was all that was permitted, and he missed. His aim was off, and the wind current carried the arrow further away. That was all the deer he targeted needed to notice them and escape. How disheartening it was to fail in front of them.

But Van did not give up and eventually shot one down.

It felt wonderful to be the one bringing the family something for a change. He found it fulfilling to know he could handle that responsibility, to know he could do something for them.

It was later that day when he met the bear that nearly maimed him.

"Okay, okay! I give!"

Memory lane had been wrecked by Wally's shouting.

While Van was recollecting good times, Rubi had already settled her match with Wally. She had him flat on his back with her axe held just a hair's length away from his throat.

When she thought the poor fool had enough, she took the blunt weapon away from his throat and stood tall and proud. She was out of breath for a moment, but quickly regained her strength and turned her attention—and her weapon—to her spectator. "You're next, Van! Pick up that sword and come at me!"

Her energy was infectious. With a confident grin, Van took both the sword and scabbard in hand and marched toward the fierce young woman.

This time, he was going to enjoy confronting an angry bear.

Two days before the lessons were scheduled to begin, Lord Estrine took a number of pages into the city. It was just after sunrise. Merchants were still preparing their stalls and shops for their customers' arrival. Mothers were opening windows to let sunlight into their homes and wake their families. It was the only time of day the streets were clear and quiet.

That made it harder for the pages to get away with whispering gossip or asking questions. Such a shame. Van wanted to hear what the others thought about their little outing. He did not know what they were doing.

While the pages were supposed to keep a dignified appearance in public, he found it more difficult to hold a straight face when the sun had been blocked out so suddenly. He had never been so close to the royal palace before. He only saw it whenever crossing through the square, when it appeared the size of the Estrine Chateau from a distance. Standing in front of the colossal gates alone overwhelmed him. The tallest tower stood so high, looking up at it nearly snapped his neck. The only people who looked directly upward at the sky were stargazers and those praying to the gods.

A rattling metal screech shook Van from his thoughts. The gates pried loose from the ground, opening a way for the arriving party.

We're ... going inside the palace!?

Van breathed deeply. Were he to get too excited, he would perspire, and everyone would see the vapor coming off his skin. He needed only to keep a stern face and straight posture, as an unwavering soldier would.

Van averted his eyes before the gates opened all the way. The sun's light gleamed brilliantly through the gate, as if it were inside its very confines. It was only its light reflecting off the knights suited in pearl-white armor standing at attention in two rows of three.

He had heard about them. Those Holy Knights were a special unit of soldiers blessed by the church. They were as revered as the Six Champions, though not as powerful. Protecting the capital and the royal family from imminent threats was their sole responsibility, which explained why many outside the capital had not heard of them. He did not understand what set them apart from other knights aside from that.

A few of the Holy Knights approached Sir Charleston and Lord Estrine, both of them saluting out of courtesy. The Estrine knights offered them the same formality in return. The Holy Knights exchanged a few words with them, then turned to the pages. Even though their exquisitely forged helms covered their faces, their heavy stares could be felt as they drew over Van and the other children.

Their conversation concluded, the Estrine knights and pages followed the two Holy Knights. Van kept his guard up when crossing the four Holy Knights at their posts. Their valsara was intense, unnaturally intimidating, yet seemed eerily calm all the same. It was unnerving.

The palace grounds spread farther out than the chateau's vast fields, although it was also much more crowded with useless adornments and these complex hedge mazes. A straight path paved with marble and granite led them to the palace.

Van struggled to avoid looking ahead instead of up at the clouds, where he assumed the tower spires reached.

At the path's end stood the palace entrance. The Holy Knights went ahead to open the gate. By the time their guests caught up, their way in had already been prepared.

The hallways shared an intricate design similar to the ones in the Estrine Chateau except they were lined more so with empty suits of armor than vases and paintings. The armor was especially impressive, casting reflections of the passing pages.

Van was not comfortable with the new environment. Ever since he learned Lyn might have learned of his secret, he became suspicious of approaching others.

After a day, he knew Lyn could be relied on. She stepped away from her duties whenever she spotted him in the halls and knocked at his door every time she walked by it. It was all to see if Van needed anything, be it clothing or tea or even a friendly chat. Never once had he sensed hostile intent from her.

She could be trusted, whether she knew or not, but that could not be said for others. It was bad enough so many knew about his true colors already. If the wrong person found out, his life would be forfeit.

And the royal court must have been filled with as many people who despised Victoriah the Wolverine, his mother, as there were who revered her. Short as his stay would be, he could not relax.

"We'll reach the throne room shortly," said a Holy Knight.

The pages became excited after hearing that. Van, however, did not notice. He heard something unusual come from the hall to his right. The sound did not ring clear, so it had to have been far away or came from something small. When he turned to the others to ask if they heard it, everyone had already gone ahead.

Since everyone already went on, never noticing they left him behind, Van decided to investigate on his own.

Every hall looked exactly the same no matter which way he turned. He would have lost his way if the noise had not kept echoing through the halls. Following it was easy. It became chirpier and whinier the closer he got to it. Not even an infant human could imitate such meek mewling. It belonged to an animal.

A humid breeze carried the next cry directly to him. He followed the trail, relying on the feeling alone rather than the sound.

He eventually happened upon an open window. As strange as it seemed, that was the only window without any glass covering it. He could not comprehend if it was a style of design or if someone broke it and never had it replaced, but he did not bother caring. Outside the window, he found a branchy tree holding the thing crying for help.

It was a small kitten.

The helpless thing perched itself on the tree's highest branch and stared up to the palace walls. It kept looking that way and letting out this squeaky mewling.

The poor thing must not have learned how to climb down trees yet.

Without any other thought, Van clasped the windowsill and leaped through the opening. The kitten needed help, and he was glad to offer it. He walked up to the tree at an eased pace. If he wanted the kitten to know he meant no harm, it could not see him approaching too quickly, or it might be frightened.

The kitten turned its attention onto Van as soon as he walked under the tree's bare branches.

"Hello there," he said with a smile and gentle voice. Letting the small creature know he was friendly would reassure it to let him come closer. He was not worried it would flee if he had not smiled, but the kitten could not have been more than a year old—it was adorable.

The kitten crawled across the branch it was on to meet him, its tail swinging in a character almost canine. It cried the most captivating *mrow* before stopping in place.

Looks to be domesticated after all, Van thought, relieved.

The trunk looked too thin to support an adult, but after lightly knocking at its base, Van found he would manage. "I'm coming to help now, okay?"

The kitten mewled again in response. He failed to interpret what that high squeaking meant; perhaps it could not understand him well either. A few kind words did not go to waste, though, especially when addressing something so young.

Van removed the practice sword from his side so it would not get in the way, then gripped the tree's thick bark and started climbing. He soon got to a branch within arm's length, but its support was flimsy at best. Taking that branch and having it snap in his grip would only shake the tree and startle the poor kitten. He needed to go higher.

He continued upward, careful of where he grabbed so he did not fall, slowly getting closer to the next branch. It was tempting to jump then, but he resisted the urge, knowing perfectly well how painful the landing would be if that did not go well. His fingers started trembling. At this rate, he would fall if he did not grab a branch soon.

When the branch finally came within reach, Van stretched his left arm to grab it. His fingers could barely tap its edge. He kept pushing higher to the point the muscles in his arm began knotting up. His right hand slipped off the tree trunk as he finally grabbed hold of the branch. It was difficult to hold on, but he grabbed hold with his free arm before losing his grip.

He started climbing as soon as the feeling in his hands returned, scaling the branches like a fragmented ladder. The kitten was enthusiastic, mewling louder and scampering along the branch the closer Van got to it.

He found himself beside the kitten before realizing he climbed over twenty feet. He saw the kitten's slick brown fur glisten in the light, and when it cried, it exposed its little fangs and healthy pink gums. It was well taken care of. Van waited until the excitable little creature had settled down before presenting it his palm, allowing it to inspect his scent.

"Let's get you down now," Van said when the kitten pointed its flat nose back up at him.

He arched his hand behind the kitten, petting it for comfort, then gently scooped it by the belly and pulled it close.

The climb down was not as strenuous as going up. In fact, it was not a climb at all. Instead of taking the long route, he decided to jump through the gap in the branches. The kitten struggled a bit, flailing its forepaws in the few seconds both of them plummeted to the bed of thin grass, but calmed again after the air stopped lashing at its fur.

Van landed crouched over on his feet and his free hand, still holding the kitten up away from the ground. A numbing pain rattled all the way to his knees and elbow and lingered, but when it faded enough that he could ignore it, he set the kitten down and stood back up.

"There, you're free." It crossed his mind that the kitten lived in the palace, so he did not bother telling it to run along back home.

Yet when he turned to collect his sword and return to his pack, the kitten kept hanging on his tail. He could not go back to Sir Charleston with an animal following him and risk worsening his already anticipated diatribe for moving on his own. But he could not shoo the little thing away either. It was already cuddling up against his legs and purring euphorically.

It was neither enemy nor pest nor prey. Against animals not seen in such ways, Van only considered them as friends.

Squatting down to the kitten's level, he scratched the back of its neck before picking it up again. "I suppose returning you to your family would be best."

He went back the way he came—climbing through the open window.

The royal palace was a large place. Searching high and low an entire day would leave half of the place still uninspected. But that pessimistic thinking would only hinder his progress before it began.

Van wandered down the hall leading deeper inside. Someone would be able to help him find the kitten's owner. All he had to do was keep going and run into someone.

Strangely enough, not a single guard patrolled the innermost halls. No matter how deep he went, no one came to greet him. Somewhere along the way, however, he sensed someone nearby.

Then, when the silence seemed the most petulant, a sound finally resonated. A hoary, dry sound, it was perhaps from a wise mage. The kitten seemed more enthusiastic upon hearing it across the hall.

That had to be its owner. Van hurriedly paced down the hall to the next left turn, where the voice rang loudest. Curiosity taking over yet again, he used his magic sight to determine what sort of person the kitten's owner was. The valsara of three people filled his vision when he turned the corner. The silhouette standing tall in the middle held a spirit uncanny compared to the others. Several profound desires surrounded a single core, spiraling somewhat chaotically but still presenting a majestic presence.

What sort of person could possess such an unfathomable valsara?

Van opened his eyes to get that answer, but stood tensely when the world around him returned. He almost could not believe who stood in front of him.

It was Faustign L. S. Vermalio.

~ Sixteenth Chapter ~

Lost

"Oh ho! There you are, Lorelei."

The kitten leaped out of Van's arms and ran gleefully to the king upon hearing its name. The king bent down to pick it up, keeping a hand caressed behind its ears. He played with the little animal, then turned to the boy before him.

"And who might you be, young one?" King Faustign asked.

Van was relieved that the king did not seem too alarmed by his presence. In accordance with the custom for addressing royalty, Van waved his hand over his heart, pressed it against his ribs, and bowed his head. "V-Vandelas Kronas of Southern Valley, milord." He bit his tongue immediately upon realizing he had forgotten to address the king as "my liege" instead of as mere nobility.

King Faustign's dry laughter only made his slip of the tongue feel all the more humiliating, though it was not out of ill contempt. He seemed to be experiencing a faint nostalgia, based on what he saw in his impressive valsara. "So you are Lady Victoriah and Sir Jerrell's son? I wondered oft what the progeny of such magnificent people would be like," said the king with a smile. "You remind me much of your father."

The Shift Pendant masked Van's appearance enough to deceive even the king. It was both satisfying and left a foul taste in his mouth.

"And you are a page under the Estrine family's jurisdiction, yes? I suppose this would explain Sir Charleston's behavior during my address: one of his students had broken from his leash."

Van tried to keep composed and not worry about what awaited him.

King Faustign petted the kitten in his arm, scratching under its white chin when he looked up. "But it seems your absence resulted in finding this little scoundrel. Pray tell, where did you find him?"

"Lorelei, was it?" The kitten answered Van with a cute cry. He felt humbled to be addressed even though his master was among them. "He was outside, atop one of the trees in your courtyard down this hall."

"Hm. How peculiar. My knights have searched that area a great many times without luck." It must have meant Lorelei was much better at hiding—much like the clingy Snowflake—than the human guards expected. "Well, regardless, I am grateful for your assistance in finding him."

"I am glad to be of service. But, and excuse me for prying, my liege, how did Lorelei find himself outside on his own?"

The royal did not seem to mind the question. "This little one favors himself quite the mischief-maker," King Faustign stated while twirling his finger for the kitten to playfully bat at. He then looked to Van, his kindly red eyes in perfect view. "Whenever the queen and I are enjoying our leisure, Lorelei always makes a fuss. And whenever he sees an open door or window, he sneaks through unnoticed. There were times before when he used to nuzzle and purr at our feet or wrestle with his siblings, but he stopped that about a month ago so he could torture us instead." Many would normally throw a cat out to fend for itself for things like that, but King Faustign spoke as though he enjoyed the mischief.

Looking down at the kitten, who spent his time overly excited by his master's taunting, playfully sinking his incisors into the man's thumb, his actions appeared to contradict with the king's words. He had fun with him.

Lorelei looked to the king with absolute glee, so much that he gained an energy merely from hearing his voice.

It must have been lonely. The kitten was not trying to misbehave; he only wanted attention from his favorite human and found a means to get it.

By the time Van realized that he had been speaking his thoughts aloud, they had already been conveyed to the king.

King Faustign looked at him with mild surprise. He probably had not heard many children so bold as to correct something they knew nothing about. It was difficult to determine what he thought.

Then Lorelei started mewling in a timely manner, letting it be known the stranger was correct. He stopped after the eleventh *mrow.*

The king laughed drolly. "It would seem I need to spend more time with this little one at my lap." He continued to pet the kitten, moving his hand vigorously to tire the little thing out. Lorelei sounded so happy purring with such euphoria. "Quite remarkable, to be able to read Lorelei so well. Perhaps you have an innate ability to connect with animals."

Innate was an interesting way to put it. Van always had a way with animals before his death, but could never communicate with them so well without Pruina's influence.

"How would you like to learn how to train the hunting dogs here?"

If anything else had been said after that, it went unnoticed. It was not so surprising that he would be treated kindly by the king, but to be so casually given such an amazing opportunity, it was unnerving. Refusing such a generous proposal from the king would be entirely unforgivable, so to avoid confrontation, but mostly because he would love to work with animals, Van gave a simple nod.

The smile drawn across King Faustign's face showed he was pleased. He looked over to one of his knights, giving him a silent motion.

"It was a pleasure to meet you, young Vandelas. I look forward to seeing your growth in these next few years."

Van watched how the knight approached him, then looked back to the king and again saluted him. "Thank you, Your Majesty."

The knight escorted Van back to the Estrine Chateau. When stepping away from the palace grounds, Van noticed several commoners had turned away from their tasks to stare at the Holy Knight. It made him uncomfortable, but he could not do anything about it.

What happened upon his return was all too predictable. Sir Charleston barked such vile rebukes at the page for losing his way that it almost shook the chateau's foundation. He had never been so furious as to express his disapproval so loudly for those eavesdropping. It almost made Van question the choice he made in following Lorelei's feeble cries.

The Holy Knight said nothing, remaining patient and at attention during the diatribe. But when Sir Charleston approached him to apologize for taking up his time, the Holy Knight explained to him the proposal from the king.

It left the stern instructor suddenly inert.

All those eavesdropping began making more racket than the knights in whispering to each other, curious why the conversation suddenly died down. Van only heard offensive words—nothing he wanted to repeat.

The day lessons began was the same day squires and young knights at the palace learned to train the hunting dogs, but attending was impossible.

Four days had passed since the moon transitioned into its second waxing phase, meaning the full moon was expected to rise that very night. Van needed to remain locked inside his bedchamber for everyone's safety. There he remained until the moon finally began its waning phase again.

Time could not have moved slower.

While Snowflake relished in having time with her compliable pet, Van became depressed before the first evening of captivity ended. He needed to keep himself occupied. The most he could do within the confined space was continue his studies and perform simple exercises.

One hour made him realize how small his bedchamber was. Soon after, he became claustrophobic. He grew irritable before the sun even set.

Had Snowflake not been there to keep him company, he was not sure he could bear the isolation. Her constant demands for pets and brushing kept the illusions of walls closing in at bay and distracted him from the pages training outside. After a few days, she even started bringing him snacks to cheer him up, although he was not comfortable eating mice. At least he learned she did not have to steal food to sustain herself.

Just as a precaution, Van chose to sleep before the sun set. The decision, however, left him restless until it became dark.

The night after that, he decided to use the time to strengthen his mind so he might conquer his instincts. He sat quietly in the middle of the room, his mind blank.

Thinking about nothing reinforced his irate mood even more. The impatience at being confined made his teeth ache for something to chew on. To distract him from that, he began thinking about the exciting hand-to-hand combat exercises Sir Charleston began teaching the pages.

Without the need to carry anything in hand, Van felt more adept in a fight against the other pages. The training he had given himself, wearing the weights to strengthen his muscles, resulted in quicker movement and stronger strikes.

For Van, who had always been bested by everyone in swordplay exercises, finally being able to beat them was as savory as the tart juices of midnight vipers. And it became all the sweeter when he fought Kallant.

Many of the pages, however, did not take kindly to his way of fighting. They thought it cheap, shameful, unknightly even. Perhaps they were right. He basically imitated moves his mother demonstrated to him. She often took her "survival is all the matters" philosophy too far.

However, their combat instructor said nothing against it, and instead punished the pages for their poor behavior with cleaning duty.

Since he would not say anything bad of the fighting style, Van stopped thinking badly of it himself. That did not mean other pages felt the same. Everyone began calling him "the beast spawn."

One afternoon, when everyone regrouped to find new sparring partners, Van ended up with Rubi. For a moment, he thought he could enjoy the exercise, but as he took his stance, he suddenly felt afraid. The abrasive girl leered painfully at him, her eyes masking any kindness she had. Less hostility had been there when she attacked Wally.

Those cruel eyes reminded him of a mountain cat that sought him for food on his hunting trip.

When the round began, Rubi lunged at him, prepared to knock him to the ground. He narrowly leaped out of the way before then. Had Van been any slower, the fight would have been over in that instant. She was really serious, more so than he had ever seen of her. Rubi's stance left no openings despite the rash advances she made.

Van kept his distance. He could not find it in himself to get too close to her without flinching.

Everyone had seen what she did to the poor northerner after he spoke to her so condescendingly for acting tough, instead of prim, proper, and polite, because she was a girl. No one had seen him after the lessons ended that day, and when his faction next saw him, the northerner was completely unrecognizable under the bruises and throbbing black eye. No one spoke a word of it to the Estrines. The boy was worried about whatever pride he had left, and the others were terrified of being Rubi's next victim.

The look she gave Van showed she intended to disfigure him next. Fortunately, he escaped her. Shameful as it was, all he could do was keep evading the punches she threw, fleeing from her every chance he got, until Sir Charleston called for another change in partners.

There were some maneuvers that could have been used against her, recalling how she slowed down slightly whenever throwing a punch. But fear of what she might have done to him left him incapable of implementing them. No one ever rattled him so before.

Even when the fight ended, Van could not relax when Rubi looked back at him. She raised her right hand into view and clenched a fist as if to say, "I'm not done with you yet!"

This year's hunting trip came earlier than anyone expected. The sun was still buried behind dark clouds and snow still blanketed the land. Winter had yet to leave Vermalio.

Prince Aeron explained to his friends how the Estrines preferred to set the trips at different times of year, and they were especially careful when planning hunts in the winter. They relied on mages from the palace to predict whether the winter would be harsh or merciful.

The mages must have given positive predictions to allow one group to explore the northern mountains.

Lord Tamsilac himself guided a group of pages through a ruined tor called the Ravaged Precipice. Tales of dragons having once done battle in those mountains spread across the country. It was the very reason travellers stayed clear of the range and the valley carved through it.

East to the Ravaged Precipice lay an abyssal chasm where it was said the stronger dragon dug its nest. A great many bold adventurers ventured into it to discover what secrets the chasm held. None of them were heard from again.

Thankfully, dragons were only an old myth, otherwise everyone would have been terrified to journey there.

The first mountain towered over the land where the chasm ended. Several more stood after that one, each taller than the last. A deep valley cut through the center of the mountain range, appearing as though something tore through it.

Taking children to such a dangerous place made about as much sense as having a brittle old man be their guide.

The party arrived at the Precipice in coaches. Lord Tamsilac ordered the pages to vacate them before they reached the mountains. All thirteen of them obeyed without complaint, but they wished they had done otherwise when the elderly Estrine told the coachmen to head for the nearest settlement. "If you don't find us here by the time you've returned, assume the worst and don't bother with a search." The coachmen laughed at the old man, assuming he was joking, but the pages were not convinced.

It was hard to believe Lord Tamsilac was so upbeat about the outing when no one else even cracked a smile.

The party hiked about ten miles across the flat landscape before reaching the first foothill, then climbed until it got dark. They finally stopped to set up camp once they came upon suitable ground. It was flat and covered by a layer of snow. A few blades of grass could be seen here and there, so it meant the powdery blanket was thin, making it easier to set everything up.

The pages collapsed when finally allowed to rest. Lord Tamsilac, unbelievably, still had more energy than a spry hare. He probably could have set up the campsite himself, but he made everyone play their part regardless of how tired they were.

Since so few pages had been selected to endure the trip, there was more to be done around the campsite. Most of the pages were slowed by fatigue and the chilling grip of winter.

Unaffected by the cold and still with energy to spare, Van volunteered to set up a few tents other than his own. He did not beg for unfrozen air or give in to fatigue like the others.

This climb is nothing compared to the Sperov Mountains.

While he set up tents, allowing a few to rest, he spotted Rubi doing the same at the opposite end of camp. She was the only other part of his faction to join Lord Tamsilac's party—the worst possible one.

She had been giving him and the rest of their faction the cold shoulder since autumn. Everyone tried approaching her at least once—even Wally—so they could figure out what had been bothering her. She only answered their questions with a clenched fist or a venomous tongue.

Van made the most effort to confront her, only to be rewarded with bloody screams and bodily injuries. Everyone thought he had done something terrible for her to react that way toward him.

He flinched when Rubi's stare fell on him. They locked eyes for but a moment, then she returned to her work. Van felt relieved she had not gone after him again, but he also regretted feeling that. He did not want her to stay away. He wanted them to get along again.

The tents had been set up without a word spoken.

It was too late in the day to begin the hunt, and everyone was exhausted. Lord Tamsilac could not have his pages too weak to do anything in the morning. He rewarded their efforts thus far by building a great fire and handing each page a pouch of emergency rations. The pouches held enough to sate their hunger for the night.

Everyone gathered around the fire to enjoy some form of comfort before the day ended.

Van sat alone against a tree while sinking his teeth into a sandwich made of stale biscuits and dried ham. Someone needed to keep watch: that was the excuse he made to keep away from the fire. The heat that comforted the others would only wear him out.

The fire lit up the entire site. Just looking at it from where he was, Van could tell it would keep everyone warm well until they went to sleep.

"Hey."

Van swallowed what he had left in his mouth before looking up. Rubi stood before him, arms crossed. She did not appear as intense as before.

"Come on over to the fire. You won't be of any use if you catch cold." That was the first thing she said to him in the four months her silent treatment lasted. Her words came across as cold, callous, and sharp, but for her to say that, she had to be concerned for him to an extent.

It meant a lot that she chose to speak to him again. And yet—

"Don't worry about me. I'm keeping watch."

He gave her the same response everyone else heard from him. It was not just because he did not want to go by the fire. She chose not to speak with him for so long, to treat him like he did something horrible. It wounded him, and even though he tried to overlook it, he could not ignore how much it hurt.

He had been waiting for Rubi to feel she could approach him again, and now he was brushing her off, turning her away.

He thought he was in trouble when she inhaled and puffed out her chest, a sign that she was going to lash out. Relief washed over him when she only exhaled a heavy white breath and turned around.

It seemed she would actually let him eat in peace.

A heavy pressure lifting from his shoulders, Van focused again on the last piece of the biscuit sandwich in his hand. He stopped it halfway toward his mouth when he heard a stern *thump* by his head.

A snowball had been thrown at the tree trunk, narrowly missing his head. The impact was hard enough to shake some flecks from the branches.

"Get up. Now!"

There it was—the blind desire to fight.

Van looked aghast at Rubi as she readied herself for hand-to-hand combat. From looking into her eyes, he could tell she would charge at him if he did not face her, as she had done time and again.

It had been the same routine again and again, again and again and again, for months. He had enough. Van tossed the sandwich piece into his mouth and swallowed, then stood and stared her down.

She stopped speaking to him and retorted to any kindness shown with hostility. If a good scuffle was what it took for Van to gain any grasp on what was going on with her, then he would do it.

Rubi rushed forward for the first strike. All too predictable.

Van took a sidestep and tripped her against the tree. He did not feel any guilt. It revealed how much pent-up hostility she held on to since the last time she challenged him, allowing herself to fall for that.

Unamused by that unsightly trick, Rubi gave Van a mean glare. She got back up quickly and charged again.

This time, he did not move out of the way. His training these past months made him strong. He felt confident he could withstand Rubi's attack.

Her first strike pounded at his rib cage, sending rattling shocks over his chest. It was like being hit by a club, but Van endured. He blocked her next swing and repaid her twofold, throwing a fist into her stomach. When she stumbled back, he tackled and threw her to the snow bed, and tumbled down with her when she grabbed his collar.

The two of them began wrestling around on the ground. Neither of them allowed the other the advantage of getting back onto their feet. They shoved each other's faces into the ground and rammed the other into thick trees and bristly bushes.

They got so caught up in their brawl that they failed to pay attention to their surroundings. That carelessness cost them.

Unable to keep up with Rubi, Van lost the upper hand to her and was pinned to the ground. The force she used was unreal. He no longer felt the snow encasing his body, but instead the world around him breaking apart. It all slammed into his back in an instant, and the weight pressing at him from all sides nearly crushed him.

By the time he realized what happened, his vision faded.

Rubi's voice soon called to him, keeping him from slipping away.

When next he opened his eyes, the sky had become pitch-black. Everything looked much farther away than it was before. The clouds dispersed, giving way to the twinkling stars. A moon almost nonexistent hung behind the frail cliff from where they had fallen from.

How long had it been since they began fighting? How far had they strayed from the camp?

"—hear me?"

Van glanced weakly to his side. Rubi had her hands on him, shaking him. Her face expressed more concern than he had ever seen from her. Once she noticed he looked to her, she pulled away and fell silent again, her eyes wide with alarm.

Van struggled to sit up, unable to move competently atop the heap of loose snow and torn fir branches beneath him. Breathing became difficult; his chest palpitated uncomfortably whenever he inhaled. His spine felt like it might collapse no matter which position he sat in.

A rough tear ran along his back. Van turned back to see Rubi had pulled a barbed twig from his chain mail.

"Thank you..." It felt difficult to say that to her after they had gotten into such a frenzied scuffle. "You're not hurt, are you?"

"No. I'm fine. You cushioned my fall. I doubt I'm in any worse shape than you."

Van managed to stand despite the splitting pain in his tailbone. While hunched over, he noticed the small pouch with his emergency rations was gone. It must have been ripped from his waist during the fall. Nothing hung from the tree branches above except the occasional icicle.

He consulted Rubi about her rations. She nearly panicked when she found out her bag had disappeared too. The icicles nearly rattled at the volume her voice rang. When he thought she would alert the wildlife, he went up to her and firmly cupped her shoulder. For a moment, he thought she would scream even louder, but somehow, it had the opposite effect. She went silent and looked at his hand on her shoulder until he pulled it away.

What was most important was getting back to the campsite.

They agreed on that at least. Using their knowledge of the shape of the valley and the position of the new moon from where it rose, they determined where they should go and went down a stone path devoid of vegetation.

A soft breeze swept snow off the cold stone path.

They kept close to the mountain wall as they moved, wary of the ground breaking apart from under them again. Perhaps it was not the best option, but it was smarter than wandering blindly in the open. Even with their eyes adjusted to the darkness, it was difficult to see what was where.

Along the way, Van stumbled over when his hand did not lean against anything. He found a small opening in the wall upon picking himself up. It was a lucky find.

Rubi punched him in the back. "Why did you stop?"

"Let's rest here for the night."

"We don't have time for that! If we don't hurry, Lord Tamsilac will leave without us!"

"We're not the only ones out here for the hunt." He tried to contain his frustration, but could not help growling a little. "If we don't take cover for the night, getting back to the others will be the least of our worries."

A frightened expression drew over Rubi's face. If she planned to further protest, she lost all will to when looking directly at him.

Van walked into the opening but did not sit down until Rubi conceded and joined him. She took to the opposite end of the small opening, practically pressing herself against the wall.

"Don't even think about huddling up to me for warmth. It's your fault we're in this mess."

"Yes, Lady Ivanstronge," he groaned.

Rubi punched him again for the last time that night. She hated being called that. She hated being reminded of her place in her family.

As insufferable as her behavior was, Van still felt relieved Rubi was acknowledging him again. He looked up to the stars, thinking about everything he might have said to upset her—as he had done many a long night—before falling asleep.

Van awoke to an intense throbbing at the side of his head. He had fallen against a rough stone protruding from the wall. Rubi stood above him angrier than ever, having shoved him hard enough to leave a mark.

"What did you do that for?"

Rubi scoffed coarsely and turned away from him. "I told you not to huddle up to me," she said aggressively. "Pay attention to what I say."

She was acting ridiculous. Van had been sleeping the whole night. Even if he did wake up, there would have been no point in leaning against her to keep warm. He was physically incapable of feeling it.

Regardless of his unease, Van made no unnecessary retort. They did not have time for this.

The sun had risen. A new day was upon them. What mattered was getting back to the others before Lord Tamsilac really did leave them behind, preferably before the moon rose again.

They were not wrong to fear abandonment. Lord Tamsilac gave less sympathy to the pages than Sir Charleston. He was blunt with his disapproval and harsh in his punishments. It made Van wonder what sort of knight he was in his prime.

"Get up already! We can't waste any more time."

Van listened to Rubu without revealing his burgeoning frustration. It was best to express it after they safely returned to the group.

"It's already past daybreak, so everyone will already be advancing farther into the mountains. We need to pick up the pace."

Van nodded, to which Rubi glared bitterly at for a brief second. The angry girl turned around to lead them, then abruptly stopped. "How are you at foraging?"

The subtlety she used when asking told Van she was not the best huntress. He kept that to himself to avoid confrontation. "We should be able to find something. We'll walk and search."

That answer seemed to be enough to put her at ease for the moment.

Although they lacked the arrows they would normally be given, they still had sharp short swords given to them in place of their practice ones. If they came across something small, they had the means to give it a quick death and give them something to eat.

Rubi led the way. She knew the plans Lord Tamsilac told everyone that gathered around the fire the night before. She was their best hope of getting back.

The valley fostered many obstacles—large stones obscuring their path, sudden gaping tears in the ground—that impaired their journey. The two cautioned against approaching any dead ends, still shaken up from when they fell from the cliff. There were as many beauties to this place as there were perils. The landscape, while wrecked and torn apart, still kept together enough for plants to grow unimpeded. Trees grew from the rocky walls, bending upward over patches of grass that would have otherwise been buried by snow. Fruit grew from the branches underneath the protection. Some were not suitable for human consumption, but Rubi managed to weed out the ones they could eat.

A few berries were not enough to fill their stomachs, but they would give them a little more energy. A little was better than nothing. Northern Vermalio was frightfully cold in the winter, and the nights were much worse. Their bodies used more energy just to survive those nights.

At least Rubi's did.

While Van no longer felt warmth, the cold never affected him, no matter how frigid it became, and his body, thus, did not need to use the extra energy. He remembered how it affected normal people, though, from his time with his father in the Sperov Mountains.

When they sat down for some rest, Van talked of how impressive the Ravaged Precipice's valley looked. He imagined what changes there would have been in the spring.

His vengeful companion was not amused by the wonder he saw. "Van," she growled, "have you forgotten how this valley was formed? The mountain that once stood here was reduced to rubble. Dragons destroyed this once beautiful land and made it into this ... mess." Her voice was brooding the entire time. "Didn't Lady Victoriah teach you not to revel in the things evil beings create?"

Even though she said that, he did not feel the same. How could anyone not be amazed at what they have seen? It was true the valley had been destroyed—maybe not by dragons, but definitely by something. That was not what he found amazing. The fact that life prospered and adapted to the changes so magnificently was what captivated him.

The conversation died. Rubi did not want to talk to him. Van's frustration made him cave into snacking on a few midnight vipers he found.

He doubted she would care if she saw him eating the poisonous berries, but there would be less fuss that way. Even if he was mad at her now, he wanted her to keep her energy up. The midnight vipers did not poison him. Eating them meant she could eat the safe ones.

Night had fallen than they anticipated. It was time to once again stop and rest after an excruciating trek. But they never crossed the valley. They never found a safe place to hide. If they spent too much longer wandering in the open, the local predators would have some rare treats to share. They needed to hurry to the mountain walls.

Van and Rubi kept to the bushes and trees, relying on them for protection if they should need it. Nothing short of a long reach would be of any imminent threat to them within the camouflage.

Every few feet or so, Van could hear his companion saying something under a heavy breath.

Great Gaia, grant me sanctum.

Great Gaia, grant me sanctum.

It was a chant that travellers often said when they traversed dangerous places.

When he stepped closer, Van saw her eyes frozen open. Her hands were trembling.

It took him aback. Rubi always behaved so brash and confident, even when addressing a knight of high rank or a noble outclassing her. He had never seen her afraid before.

He wanted to wait a little longer before addressing the matter, but if nothing else, it would at least distract her from her fear.

"Rubi ... why are you upset with me?"

The redhead came to a complete stop when he spoke. Van thought it best to talk while they were on the move, but knew rushing her would only make the friction between them unnecessarily awkward. He could not have that, and waited patiently for a response.

He wondered what was going on in her head. Her valsara changed hues again and again so quickly it made identifying emotions impossible. How one person changed moods so quickly befuddled him. The milieu in Rubi changed between several different hues until they began converging.

What could it mean? Van asked himself.

Finally sorting out what she thought, Rubi turned abruptly around. Her eyes portrayed anger. "Stop saying stupid things now of all times!" She tried to intimidate him into not asking any more questions.

It was a mistake to ask, but not because it upset her. Her hostility and dismissive attitude these past few months have been bothering him so much. And that snippy response pushed him over the edge.

"All this time, I thought you constantly fought with me because you are upset about something."

Rubi tried interrupting, but Van would not have it.

"Anyone who has seen us fight thought I did something terrible to you. I've been pestered with questions asking the same thing, even by our own friends, which you dragged into your little grudge against me. Tell me, Rubella! Is that why you're so angry? Did I do something to hurt you?"

"Van—"

"What is it? What did I do!?"

Rubi cupped a hand over Van's mouth roughly, muzzling him, and tackled him into the bushes. He resisted a moment, then saw the anxiety in her eyes swell franticly.

Leaves rustled twenty feet away. Branches snapped.

Suddenly, Van began to feel they should not be there—they must run away. As if reading his thoughts, Rubi pressed her other palm at his shoulder, forbidding him to move an inch.

Footprints trotting against the snow could be heard not far away. They kept getting louder with each step. And when Van's instincts begged him to run away the most, he saw a huge coyote covered in silver fur through the webbed branches and leaves concealing him and Rubi.

More of them approached. Two. Three. Four...

Van was amazed at their surreal size. They were large enough for him to have heard them earlier if he were not shouting. He ended up calling the predators instead of hiding from them.

A frightful thumping thrashed against his chest. For a moment, he thought it to be his own heartbeat, but that was not it. It was Rubi's. Though they never touched, her torso was very close to Van's. She attempted to mask both of their presences and even silenced her breathing, but her heart kept beating dramatically.

The beasts would hear.

Or so they feared. They instead began passing through, finding nothing of interest.

Even with them gone, Rubi did not release him quite yet, for good reason. The pack was out of sight, but their ears were dangerously acute. Steadily moving one limb at a time, she got off of Van, saving her hands for last. She breathed harshly, quelling her heart to slow and urging the blood in her face to run again.

Van strived to keep his breathing steady. "Praise Gaia... I've never seen such huge coyotes before."

Rubi gasped harder. "If only ... they were," she forced herself to say. She took one last deep breath and looked his way again. "Those were wolves—bigger, stronger, scarier cousins to your southern pups. One of them alone can put an end to the both of us. And if there are a few scouting the area, there are bound to be more lying in wait." She stopped to collect her thoughts and draw the short sword at her hip.

Van was never scared of crossing a coyote. He even wrestled one not long ago for a hare's meat. But those wolves were different. He might not have gotten the prize if a wolf took its place instead.

"This spot won't be safe for long."

Van nodded in agreement with Rubi. They were lucky they went unnoticed the first time.

They fled in the opposite direction the wolves went, hoping to gain some distance. The branches and stones in the way no longer became a problem. They ducked under, leaped over, and passed every obstacle before they came too close, almost anticipating where and when they would appear. At the risk of getting caught from the tracks they left behind, Van and Rubi ran past their limits.

Wherever they went, Van never sensed the wolves' presence lingering. It looked like they were actually going to get away.

The walls of trees broke when the two of them finally reached the mountain wall again. There was nothing but stone and frozen soil in sight. The air was still. No wind blew. The cold began to feel less of an embrace, more like a strangle.

A path leading up the mountain arched to their left. Climbing to higher ground would not ensure escape, but their odds favored better doing that than wandering around like lambs on the ground.

"Come on!" Rubi already ran on ahead.

Van could not blame her for being so impatient now. After everything that happened, they finally managed to catch a break. It was very lucky.

No matter how benevolent Lady Sundralla is, luck only lasts for so long.

Those were words Sir Charleston was fond of saying whenever he overheard a page call themselves lucky.

Van did not let his guard down.

After catching up with her, he noticed something off about the air. There was a reason the tension was so tight. They had not escaped yet. Something else was there, watching them.

"Rubi, stop!" He kept his voice low but firm.

She did as he asked, knowing full well he would not pick that moment to talk about anything other than survival. They scanned the area, searching for whatever it was he sensed.

Then suddenly, a dark howling disrupted the silence, resounding from every direction around them. They had been found!

And Van found the presence hiding directly above them on the mountain rock. One of the wolves—one he could only assume was their leader—stood ready to pounce from the edge, eyeing its first kill.

Without a thought, Van shoved Rubi to the ground and threw his body over hers. He screamed as dozens of long, sharp blades dug into his back. The chain mail kept the canine behemoth from splitting him in two between its teeth, but the strength it exerted nearly made his muscles shut down. Van kept himself from falling over to shield the wolf's intended target.

He wished he had not opened his eyes. The sight of Rubi in front of him nearly made him lose hope. Pure terror rattled her once resolute eyes. Her skin turned so pale that she nearly blended in with the snow.

More wolves—counting six—came answering the call of their leader. Van recognized a few of them by the slick patches of fur around their legs.

There was no possible way either of them could escape ... except one. The only chance they had was for Van to use his Second Verse, ultimately revealing what he never hoped to show another soul.

There was no choice, not with the life of another at stake. Not with her life at stake.

The beast made direct contact with him. All it would take was a thought, and he could freeze it solid. But he shuddered from the pain shooting throughout his body and lost the focus he needed.

The wolves began howling one after the next. Their bellowing tore through his mind more mercilessly than the beast's fangs.

Then he realized he was losing his mind in slipping into the clutches of death. A glance at the pack showed him they did not howl. They only slowly approached, eager to feast on the human children.

The maddening cries were all in his head.

Why are you cowering?

The cacophony of voices belonging to Pruina echoed through the howling. He thought it to actually be the ethereal being for a moment, then, surrendering to his senses, thought differently. It was not Pruina, but something else entirely. It came from him, his thoughts, his valsara.

An answer came to him in listening to those voices shrouded in the fog of pain plaguing his thoughts. There was a way to confront the wolves even in his current state, but he failed to see how.

Show them you aren't a force to be trifled with!

The primal voices guided him to the answer that kept eluding him.

What could a child do against such monstrous creatures? Doubt conflicted fiercely with the force compelling him, both fighting for control of his volition. Then he looked down at Rubi again and saw the tears burning down her face. Seeing her completely submit to defeat froze every emotion in him except one: fury.

You are not prey. Show them that! Show them where they stand!

Van struggled to maintain the strength in his muscles as he turned to gaze at the wolf enjoying the way he squirmed between its fangs. It tightened its jaws, toying with him further, wanting to see how long he would resist until finally breaking.

Bloodlust coursed through him as the snow began to stain crimson. And when he turned to stare the wolf in its dead blue eyes, their roles reversed. Van had no longer been stricken by fear of the wolf, whereas the beast cowered and leaped back to escape from him.

The fangs retracting from his flesh felt more excruciating than when they were burying themselves deeper into him, angering him further. There were others still approaching. When he turned to the grunts, they gave the same frightened response their leader had.

The predators became the prey and the prey became vehemence.

It all ended too quickly. Everything faded to black after Van met eyes with the pack.

He and Rubi managed to escape somehow, that much he understood.

He was lying against the rock wall while she was dressing the bite marks over his abdomen.

Where had she gotten the material? How did he not know she removed his chain mail and tunic? The Shift Pendant still rested around his neck and his skin, its magic still at work. How had they gotten out of that without his Second Verse? Did he really scare off the pack?

"Van?" Rubi called out to him after realizing he had awoken.

"Ru—"

"Don't talk! Just rest."

His sides ached too much to make any argument. He could feel a few ribs had fallen out of place.

While she continued to treat him, Van tried to make sense of what happened, but everything was too hazy. The unbridled fury he felt against the wolves for attempting to steal something important was all he could cling to. It felt familiar.

Yes... I remember.

But not what happened to the wolves. He remembered the night Sir Charleston visited his home. It was exactly as it was described—walking out to see the two colleagues conversing, alerting them of his presence in an angry howl, charging at Sir Charleston, wrecking everything around him. Everything going black must have been when Sir Charleston knocked him out.

It was the same. His rage then and when confronting the wolves were the same. The beast in Van awakened again, but instead of taking over, it guided him.

"Help is coming," Rubi spoke, her voice rushed and heavy with worry. "They found us. It won't be long until the others come and take us back to camp."

It was a great relief to know the pages found them before the wolves regained their senses and returned for revenge.

Her arms had not pulled away even after she finished treating him. They instead weighed on him further, holding him from behind. More pressure had been applied to the hand she intertwined with her own.

"So ... endure it until then. Got it?"

She was still tense, angry, but in her voice rang compassion. Rubi was trying to keep him warm—though futilely—and offered her own strength to put his weary mind at ease.

Her grudge against him had finally stopped.

Resting his eyes, Van dryly muttered, "I understand."

Rubi's muscles tightened around him. "...I told you not to talk!"

<h1 style="text-align:center">~ Seventeenth Chapter ~</h1>

<h1 style="text-align:center">Territory</h1>

Lord Tamsilac did not pity Van or Rubi for being injured and tired. For strayed from the group, he put all the responsibility of setting up camp, cooking everything that was caught, and salting the leftovers on them.

The friction between the two finally faded. They barely had time to reconnect during their punishment, but Van and Rubi made time during the hunts and before resting for the night.

Rubi expressed her dissatisfaction with how little time they had together after the lessons began. She felt Van had been avoiding her when he locked himself in his bedchamber and left for the palace. Loneliness chimed in her valsara when recalling those times, and with it, aggression.

When Van asked why she did not say anything, she first tried to feign ignorance, then awkwardly chortled. Having been raised in a family handling the relations with Ederea, Rubi learned to express herself through actions rather than with words, as it was the Ederean way. Simply stating what was on her mind became a foreign concept to her.

Having heard her story, Van then explained why he had been away so much. Although he could not tell the whole truth about why he hid in his bedchamber, she seemed to understand after he said Sir Charleston had him confined. And she was very surprised to hear about his encounter with the king and his generous offer.

After hearing everything for herself, Rubi apologized for her behavior. Van felt he, too, should apologize for causing her such discomfort, but Rubi punched him in the shoulder for it.

"Why are you apologizing for trying to be the man you want to be?"

It seemed ridiculous after hearing her put it that way.

Everything returned to normal after they went back to Brigadier.

Rubi's return to the faction excited everyone. She was happy too, enough let go of what Wally said about "the uppity princess breaking from her confines." The circle of friends was whole again; they ate together every meal, got together for studies somewhat periodically, and enjoyed their peculiar banter as they had the previous year.

Except from then on, Van and Rubi brought themselves in each other's company more often.

Sometime in late spring, Rubi began sneaking into the boys' wing and sat outside Van's door when he was confined. They spent plenty of time talking to one another through the door. How she avoided getting caught by anyone amazed him. She never told him how she did it.

She clearly had a trick up her sleeve, and judging by the energy that exuded from outside his door, it was a magical one. Why she bothered with the risk eluded him. Meeting for a little "tête-à-tête," as she called it, was not worth being expelled from the chateau.

How hard it was to know whether their new situation was more or less strenuous.

Spring and summer went by before Van realized it. He had been focused so strictly on his training that he had not noticed the time pass.

At least, that was what he tried to convince himself.

Try as he did to deter thoughts, Van kept thinking about Mini. He got a letter from her before he returned home and was not pleased with what he read. While he was away, the blossomed seamstress had gotten engaged to a visiting duke's son and was due to leave the village to live with him before the next turn of the seasons.

At first, Van was happy for her. But his outlook on the matter changed halfway through the letter where Mini wrote it had been an arranged marriage made between Pruella, her mother, and the duke. It seemed a simple proposal—Mini married the duke's snide child, and the duke used his influence to make Pruella the most beloved seamstress in the region.

Simple as it was, it did not seem right.

Her worn handwriting spoke volumes; she found the arrangement unpalatable, but she explained why she had no choice but to go along with it. Her mother's business had been lapsing as of late. Customers have been scarce. Prices for the needed materials became ridiculously high. Her livelihood was in danger. If Mini married, she would save her mother's business and reputation.

Noble a goal though it was, it left Van feeling disdain. And unfortunately, by the time he returned to Russalin, she was already gone.

Still upset by the whole situation, he asked his father, "Why do people marry?" when he got home.

There were those who married for love. But in many cases, as it commonly was among nobility and those carrying a certain power, marriage was used as a bargaining tool to settle disputes or secure wealth.

Van wanted to say the marriage Mini went into was a mistake. She was not happy with it. He wished he could have told her that himself.

All of his friends were gone. He missed Mini, who married herself off for her mother's sake. He missed Brute, who left to become a blacksmith's apprentice and build his future. He missed Mari, who returned to her homeland after being dragged along by her mother's whim. He missed Davern, who departed for the Elysium. And in the slow pass of summer, Van began to miss the friends he made at the chateau.

Long since he left the village to start his training had Van accepted the broken ties that would inevitably be made, but he could not help cling to the strands all the same.

He felt empty without his friends, even after returning to Brigadier.

Following the same pattern as the previous two years, Van walked to the banquet hall eager for a filling feast after locking up his belongings.

He perked up when he saw Gal and Lelia eating at their table. His lonely mind beckoned him to meet with his friends, but his stomach tugged him toward the servants handing out food.

After getting his hands on a full plate, he went to join his younger friends. The twins looked as pleased to see him as he was to see them. As always, Gal was quick to loudly call out to him while the composed Lelia waited until he was in earshot before calmly greeting him.

The two of them have grown again and changed even more.

Gal was half a foot taller, his height accentuating the developing muscles on his arms. His eyes lost the once precious innocence, turned a dark bronze. From his wide smile, it could be seen that he lost one of his upper front teeth, which still allowed him to retain a child-like charm.

Lelia no longer shared her brother's height, falling a few inches under him. Her eyes kept the same wonderful glimmer but displayed a calmer spirit. She began wearing her gold locks in a ponytail, probably from letting them grow so long.

It was unusual yet oddly refreshing looking at them so differently.

"What are you wearin' that ridiculous scarf for?" Gal spoke as bluntly as ever.

Van took to a little change himself. He donned an amber scarf thick enough to completely bury his neck in a single loom. Too much cotton was used in making the plush accessory. No matter how he wrapped it around his neck, it always left a fair length of it covering his lower jaw. His mother made it for him; he could not likely say anything bad about one of her few woven works. Van only thought of the extra cotton as a comfort. The only flaw it had was that it kept him from getting any food.

When he pulled it down to eat, Lelia stared coldly at her twin and called him out loud enough for others to hear. "You mustn't speak such rudeness to our friend." Her speech became much more eloquent.

It was hard to hear what the growing boy said to his sister, with his voice so low and Van hungrily munching into venison. From the smug expression on his face, he seemed to be having a bit of fun.

Lelia, however, did not appreciate her brother's tone and kept reproaching him as if he were a younger sibling instead of her twin.

When she began using words like *incongruous* and *repugnant* to describe his behavior, it became clear she only wanted to show off her speech abilities.

It was getting to be too much for poor Gal to bear. "All right, all right! We get it!" he snapped, finally breaking. "You're a sophisticated girl who can use big, confusin' words now. Just stop it already. I miss the ol' Lelia..."

That last comment left Lelia bitter.

Van stopped eating a moment to intervene. "Your sister is just proud that she learned so much, Gal. You should be proud of her too."

"I am, but I like it better when she's not tryin' so hard to pretend to be someone she ain't."

"I am not pretending to be anything! I have no trouble speaking as I normally would, but I need to continue practicing. Using proper speech will be of great benefit to me in the future."

"If you don't give it a rest, that *will* be the way you normally talk."

"We're friends, Lelia, not some strangers," Van picked up on what Gal said. "Just speak freely with me and your brother, all right?"

"But are you not nobility yourself?"

"I am, but I live rather modestly compared to other nobles." Telling them that he was a fallen noble would only dull the conversation, so Van did not mention it and kept a kindly tone. "To be honest, the eloquent way you're speaking is a little intimidating."

Lelia loosened up shortly after hearing that.

Truthfully, Van preferred the way she naturally spoke, but he understood that she liked what she was becoming. She was ashamed of the way she used to speak. She wanted to speak more properly so she could feel a more competent woman. It was a change she wanted for herself, so he supported her, even if he liked her as she normally was.

Lelia gave an awkward smile and glanced to the side. "I guess I was acting a little snobby."

"No, not snobby. Just a little forced."

"I told you so," groaned Gal.

"But you also sound very mature and confident. Who has been teaching you?"

The male twin sighed curtly while his female counterpart's eyes lit up. He kept eating as Lelia kept speaking with Van.

"Lord Xanlir."

"The Champion of Duty?"

She nodded. "He was kind enough to teach me in his grandmother's place when he returned. He was very patient with me ... even when I kept misusing the phrases he taught me and lost heart when I couldn't learn how to use tongue twisters."

Van smiled. The generosity of Lord Xanlir knew no bounds. It seemed he had not changed much.

"'A knight's solemn duty is to his people and to those his junior.' That's what he said after I thanked him."

In that instance, Lelia's valsara changed tone. A wide array of emotions began to form one after the next. It was a familiar pattern, a vibrant phantasmagoria he had seen before, but Van could not recall when.

"Watch out, sis. If you're not careful, you'll—"

Gal's teasing came to a rough halt. His face once expressing impish delight trembled with pain. The impression of Lelia's suddenly bitter expression expressed that she kicked him under the table, spitefully.

"Shut yer trap, ya bloody devil!" She covered her mouth with both hands after hearing what she said.

Gal seemed just as amused by it as Van. "Now *that* sounds more like the Lelia I know," he said, then recoiled when she glared at him. "But it doesn' much look like her..."

The twins argued on occasion. Sometimes, they had little arguments for the fun of it. But now, Lelia looked more tense than usual.

From there, they ate their meals in silence. They only spoke when commenting on how good their food tasted.

Afterwards, Van excused himself, promised Gal that he would help him train later, and went to the stables. It felt like ages since he saw Nightshade.

"Oh. Good day, Young Master!" Lyn called out to him when he returned to the boys' wing. She was stepping out of the maids' chambers when she saw Van covered with dirt and sweat.

He did not cower at her approach as he used to since their reunion the year prior. He never found out what she knew about his power, and there seemed to be no need to ask. He warmed up to her once more, and Lyn became much more attentive since then, like a caring sister.

Van smiled broadly seeing her come his way—never minding that it could not be seen under the scarf.

"My, how you've grown since I've last seen you."

"Please don't give me any insincere flattery," Van said flatly. "I know I'm not as tall as the other boys."

Lyn stood before him, running a hand through his hair. "Nothing I say about you is insincere." Her hand fell to his arm, then she lifted it to inspect the muscle. She then moved on to a quick inspection of his shoulders and waist. "We will have to get your measurements again."

Thought of his own growth never crossed his mind. He barely noticed the ground gradually getting farther away and the hair budding under his arms. His build remained about the same, but the edges around his face slowly evened out, giving him a more mature countenance.

"Do you have time now?"

She smiled warmly. "I always have time for you."

As time went on, they stopped worrying about appearing unacceptable in the eyes of others. Despite how careful they were, someone found out about their relationship and spread the rumor that he let servants treat him like a pet. Lyn came to openly coddle the boy; Van did not put up any resistance. It did not matter. The pages taunted him every chance they got. Their words were weak, much like their minds.

Van and Lyn turned around for the maids' chambers again.

He noticed Lyn's eyes on his neck where the bulky scarf hung. It did not take Praecur to know what she was thinking. He grabbed one of its arms. "Mother made it for me."

Lyn's vague scrutiny eased into a weak smile, something rather forced. "Ah, I see." She wanted to be polite, but could not quite help sounding bewildered. Realizing he noticed this, Lyn quickly recollected her composure and added, "It certainly is a ... uniquely thick one."

"I'm just glad it keeps together. Knitting is not one of her many strengths." Had Van not said that, Lyn might have continued to feel awkward about saying something offensive.

Her slowed heartbeat indicated that she calmed down. "It is very sweet of you to wear it for your mother, but you shouldn't force yourself to wear it when she's not around to see if you do not like it."

Van shook his head. "I do like it, though. I like how soft it is." He held up the scarf's arm to her, wanting to prove it. It looked she would politely reject the offer, but then she reached for it. A gasp escaped her upon feeling the fine material, followed by a soft hum.

Victoriah might not be the best knitter, but she certainly knew how to find the best material.

Lyn let go, reluctantly, when they arrived at her chambers.

The procedure was relatively quick. Each measurement only took half of a second once Lyn wrapped the measuring wire around his frame. He grew a little taller, and his shoulders and abdomen gained some mass.

When she said she would have everything prepared right away, Van made his exit.

A look out the window at the end of the hall showed the sun slowly dipping over the horizon. Still hours more until the evening meal was served and no one asked Van for his services. He decided to return to the training grounds and practice his swordsmanship.

The early morning had this unusual lonely air. He was not sure what it was, but it was a bit bothersome. He chose to focus on getting breakfast instead of that.

"Is this seat taken?"

To Van's delight, Ccuivr joined him at their table not long after the bell rang. He took the seat across from him while carrying a bowl of porridge and a mug.

"How has my protégé been?"

"Rather well," Van replied. "I've been getting a better grasp on my swordsmanship. It has taken a lot of work, but I think I have a few ways I can improve it."

Ccuivr grinned. "Interesting. You'll have to show me once you do."

"Will do."

They had a nice talk about different fighting styles before Gal and Lelia arrived. Ccuivr only spoke when he needed to and kept to his meal quietly. He did not look the twins' way if he could help it.

Lelia tried speaking to him now and then, but gave up when Ccuivr began slowly nursing his mug without coming up for air. Gal had seen him swim before; he knew how long he could last without taking a breath.

Ironically, his charade caught Lelia's interest.

Van focused on his meal while the twins entertained themselves with Ccuivr, only to be disturbed after he started gagging on his drink. Jumping from her seat, Lelia rushed to his side to see if she could be of help, but Ccuivr calmed down seconds after.

"Are you all right?" she asked him.

Ccuivr did not speak right away, still taking the opportunity to replenish his lungs. "Yeah ... I'm good."

"What got ya so spooked?" Gal asked.

"This may sound insane, but for a minute, I could have sworn I saw—" He stopped speaking suddenly, surprise flickering in his eyes. "Huh. Well, now I've seen everything."

They all turned in the direction he looked to find an attractive young lady wearing a night blue dress marching their way. Her dress shimmered with every step she took, rippling like water. And the few pieces of silver jewelry she wore on her wrists accentuated a serene beauty.

"Hey, guys!" No one could believe that lady was Rubi.

Out of everyone, she seemed to be the one who changed the most.

Her abdomen took a more curvaceous shape, accentuated by the beautiful dress. Her smile looked sweeter. Her red hair glistened in the light she was under. And her eyes glittered with a radiance Van never saw before, as if she had taken the essence of a finely cut garnet.

The girl had transformed into a person he barely recognized as the rough, abrasive Rubella everyone knew.

When realizing he never finished off the meat dangling from his jaws, Van slurped it up before anyone noticed, and chewed hurriedly. Looking back at Rubi, he quickly scanned her valsara while she was griping at Ccuivr for something he said. Van was almost worried that was not Rubi at all. But her valsara shimmered in a radiance he recognized, only brighter. It was the same Rubi, but different somehow.

When she looked his way, bearing the same surly expression he was used to seeing, he winced. She seemed to have said something while he was not listening.

Then Gal said, "Aw, you can't be askin' him. Any fool can tell he'll side with you."

What were they talking about?

Rubi looked a little more upset when he did not say anything. "I make this look good, right?" she repeated.

When Van finally understood, he motioned to respond "Yes," but then found his tongue in a knot. Showing any more hesitation would rile Rubi up more, so Van forcibly tore the knot up and replied, "Of course. You look very nice, Rubi."

"I agree. You look positively lovely," Lelia added.

Rubi grinned widely, showing her teeth and leering at the two who said otherwise. "See? Told you!"

"Why're you even wearin' a dress anyway? You're a page."

It could have been Van's imagination, but he thought he saw Rubi flinch at that question, her skin crawling.

She then narrowed her eyes, that frightened gaze turning ruthless. In anger, she slammed her hand against the table and stared Gal down. "I am a woman, twerp! A proud, strong noblewoman! And a lot of the snobby little boys here have been forgetting that just because I wear the same uniform. And they still *somehow* think they are better than girls. I don't care if I have to wear a dress to prove it. I'm putting pompous little boys like you in your place and showing you that girls are just as capable as you lot!"

Repressed hostility gave her words terrifying weight. Her voice rose an octave higher for nearly every anger-riddled syllable she said. By the time she finished, she was standing so tall over Gal that it looked like she was going to devour him.

All of the color faded from poor Gal's face. Lelia scooted a foot away from her brother, afraid she would be caught in the middle.

Likely as it was that her hostility came from Gal hitting a sore spot, it still showed how her skills of intimidation have grown. Gal babbled an apology out of fear of what it would lead to.

No one mentioned anything about the dress again, apart from the most sincere compliments. Gal did not say anything else.

When exchanging stories about what they did over the summer, Rubi mentioned joining her family's messengers on a march to the northwestern border. She rode with several soldiers for fourteen days through perilous terrain. According to her parents, the message contained vital information about the Renegades that needed to be delivered at the earliest possible time, leaving them little option about how to get to their destination. It was the only reason Rubi volunteered to accompany a small party of men.

No matter how clear she made it that she did not want to be treated as the duke's daughter but as a fellow warrior, they kept pampering her. She almost felt that the journey was not worth it, until a group of brigands attempted to ambush them. Only in the thrill of battle did she feel alive. She used everything taught to her and felled every enemy that dared cross her. The remaining few who could not fight back were captured.

"It was a fine excursion," Rubi claimed proudly.

Her tale invigorated Van's appetite. How she depicted the enemy as revolting lamps made him laugh. He ate everything on his plate, but he did not want to leave the table for more until Rubi finished.

Despite the earlier upheaval, the four were laughing heartily and having a grand time in each other's company. It was not the same without the whole faction, but they enjoyed it nonetheless.

When Rubi finished her eggs, she decided to take her leave. It was a little disappointing to see her go. Seeing her leave made Van want to follow, but he kept that impulse in check.

"Hey, Van." Rubi turned back to face him. "Would you mind practicing archery with me before lunch?"

He felt both delight and confusion at his dejection suddenly slipping away. "Sure."

She gave a broad smile before she turned to leave again.

When she was no longer in sight, he got up to get more food.

He stopped again, begrudgingly, when Cciuvr tapped his shoulder. "When you get the chance, ask her about the encounter with the brigands again. I'd like to hear the rest of her tale."

"The rest?" Van echoed.

"What do you mean?" Lelia asked. "Didn't it end with the brigands' death and capture?"

"She never said what happened to them when they arrived in the city—the one *she never named*. There's something she's not telling us."

What Ccuivr said sounded paranoid, but it made Van think.

As they always had, Van and Rubi trained together competitively. They each selected the other's targets before they fired their arrows, trying to make it more difficult for them to shoot each time. It was an enjoyable exercise. Rubi's suggestions made it more entertaining, and she was kind enough to put their game on hold if she noticed either of them needed to adjust their form.

Neither preferred the bow to the sword, but they knew to learn so they could be more useful in times of need.

When firing arrows in place became boring for them both, Van suggested attempting to practice their archery while on horseback. The idea excited Rubi as much as it did him, her smile drawn across her face, cheeks almost bulging.

Shooting arrows on the move was difficult. Keeping focus on the target was very trying while being jostled by the running horses. And it became worse for Van when Nightshade shook every time she heard the bowstring's twang.

It came as a surprise when Rubi fell from her mount before he had. She looked okay and insisted she was, but her training partner insisted on taking her to the medical ward in case she hit something.

As Rubi insistently protested, there were no major injuries anywhere; the servant who examined her said so. But she was still disoriented, so she was allowed to rest on the bed until she felt stable again.

It was already midday. Van thought to leave and fetch her some food so she did not miss a meal, but Rubi made him stay. He listened but became a little antsy when the room became too quiet.

Fortunately, Rubi got herself settled before long. "Thanks, Van," she said when she stood from the bed. "I'm glad I have you around."

Her voice rang more sincerely than it ever had before. He could hear her relief. It swept against his ears in a gentle brush and left him at ease yet feeling faintly forlorn.

Something *was* wrong after all, and she did not want to share.

Rubi headed straight for the door, but Van held a hand to her shoulder before she could step outside. She flinched, then calmed down. Her grin expressed a bittersweet joy.

"Still got cold hands, huh?"

"Rubi."

"Hm?"

"Is there something on your mind? Something you're troubled by?"

The comfort she felt faded with her smile. The glimmer in her eyes vanished. Her muscles became tense again. Her hands clenched into trembling fists. Her whole body became agitated with strife. How had she managed to hide it for so long?

"I didn't want anyone to find out," she finally spoke a voice devoid of joy, "least of all you... I didn't want you to think any less of me. But I guess I can't hide it forever."

"What reason would I have to think less of you?"

Rubi took a deep breath, then dryly exhaled, allowing her shoulders to droop. She scrapped the friendly cold hand off her shoulder before facing him again, unable to look him in the eye. "I regret ever going back home. I never should have gone with the messengers ... and I should have never returned home afterward." Those miserable words completely contradicted the pride she beamed with earlier. "I met with the nobles there. They were impressed with me, too impressed. The lord wanted to offer my hand to his son. I refused. I plainly said 'No way!' ignoring the manners I was expected to show. But he wouldn't let me get away. My parents caught wind of the proposal and practically gave me away upon my return to Cragfill."

The strife weighing her down hit Van hard. The shock left him thrown off, unable to give a coherent response.

"I only returned here because my parents thought I could use a little more training. They want to give a strong, capable wife to the northern lord's runt in case he doesn't prove useful. They don't even want me to be a knight, just a useful pawn they can have get rid of anyone who stands in the way of their success." She spat venom when mentioning the lord, the runt, and her parents. "This will be my last year here... I won't get the chance to be a knight. I already lost my shield, my freedom, and the worst of it—" She held her tongue, neither able nor willing to say any more. Her arms trembled with the malicious rage she kept bottled up inside. It took all her will to keep from lashing out at the person nearest to her.

Van could not stand seeing her like this—tortured, rattled, broken, so much unlike herself. Seeing someone as strong as her suddenly lose all hope sent cracks running across his chest and rage pumping through his veins.

"You can't just accept this, Rubi!" he spouted. "Just refuse what your parents did to you like you refused the lord."

"I can't do that... I can't turn against my own family, Van. I— I just can't do it." Her words broke him. Her voice became bereft of her once fiery ambition. "Believe me when I say I don't want this, but ... there's nothing I can do. My parents have made the choice."

And with that said, she could no longer bear the scorn she held toward her weakness and the situation, and she left the room.

Van could not comprehend what just happened. In that instant, the once mighty page Rubella became a mere shell of herself, trying to flee from her anger and grief.

Gritting his fangs and clenching his fists, he cursed under his breath wondering what dreck could have broken her. Whoever it was, he was a dead man.

Three days passed. Van had no luck in finding out who the boy engaged to Rubi was. He was certain whoever it was trained with the same noble family.

It was a gut feeling—not much to go by, but he knew it was not wrong. Somehow.

He had nothing else to go by and no one to turn to. If he got the others involved, he would have betrayed Rubi's trust after she confessed her defeat, poured her heart out to him in confidence. It took some effort, but he managed to throw his faction off his scent for the time being. It would not last forever. He had to work fast.

And soon enough, he found him.

How tempting it was to lash out at the haughty child and forbid him from marrying Rubi and taking away her freedom, but Van knew fully well that was no way to settle the matter, especially not with another noble. There had to be a way to settle it civilly, or however way it could be done to officially void the betrothal.

And though he hoped it would not come to this, he knew he had to rely on someone. It was a long shot, but Van decided to consult the one man he knew could help with such a touchy matter: Sir Charleston.

At first, the knight was surprised to be approached with this and was ready to send the boy away. Fortunately, he took an interest in the matter. When asked who it concerned, Van only gave the name of the boy, trying to protect his friend. It seemed to be enough for Sir Charleston to figure out who the other one involved was, though.

For one reason or another, he told Van what he needed to know.

A matter such as this would not be easily negotiable among commoners. There was, however, an old tradition among Vermalian nobility that had been used to settle objections such as his. Instead of the arrangements being handled by the parents, the boys would duel one another to decide the fair maiden's fate. Of course, according to Sir Charleston, there were repercussions.

So long as it got Rubi out of that marriage, Van did not care.

One late afternoon, Van went to the training grounds and stood in the center of the earth everyone practiced on. His shoulders were stiff, arms crossed. His forehead wrinkled from agitation, eyebrows furrowed, his glacial eyes leering menacingly at the empty space. A ticklish autumn breeze swept across his mien, bending his locks to the wind, but he did not respond to it. The frozen boy became a gargoyle waiting for his prey.

The only one with him was Sir Charleston, who Van asked to observe the duel. He was a difficult man to persuade, especially since the good knight vowed to put Van down if he proved a threat to anyone. Perhaps that was why he agreed to do it.

Van asked him to be the witness as sternly as he demanded the challenge of his foe, sparing only ferocity in place of cordiality.

His attention turned back for the chateau as his enemy drew near. "You're late," growled Van.

And yet *he* came prepared with swords—sharp, unshaven ones—in hand for the very occasion. Although reluctant to get close to him and remain cordial, Van accepted a sword from Kallant.

The sword was heavier than the ones the pages trained with and even the weighted one Van normally used. Its heavy metal would definitely slow his movements, but not enough to make a difference. Both pages seemed capable of handling the weapons without any complications, seeing as neither needed time to get used to the weight.

"Shall we begin?" Kallant asked.

Van shook his head. "Not yet. I would like to propose a wager."

Kallant's sneer grew wide and sinister. "I'm listening."

"If I win, you, Kallant Ginnstom, will forsake your betrothal with Rubella Ivanstronge of Cragfill."

That smug smile twisted with anger, and irritation had traced itself across his forehead. "That's rather rude of you, bringing my family matters into your grudge against me. It doesn't involve you."

Van gritted his teeth. "I became involved when she told me about it. She doesn't want to go through with it."

"And you think I do?" the thug scoffed. "Being told to I am to marry such a vile shrew sickens me, but my parents want the power that comes with being the envoy of Ederean relations. Even I know it's better than just watching the northern waters, waiting for a disaster that never comes. If I go through with this, then there will be more in it for me in the end. So why should I agree to risk that?"

The idea of treating Rubi like a tool, using her for material gain, made Van's taste for blood grow. He could barely contain himself, but he bit an incisor into his tongue to distract from the anger.

"Should you win, I'll return to Russalin and never return. I will live the remainder of my life as the pitiful peasant you see me as."

It was the best possible bargain he could make the unworthy adversary. Kallant despised anyone from the lower class associating with nobility and looked down on those nobles who treated the commoners with so much as a shred of humanity. The Kronas family was fallen nobility, putting Van on the same level as one without any noble ties. Not many were fond of him, but Van's presence in the Estrine Chateau held some meaning for the lowborn. Were Kallant to remove Van from the picture, it would bolster the sway he had with the arrogant noble pages and break the confidence of those without wealthy families striving for knighthood.

It was a risky gamble, but one worth taking.

Judging by the widening grin across Kallant's face, as Van predicted, he could not resist the opportunity. "Then we're in agreement," he stated malignantly. He already drew his sword, eager for the coming bloodshed.

Taking a step backward, Van took his sword and scabbard in hand, and glanced back to the knight.

Their observer stood in place, watching the two boys before him with, surprisingly enough, an unexpected speck of sympathy in his eyes. It went away quickly and his expression became stern again. He uncrossed his arms and held one up, waiting a moment to test their patience.

Once he swung his arm downward, the duel commenced.

At that very moment, Kallant rushed at his foe. Van stood motionless as the enemy drew near, and when he came close enough to strike, he blocked the attack with the base of his scabbard, then thrust forward to throw him off balance.

Kallant was clever. He recognized that technique and responded by rooting his feet firmly into the ground to keep the distance he closed. It left Van little option but to step forward and strike. Kallant was prepared, though. He brought his blade at a higher angle to block the horizontal swipe. Metal barring metal, grating against each other forcefully, it came down to brute force to see who would take the upper hand. The bloodlust coursing through his veins filled Van's throbbing muscles with strength. Against any other adversary, he would have already forced them aside, but Kallant remained stalwart and slowly overpowered the smaller boy.

Van clicked his tongue in agitation and moved back before he was thrown off balance. Relying on his techniques alone was not enough. Kallant was many things, but accusing him of being a fool who did not learn from his mistakes put Van in an unfortunate position.

Rather than remain on the defensive, he closed in on Kallant, followed his rhythm and stepped past the wave of his sword, and brought his weapon down at his shoulder. Kallant narrowly avoided it and, quickly taking back his balance, thrust at Van. That counter was repulsed by Van's scabbard, allowing him to move in and aim his sword low.

They clashed with one another viciously while studying the other's moves and breathing, searching for any fault in their forms as the cycle continued. Each time Van struck back, his movement accelerated, causing the power in his attacks to become even more devastating.

Kallant could not follow the flurry of attacks that rained down at him and gradually began to lose his footing. He held strong and attempted to push his opponent back. It looked like he was about to fall over when, by some stroke of twisted luck, he met his sword with Van's and pushed back with enough brute force to knock the weapon from Van's hand.

No way...!

Van stared at the falling sword with disbelief. His throat closed, shock freezing his whole body, until he found the strength to leap back.

"Well?" Kallant scoffed. "Do you yield?"

There was no way he would let him take back his sword. Without a sword, how could he fight back? All he had on hand was a dull scabbard unsuitable for bloodying anyone.

But surrender could not be allowed.

Van held his scabbard up, retaking his stance. First blood had yet to be drawn, and he would keep fighting so long as that remained the case.

Kallant's smirk widened, blatantly showing how foolish he thought his practically defenseless enemy, and went on the attack. His sharp blade lashed at his foe incessantly, urging Van to keep moving.

All he could do was defend and evade. He danced at his enemy's mercy, keeping focus on his empty hand as well as Kallant's grasp around his sword and the angle he held it.

Kallant's grip loosened ever so slightly with each frenzied swing. All it would take to have the battle in Van's favor again was a brunt where his hold was weakest. If he struck when the opportunity was just right...

The thug thrust his sword for Van's head. Van leaned to the side, narrowly evading, and drew his scabbard along the blade. He dragged it the sword until he heard it tap the guard, then flicked strongly upward, prying it from Kallant's hand.

The sword spun dangerously through the air. They watched until it slowed and began to fall. Kallant staggered backward, but Van remained where he was, tracking its rotation. When he learned where and how it would move, he reached out to catch it at the handle, spun, and fervidly swung skyward at Kallant.

Blood peppered the dirt from both the sword's tip and Kallant's vacant face. He fumbled back, falling on his backside. They locked eyes only for a moment before his forehead had been grazed, and he saw the extent of the malice exuding from Van and connecting with the stolen sword.

Van looked down at his enemy, still brimming with hate. The desire to keep fighting, to make Kallant regret everything he had done, threatened to overwhelm him. Just a scratch was not enough. He held in his hands the means to make him suffer.

But Van continually reminded himself that he had already drawn first blood. The duel was over. That barely kept his rage in check. But he managed and sheathed his sword into its opposite's home.

"You lost."

What he said went ignored. Kallant had yet to shake the terror gripping him. His eyes were frozen open, his pupils trembling from both the malice he saw and the sunset's light glaring over Van's shoulder.

Pathetic.

He tossed the sword back to the quivering slime on the ground, no longer willing to touch the same steel he owned.

Van then turned to face Sir Charleston, who tried to keep his surprise in check. He ignored how the knight's hand reached for his sword and humbly bowed to him. "My thanks for your cooperation, Sir Charleston."

Showing respect to the victor, the good knights nodded his head. "Congratulations, Page Kronas."

Van left them behind, no longer needing to be in their company. Tired from the struggle, he began to slow his breathing, relaxing his heart rate.

The fight taught him that he still needed to improve. He needed to keep training harder. But for now, he could relax.

Or at least, he wanted to. His senses warned him of approaching danger. The moment he heard metal dragging against metal, he found it.

Kallant snapped out of his state of fear and became possessed by anger. He rushed at Van with the sword in hand. Pride wounded and ambitions sullied, he fully intended to make him pay with death.

He swung, but the attack did not connect. It was interrupted by Sir

Charleston, who stepped in to shield the unarmed boy, with his mighty blade. Fury guided the knight to repulse the page and throw a closed fist across Kallant's face, knocking him to the ground. "Kallant Ginnstom, you disgrace yourself in attacking someone unarmed!" His voice boomed across the entire courtyard, rage and intolerance carrying it far. He walked over to Kallant and ripped the sword from his grasp. "Return to your bedchamber and await your punishment!"

Kallant looked up at the knight bewildered, unable to believe what he had been told, then caught a glimpse of Van and leered at him.

"That's an order, boy!"

Defeated, Kallant stood and walked back to the chateau in shame.

The knight watched him go with a scornful gaze as he sheathed his sword. All the while, Van looked up at him overcome by disbelief.

"You ... saved me?"

Sir Charleston looked back Van's way. "There is a code that all knights must adhere to. It may well only serve to shape an ideal, but that ideal is the very foundation on which we are brought up. Had I let that disgrace do as he pleased, I would have been disregarding that code."

Van listened to every word said and understood them perfectly.

"We are done here. Go about your business now."

The page saluted his superior and did as he was ordered.

Early the next day, Van was at the training grounds smacking around a wooden dummy. The results from yesterday's duel left him up late last night wondering how else he could improve his techniques.

Practicing with a wooden dummy was not the most beneficial way to improve, but the marks he left on it showed how much damage he could cause. The more he moved, the more ideas he formulated. When he got a clear idea, he could try it out.

"Van!"

Rubi's fierce voice broke his concentration. The air was quickly being torn by a thick surface heading straight for him. Van quickly turned around, shielding himself with his scabbard.

After dodging him and the others for days, her finally showing up with anger in her eyes really surprised him.

"What's the matter with you!? Why couldn't you stay out of it?"

She could only be talking about her betrothal to Kallant.

Van leered at her assertively as she threw her dulled sword at him again. He intercepted the attack and danced around her, throwing her off balance. "You were going through with a marriage foisted onto you against your will—with Kallant, that arse, of all people!"

Rubi huffed violently in her next swing. "I didn't have a choice! I told you that!"

"That's why I intervened. Someone had to if you weren't going to say anything for yourself." Van sheathed his sword when Rubi distanced herself. He did not want to fight a friend when he was upset. He did not trust himself to hold back. "There are a great many things I have to be silent about, but I'd be a fool to not do anything about that."

Rubi's eyes glinted with frustration, but her relentless assault came to a halt. They stared each other down, wanting to assess everything about the other, trying to figure out what they were thinking.

Soon, she calmed, exhaling heavily and lowering her blunt weapon. Rubi hid something when looking away; the brief glance Van got was not enough to figure out what it was. Even when examining her valsara, he could not ascertain what she tried to hide.

Then Rubi stepped up to him and punched him in his shoulder. "You better know what you're getting into."

Whatever she meant by that remained unsaid. She left without another word—done with their conversation and with attacking Van.

Although he thought to pursue her, Van decided against it. She was free again and able to chase her dream. If she wanted to talk again later, he would gladly listen. For now, they needed a moment apart.

~ Eighteenth Chapter ~

Visiting

The rest of the faction heard about what happened between Van and Kallant before long. As it turned out, Wally had spied on their duel from the beginning, and the results left him ecstatic.

As much as the others enjoyed what he told them, Rubi made it very clear she did not want to hear about it again. And the praise and pats on the back they gave Van made him a little uncomfortable. They were both embarrassed (though not in the same way) about the matter.

But the others kept wanting to hear it, especially the part when Van drew first blood. Gal and Ccuivr wished they were there to see the look on Kallant's face. They had their own grudges against the bully and wished for the opportunity to pay him back. Stevene thought about the three of them finding Kallant and having their own revenge for pestering their friends, much to Rubi's disgruntlement.

Van could imagine how that would go; they would return wearing thick bruises and proudly tell their friends of the harm they caused.

But by the time Wally let the secret out, Kallant was no longer there.

He left the day after the duel. The cost of going against the knight's code was severe. For attacking Van when he was unarmed, the Estrine family banished Kallant from their home, taking away the opportunity for a knight's shield, and sent him back to Starscape to inform his family of his disgrace.

It was almost a shame he departed so soon, as Rubi—and it clearly showed—wanted to exact her own revenge. Though the decision for them to marry was not his, that did not make her less spiteful toward him.

Without Kallant, most of the other delinquents quit messing with the weaker pages, or at least acted more carefully. Not much time had passed, and yet every page that heard what happened became more confident. They already began standing up against their bullies and for each other.

It was a wonderful step taken towards knighthood.

When the lessons officially began, Van and his faction were provided with fewer lessons per day than usual. Those attending their third year and so on mainly attended their lectures on tactics, geography, and etiquette and language. That did not mean there was any time for leisure.

While the first- and second-year pages had more strict schedules, the more experienced pages were given tasks at the most unexpected of times, leaving them very busy. The various tasks practically took away all chances to act independently. Most helped the servants clean and the chefs cook while others delivered messages, carried back food from the markets, basically anything the Estrine knights could think of to keep them busy. And all the while, they were still expected to practice swordplay, archery, and everything they used to do in the form of lessons.

Denying the requests of the knights was unacceptable. In military terms, they ranked higher than any of the pages, no matter their status. Rejecting an order from a superior showed they would be unreliable as a knight and a liability, a perfect reason to deny them the Rite of Chivalry, a rite of passage every Vermalian page had to take.

The change left Van depressed a majority of the time. His friends were almost always busy. He barely saw them. To make matters worse, the knights enjoyed abusing their power over him. He noticed how they addressed the other pages with his experience who looked to be free from any orders. They did not so much as turn their direction, always going straight to Van for their worst tasks when they saw him.

He suspected it before, but said nothing. The knights looked down on his differences as coldly as the pages had. Neither age group would care about anything he would say, and the knights could actually punish him. It made things easier to just endure their judgment in silence.

It was not entirely unbearable, though. Lord Xanlir was around frequently during that time. He sometimes offered Van extra training in the form of an order. Even when the page was already performing a task, all he had to do was tell whoever was using him, "I'll be taking him for now," and they stripped Van of his current responsibility to go with him.

Van enjoyed sparring with Lord Xanlir, heavy-handed as the knight was. He always reminded him to think quickly on his feet even in a trying situation. Sometimes, he would suggest taking their horses for a run after he ran Van ragged, and he even took time to sit down and regale him with fascinating stories of his travels.

Running across the entire country, going where his abilities and influence were needed most, and even taking the time meant for rest for those who needed a little compassion, Lord Xanlir was a man worthy of praise—one Van came to truly respect.

After a few weeks, it was rather easy to respond to an order without feeling much hostility. It was a simple procedure: listen well, get the job done, ask if they needed anything else, then get lost. He was starting to get used to his duties.

A new arrival, however, disturbed everything.

One evening, the pages had sat down for dinner and patiently awaited the Estrine family's arrival. Another day of lectures and servitude passed. The pages silently groaned in irritation, for there was nothing to eat. The servants usually brought food out before half of the pages arrived, but there was not even so much as a scrap of stale bread.

It was not until Lord Estrine and Lord Xanlir arrived that the pages withheld the commotion they were ready to cause. And with them were a few guests. Following their hosts were King Faustign, a burly man donning enough rich fabric and jewels to be considered as a high-ranking noble, a radiant girl, and four women—likely servants—in frilly garments.

The girl stood out more than anyone else, her captivating appearance capturing the most attention from the boys.

The newly arrived gathered around the Estrines' table, joining the rest of the family, but turned around to face the pages instead of sitting.

"Everyone, listen well!" bellowed Lord Estrine. "You may have noticed the new faces accompanying us here tonight. These two are members of the illustrious Ederean royal family, His Illustrious Majesty King Godefroy du Joiec II and his daughter, Princess Camellia."

Those few not already taken away by the girl, the princess, had been when they heard Lord Estrine. It was hard enough to believe that the king of Vermalio would be joining them, but the king of another country and a princess as well? Many could not help whispering among themselves they were so surprised.

King Godefroy held his daughter's hand while facing the pages. Princess Camellia released his hand to curtsy. "Well met, young progeny of Vermalio!" spoke the foreign king. His voice was rough but rang with a tone of imperial refinement. "'Tis a pleasure to be here with you on this fine autumn eve. We come here as friends to renew our relationship with your great kingdom. And while I am here to discuss matters with the good King Faustign, my daughter is here to learn from you all. She has grown curious of how Vermalian warriors are raised and wishes to learn firsthand. I hope you will be good to dear Camellia during our stay."

A princess? From Ederea? Coming to learn about the Vermalian pages? As fascinating as that sounded, it was also quite unusual.

Lord Estrine stepped forward to speak again. "At His Majesty's request, Princess Camellia will be staying here. While she is here, a select number of you will be assigned to act as her escorts. Those who do are expected to fulfill her wishes and curiosities. I expect you all to offer her an enjoyable time without *any* issues!" His booming voice echoed forcefully, carrying a great weight for his warning.

Then he lowered his head to gruffly clearing his throat and clapped his hands. Several servants marched into the banquet hall carrying trays of food at his signal.

"Now, without further ado, let's eat!"

The pages were given their usual gruel and the Estrines and royals were brought the most heavenly food befitting those of their stature. Some pages tried not to focus on the actual food. The way it looked and smelled, but not being allowed any of it, was a punch in the gut.

Not many of the boys focused on food, though. They were much too occupied with looking upon the beautiful foreign princess.

The girls were either admiring her as well or giving the boys the evil eye for fawning over her.

"Man, she is one lovely lady," Wally hummed.

Stevene and Gal were in agreement, neither one resisting the chance to glance past him for another peek.

"She's a princess, ape," Rubi retorted. "Of course she's pretty."

"Pretty? No, no, no!" Stevene wagged his finger discerningly. "That trifling word doesn't do a radiant flower like her justice. Exquisite, perhaps. Or maybe dazzling. But 'pretty' is much too lackluster."

"Fancy yourself an aspiring poet there, Stevene?" Ccuivr asked. "She's just a girl. No point losing your heads over her."

"Says the brooder who turned bright red at the sight o' her!" Gal's taunting left a mark. Ccuivr's eyes darted opened and his mouth fell short of his spoon. "I knew it! You're as hooked as the rest o' us."

"You are being ridiculous. I never even looked at her."

"Then who were ya lookin' at, eh? One of the ladies followin' her?"

"Shut up and let me eat!"

Van did not pay attention to their teasing Ccuivr. His only interest was in satisfying his hunger. He kept an ear out in case anyone was to address him, but the topic of the princess' beauty meant little to him. How they could be so fixated on someone's appearance was a mystery to him.

Then he recalled how taken he was with Rubi's metamorphosis after she called his name. The thought was a recurring one as of late. Her changes still baffled him. It was mystifying, like a beautiful butterfly emerging from her chrysalis.

Hearing her call him again, he put down his spoon and looked her way wondering what it was she needed.

"What do you think of her?"

It again involved the visiting royal girl.

Van turned around to catch a glimpse of Princess Camellia du Joiec picking up a fork carrying the tiniest slice of juicy venison. The girl had this enchanting smile that lit up her entire face. All of her features were smooth as porcelain, her nose a tiny little dot in the middle of her face. The long, starlight gray curls atop her head had a bounce and lusciousness that trumped beautiful fox fur. Her most interesting feature, though, was her eyes; although she was far from where he sat and they were difficult to see clearly, something about them appeared almost ... spiritual. It would be impossible not to notice her, no matter who else was present.

And yet Van was not as enchanted by her as everyone else was.

He faced his friends again and said, "I don't see what you all do," then turned back to his meal.

That did not stop Wally and Gal from trying to get whatever it was they were looking for from him. They pestered him in unison, poking fun like they did with Ccuivr, but after hearing him say it again, they backed off. They knew that he meant what he said.

The other boys were not the only ones affected by what Van said. That irate flare whelming up in Rubi's valsara vanished upon recognizing his words to be true. Having only seen it briefly before looking at the princess and now, Van was not certain what she was felt.

He ate his meal quicker than he usually would, jamming the swill down his throat and washing it down with water, then left. He wanted to get some time in to practice his Second Verse.

Over the summer, Van came to understand the importance of daily practicing use of his unusual power. Although he had adequate control, he noticed how it occasionally slipped when he was alone.

There was no room for mistakes. Small as it started out, he could not allow himself to lose any control.

The halls were empty when he returned to the boys' wing, which was not so surprising considering their latest guests. That was good, though. No one would be able to suspect he wielded otherworldly power if they were not nearby to sense it, assuming they could.

When he opened the door to his room, he found he was not alone. Lyn had entered the bedchamber in his absence again to trade his dirty uniforms for clean ones. Seeing her in there was not that unusual; finding her on her knees looking under the bed, however, came as a surprise.

"Oh. Good evening, Van," she said, getting back onto her feet.

"Evening, Lyn... What were you doing on the floor?"

Her eyes flickered with a mild worry and a hint of fright. "I heard something move underneath and thought to see for myself. I thought it might be a rat."

It definitely was not a rat. Any vermin that entered usually got caught and snacked on by Snowflake.

It might be her— No, it was. Her scent was still fresh, so she had to be close by.

"Perhaps you were just hearing things."

"Yes ... yes, perhaps you are right. The vermin always wonder closer to the kitchen than anywhere else."

Van sighed silently, making it look like a yawn. He doubted she would be convinced so quickly. "I will be turning in early tonight. I feel a little out of sorts."

"Then I will be taking my leave," she said professionally. "Good night, Van. And congratulations."

"Congratulations?" he repeated, perplexed. He had not even done anything worth the praise. "For what?"

The maid turned back around as she was leaving, expressing a brief surprise before looking at him with more caution. She dryly laughed a little. "Forgive me, but the servants cannot help spread whatever gossip they hear. I heard the good news of your betrothal the oth—"

"Did you say *betrothal*?"

Lyn looked as confused as he was. "Well ... I heard about it from one of the servants. You see, he heard of your duel for the hand of a young lady, and that you won."

Van's stricken mood lifted. Relief washed over him when he realized that it was a misunderstanding. "Ah. No, it's not what you think. Rubi did not want to go through with her arranged marriage, so I fought for her choice to be free since she couldn't."

The only changes to the maid's demeanor were a pursed frown and slanted brows. Her very valsara trembled with concern. Walking back into the room, Lyn approached Van and kneeled down to his level, planting a palm onto his shoulder. "Van, did you not fully understand the kind of duel you took part in?" Her voice wavered with her valsara. It began to worry him, greatly. "When young men make the challenge to void an engagement through combat, it has a deeper meaning. It is a traditional test to determine who is the most worthy—whoever takes victory takes the girl's hand in marriage. Since you won—"

Van did not bother listening to the rest. It was too much. He thought he freed Rubi from the shackles called marriage the moment he drew Kallant's blood. The thought that he failed her irked him for every word Lyn spoke.

"...And it is impossible to annul the betrothal altogether?"

"No, Van. You mustn't do that," she spoke firmly but with a gentleness that would not startle him. "Completely rejecting her would dishonor her. It would mean the worst humiliation for a woman, even one as rough-and-ready as your friend."

Her words left Van in disarray. Shaming her was out of the question. But blindly following the tradition did not sound very appealing either.

This must have been what Sir Charleston meant when he said there would be repercussions.

Lyn stood up, offering him a sympathetic look, then excused herself to leave.

When aware that she had gone a fair distance from the room, Van slid down to the floor and called for Snowflake. As suspected, she was there, hidden in the shadows underneath his bed. She came out to nudge her head against him. He petted her down her head and along her back, finding the slightest relief in running his fingers through her lush fur.

So he could take his mind off the matter, he started his training right away. First, he formed an area of influence. Then he used the obscure images that went through his mind to make a small sculpture. Once a sculpture was formed perfectly, he then shattered it for the next one. His thoughts became clear after repeating the process a few times. Then, centering his focus, he sought to shape the ice into things that would be useful in a fight.

It was the same procedure he did every night since returning to the chateau for the third time. During the time, he discovered he had a particular liking for swords and knives.

Snowflake liked to bat at the harmless-looking pieces before he destroyed them. They proved too sturdy for her to break, so he did not mind.

After a while, he began to lose focus again. He could not forget. Lost had his mind been to the unusual concept of marriage the Vermalians held. Through the circumstances he engaged in, it better resembled a game than the commitment of love and devotion he had been told of. It was unsettling. There was no way for Rubi to escape what had been foisted upon her. Van could, but in doing so, he would humiliate Rubi. He could not do that to her.

As he was inadvertently sculpting a rather entangled piece, he stopped midway, forming a bizarre spiraling head for a pike.

"You better know what you're getting into."

Those words Rubi spoke to him now told him more than they had previously. She was counting on him to interfere.

Wearing the dress she had on the day she told him, falling apart when she did—they were, to an extent, things she planned to do. It was to lure him in. She relied on his soft heart and respect for her, even his lack of knowledge for things other noble children learned while young, to work around her parents' decision. She planned this.

She knew he would find a way to help her, hiding her uncertainty about dragging him into the binding matter. She believed he would win the duel, strongly enough to bury the guilt that came with her fearing what awaited him should he have failed. And to make the illusion last a little longer, she feigned frustration when she next approached him.

It all sounded preposterous at first. That could not have been it. But the more Van thought about it, the more he remembered what he saw expressed on her face, in her eyes, and in her valsara. And she warmed up to him again so quickly too.

He could not explain it, but Van did not feel as angry about that as he thought he should be. No matter how he looked at it, Rubi was using him to suit her own ends. He should have been upset, and yet he could not help but crack a smile and laugh about it.

No anger. No resentment. He was genuinely impressed with her.

A paw pressing at his leg got his attention. Snowflake looked up at him curiously, wondering why he stopped his performance.

Collecting his focus again, Van finished the sculpture, making it into something he knew she would enjoy. He brought thorns to rise from the center of the pike head, forming a base, and then sprouted arms from them that swirled into petals. It looked like the fabulous flower she had taken a liking to during the summer.

The petite fox leaped for joy at the familiar sight and got close to see if it had the same scent.

It brought the smile on Van's face to grow seeing how excitable Snowflake reacted. She had an energy that always made him forget any dreariness and uncertainly.

With his thoughts back in order, he put focus back on sculpting better weapons.

The Estrine Chateau had become exceedingly lively as of late due to the presence of the Ederean royalty. As previously explained to them, the princess took an interest in learning about the lives of the pages. So she could, Lord Estrine selected a few pages every day to serve as her guides and bodyguards. They accompanied the princess to wherever she wanted to go and kept her safe.

It must have been relatively peaceful in the capital for a foreign king to entrust his child to inexpert pages.

While the others tended to their guest, Van was buried in the work the knights had given him. They never gave him a break, even when he was walking from one lesson to the next. He could not disobey them, and simply completed the work and hurried to the lesson only to be punished for his tardiness.

He needed to figure out a solution if he wanted to keep training there. And as it would happen, one was given to him during Lord Tamsilac's lecture while he was being punished. He stood in the corner, balancing a book as thick as a mace on his head, as the elderly knight discussed different strategies to rout enemy soldiers.

Slowly but surely, Van learned where his enemies patrolled and, unlike those in Lord Tamsilac's plan, took routes to avoided them and secure his attendance. After countless careful calculations, he found a safe path to each of his lessons without being spotted. It took a lot of effort, but he was never late again.

That did not fix his problems with the knights. Two in particular liked to give him a hard time for trying to avoid them and accused him of trying to run, calling him a coward.

He endured the abuse. Their words amounted to nothing. As he grew older, Van saw the value in people's disrespectful words diminishing, and they practically lost any worth once he turned thirteen recently. Unless they left a particularly sharp sting, their words went unnoticed.

While he focused on completing a task from the knights, Van constantly kept an eye out for Lord Xanlir, hoping he would strut by and save him again. Clinging to the man like he would his parents, like a sad cub, seemed pitiful. He really looked forward to the training sessions they got into.

Do squires admire their meister knights in that way?

The thought crossed his mind a few times—the potential of Lord

Xanlir making him his squire.

Even the other pages thought the Champion of Duty was particularly fond of him. It was another reason why they were so scornful toward him, being favorite to two of the Six Champions.

Van spent a long while polishing the halls with nothing more than a bucket of filthy water and an old rag stained by dirt and grime.

"Make 'em shine!" the two disciplinarians often said curtly.

They never specified where to begin and where to stop. Even if Van picked a wide vicinity and made it cleaner than anticipated, they would still scold him for a job he did not do right and continue to if he were to say anything about them not giving him proper instructions.

The thought of how much barking and spit he would endure brought his teeth to grind. Their annoying voices echoed through his head. And he could only swallow his rage and continue working.

Footsteps sounded through the halls. Van groaned to himself. He just finished scrubbing down half of the stretched-out floors. The thought of scrubbing away the fallen dirt from passing peoples' boots and shoes made his pent-up frustration boil.

How he wished he was practicing swordplay that very moment.

As the bystanders passed on through, Van kept his back to them, unwilling to show his temper to those undeserving of it.

"You know, it's rude to not say hello to a lady that passes by."

Van stopped cleaning, confusion etched on his face. That voice belonged to Wally. Why would he say something like that? Humoring his friend, Van turned around to find him and several others around the Ederean princess and her servants. He stood back up while Wally gestured in his direction.

"Princess, may I introduce to you my good friend, Vandelas Kronas of Southern Valley." From the cheerful disposition and clear annunciation he used, it sounded as if he were practicing to be a crier.

The foreign princess turned to Van's direction and curtsied with the grace of a petite faerie descending to perch atop a thin leaf. When she looked him in the eye, she actually resembled the mythical being.

Van's heart stopped for a moment. Those eyes were beauty perfected, the most precious white pearls glistening with the purest silver stardust under the shadow of her gaze. It was not her stare that briefly obscured his mind. The anger he bottled up began to stir like a captured raptor trying to break free from its captor's grasp. Anxiety spiked and began mixing with his blood. Those eyes, those transfixing eyes greatly resembled the magnificence of the full moon that compelled his inner emotions and set his instincts free.

Worried about losing control, Van turned his attention slightly upward enough that he no longer felt any compelling urges to suddenly attack. Hopefully, no one would notice he looked to her forehead.

"Well met, good sir. 'Tis a pleasure to make your acquaintance." Her voice rang a fair melody befitting a budding royal girl and with a charming accent. He heard it once or twice from Rubi and a few others who lived close to the eastern border.

Not wishing to be rude, Van crossed his arm over his chest to properly salute and bowed to her. "The pleasure is mine, Princess."

Princess Camellia laughed a moment, trying to conceal a broader smile behind one of her petite hands. She seemed charmed by his effort, but also a tad entertained. By what, Van did not know but he kept his curiosities to himself.

Wally jocularly applauded him. "Bravo, mate! Even after being worked like a dog, you can still pull off a knightly standing. You've been practicing better than those louts over there."

Had all of the labor he endured really shown so much?

Faint growls could be heard among the other pages. They could barely contend from reaching out and strangling him then and there. Obviously, they were not amused by Wally's attempt at humor.

The princess, however, laughed a moment more, finding him the jester he was.

If Van knew Wally the way he thought he did, he would next attempt to make a quick escape before his audience lost their composure.

Wally walked up to his friend, patting him on the shoulder sternly.

"You could use a breather. Tell you what: why don't I finish your task here, and you can guard Princess Camellia in my place."

And there was the escape they both needed.

Then he turned back to the princess and added, in a more flattering tone, "Of course, only if it is all right with Her Highness."

Princess Camellia nodded in agreement. "A grand idea. You may go then, Page Alivvrn."

The two followed the princess' word and traded places. Van offered Wally a quick smile as thanks for the rescue, then stood by Princess Camellia while his friend picked up the old rag he left on the floor.

He allowed the other pages to pass first so they could get their distance from the jester.

"Page Kronas."

Van stopped upon hearing the princess' voice. Turning back, he saw she had extended her hand to him. Her long white gloves glistened in the light. From his extensive studies in Ederean culture, it was common courtesy for a man to introduce himself to a lady by planting a gentle kiss on the back of her hand. Van almost grimaced, as he was not particularly fond of that custom.

"Your hand, please."

Suddenly, he felt reassured that it was not the traditional Ederean greeting she wanted, but a more direct way to guide her.

How strange, Van thought curiously. From the faint glance at her valsara, she seemed to *need*, not want, someone to lead her. But why?

"Just go along with it," whispered Wally as he walked by carrying the bucket back where he and the others came from. A few mucky tracks left their impressions on the once clean floor.

He was right. If a princess requested something of a servant or soldier, it was their duty to comply. So Van turned his hand over and cupped it under Princess Camellia's. Immediately on contact, she winced and shivered, barely able to contain herself.

"Is something the matter?"

"N-No," she replied in a shaky voice. "My apologies. Your hand is just so very cold."

Van silenced a groan under his breath. Having spent five years like that, he had gotten used to how cold his body was.

"Shall we go then?" asked Van, keeping a calm tone.

"Aye. Let us be off."

They walked on together, catching up with the others at the end of the hall before they went too far. Van noticed the princess had not so much as taken a step until she felt the slightest tug in the direction he guided her in. Strange as it was, he decided to leave alone calling her actions odd until he could determine why she did them.

What he could not dismiss, though, was the sense of discomfort he felt whenever someone looked at him coldly. The maidens must not have taken a liking to him after seeing their lady shake from his touch.

When they caught up to the group, Van bowed his head to them humbly. "I apologize in place of my friend. His jokes can be provocative at times, I know."

A female his size with piercing eyes sighed and said, "So long as we get away from him, all is forgiven."

"How are you friends with that fool?" asked the taller male with messy dark brown hair.

A vein under Van's hair throbbed from that callous remark. It was strange to hear someone say that about a friend instead of about him, but it was agitating nonetheless. He kept calm by briefly clenching his fangs. "His jests aside, Page Alivvrn is a kind person and very reliable."

The tall boy backed off after that. Quarreling would only make working together for the day all the more irksome.

Having already been shown the chateau and a fair portion of Brigadier, Princess Camellia decided she wanted to better know the everyday life of the pages.

Having already been shown what the lectures were like, the group took her to the training grounds. One of the instructors was still outside shouting at the pages as they practiced swordplay. He often had something to correct, and did so loud enough for the princess to hear from afar. She did not seem shaken by the instructor's harsh tone or how he threatened to put those who would not follow into the ground.

When the instructor noticed the extra people, he practically changed into a different person. He offered the princess a cordial greeting and, after hearing she merely wanted to observe, put a stop to the exercises being done so he could pick out pages two at a time to give her a show.

The pages fought their hardest, believing their display would impress the princess. As they fought on, Van believed in the opposite.

He noticed, as more and more went against each other, how Princess Camellia's attention had not turned to anyone in particular. She did not react at all to any particularly brutal strikes the other onlookers jumped at. A gentle smile remained on her face no matter who lost or how. Those of royal lineage were taught to behave and react in certain ways, but her calmness was too perfect to be rehearsed.

Her countenance and valsara both remained stagnant every match. She would always say, "A marvelous performance, the both of you," at the end, even when the round was quick and dull.

The instructor soon inquired if she would like to see how the pages guarding her would do. They were very excited when she approved of it.

When Van's turn came, he began fighting with the Vermalian swordsmanship, as it was expected of him. As he began to stagger, he looked to Princess Camellia's stagnant smile and thought of an idea. His opponent came close, and when he did, Van took his sword in one hand, drew his scabbard, and turned the tables. He ended the match before his opponent could retake his balance.

The princess made no spontaneous reaction, unlike her guards and servants, except when the instructor called Van out for his "outlandish display," as he put it. She seemed confused, unsure of why the knight was so upset or what he meant by Van "treating this like a dance troupe."

It was very peculiar.

When she grew bored of the combat demonstrations, the princess requested that they show her something else. The boy with glasses suggested they make way for the observatory. The tall girl thought they could attend another of the lectures, particularly one on etiquette. But the princess showed mild interest in all of that, delicately stating she wished to see "something rousing." She did not seem to comprehend that a page's life involved more education than adventure.

There was something that might interest her, though.

When Van made his suggestion, the other pages were against it, but the fair princess seemed intrigued. Begrudgingly, the other pages showed Princess Camellia the way to the stables.

The others went on ahead while Van guided the princess through the tall grass. She moved slowly, careful of where she stepped along the trail. Her guide moved at the appropriate pace so she could keep up without tripping over. It was strange how no one called out to the others for them not to go too far; they were supposed to behave like guards as well. At least she still had one, joined by the hand.

Van directed the princess to the flat path around the steep hill by the stables. When it came into view, he became a little anxious. It had been a while since he gave Nightshade a proper run, having been run ragged by the tasks given to him.

Everyone was already inside, tending to their mounts, checking their feed, brushing their manes. They interacted with the horses more attentively than usual, showing more care and consideration than Van had known them to.

Prompted to stop when he felt the princess did not follow, he turned back to see what the trouble was. One of the beasts had gotten her attention, nuzzling its nose against her thin arm.

It was the brown warhorse Stevene's parents gave to the Estrines. The gelding lacked the grace and allure he had in youth. Having lived for thirty-one years and seen many battles, galloping away from them all, he received many injuries for the men he served. Since he could keel over any day, Stevene's family thought it fit to have the gelding serve the remainder of his life peacefully running at the service of a page. They did not want him dying in battle and putting his master at risk.

Princess Camellia gave into the stallion and caressed his long, white-speckled snout with her small hands. Unlike when she watched weapons clash, her white eyes showed vivid delight. "Such a handsome creature," she said, stroking the sores along his face and the scar close to the missing left eye.

She did not so much as flinch in the presence of the disfigured gelding and even called it handsome. Everyone who caught sight of the beast reacted frightfully in one way or another, be it man, woman, or page. Even Van leaped upon seeing him the first time. And yet the gentle Ederean girl gazed at the creature with nary a shred of fright and showed it affection.

It brought about an unsettling jealousy in Van. Could her reaction have reflected a greater love for animals than his?

Perhaps, but there was something else. In her valsara was this slowly settling ripple of ignorance.

His inquisitiveness had been trampled back into place upon hearing a familiar call at the back of the stables. Nightshade knew her master was among the human children. Her hooves trampled an energetic *bang, bang, bang* against the ground. She so terribly wanted a run.

"Your Highness." Van turned to Princess Camellia, who continued petting the scarred warhorse. "Would you care to go for a ride?"

She seemed tempted at first, but leaned away from the idea for a moment. Her gaze drifted here and there until looking back to him. "So long as my ladies-in-waiting accompany us, it sounds grand."

How kind of her to think of those who served her as well.

The four ladies each went along with a page, accepting their help in mounting a horse out of courtesy. Princess Camellia chose to remain guided by Van and followed him to his horse's stall.

Nightshade did not expect to carry two people, but she showed no protest. Even a horse had its pride to bear, and Nightshade did not wish to wound hers through complaints of who else the boy she respects as her master wished to bring along.

She ran as fast as she always had, passing the meaty horses that raced with her and tearing through the breeze. The wind assailed both of her passengers playfully. Lashes of the princess' shimmering silver hair occasionally drifted in Van's vision, nearly blinding him when aligning with the sunlight. When he turned back to check on her, he saw the princess with her eyes closed tight. Her arms were wrapped firmly around him for fear she would fall.

Every now and then, her delicate laughter pushed through the heavy brushes of wind and reached his ears. Despite her startled appearance, she was having as much fun as her guide.

Eventually, it came time for a little break. Van could feel Nightshade's lungs pulsating fiercely against his legs and Princess Camellia's heart against his back. He steered his mount toward the hillside.

Upon coming to a stop, he heard the princess' heavy breathing and saw her forehead glisten. She must have taken more excitement than she could handle. Her guide waited until her arms slackened from his back, then climbed down Nightshade's back. He offered her an outstretched hand and helped her dismount as well. It took a little reassurance, but she came down when she was certain she would not fall over.

He brought her up the fairly steep hill under the shade of the towering oak—the spot he found most relaxing at that time of day. They sat on the grass and allowed their bodies to be caressed by a breeze much gentler than on their run.

"That truly was exhilarating. I do not ride horses very often."

It showed, though Van did not want to be rude and say as much. "I'm glad you enjoyed your time, Your Highness."

"Oh, I did."

The two had a leisurely conversation while they rested. She seemed to be impressed by the Estrine Chateau and the way things were run there. They spoke formally about what she had experienced so far and what she had yet to see.

When he relaxed again, Van thought about what he had seen from the foreign princess throughout the day. After letting his mind run, after weighing what he had gathered, he came to a conclusion that he was not quite certain about. Curiosity urged him to find out, so he ignored his better sense of judgment and looked into her eyes.

The princess looked out to the chateau, unfazed by the movement in the scenery before her. She did not react to the horses still racing in the fields, or the pages still training, or the sun's rays glaring above the towers of the distant palace. She did not seem to be in deep thought either; her valsara was still settling after the exhilarating run.

So that's it.

Another unique individual came into Van's life, and he had this inexplicable feeling that there was still more to uncover.

~ Nineteenth Chapter ~
Who Would Have Thought?

After experiencing how it was to be her guard and guide, Van began taking measures to avoid Princess Camellia as well. It was not that he found the time with her unpleasant; it became all too tempting to look into her eyes the more he saw them. How their likeness matched that of the full moon was uncanny. It made his impulses harder to control.

Such beauty could not have been recreated. And yet it was, through that girl.

There was something about her that Van wanted to comprehend. She had a numinous valsara that could inspirit others with ease. It was warm, comforting, but something about that radiance, that purity, compelled him to adhere to caution.

Tempted as he was to find out why, he resisted his curiosities and did approach her. He had other things to worry about anyway.

Rubi had been acting especially aggressive lately, challenging more pages to fights and mocking them if they tried to avoid it. It began around spring the previous year; for some time every month, she shifted into this maddeningly belligerent phase where she goes throughout her day with a frightful temper. Her faction called it her mood.

And the boys were usually the ones to bear the brunt of it.

Rubi would go after any page, but since she interacted with her faction often, inexplicable temper was usually turned against them. She never showed that particular rage toward Lelia, though—just the boys.

During that time, everyone knew to mind what they did around her, even Wally, who found joy in pestering the fiery redhead. The slightest upset would send her off charging with a look in her eyes that could paralyze anyone. Her temper usually dissipated the following day. So long as they were careful with her for the day, they weathered her wrath.

That did not save them this time. Rubi had been holding on to her temper for the last week. Whatever bothered her so much must have been incredibly irksome. No one said anything about it, but Wally could not keep from taunting her for more than a whole day. If nothing else, his impulsive antics tired her out.

Van began to worry about Rubi. Her actions kept getting her into trouble with the Estrines. Punishment after punishment had been placed on her, and it only made her mood worse.

In hopes of appeasing her, Van tried offering her a helping hand whenever he saw her on her way to a punishment. The weight put on her seemed to lighten when he offered, but she rejected his help each time. "I can take my own lumps. Thanks anyway," she always said.

He thought Rubi's temper would dissipate with time, but that was not the case. Her mood still persisted regardless of the kindness shown to her. Although, she addressed him with less hostility.

All her friends could do was wait until her mood finally passed.

In the meantime, each of them took turns watching over Rubi by the day, thinking of ways to help put her in a good mood.

To satisfy her growing thirst for combat, Van sparred with Rubi when his turn came. As always, she accepted the challenge, facing Van with a broad grin and burning excitement in her eyes. They clashed fiercely, Rubi using her strength to throw the boy off balance, Van defending and countering with impressively fluid movements. And in their resolve to overpower the other, never giving an inch, they kept at it until they both fell from exhaustion.

It was never easy holding out against such a vicious foe. Those muscles held more animosity-born strength than most of the boys at the chateau, and her fighting style developed into something brutal. She made it quite clear without words how determined she was to be chosen by Victoriah the Wolverine.

She bore such ferocity, and yet when Van glanced over to her fallen body lying beside his own, it was not there anymore. Rather than the warrior who tried to tear him asunder a moment before, there was instead this ravishing young lady. An enrapturing aura enshrouded her as she looked peacefully to the open sky. Her chest rose and fell at a slow, paced rhythm depicting her relaxed demeanor. Again, he saw Rubi in a light unfamiliar and unnerving, but it captivated him all the same.

It was enjoyable just lying by her side, watching the clouds roll by, taking in the soft breeze. He only noticed he had fallen asleep when Rubi shook him awake. Even when she jostled him from rest, Van saw the lovely Rubi looking down at him with a bright smile.

"Hey slugabed," she said in a chipper voice, "are you going to keep sleeping the day away, or are you going to give me a rematch?"

Her smile invigorated him to get back on his feet, though he felt conflicted afterwards. He still saw the maiden he had become charmed by, at least until she took her sword back in hand.

They continued to spar until the chateau bell rang. Time went by so quickly that they had not noticed dinner was already being served inside. Gruel never tasted so good after all the energy they put into swinging at each other.

With Rubi's mood finally faded, everyone interacted with one another the way they usually had again.

The times when the whole faction came together were few, and always precious. With the years passing by, Van came to realize how little time he had left to be with his friends. This year would pass before they knew it, and knights would eventually choose them to be their squires. Once that happened, there was no telling where they would go or when they would meet again.

He wanted to spend all of the time he could with them.

And as it would happen, a great opportunity came for them to spend an entire day together. One evening, Sir Charleston summoned the faction to inform them they would be Princess Camellia's guards the next day.

It seemed too good to be true. And, according to Wally's grin broadening by the news, it was.

Apparently, he had been telling the princess stories about him and his faction, and they seemed to have amused her. Everyone was suspicious of what he may have said. Not all of their experiences were ones they wanted to remember.

Van thought he knew of a few of them, as he was well aware of how much his devious friend knew, but never spoke a word. His plans to send them into disarray would be for not if he spoiled them. Perhaps the princess would enjoy whatever inventive performance they were led to play as much as he always had.

Van did what he could to hold his head high the next morning. He had a wretched time sleeping the night before.

A part of his mind, active in a cryptic process all its own, kept waking him throughout the night. He unconsciously looked out the window every time he did, though he was not sure why. No nightmares tormented him, but he still felt he was in one, a faint anxiety keeping him wary.

He felt out of sorts the next morning. He remained on alert while walking through the halls to meet his friends, almost expecting something to leap out from out of nowhere.

"Van."

His hand immediately drew to the sword strapped to his side when that voice broke the silence. Instinct overshadowed thought in that brief moment when he failed to recognize it belonged to Rubi. She stood promptly behind him when he turned around.

Either her steps were so soft they became untraceable to his keen ears, or he lost too much sleep to notice what was happening around him.

As much as he would have liked to contemplate which seemed more likely, Rubi's unusually worried expression took his full attention. It looked like she planned to say something, but she recoiled, withholding whatever it was and looking away.

He tried to determine which Rubi it was that approached—the warrior or the maiden—in order to anticipate what was on her mind, but it was unclear. The resolute flare he knew and the new gentle wavelength exuded from her valsara in an intimidating yet harmonic discord.

The silence between them began to feel awkward. Van felt he should speak since Rubi lost her tongue, but fell short when he saw her lips twitch. "Here!" She took her hands from behind her back and held to him one clasping a white flower.

Is that ... for me?

The flower's fragrance diverted his focus to it. Its stem and petals were both exceptionally long and captivating to the eye. Each of the flowing white petals curled back elegantly and showed bright yellow markings underneath, exposing its wavy pollen-covered anther. It smelled sweeter than the finest golden honey harvested in the springtime. One sniff made it impossible for Van to turn away. He wanted a better smell.

So he accepted the flower from Rubi, who struggled to hide how her hand trembled, and brought it to his nose. It had such a glorious scent. Fatigue and weariness melted away from a single smell. Suddenly, he felt ready to oppose anything that came his way.

Van sighed blissfully, enticed by the fragrance. "Thank you, Rubi."

Rubi stopped trembling and her cheeks grew bright red. A delightful smile bloomed across her face, reaching her rosy cheeks yet appearing small, almost delicate. "Glad to you like it," she boasted proudly, her rough voice portraying her usual confidence. "Let's get moving."

Van nodded and followed her down the hall. He carried the flower tightly so as not to drop it but carefully so he would not crush it. Even though he knew it was destined to wilt, it was precisely the reason he treated it with care. It was not every day he got a gift from Rubi.

As they strolled through the halls, he noticed how she was walking unusually close. There was not even an inch between them. She never got so close to someone unless it involved hitting them. While pondering why she never cringed and leaped back from the frigid air encompassing him like she always had, Van wondered why he thought that. The closeness did not bother him, and she seemed content too.

Why say anything if neither of them felt anything wrong?

"Ack, fie!" Rubi groaned in the rough Ederean accent she occasionally used, and came to a stop.

Van suddenly felt his heart sting. Ignoring that, he focused on the distress he heard from Rubi. Seeing nothing out of sorts calmed him down, but it bewildered him as to what startled her. Rubi straightened herself when she noticed him looking her way, then flashed him a broad, clumsy smile. "S-Sorry, Van. I forgot to strap on the sword Sir Charleston gave me last night. Stall the others for me until I get back, okay? I'll be quick!"

She ran out of sight after shouting what she needed. He did not even have time to tell her that he would.

Does she trust me that much?

It felt so strange now that she was gone. The loneliness he felt, something he had not noticed for a while, crept over him again. When she showed him that sweet smile, when she walked so close that he could almost feel her touch, he noticed how he enjoyed having her close by. It was almost like the cold had stopped biting into him for as long as she remained by his side.

While lost in thought over what that could be, Van kept his course to the chateau's main entrance where everyone agreed to meet. As he walked down the main stairway, he kept smelling the white flower. Its aroma was irresistible. He almost did not have the strength to pull away.

Catching traces of human scents brought him out of his trance, urging him to pry the flower from his nose before anyone saw. A lot of boys teased each other for playing with flowers.

He got a lot of attention for being so different from everyone. They already thought him spineless for letting a servant treat him as she liked. Such cruel jokes were made about him for spending all the time he did in the stables. He would likely become a laughingstock when they saw him carrying a flower.

Hiding it was no longer an option, and he refused to get rid of it.

Let them say what they will. It doesn't mean a thing.

With the white flower away from his nose, the scents became much clearer. One was a musty odor that lingered, the other a stale, and somewhat salty, scent similar to old bread.

Ccuivr and Wally—without a doubt. Even they would not go easy on him. Wally would joke about him losing a piece of his masculinity and Ccuivr would just scoff at the feeble plant.

Both boys stood alone at the bottom of the stairs waiting for the others to arrive. Already he could hear Wally's complaints about everyone "taking their sweet time." Ccuivr, on the other hand, merely demanded Wally be silent.

The soft echo of Van's footsteps against the stairs put a stop to Wally's complaining and directed the boys to look to him.

"What took you so long, Van? "You're usually the first one to show whenever we meet in the banquet hall." As per the norm, Wally's voice enunciated a jocular tone no one took seriously.

Van waited to respond until reaching the bottom of the stairs, where their conversation could continue at a volume that did not disturb anyone. Speaking with someone as loud as Wally always drew attention, especially when he tried to make jokes.

Then Wally whistled, his eyes widening at the sight of what was in Van's hand. "Well, well, *well!* Look what we have here." He invested so much attention in the white flower that it seemed natural for a boy to carry one. Then Wally's stare became bothered, darting toward Ccuivr. "Hey gruesome, I'm talking to you!" Without warning, he shoved him.

Ccuivr tumbled before catching himself. He stood again, ready to get even with the fool, but—to both his and Van's surprise—he stopped to stare at the flower too.

Van no longer knew what would or would not set others off.

Ccuivr blinked. "Is that what I think it is?"

"No doubt about it," said Wally. "It's a pearl orchid like any other."

Apparently, the flower was popular enough for them to know it by name. How curious.

"Good going, Van!" Wally enthusiastically wrapped an arm around his friend's shoulders, shaking him like a drunken oaf and roughly messing up his hair in a hearty laugh.

Van had never seen him so excited before. It was almost concerning. He tried to speak, but being shaken about so wildly made it difficult to strain so much as a word from his throat.

Fortunately, Wally let him go, only to get more answers from him. "Well, out with it, mate! Who was it?"

Wobbling to and fro from his friend's careless handling, Van attempted to regain his balance. Even when he found his footing, it did him no good. The room still twisted in unsettling distortions—the floors rippling like water, the walls inverted, his friends receiving extra appendages, then losing them the next moment.

"H-Huh?"

"Come on! Don't keep us in suspense here."

As soon as his senses were reset, he took a step back as Wally was about to step in closer. Sudden movements brought back the dizzying sensation again, but they faded fast.

"Who gave you the flower?"

Van rubbed his temple so that he was certain he regained his composure. Then he looked down to the flower, concerned whether Wally's reckless behavior damaged it. He gave a sigh of relief when he saw the petals did not suffer even the slightest wear. "It was Rubi."

Suddenly, Wally and Ccuivr looked completely dumbfounded. Both of them stared at Van wide-eyed, their jaws dangling from their joints. They almost appeared to have turned to stone, but quickly their faces loosened. Ccuivr was frowning, looking as disgruntled as ever, while Wally smirked devilishly.

"So she decided to tell him after all," he snidely spoke to Ccuivr. "Told you she would! Now, where's my gold lev piece?"

Van cocked his head. *What does 1000 lev have to do with this?*

"You'll get it. You know I'm good for it."

From the sound of it, both Wally and Ccuivr had made a gamble of some sort. That did not surprise him much, but the amount of money Ccuivr just lost certainly did. "What are you two talking about?"

Wally faced his friend again with a smile that lost its impish appeal, one that instead begged sympathy. "Sorry about getting involved with something so personal, mate, but we couldn't help ourselves. We made a little wager to see if Rubi would confess her feelings to you or not."

And those words raised many, *many* more questions. Rubi confessing her feelings?

The two boys stared at him, expecting more information. They knew more about what was happening to Van than he did, and they caught on to that impression the longer he remained silent. Their excitement faded in the coming disappointment they emphasized in their groans.

"You have no idea what just happened to you, do you?"

Van blinked. It was the first time Wally sounded like he was talking down to him.

Ccuivr slapped himself in the face rather fierce and shook his head. "I knew something wasn't right. The boy's too clueless to even realize it."

Now their arrogance was striking his temper. "Realize what? Someone tell me what's going on!"

Wally expressed more sympathy upon hearing Van's frustration. He understood what little more Van could take. He put himself between Van and Ccuivr, possibly so he paid less attention to the snide young man behind him.

"You see, Van, what you have there is a special flower called the pearl orchid. It's a thing of beauty, yes? Pretty. Delicate. Such a flower is beloved by the young women who receive them from their men as much as the men who are given one by their women. As such, it is often called the 'flower of love.'"

Wally spoke in a poetic tone normally heard from eccentric bards. He took a moment to pause, glancing at Van to see if he had gotten the point. And he found he noticed nothing. The bitter look of disappointment he had showed that he conceded to agree with Ccuivr.

If they saw the point and he did not, Van wondered if they were right.

"Plenty of pages are given pearl orchids, Van," he continued with empathy heavy in his voice. "Whether they're young lads or fair ladies, they muster the courage to express the feelings they cannot keep concealed by offering whoever they adore one of those."

It was plain and clear what he was saying, and yet Van could not quite process it. He thought over everything again and again, for some reason trying to reach a different conclusion. No matter what, every thought led to the one single truth.

Rubi liked him.

His mind froze as he came to that realization. It was difficult to know why. Was it fear? Overwhelming excitement? Anxiety? He remembered the discord he saw in Rubi's valsara, and now felt he could make sense of it.

What he saw on Van's honest face let Wally know that the message got through. "You've barely scratched the surface."

"What do you mean?"

"She feels really strongly for you. It's not some fleeting calf-love."

"How do you even know this?"

"Funny you should ask. For some time now, our dangerous girl has been confiding in young Lelia about her forbidden feelings for you. I got the inkling Lelia was hiding something one day and 'persuaded' her to tell me everything. Though, honestly, I wasn't expecting this! Rubi's been going on and on about what she feels for the past year now, never really coming to an answer on whether she should say anything or actually try to attract you."

Wally paused again, unable to keep a chuckle from escaping him. He restrained himself so it did not go on for too long. "The point being, Van, she's heart-bound to you. Otherwise, she would have never given you that flower."

Van glanced down at the pearl orchid in his hand, proceeding deeper into his thoughts and allowing Wally to have his laugh. For someone who could only see select sides of her, he could not imagine Rubi trying to attract someone, and found it laughable.

But Van did not find it hard to believe.

Rubi was a wonderful girl—passionate, determined, beautiful. She always knew what she wanted and worked to seize it no matter the difficulty. She took pride in her strength, always brimming with confidence in what she could do and how far she would go with it. Though her smile sometimes had a boyish quality, her eyes glinted with a charm that had captivated Van.

Where did that charm come from? He never noticed it when they first met or very long after.

Van wondered why he had not seen her feelings before, why it took being blatantly told to realize them. And then he remembered the moment they shared just now. They were close, and they comfortable with it.

It was no ruse. She was genuinely happy when he accepted the pearl orchid from her.

And he did not even know the significance of it.

"Wally."

It seemed while he was deep in thought, Ccuivr was chiding Wally about how duplicitous his laughter was. Wally immediately focused on Van again, plainly ignoring his other friend.

"Can you do me a favor?"

This question stunned him a moment because Van never asked for anything of him before. "Sure. Name it."

"Make an excuse for me, something convincing."

Wally did not need any further explanation. He smiled and nodded, understanding what he planned to do.

Van immediately ran down the hall behind the stairway.

When he reached the training grounds, Van took no chances. He kept himself pressed to the walls to avoid being seen. The Estrine knights changed shifts immediately at dawn—assuming what he overheard from the lazy knights who worked him like a dog was true. Whoever kept watch now would be fully rested and capable of spotting disturbances.

He did not sense many present above or on the ground, but chose not to risk any daring moves to save time. The plan was to simply find where the pearl orchids grew, pluck the most beautiful one, and bring it back to present to Rubi.

Then—and he would have slapped himself for it were he not afraid to draw unwanted attention—Van realized he never knew where to search.

His brows sank and furrowed from thinking of the gaps in his plan. A vein throbbed painfully on his forehead. Van tried to keep calm and brought the flower back to his nose. Its fragrance soothed him.

As he lowered his hand, he found the fragrance's pungency had yet to pass. It was as though the pollen had scattered to the air around him. Curious, he inhaled again and found the scent concentrate more around one major point. Every breath he took etched something into his mind until he had been drawn an invisible path to the eastern grove.

Seeing no other option, he dashed across the yard and dove straight into the tall grass for cover. The only sound to alert him was the soft wisp of wind brushing the grass and making it dance, which effectively masked his presence. He continued on, crawling through the tall grass.

In every direction Van turned, he only saw the gently motioning green. Left. Right. From behind or in front. All that surrounded him was the untamed grass swaying to the breeze. Van relied only on his nose to guide him through the walls of green, smelling the white orchid again whenever another scent filled his nostrils.

Time seemed eternal yet dissipated quickly all the same. He worried about being gone too long and leaving Wally to answer for it. Even he could not make enough excuses to stall forever.

Upon reaching the small grove, he bolted out of the grass and rushed down the trail made by the orchid's scent. It did not take long to find what he searched for. Deep in the grove's clearing, hanging on every tree from every branch, dozens of pearl orchids were in full bloom, each more alluring than the last.

It was a breathtaking scene, but there was not time to take it in. Van glanced at the nearby orchids before proceeding farther, wanting to be certain he did not pass the perfect flower.

As he searched for the flower worthy of gifting Rubi, he began to wonder why he was doing it.

While it was true he was attracted to Rubi, he was not sure where his heart lay.

His feelings about their betrothal were rather mixed. He thought she was only using him. But that was not all there was to it. If it were, she never would have expressed her feelings through the orchid. She would have gone through their time together in silence, or perhaps even ignored him for going behind her back.

Now that he knew of her true feelings, his were put into question. Did he feel the same way? And if not, wouldn't it be unfair to her to give her an orchid? She deserved an honest answer if he was going to do something equivalent to saying "I love you."

There was no questioning he cared about Rubi deeply. What he had done for her shows that much. He enjoyed the simple moments they shared. When she was with him, he felt happier; when she was not, he realized how cold he was.

All of his contradictory thoughts failed to sway him from the notion that it was what he should be doing.

All thought stopped when he saw the orchid he knew Rubi would love. It hung precariously from the tip of a sturdy tree's flimsy branch. He went to harvest it immediately. Pressed for time, he did not worry whether or not the branch could support his weight. He only kept sight on the flower while climbing the tree and slowly slinking along the branch—until it snapped under his weight.

His body ached all over, but he shrugged off the pain that would eventually heal and kept focus only on the goal at hand.

Shaking off the disorientation, he looked over each and every last orchid that fell, even the few that were crushed under the branch, until spotting the one he was after still barely hanging from its edge. He stood and gently, making absolutely sure he would not damage it, picked the pearl orchid from its perch.

Van did nothing but stare at the perfect orchid with pride, wondering how happy Rubi would be when he presented it to her.

As he realized that was precisely what went through his mind and before he could question it, he started to imagine that big, cheerful grin on her face. He thought of how her eyes would sparkle, how merrily her smile would shine seeing her feelings returned. She would quickly regain her tough girl exterior and keep her true feelings hidden until finding herself alone, where she would allow her glee to overcome her and hold the flower close to her chest.

All of the doubt Van harbored vanished.

Delicately, he pulled the pearl orchid Rubi gave him next to the one he planned to give to her. Earlier, he saw them as nothing more than flowers that would quickly wither. But now he thought them more.

He wanted to be with Rubi as long as he possibly could; that much was certain before the day began. That now took a new meaning. A word, a name, a single thought—it was amazing how much that could change.

Rubi had given him her heart. And now, he was going to give her his.

He could not wait any longer. Van rushed back in the direction he came, all too eager to see what he envisioned come to pass.

Avoiding getting spotted when he left the grove's cover suddenly did not seem very imperative. He saw no guards at their posts when looking to the chateau from afar. It would not be much trouble getting back.

Wait... Something was not right. Lord Estrine never left any area of the chateau exposed to threats.

He needed a closer look. Van sprinted through the tall grass, not bothering to duck for cover while keeping the flowers safe in his hands.

The air tasted of danger. Every step he took broadened his caution. After he determined there really were no knights on lookout, Van heard an echo of terrifying screams break over the Estrine Chateau's solid walls. Fear rushed through his body as they reached him, bringing him to writhe until falling to his knees. Losing all regard for the flowers, his hands clasped firmly against his skull, desperate to suppress the pain threatening to split it open.

Roaring explosions echoed in the depths of his mind, magnifying the terror overcoming him. The visions of blood staining the earth and ghastly faces frozen in terror tormented him once more.

No... Not again... Leave me alone!

He begged for the images to leave him, hating them more than when he witnessed them the first time two years ago.

More screams filled the air and drove out the images plaguing him. Not all of them were in his head. They were coming directly from the city.

He never thought much about those hallucinations, but knowing he only saw them whenever fighting in the mock wars the Estrine family organized troubled him. He stood and ran back to the chateau, failing to notice he let the flower Rubi gave him slip from his grasp.

I have to hurry. And fast!

Not a soul roamed the entire chateau. No guards patrolled the halls, or pages, or servants for that matter. The entire facility seemed devoid of life. But through Van's magic sight, he noticed those unable to do battle have already locked themselves in their rooms.

No destruction took place. The enemy had not yet breached the chateau.

In his search for the others, Van rushed past the windows overlooking Brigadier's main district and witnessed a terrible scene. Dangerous men armed to the teeth had somehow gotten past the city walls and were slaughtering people one after another. Any able men—foot soldiers, Estrine knights, Holy Knights, even armed civilians—raced to intercept and rout them.

From the looks of it, it took three men to eliminate one. But then more began to rear their heads, leaping from the buildings they set fire to, ambushing the knights off guard. Soon, they outnumbered the knights.

At this rate, Van feared the enemy would soon breach the palace, or worse yet, the chateau. The royal palace would remain safe under the protection of the army of knights, said to be the best of the best, at its disposal. The chateau, on the other hand, did not have as many trained knights. And they had Princess Camellia. There would be more to lose if the enemy set its sights on the smaller estate.

Time was of the essence.

He tried tracking her down the only way he could, but he was not picking up anyone's scent. As he was not with them to greet the princess, he had no idea where they would go. They could not have gone far, though, and since Princess Camellia required someone to guide her, they could not get anywhere fast.

The ground and second floors were the only possible places they could have gone in such a short time. Van began his search on the ground floor. Even if they were not there, he needed to make certain. Before they became compromised, it was best to check the places where danger was bound to strike first.

Van kept his sword and scabbard in hand, readying himself for anything. He muttered a curse to himself, wishing he had earlier accepted a real weapon from Sir Charleston as his friends had instead of relying on his father's old practice sword. This was supposed to be training; he could not have known that they would be attacked.

When making his way for the foyer, Van detected something lingering across the corridor. It eluded him a moment, but then he recognized that dry, peachy scent with a hint of earthiness—it was Rubi's scent. Wherever she was, the faction, the princess, and her loyal servants were bound to be. They all left the hall to the main gate and hurried into the eastern corridors.

He followed the trail quickly, desperate to catch up with them. As he passed the windows leaking traces of the morning sun, he detected another scent he thought he recognized, but it had been shrouded with another unpleasant odor, masking any familiarity.

The trail led to the left across the expansive hall of portraits. As Van made a sharp turn following it, he found it led to a dead-end. Nothing but a wall stood in the way.

That could not be. The scent grew stronger as he followed it and continued past the wall. It made no sense.

Van crossed those halls more times than he could recall in avoiding the Estrine knights. Never once had he found anything more than the wall that was there. His senses never deceived him before. They had to be right. There had to be something on the other side.

Wary of the imminent danger, Van slowly walked down the dead-end with a hand against the wall, examining it for any fault or opening. For the scent to travel farther, it meant the way forward had to be hidden. He made it toward the end without finding anything, then stopped inches from the dead-end. He pulled back, flinching, like he was frightened something would happen.

It felt all too familiar.

Van carefully looked over the wall, making sure not to miss the slightest detail. Nothing was revealed to the naked eye, but when switching to magic sight, he found what had him so cautious. Something hung directly over the wall, a talisman of some sort with a cryptic rune at its center. It vanished when he relied on his eyes alone and appeared again when using his magic sight.

Whatever it was created the illusion of a wall behind it while, at the same time, masking its presence.

It served to protect something, but Van did not like it. His heart trembled when he looked at it, adrenaline rising. Something warned him that it played a malignant role.

That was all he needed to know.

Coaxing the power inside him to build, he sheathed his sword, a frigid vapor now permeating from his arm. Then he thrust directly at the talisman and clasped his hand around it. Its magic reacted to his presence and immediately retaliated, quickly warping his mind. Before it could strain it, he quickly froze the talisman, nullifying its magic.

There was more to the talisman than he first thought. Its magic tried to do something to him. For a moment, he forgot what he was doing and thought he was still looking for a pearl orchid, but Van got a hold of himself and remembered the mission at hand.

On impulse, he inspected his skin, which reverted back to its true russet hue. He reached for the Shift Pendant underneath his tunic, squeezing it. The spell reactivated and his disguise was restored again without delay. Enough of his Second Verse must have been integrated into the Shift Pendant so that it could reactive without the need for a recharge.

He smashed the talisman against the wall, shattering it. A darkened stairway then appeared where it once hung. When looking down into the shadows, dread rooted itself deeper inside him. With the obstacle gone, the scent he followed grew stronger, as well as another strong odor following them: blood.

The enemy has already broken through!

Without another thought, he armed himself again and descended the stairs. He saw that he dropped the pearl orchid for Rubi onto the steps, but he could not go back for it now. They were in danger. Rubi was in danger!

Barely any light illuminated the dark passage and its cobblestone floors. The air became heavier the deeper he went, something sinister polluting it. Occasionally, another path would open up and force a decision to be made. Van was not afraid of taking the wrong turn. Despite the heavy, dank smell of decay, he could still track everyone.

An array of those scents grew very strong. A group of people was straight ahead. It was relieving to know he found them before anyone else. But as the scent of blood mixed into the air, he realized he was mistaken.

When Van saw shapes manifest in the darkness, he gradually slowed and came to a stop. He could not move. Horror paralyzed his limbs and shackled his mind. Not even in his most disturbing nightmares had he witnessed anything so gruesome.

All four of the princess' ladies-in-waiting lay dead on the blood-soaked floor. Every quarter of their bodies had been maliciously rent asunder, their abdomens ripped open, their organs squashed like old grapes fallen from the vine. They were drenched in each other's blood, sharing in their dissipating warmth. Their eyes remained frozen open, expressing their lingering guilt and despair.

It was horrific, but Van could not look away. Bile rose up in his throat, but he kept from vomiting and lost his balance, backing away from the gory sight. The intense smell of blood was becoming too much, the fumes veiling his mind in a haze. The four having been killed just recently, he could practically feel their pain still in the air.

It would have been less horrendous if they had merely been slit at the throat or stabbed. They were not just killed. They were butchered.

A terrified scream pulled him back to reality. The others have not yet met the same fate, but time was running out.

Van followed the scream down the left corridor, careful not to step on the deceased. He tried to block the fresh image out of his mind, worried it would hinder him from his objective, but the effort only weighed against him further. What sort of monster would deface someone so heinously even after killing them?

Another body was left across the hall. And the weight continued to crush him. This time, it was Ccuivr's. Whatever the enemy did to amuse himself with the four women had not been wasted on him. He had been felled with merely a small slit above the heart.

Van averted his eyes and kept running. As he did, he felt a crack form over his heart. If he stopped, he would not be able to continue. He clenched his fists over the cold metal of his weapon and gritted his teeth to suppress the pain.

It was all he could do for the others. Stevene and the twins, too, had been slain.

Seeing the look of utter terror frozen on Lelia's face slowed him down, tearing at his heart further, but he refused to stop.

Someone was still alive deeper inside and needed help. The dead could be mourned for later, but limiting the casualties could not wait.

The screams became louder as he went on and more sounds were heard directly ahead. A struggle was still occurring. Van rushed forward in hopes that he was not already too late.

The darkness parted as a dying cry escaped from the form taking shape inside. Soon, he saw the one body was actually two; one stood over the other that just fell to the ground.

When his vision fully adjusted, he lost all strength to keep moving. The body falling to the cobblestones before his very eyes was Wally. Van felt his blood run cold when he saw the life fade from Wally's eyes and collapse directly in front of Rubi—or rather, her corpse.

"So you finally decided to join us."

Van thought his mind was going to snap. The one before him, the one who murdered his friends, was Lord Xanlir.

Van could not move. His entire body became paralyzed by the reality before him. He could not believe that the honorable Champion of Duty did this, that he was capable of butchering four defenseless maidens and killing the pages he once guided and protected.

A malicious smirk etched across Lord Xanlir's face, complementing the eerie gleam of malice in his eyes. The man Van once admired completely vanished under that guise. "What's the matter? Too astounded to speak?" His voice flung cruelty and enmity, the valiance he once had gone.

"Y-You ... You did—"

Lord Xanlir nodded. "Yes. Sadly, your friends left me little choice but to kill them after they so refused to hand over the Ederean princess."

The princess?

Van shot his gaze beyond Lord Xanlir where the last of the darkness clustered. It ceased to hide Princess Camellia, who clawed at the walls desperately like a cornered mouse trying to escape.

"Had they not stood in my way, they could have lived a longer life, perhaps with more reward. And now I have to deal with several more dead pages weighing on my conscience. You have my condolences, Vandelas. But now, if you'll excuse me, I must confront my prime target." Lord Xanlir turned around to close in on the princess. He carried the blood-coated sword he used to murder everyone, dragging it across the ground, cracking sparks in the friction it made, to taunt her.

Van's heart trembled, more cracks forming. *How could he do this? How could Lord Xanlir kill them?*

The trembling intensified, bringing Van to wither from pain it brought. *My friends... He helped them to grow as pages with all the kindness a man could have ... then killed them in cold blood?*

It was becoming too much. The cracks surrounded his heart in a web of pain. *And now ... now he's turning his blade against a defenseless girl without a shred of remorse!*

The loss—the murder—of his friends, the callous betrayal, it all came down on Van with such oppressive force. His fragile heart, unable to take anymore, then shattered.

All of the dread inside Van soon evaporated in face of the violent rage that overcame him.

"Xanlir!" he roared a terrifying scream at the top of his lungs. Taking a strong hold of his weapon, he sprinted straight for the knight and swung for his back. In the instant Van swung, Xanlir turned and successfully blocked the hate-filled strike with unwavering strength.

Unfazed, Van continued his relentless assault. He swung both his sword and scabbard in wild yet precise strikes aiming for places he could leave ample damage. Without the weights he usually wore holding him back, he moved at speeds he could barely keep up with himself. Sheer rage only pushed him to strike more, to strike faster, to look for every chance to attack at his foe.

As fast as he was, Xanlir watched carefully his movements and fought Van off with fierce strength.

"Why?" Van snarled in between swings. His voice was hoarse, carrying the sorrow and fury guiding him. "Why did you do this? How could you betray us? How could you kill my friends? We all serve under the same rule. We're all on the same side! If King Faustign knew of this—"

Van was soon unable to match Xanlir's power. The fallen knight held his blade forcefully against the page's, stopping the haphazard strikes thrown against him. He applied pressure against his sword, pushing the boy back, toying with him. The evil glow Xanlir's eyes flickered heinously. "Everything I do is for the king."

He killed innocent women and the pages he promised to guide, spat on them for believing in the mask that he created, and now mocked the very man he swore fealty to.

It all pushed Van too far. He tasted blood between his teeth, not from pain but malice. It quickly took him over and he let it.

He saw him now for what he truly was behind the broken façade of benevolence. He was a monster.

Van knew he could not cut Xanlir, but he did not care. He just wanted to keep attacking, to hurt him, to spill his blood and see his lifeless corpse on the ground.

I'll kill you... I'll kill you. I'll kill you!

He assailed the detestable knight in a flurry that nearly blurred his movements. Van lost track of where he tried to strike. The malice burning within him intensified from hearing the snide laughter Xanlir breathed.

Deciding he had enough horseplay, Xanlir met an incoming strike and pushed it back, easily throwing Van off balance with just one swing. There was not any time for Van to react when he closed in. With another mighty swing, Xanlir brought his sword against the practice weapon with the force to snap it in two. Finally, he thrust his sword and pierced Van's chest.

Three strikes—that was all it took for Xanlir to dispose of the boy. He did with three strikes what Van failed to do in over fifty.

Flashing a heinous sneer, Xanlir flicked the boy off his weapon. Blood spattered against his skin and armor, but he did not even wince.

"I enjoyed playing with you, Vandelas." Even through the agony, it stoked Van's anger to hear Xanlir speak so casually. "If you hadn't interfered like your little faction had, you might have survived this incursion." Xanlir turned to advance toward the princess again, but paused a moment and turned to glance back at Van. "A terrible shame about you and Ccuivr. I'd honestly hoped to take one of you as my squire. You two would have done better than the rest I liberated."

Van froze from shock. Long before this madness, he hoped that a knight like Lord Xanlir would choose him. But now he snarled at the poison in his words.

Van desperately struggled to get back on his feet, but pain pinned him onto the cobblestones. Blood seeped and spurted from the hole carved between his ribs. Even as his body became heavier, he could not remain still as he watching the fallen knight close in on Princess Camellia.

The princess turned from the wall she clawed at as he approached. Her breathing stopped and her terrified voice shook at the tangible malice closing in.

The sight of her pearl white irises shrinking tortured Van more than the pain splitting his body. The sheer terror ringing from her valsara fed his resolve to stand and fight. Fending off the burgeoning pain grew all the more difficult, his muscles growing weaker as his body became heavy as stone.

His vision began to flicker, his consciousness slowly slipping away.

No... No! Not like this!

Fighting through the tremendous pain and the increasing weight of his body, Van began seizing strength he did not know he had.

If I die here, then ... I'm taking him with me!

Maybe his swordsmanship was no match for Xanlir's, but there was one last thing he could do. He was going to die anyway. What did it matter if he saw?

He heard the howling that filled his head whenever his inner beast, whenever his malice, wanted to rage. It derailed his thoughts, but Van shook the hold of his primal instinct before it could take full control. It motivated him to move faster, and he wanted that, but he did not want it controlling him. That would not save the princess.

With all his strength, Van struggled until finally standing back up and raced to the princess' side. The pain meant nothing anymore. He still had the chance to save one person. So long as he did that, he could deal with a few more agonizing last moments.

Xanlir already stood over the terrified princess, taking in the stark fear shaking her very soul, ready to skewer her.

Taking one final sprint, Van closed in on the fallen knight and Princess Camellia. Right as Xanlir thrust his sword, Van got between them and clasped the blade between his hands, holding it at bay with brute force alone.

At first, Xanlir was shocked to see him muster the strength to keep resisting, but then he smiled maliciously. "As tenacious as ever, even on the brink of death. You always impress me, Vandelas. But it's futile." He forced the sword back into the freshly carven hole it slit open. With the blade connecting them, Van could feel how he enjoyed the hunt becoming such a challenge. "You are but a child and I am a knight among knights. There was never a chance for you to stop me."

Van refused to let this continue any longer. He looked Xanlir directly in the eye and watched his confident leer break apart. He roared with all of the air he had left in his lungs as he tightly gripped his hands around the blade and mightily pry it from his wound. "By the gods..." Upon looking into the boy's cold eyes, he lost his composure. Fear flickered where there was once malice. There was no doubt he saw the beast he truly was. All of the extra stress Van put his muscles under made the vapor seeping from him so thick not even the darkness could hide it. The dark space around them gradually turned white. "Wha—What in the seven hells are you?"

Seeing the astonishment on Xanlir's face let Van know exactly what he saw. As his power surged dangerously, the Shift Pendant deactivated and his disguise faded, revealing his Kindhrin skin. In an instant, ice clustered around the sword and clung to Xanlir, tracing up his arms, and freezing him to the core.

Van's vision began to fog, but he still clung to life. The enemy still stood before him. That could not be allowed.

He pulled his trembling hands away from the ice, synching the energy inside him with it. Then, allowing that energy to intensify, he clasped his hands together like a great beast would clamping its jaws, shattering the ice and the knight inside.

No corpse remained. No dismembered limbs fell from the instant destruction. Not even droplets of blood were left behind. Only the smallest specks of ice scattered about were proof of the man's demise.

With the threat eliminated, the adrenaline that kept Van standing vanished. All of his remaining strength dwindled into nothing. He fell to his knees, unable to withstand the weight of his dying body any longer. His vision began to fail him. Then suddenly, he could not hear anything. Even the cold began to disappear, leaving nothing behind.

"Princess ... you're safe..."

Everything faded to black after saying what he needed to.

At least she was safe. At least one of them was still safe.

*   *   *

...I failed. My friends have all been slain, one by one, all given a cruel end.

The man responsible for their deaths was someone they trusted. Xanlir... How could I have been so blind to the evil in his heart? Why haven't I noticed it before?

No ... the sad truth is, I had noticed. I had to have noticed that day, when my instincts awakened and I discovered my swordsmanship, my way to fight.

I knew something was wrong, but I was too ignorant to notice a thing. How many times has my ignorance blinded me? My lineage. Xanlir. Rubi...

I was clueless, and that cost us all our lives. My life—all of our lives lost for one girl. Was it really worth it?

Why am I thinking that now? Why am I putting so much thought into all that has happened? Perhaps an untimely death really does leave the soul restless.

And yet I am still here, in this frozen wasteland. I was always told that the good were whisked away to the Elysium, a paradise garden, for an afterlife of bliss after they died. I should be in an everlasting glen abundant in the tallest trees, endless bounties of heavenly fruit, groves with the most enchanting flowers in perpetual bloom.

All that surrounds me is Prunia's frozen world, without a single familiar soul to greet me.

So here you are again.

How foolish I am to think the spirit wouldn't appear.

There he is, sitting atop a small pillar of ice shaped like a throne overlooking the dark ocean, staring blankly at the water. He does not look at all like his usual self, even as he descends his perch to come to me.

How tragic it is for you to have perished again so soon. I hoped embodying a young vessel would result in exceptional longevity. Alas, your conclusion ended no differently than those who came before you. There is only so much a human can accomplish, even with the power of nature. Most have their second chance at life cut short in search of the answers they seek … as you have.

How dare this spirit speak so tediously of my death! It doesn't surprise me that he only saw my Second Verse as something insignificant, an experiment. And my life wasn't the only insignificance in his eyes. The power that flowed through me—I know he didn't just watch the battle with Xanlir. His very being resonated with my own in those moments.

"Are you through?"

I once feared Pruina. I've already died twice and suffered something far worse. I can never forget the emptiness that grew inside me seeing everyone I cared about dead one after another. There is nothing he can do to me that amounts to any of that.

"Release me then. Let my soul finally find peace. Let me return to my friends … please."

No response. The deafening silence stings more than his words.

That cannot be done.

For the first time, Pruina's demeanor has become remorseful. And … is that sorrow in those blue eyes? They are showing genuine regret.

Look to your feet.

What is he— Is he— No… Why are my legs solid ice? W-Wait! Did it just climb up me? I'm being frozen!? What's happening to me?

In resurrecting you some time ago, your soul established a link with my entirety. That link served to provide enough strength to return you to your mortal body and restore the fatal wound, as well as alter your body's capabilities for easier survival. That link is a perpetual bond. It still exists even now. As we speak, your weaker spirit is being assimilated into my entirety, never to traverse to whatever fates become of the dead.

This can't be. I'm just going to … disappear … without anything left of myself? The last time I will ever see my friends will be as the corpses I left them to be. I will never see anyone again. I will never think or feel anything again. I'm ... I'm just going to disappear.

I will let you have your final thoughts in peace.

No. Not yet. I can't just watch him go without the one answer I need right now. Pruina was right—I am inquisitive. I need to know things to make sense of how to react. Maybe that makes me strange, but that won't matter for long.

"Wait!"

Thank goodness, he stopped. And he's looking back to listen.

"If this is happening, if I'm really going to become a part of you, then I need you to tell me one thing. What are you? What is it you do with all of your power? ...What am I going to become?"

This must be the first time I have seen Pruina look truly surprised. It's just a raised eyebrow, but he is definitely surprised.

That blank, curious stare makes me a little uncomfortable. Did I upset him? No, he's giving it actual thought. He's even holding his icy hand to his chin like a pondering philosopher.

Mm... I wondered about that myself these passing millennia, and still question it now. Like you mortals who bear consciousnesses, I came into existence without knowing of my own role to play in our entwined order. Never once have I found an answer suitable enough to satisfy my curiosities, so I created one. My existence as a spirit of nature is meant to make necessary repairs to the scars you mortals inflict upon your world. Although we exist in separate realities, there seem to be ties between myself, beings like myself, and the natural order in the realm of Avariu, ties I cannot allow to be severed or erased. Put simply, I use souls with questions they cannot leave unanswered to have my own, more personal interaction with Avariu, your world, so that I may restore and preserve the complex balance that is nature.

He makes things right? I see. So, in his own way, Pruina works to ensure everything is as it should be. I suppose that is enough.

I hope that gives you a semblance of peace, Feroxis Maveronyn.

And there he goes, gone in a cloud of frozen vapor. It's just as well— my vision is starting to go white.

The ice continues to spread and take root into me. It stings so badly, like the cold is being infused with me. And yet ... the longer it happens, the more it feels like an embrace. It's a comfort—a small one, but one I can hold onto as the light grows brighter.

The light. The cold. It all feels so inviting, comforting. And yet... And yet I cannot help but be terrified all the same.

Davern. Ccuivr. Stevene. Gal. Lelia. Wally. ...Rubi... I'm scared. I don't want to be without you. Please ... don't leave me alone.

Please...

~ Twentieth Chapter ~

The Final Test

Darkness swallowed the blinding light from the center out. Every ounce of comfort had been erased, leaving no place for bliss.

After what felt like an eternity, one of his senses finally returned. He could hear a muffled call from someplace far away. It kept ringing through the void, shaking the very space, but the sound was something undefinable.

Was it one of the souls dwelling within Pruina?

The infinite black shifted into a brighter hue, quickly turning a rigid gray. It looked to be stone. Van found its depth familiar. His vision further expanded as he realized what it was—the ceiling of the medical ward in the Estrine Chateau.

He left out a dry, frightened gasp as he regained consciousness and recognized the world around him again.

Van returned to the chateau, to his body.

Bewilderment clouded his mind as he stared blankly at the ceiling. Everything was a blur. How he came to be in the medical ward, how much time had passed, and what happened to him eluded him entirely.

All he knew was that he was supposed to disappear, but didn't.

The sound that called him back to the world became stronger and clearer, allowing Van to identify it as the voices of people. But the voices were still too muddled for him to make out who they belonged to or what was said. He tried to look for them, but he became distracted by the white blocking out his vision again—as a puff of fur. When it pulled back enough for him to see, Van could make out a face with precious vulpine features.

"Snow...flake...?"

He began to question whether or not what was happening was actually real. Was it all just a cruel hallucination, or had he really escaped death once more?

Snowflake's big blue eyes gleamed with vivid relief. She leaned in close and nuzzled him gently. *I am here*, it tenderly implied.

That possessive kindness could not be fabricated by an illusion. He really had returned. He was alive.

Though he found his anxiety lessen while Snowflake cuddled with him, Van wanted to know who else was there with him. The voices he had been hearing became inexplicably clear.

To his left were the two women in his life who have looked after him: Victoriah, his mother, and Lyn, his sisterly maid. Both of them wore countenances etched with grief, exhaustion, and relief. Victoriah spoke something that could only have been a command to the maid, who bowed to her and left the room with haste.

Van noticed he looked upon his beloved mother with strong grief. He should have been happy to see her. He wanted to be, but he felt so many tight knots in his chest and head that he failed to muster any euphoria. For a moment, he thought she was not as she appeared to be.

"M-Mother...?"

Victoriah turned to her son immediately upon hearing his tattered voice. She walked to the bed with a worn smile to see her son, caring for nothing more than his well-being.

She was real too.

The maternal knight lowered herself to Van's level and reached out to cup his cheek. He felt the flinch she tried to hide as well, leading him to wonder how cold his skin must have been.

As his mother whispered his name and bade "Shhh," to soothe him, Van realized his skin was not the true dark hue it naturally was, but instead the deceptive pale peach resembling that of any other Vermalian.

It was wrong. He recalled his true colors having been revealed, as well as the moment when his life was once again taken. A terribly sharp pain twisted his chest as his fragmented memories returned. The scar across his abdomen pulsated agonizingly where his ribs met, a familiar but dreadful feeling.

"Why...? How am I still alive?"

His mother caressed his cheek so she may distract him from the pain. "I don't know whether or not I should tell you how fortunate you are after coming so close to dying twice in your young life. It is a miracle, truly." Victoriah paused for a small breath. "Princess Camellia brought you back to us. She has healing magic."

There was always something pure and radiant about the princess' valsara, so it did not surprise him that she possessed such magic. It made sense. She was the only one who could have saved him in time.

"I still can't believe it. It's too good to be true. Among the handful of healers I met in my life, none of them are as gifted as her."

It startled Van to feel his mother's tender hand tremble and hear her voice to do the same. Her face had sunk from his sight. She did not want him seeing her quivering lip or the tears falling onto the sheets.

"Even if all of those healers put their power together, they would never have been able to mend that gash in your chest and keep you with us ... but Van ... that little girl did it alone."

A proud knight, Victoriah never allowed herself to show any vulnerability to another soul, even her own family. She always acted with pride in her power, anger toward the unforgivable, and compassion for the small and weak. But she never let anyone see her cry.

How badly had he been maimed for her to crumble like this?

Sadness was not all she had to endure. In her valsara festered the colors of murderous rage, grief, and the one thing Van would never expect: helplessness. It was hard to look at, but even harder to look away from.

The rage she felt—it had to be for the traitor. Not even she could fathom how someone of like him was capable of such madness.

Van's thoughts grew darker with the terrifying images of his friends' fate returning to him, and as they did, the pain in his chest worsened.

He did not want to believe it. "My friends. W-What became of them?"

Victoriah's hand tensed up. She looked back at Van, fright in her eyes, contemplating if he had truly forgotten the tragedy. Her hand drew from his cheek and gripped the boy's hand buried underneath the sheets. Her eyes glistened brightly, more moisture whelming inside.

She did not need to say anything. Her expression told him everything.

His breathing went still. His eyes lost their light. Van still refused to accept it. He could not bring himself to. It ate him alive inside to remember that man had slaughtered the friends he left alone to pick a flower. Their lives were much too important to have been forsaken for a symbol.

If he had been there...

Guilt racked at Van until bringing tears to his eyes. Those bitter droplets trailing down his cheeks froze solid upon falling off. He turned away from his mother, not wanting her to see his tears either. Snowflake crawled closer and brushed her face against him. She wanted to comfort him, understanding well his pain.

Struggling, Van lifted his arms up out of the blankets to hold her close. Though it tore at the muscles in his chest to move, he felt he had to hold on to her. He did not care about the tears chipping off his cheeks or the pathetic squealing he let out in his cries. He only wished to mourn for those he lost.

Wallace Alivvrn was the first friend Van made outside of the only home he knew. They could not have been more different in personality or upbringing, but Wally fully accepted him, even after learning Van was a Kindhrin. He was a true noble and a true friend to the very end.

Gallelia and Galvven Erite were wonderful children. Kindhearted. Strong-willed. Brave. Although they both depended on their older friends for many things, they learned quickly. Every accomplishment they made left Van proud and inspired him to do more.

How brokenhearted poor Lelia must have been to be attacked by a knight she idolized.

Stevene Inverg always liked to challenge everyone's intellect. Boastful as he was, when times were tough for any part of the faction, he would them help in any way he could. All he ever wanted was to be useful.

Ccuivr was always looking for someone to challenge. He enjoyed rivaling his physical strength with others he recognized. He was cold, standoffish, but he cared about his friends a great deal, even if he would not say it aloud.

And Rubella...

The remnants of Van's heart trembled at the thought of having lost her. He felt himself a fool for not noticing her feelings and kicked himself for failing to return them. That rowdy girl was disagreeable at times and liked to be rough, whether in a fight or just making friendly conversation, but Van loved that about her. Remembering the reaction he hoped to see from her upon giving her the pearl orchid, what once made his heart soar, now crushed what was left of it.

Van cursed himself for not realizing what Rubi was to him before.

Hoping to be the one to comfort Van instead, Victoriah reached out her hand, but he recoiled, facing the window and hiding from the sunbeam. He felt her regrettably pull away; his mother's sadness was palpable.

Perhaps it meant he was a terrible son for rejecting his mother's love, but Van could not bear to look at another human.

His face soaked in frozen tear trails and voice broken and withered, Van bawled into his fox's fur.

He cursed himself for not being there for his friends. He cursed Xanlir for taking them away. And he cursed Princess Camellia for not saving them instead of him.

The minutes went by in silence. Not a sound rang across the stagnant air. And yet the mood could not be heavier.

Van had fallen silent, having let all the hateful things on his mind be said. He kept a firm hold on Snowflake, fearing that she, too, would vanish from his life.

Victoriah remained close so Van could cry into her if he needed to. She wanted to hold her child like he held his pet, but he already pushed her away once. It saddened her to see him suffer so.

A soft knock at the door disrupted the dreadful silence. Victoriah stood to answer the door while Van, his arms tightening around Snowflake, remained where he was. Though unable to see her, he sensed the tension in Victoriah the Wolverine rise as though expecting another attack. The betrayal left her cautious and on alert.

"I've returned, Lady Kronas." That sweet voice belonged to Lyn.

Van thanked the gods—something he hadn't done in a long time—that his weary mind did not imagine her, that she survived as well.

She entered the medical ward, but not alone. Several footsteps resounded across the stone floors. Whoever it was came in no further than the chair where Victoriah stood.

The grieving child closed his eyes and heightened his senses to detect everything throughout the room. Along with Alicalyn approached the harsh demeanor of Sir Charleston, the hearty and strong Lord Estrine, and— Van almost stopped breathing when he detected the infinitely chromatic valsara that could only belong to King Faustign, who was accompanied by King Godefroy du Joiec and Princess Camellia.

It was tempting to look, but Van remained still where he was.

"I see he was informed of what happened," said the Vermalian king with a voice ringing sympathy.

"Yes, Your Majesty." The silence, painful, potent, and heavy, followed a moment longer after Victoriah spoke. "He's been like this ever since."

"Mayhap he's gone into shock. The poor lad." Those words were spoken by Princess Camellia. "Does he yet know my assailant's true identity?"

"No, Princess. I haven't told him yet," Victoriah answered.

"Then may I?" King Faustign offered.

"Of course, Your Majesty, but ... I doubt he'll respond."

"He will," Sir Charleston insisted. "Page Kronas, present yourself."

"Charlie, leave him be."

"If he truly wishes to be a knight, then he should accept this as a normalcy in his life, not fall into this—"

"This *what?*" Victoriah interrupted with a sharp tone and a click from her scabbard.

Van recoiled from the horrible sound. Knowing whose weapon it was meant nothing. The sound followed a weapon being drawn, and the weapon would promise bloodshed.

He coiled his arms around Snowflake, fearful of the outcome.

"Enough, the both of you!" commanded Lord Estrine. For the first time, his voice was not deafening, though it was not quiet either. It remained firm while also having concern for the heartbroken page.

"Sir Charleston," gently spoke King Faustign, "a soldier though he may be, you must remember that he is still a child, one who has lost friends in battle. You know well what it is like—what it was first like for you."

The knight offered no retort and remained silent. A wave of strife brought his valsara to ripple.

Footsteps clopped across the floor and approached the child, but they stopped halfway across the room. Snowflake perked up, prone to growl before Van held her down.

King Faustign could be trusted—at least he hoped.

"Poor child—to see such a twisted side of someone you valued and trusted. I have heard much talk about Lord Xanlir taking interest in a particular page. And here you are, bereft, robbed of your friends, your trust, and quite nearly your life." The voice of the king was burdened by remorse and guilt. Despite that, he spoke clearly, gently, as one would to a frightened animal. "He was my champion; I bear responsibility for his sins and the pain he has wrought. Although it may mean little after all that you have suffered, know that you have my heartfelt sympathies, Vandelas, and my deepest apologies."

King Faustign paused a moment, hoping his Champion of Heart had been mistaken about her son's silence.

But he said nothing. Their sympathies amounted to little more than a mild agitation. He did not want their pity.

"It is only right for you to know: his loyalties were never with us."

Though he thought he could not be surprised by anything else, Van stirred a little.

"This entire time he was a Renegade, and one of great importance to their cause. He stole information, relayed it to the hidden enemy, sabotaged operations to subdue and repress the Renegade forces, all the while continuing the ruse and behaving the loyal knight."

It hurt all the more to hear that. It meant nothing Xanlir did was real; everything was meant to deceive them, lead them astray until he did what he needed.

"The incursion that devastated Brigadier, he was responsible for orchestrating it. The chaos sown served as nothing more than a diversion; while the insurgents fought, he took the opportunity to secure and slay Princess Camellia. The Renegades wanted the princess to die at the hands of a Vermalian knight so that it would create strife between Vermalio and Ederea, and inevitably lead to war between our two countries."

It made sense. The Ederean royalty came to discuss and further develop their relations with Vermalio. If a Vermalian knight were to murder either of them, that peace would crumble. War would ignite. So many more lives would have been lost to throw Vermalio into instability and shake the confidence in the royal family.

Those downtrodden words doused Lord Estrine's once vibrant valsara. "It brings me great shame to know one of my own has been devising such treachery. Sabotaging us, spiriting pages away—to think my own family has been supporting this madness..."

Spiriting away?

That was what Xanlir meant by liberated. He led the princess and company down the same corridor where he set the talisman, where those pages Van once followed disappeared. Liberated, from the Renegades' perception, meant turning them away from the current ruler and the rest of the kingdom.

It was not just them he hurt. That Xanlir would be willing to go so far, that he would further beget such hatred, orchestrate the deaths of countless people, it brought something in Van to grow. It was nothing like sadness, nor pain nor loneliness. As it budded in him, it made Van want to take a weapon in hand and again hunt the monster that took so much from him.

"Whilst the truth has been learned, we cannot remain in this country much longer." King Godefroy interrupted. "Not knowing who is Vermalian or Renegade leaves us in constant danger for as long as we are here. We stayed only as long as this so my daughter could speak with her savior." That last sentence was directed entirely at Van.

A few sets of footsteps approached the bed closer than the Vermalian king had. One set was burly and heavy, the other light and petite. They belonged to the Ederean king and princess.

"I understand the betrayal of Lord Xanlir and the untimely fate of your friends has left you heartbroken," the princess spoke respectfully. "I do not wish to trouble you any more than I already have. Mayhap this is not the right time to speak, but 'tis my only chance. I wish to express my gratitude to you, brave Vandelas Kronas. Prithee—" She stopped a moment, either confused or uncertain. Perhaps she was thinking of a way to translate her thoughts. She then took a deep breath and bade, "Prithee, accept this humble lass' offer to come and enlist in our armies."

Van gave no answer, this time because his astonishment gagged him. A foreign princess was asking him to become a soldier for her homeland?

"King Godefroy, what is the meaning of this?" Victoriah was as surprised by this as Van. It was so difficult for her to restrain the shock and agitation in her voice that it almost sounded like she was choking.

Instead of the Ederean king, King Faustign elaborated. "We discussed this while you were watching over Vandelas. The boy's actions have left young Camellia impressed. He was on the verge of death and still mustered the strength to protect her. Such doggedness is rare even amongst the most valiant knights. Therefore, we came to an arrangement. The du Joiec royal family earlier bequeathed unto us a cluster aurichalcum capable of supplying us with magic charms for a long time to come, but we had nothing to offer them in showing our alliance holds value."

"Tell me you aren't thinking of using my son as a trinket for trade."

"His Majesty is proposing offering a warrior fit for their military. Regardless of his blood relations, he chose to become a knight. His place is where he is commanded to be," Lord Estrine bravely stated. "Such exchanges have been made between our kingdoms for generations, Lady Victoriah. You cannot claim to be surprised by this."

A fierce argument broke out between the two Estrines and Victoriah.

Van did not bother listening to them. Everything was happening too fast for him to keep up. He needed to reassess everything again and again.

Leaving for another county? He never thought that would happen unless war broke out. For that matter, he would be leaving for Ederea. Speaking their language always proved challenging, and following orders was impossible if they could not be understood. There would be new sights to take in, new food to get used to. And chances were, he would never see his parents again.

Those thoughts weighed heavily on him, but as he considered the options, he thought many of the changes would be for the better.

He felt anxious and unstable knowing there were others that pretended to be allies, who held knives to their backs and waited for the need to thrust. Just thinking there were more of those murderers hiding in plain sight made his blood boil.

Would his hate lead him to one day strike down an innocent?

When slowly moving his arms away from Snowflake, Van heard something interesting. Sir Charleston stated it was best for Van to first take part in the Rite of Chivalry. Though Victoriah reacted violently, stating she would rip the man's lungs out, Van thought it the perfect opportunity to prove himself. Instead of appealing to just one girl, he would show everyone his worth, like any other Vermalian page.

Only his stirring from the bed quieted the three bickering knights. All eyes were fixed on Van while he turned over to sit up. His chest still ached from the wound, but he refused to let any weakness show. He stood and faced the others, eyes reddened from the tears he shed yet hollow, plagued by dread.

He took slow steps to stand before the princess and looked directly into her eyes. "Princess Camellia ... I accept your proposal."

"Van—"

"Sir Charleston." His quiet snarl interrupted Victoriah, blocking out her concern. "I shall abide by your terms."

He looked upon Sir Charlestone with vehemence. He wanted to see what Van was capable of, so Van decided to show him much more—the beast within.

"I won't back away from the Rite of Chivalry!"

Later that day, the knights guided Van to the grand cathedral south of Brigadier. As per the longstanding tradition, a rite of passage was held there that revealed the potential of the pages chosen to be squires. That was the Rite of Chivalry.

Upon arriving, he was handed over to four pure women donned entirely in white and silver vestments, the vestals of the cathedral. The vestals were responsible for carrying out the Rite of Chivalry. Each one brandished a blessed magic that served to guide the page in question through the labyrinth of their soul. With their power, they sifted through the page's subconscious and bound them within to confront their inner demons. Should they succeed, they earned the right to be a squire.

But the rite also put a massive strain on one's mind, which often led to complications with the body. Only the resolute reemerged without suffering a relapse.

A few who watched Van enter the cathedral doubted he would leave with his mind intact; he sensed it. Their doubt only hardened his resolve.

The halls of the cathedral had an inviting atmosphere. It was almost like stepping into another realm, one of comfort and understand. Despite that, Van was rather tense following the vestals. He found their concealed forms unnerving. There was nothing particularly wrong with their vestments, but the hoods covering their heads and the veils masking their faces made him nervous. All of their human features were effectively erased beneath the ceremonial garb.

If he had not caught human scents from them, he would have thought them something else entirely.

The vestals led Van into a chamber in the heart of the building. The shallow room was lit an eerie indigo due to sunlight creeping through the dark blue stained glass on the ceiling. A delicate layer of magic covered the entrance and reverberated with each person that stepped inside.

Upon entering, the vestals directed him to the center of the room. There, an unusual symbol had been carved into the floor, the pass of time making it look almost natural. They circled around the symbol and each sat at different corners.

Van followed their silent command and sat directly atop the symbol. The magic circulating throughout the room concentrated on that spot. The vestals raised their arms, the lengths of their sleeves drawing open like wings. Their gloved hands were held to one another, their magic gathering in their palms. Van winced at the burgeoning power.

Then the vestals, all in sync, recited this eldritch chant:

"We beseech thee, Divine Cural. Guide this brave child."

* * *

Instantaneous. That was the only way to describe the change in the surroundings. The chamber completely broke apart and disappeared, revealing vast plains of gold that went on forever. The skies were affected by the spell's power as well. The sun anchored down over the horizon from where it once sat atop its peak.

Van leaped to his feet when he found the vestals were nowhere to be seen, worried over what became of them. He began losing control of his breathing before realizing what had happened.

But he calmed down quickly. None of it was real. It was all part of the elaborate spell cast by the vestals. The world around him was merely part of the rite—the colosseum where he would compete.

He cursed himself for forgetting about the rite for even a second.

The ethereal plane felt similar to the realm he nearly lost his soul in. And yet he did not feel the same foreboding as he had in the world of silver. There was something about the shifting sands that gave him a sense of nostalgia, faint and enigmatic though it was. He felt more at ease staring at the golden sands than when he had been surrounded by snow. Whatever it was, though, left afterthoughts of anxiety.

If he strayed from his goal, he might fail the rite, so Van pushed aside any unnecessary feelings and marched across the golden hills.

The Rite of Chivalry had begun. He expected to find something terrifying to confront. Something would rear its ugly head at any moment.

But he sensed nothing.

For a spell meant to bring out a person's darkest angsts, it left him disappointed. No obstacles barred his path. No threatening forces ambushed him. And he did not intend to wait. If his inner demons refused to come out, then he would hunt them down.

Crossing the towering dunes, he marched away from the setting sun into the darkness, where his tortured thoughts doubtlessly lay in wait. That was where fear always hid, along with the truth—away from the light.

Anxiety plagued his mind the deeper he went. He did not look to be going anywhere; every direction seemed the same. He sensed danger roamed nearby, but of what?

Something glimmered brightly in the darkness with the lingering sunlight. It began as a speck, but grew broader the closer Van got to it. What appeared to be a stone had a rough, glossy surface, and upon getting close enough to see something inside, a terribly bitter chill swept across the sands and bit into him.

Van stopped in his tracks. It was his own father encased in ice.

He stumbled back, struggling to fight the anxiety and rage that followed. As he stabilized himself, more came into view. Countless others—those Van had come in contact with—were in the same state.

Although he knew none of it was real, the sight still tortured him.

That cluster of voices was unmistakable. Lurking behind the frozen body of the soldier Gervall Canvast confidently stood Pruina. The spirit leaned against the frozen person, keeping his hideously ice-coated arm pressed to it, piercing Van with his icy stare. Pruina stepped into full view upon announcing his presence, his bare feet turning the sand silver upon making contact.

"You ... did this?"

Indeed, I did.

He circled the boy, taunting him, like a great predator on the hunt.

These apparitions... How inadequately fabricated. To think the mortals responsible for this world would test you with these flawed phantoms.

"What do you mean?"

These apparitions are mirrors of the fear, dread, anger, and resentment dwelling in the darkest reaches of your soul. Your presence here is merely your conscious mind, which agitates your angsts into taking form. However, they have taken the forms of mortals you've met in your life—that was the flaw. Someone like you, who has been bestowed my power, my perception over the flow of magic and life itself, could never be misled by something other than an original. No, you would likely discern them from those you truly know quickly, if you have not already, and eliminate them without remorse, even the ones resembling those you cherish the most.

Van did not listen to Pruina's words and instead focused on how he traced his icy claws over the frozen victims. His fangs were borne, his malice spiking.

You are afraid.

"Of you?" Van scoffed, attempting to sound confident.

Of yourself. Of what you can do—as a Nascitte, yes, but mostly as a human.

His façade broke apart at Pruina's words. Van knew what he could do. He knew how easy it was to surrender to his malice and kill. The beast, as it was so colorfully called it, was the primal desire that dwelled within human beings. And he recognized his well.

He knew the world around him was not real. What would stop him from figuring out those apparitions were also thus and use it as a reason to let that primal desire out?

At the snap of his frozen fingers, the apparitions he froze were completely shattered into flecks of frost.

It was more than Van could bear watching each and every one of them break with the solid ice. There were dozens of people, young and old, kind and horrendous, preserved in threatening stances—all gone in an instant.

The manner in which he bore his frozen claws startled Van into reaching for a weapon. But there was nothing at his hip. Fighting off an entity no larger than a child without a sword did not bode well when that thing only appearing as a child possessed qualities that made him omnipotent. Victory did not seem likely.

Then Pruina began to laugh, amused by some humor Van failed to see. His devilish laughter was nearly forceful enough to brush away the frost beneath him.

Upon taking a quick turn, Pruina began to slowly stalk toward his prey.

The atmosphere around Pruina grew immensely heavier, his very essence exerting a devastating pressure that stirred the air. Breathing became all the more strenuous the closer he came. And as the cold air enshrouded him in fog, Pruina's body started shifting into an even more terrifying shape. Growing to tremendous size, he soon stood taller than three human adults with a bulk so mighty that "intimidating" did not begin to describe it. His bones and ice cracked and reshaped as his body changed into that of a beastly quadruped. The lightest blue fur quickly sprouted, forming a massive pelt of winter fur. The beast grew deadly scythe-like claws on the left forepaw, the right encased in a layer of jagged ice, and tremendously thick fangs drew out of the long, narrow muzzle capable of crushing a tower. From the parting fog came a terrifying, wolf-like monstrosity that could devour anything in its path.

The wolf-beast left Van frozen in terror, not even capable of trembling.

Perfect. Now, Feroxis Maveronyn, shall we begin?

Without warning, the wolf-beast pounced.

Van quickly ran out of the way before his head was bitten off. The sand carried him farther away from the threat as he skidded on it. Pruina took only a moment to use the sand to turn back for another attack.

There was not even a second for Van to react and concoct a plan to save himself. He only had the focus to keep from being beaten senseless by those colossal paws. The forelimb coated in the razor-sharp ice, arguably the beast's most dangerous feature, followed the first disorienting swing and narrowed in on Van. It was thicker, making it much harder to avoid, but somehow managed to dive between the beast's legs and escape being trampled.

This was no mere animal. The wolf-beast initiated each attack with cunning and ruthless precision. One mistake against it would be the last.

Holding nothing back, Pruina released his power. Ice clustered into a ring around the two, effectively caging his small prey.

There was nowhere to run. Van stopped just before the ice formed before him as the threat came in close. The thing he feared most loomed at his left, ready to rend him asunder. With nowhere to go, he only watched as the wolf-beast swung its icy paw, digging through the sand with the great destructive force. Then, seeking escape, Van reacted without thought and leaped into the air. He leaped high over the wolf-beast's paw, then over the beast itself, until descending behind it and landing (somewhat clumsily) on his feet.

The incredible feat baffled Van enough to momentarily lose focus of the peril he faced. His reflexes were always surreal, as was the strength in his muscles, but he never did something so dynamic before.

Do you see now why I think so highly of your capabilities? This fabricated world reveals your strength that will be, not your strength as is. What you do now reflects what you can achieve.

Even though he just did it, he could not believe it. A human being should not be able to leap such great heights or come back down without injury. Van always doubted the changes in his body were truly animal, but after what happened, it did not seem impossible anymore.

That did not make fighting any easier, though. All he could do was run from the phenomenal power. He attempted to freeze and immobilize Pruina, but Pruina shook off the hardened ice like it was freshly fallen snow and scoffed bitterly at the attempt. Of course it would not work, but simply running would not get him anywhere. He had to fight back somehow.

The wolf-beast was relentless, charging endlessly after his prey and destroying the boundaries it set to capture him.

A primal rage was seething from Pruina and grew for every moment that went by without the kill desired. Van felt Pruina imitating the very soul of a beast, executing a performance that would have any mortal believe him an angry god. It was difficult for Van to not think the same.

Why do you flee? Do you not understand your strength here comes from willpower alone?

If that was meant to be motivation, Pruina obviously had not spent enough time observing humans, only knowing the things that weigh them down. That was what Van believed before Pruina calmed a moment and stared intently at the small prey.

I see... That is what troubles you.

"Why stop attacking?" Van panted heavily. "What does it have to do with the rite?"

You know this place. You know where you are. So why deny it?

Van went entirely still. He felt his ears crackle, his eyes almost pop from their sockets. At that very moment, he became overwhelmed by weakness, resembling the very picture of vulnerability.

This place ... is Harah Krid.

The wolf-beast had not yet gone on the attack. It stood harrowingly over Van, eyeing him with intense appraisal.

Now can you truly claim this trial to only serve as a measure for your potential?

How could he? Van longed for any answers that would tell him the fate of the land he came from, and only got stuck with incomplete history. And though it was an illusion, he was still there. His soul led him back to Harah Krid.

Those apparitions aimed to ambush you, to keep you from what rests beyond this point: the very answers you have sought all this time. Now it is I who keeps you from the memory so rooted into your being. If you truly wish to know those answers, then take them by doing away with my wrath!

The wolf-beast charged again. It leaped viciously at Van and watched as he leaped out of the way, no doubt noticing the new vigor in his step.

Whether Pruina was telling the truth or not could be uncovered later. For now, Van needed to overpower him. Somehow.

But how? Without a weapon, there was no way for him to so much as scratch the monster. And fighting off the being with a power it gave him already proved futile.

It was then that an epiphany struck.

The wolf-beast, with a satisfied malignant sneer, saw its prey had become motionless. It seized its opportunity and charged again, ready to make the kill.

No longer willing to accept being the weaker being, Van chose to fight back. He channeled his power, surging through his arms, and launched it. A silver path quickly overlapped the golden land until it came to an end, a long ice spire shooting forth and piercing the wolf-beast's ribs.

The beast let out a terrifying scream that confirmed it to be more monster than wolf. Its scream rent the sands like water in the face of a savage storm. Even the very darkness around them rippled ominously.

Van cringed from the sheer volume of the scream, but now knew he truly could fight back. Making the ice into weapons—it was something he had been doing for a while now.

Struggling to move, Pruina took its ice-covered limb and slammed it against the spire, shattering it and freeing him.

Frost crumbled from the wound like trickling blood. Furious, the wolf-beast snarled and slammed its frozen paw against the sand, forming a wave of jagged ice.

Van leaped high to the air before the wave maimed him, carefully watching how it formed. He liked how the ice flowed.

Upon his descent, he crafted a shield large enough to support him and used it to bounce and skid off the jagged ice. He bore his hands like claws when on stable ground and slammed them into the sand, forming a wave as fierce, though not as large, as the one Pruina cast. The entity stood its ground and bashed the ice wave with its paw, breaking it apart.

The wolf-beast raced across the walls Van made to slow it down. Van ran when he saw that was not working, but failed to get away before its massive claws dug into his leg. The pain felt so real, like blades digging through flesh, but Van knew he could still use his leg.

When the monster caught him again, Van quickly stopped in place and spun, using the momentum to create a spiral of jagged ice around him. The barrier managed to stand against and repulse the wolf-beast, but it failed to withstand the monstrosity wrapping its fangs around the sides and crushing it.

Those fangs cut through Van's torso and sent though him a cold so unruly he could not feel his body. They bore deep into him, threatening to split him in two. He clung to consciousness, but felt it slipping away.

Van doubted there was anything he could do, but he would not concede defeat.

Being trapped between the fangs of an animal made him recall when last that happened. Once again, Van saw Rubi's terrified face. That stoked his fury and gave him the strength to hold on. If he lost there, everything that had been lost would be for nothing. That was something he refused to accept.

Salvaging every shred of willpower he had left, Van pushed his hands against the monster's mouth and, letting out a fierce roar, forced it open enough to pull the fangs from him. Van then, exuding all of his power, crafted two broad swords with serrated edges from ice and spun, cutting through the wolf-beast's vulnerable mouth and tongue. He broke free and watched as the beast wailed, barely able to keep its balance.

Now was his only chance. Van cast more waves of ice with swift pulls of the arms, toppling the beast and rending its three limbs untouched by frostbite. Then he held his hand into the air and clenched it tightly, causing the swords to shatter. A massive glacier with sharp barbs at its bottom formed above. With a mighty downward pull from Van, the glacier fell upon the wolf-beast at breakneck speed, burying it alive.

The air was filled with white. The cold had permeated the area so thoroughly that the chilling vapor almost blinded Van. He tensed up again as it cleared, wary of how the enemy would respond. But the mountain of ice did not stir.

Finally allowed a moment to stop, Van let his breathing become erratic. The sand scattered upon him falling to his knees. As he recuperated, he looked upon the majestic golden scenery muddled by the ice cutting through it. Some of the distant hills were encased in silver, caught in the maelstrom of power unleashed by the spirit and its Nascitte.

Will I really be capable ... of all this?

His tired thoughts came to a halt at an ominous *boom, bang* shaking the ice crumbled over the monster. Quickly, Van stood back up, ignoring the trembling that came over his legs.

It could not have survived. There was no way.

Van's hopes were crushed when he saw the wolf-beast burst out of its icy grave with the otherworldly power of its roar—a mighty cry that sent shockwaves over the horizon.

The burial was a failure, as were his efforts.

The wolf-beast set its ravenous gaze onto its prey once more. Not a hint of strife or pain had been etched in its face. It seemed set on ending the hunt once and for all.

But then it bared its fangs in a way resembling a smile and let out a sinister laugh.

Magnificent! The savagery. The ferocity. The lethality. You withstood what would have destroyed the weak-willed and fought me with everything you had.

Van lowered his guard when he sensed Pruina's malevolence fade.

A mighty frigid wind brewed around Pruina as he descended the mound of crumbling ice. He reassumed his previous form upon reaching the bottom.

Van felt the adrenaline slip away and fell back to his knees. When he opened his eyes, regaining his strength, he saw Pruina standing in front of him with his frozen claw extended to him.

Unfazed by the spirit's assault, Van took Pruina's hand and accepted his help. While not as desperate for answers, he was as curious about the Kindhrin as Van. They both had a reason to go onward.

The two marched across the sands with hopes that their questions would soon be answered.

Nothing interfered with their trek through the desert. Pruina spared nothing he saw as insignificant in his attempt to push Van to his limit. The barren landscape was devoid of life save for the two of them. And yet the pressure in the air grew more overwhelming.

In the expanding darkness, a faint light reached out for them to follow. Feeling it to be a sign, Van sprinted toward the light without a second thought; Pruina continued at his own pace.

As the light grew brighter, Van felt something weigh him down and bring him to move slower—the dread he felt when he first arrived.

What stood before his eyes was not a sanctuary, but a defenseless city set ablaze. He feared the worst when he heard terrified shrieks cut through the flames.

Van rushed for the city's ruined gates, but stopped and lurched backward. A dark silhouette leaped from the shadows and tried to cut him down with a blade in hand. Seeing it had Rubi's face made him recoil.

The apparition stood between him and the memory. He felt no empathy or grief—only an untamable malice.

The apparition rushed straight for him, angling the sword to swing for his abdomen. Van quickly coated his palm in a layer of ice, then used it to block the blade and hold it steady. The ice clustered around the blade and the doppelganger. He ran his fist straight through it, shattering the entire body, acting swiftly out of respect for the real Rubi.

Nothing would stand in his way. He came this far, and after seeing the fire, there was no turning away.

The entire city was being ravaged by flames. Smoke blanketed the entire sky and stained the air, making drawing breath suffocating. The sandy streets were empty, cluttered only by crumbling buildings.

The longer Van went without finding someone, anyone to explain what caused this, the more his anxiety ate him alive.

And when he finally found someone, he wished he hadn't.

A trail of crimson led to a corpse. The body's skin was dark, and on its face were brands shaped like hooks under the eyes. It was a Kindhrin.

The poor soul was not a victim of the fire. It was murder.

Terrified screams piercing the air built upon his horror. As the flames rolled over the way he came, more Kindhrin stormed down the path ahead. Their cries needed not be said in the same language to communicate their fear.

Instinct overtook Van. He dashed straight down the path ready to confront whatever it was the Kindhrin fled so desperately from.

A few of them fell behind the others. When Van went into a full sprint to meet them, several men emerged from the flames and butchered the Kindhrin with blood-soaked weapons. Their bleached skin and wicked grins gleamed in the hellish light of the fire. They carved through the tortured Kindhrin mercilessly, as though they were lower than animals.

This ... this...!

Another scream drew Van's attention to a woman turning back for her child. The little girl with her had fallen and dropped a chimera-stitched doll. The woman scooped the girl into her arms, only to be caught by another barbarian who held a sword their way.

"Leave them alone!" Abandoning all reason, Van charged at the barbarian with as much murderous intent as he turned on the poor people. He quickly made a sword from ice and thrust at the barbarian's exposed back—and, to his horror, phased right through him.

He could do nothing but watch as the parent and child's blood was spilled over the dropped toy.

You cannot help them.

Pruina finally caught up with Van. He stood behind him as the image of the barbarian became physical once again and ran off in search of more victims.

These are not shadows of your mind, but remnants of your past. We cannot interact with them as they cannot with us.

Even after seeing it happen, Van could not believe it. How was he supposed to accept that and watch as innocent people were being slaughtered one after another? They were just trying to survive, to get away from the monsters hunting them.

Pruina's cold stare dragged over the massacre. He looked upon the dead and rampaging as a disappointed parent would at children.

So this is how the Kindhrin race came to an end...

The screams, carried hauntingly across the inferno, grew louder and louder. They stretched across the entire city and echoed in his mind.

But no matter how loud the collective screams became, one cry in particular pierced through them. It belonged to a baby.

Van felt drawn to the baby's crying. He tried following it to the grand stone building where the flames burned brightest. As he neared the crumbling structure, every other terrified voice became harder to make out, and when the baby was quelled, so were the screams.

The screams, the roaring flames—all sound had faded in the wake of one. A gentle humming rippled in Van's mind. It was soothing, offering a sense of relief and nostalgia. He could not tell where it came from, but hearing it filled him with a strong need to find the one doing it.

Space and direction broke apart and was reconstructed; he found himself behind the grand building when he never crossed its walls.

The humming became louder, and a few words were spoken in

between. He could not understand most of what had been said, but then he heard it again in the Vermalian language. "There, there," whispered an angelic voice. "Shh, now. *Sh-shh!* You're okay. You're okay, Maveronyn."

The voice was rough but feminine.

In trying to follow it, Van spontaneously found himself inside a dark hall lit by luminescent stones. The graves in the rooms to the side suggested it was a crypt. Straight ahead was a passage that branched into two directions shared by a man and a woman. Both of them dressed in heavy-looking garb and covered their heads with hoods. The woman held in her arms the once crying baby, rocking it and holding it close.

Van stared at the three with growing curiosity. The adults were both strong—he could tell just by looking at them. The man stood with great resolve as he looked at the woman with her baby. The woman kept her fear locked away so as not to frighten the baby more than it already was. They were in the midst of chaos, but still they tried to remain strong.

As the baby nuzzled against the woman, Van's eyes widened in utter astonishment. The baby, who looked barely six months old, had the same brands under its eyes as him.

"I shall fend off anyone that manages to find this place," the man spoke. "Take this chance to escape with our child."

The woman turned from her baby to face him. "Find us, Regalia. If you don't find us again after this, I'll—" She could not bring herself to speak any more out of concern she would startle the baby. Stroking the baby's head, she pulled it closer to her, leaving Van unable to look upon his newborn face.

The man leaned in to place a kiss atop her forehead. "We will meet again," he promised when his lips parted.

Van wanted to call out to them, to let them know he was there, but he could not muster a word. He had not forgotten they were only pieces of his memories; he just wanted to speak to them.

Longing overcame him when the two said their goodbyes and rushed down their respective paths. He tried chasing after them, only making it to the branch before both pathways collapsed.

Screams and savage cries from the outside shook the crypt's very foundation. Van put his hands over his ears but failed to block out the terrifying sounds banging inside his head.

Every sound painted a vivid picture of what happened on the outside. It was as though he were there, watching the massacre at its peak. Each death cry was a bash in the head and a gash to the chest. His body grew weak from the torture, and he slumped to the ground.

"S-Stop... Stop...!"

Losing more of himself by the minute, it was hard to do anything more than plea for the chaos to end.

The crypt broke apart around him, and he was outside with the pale barbarians again. They kept rampaging in every direction, leaving nothing to stand in their paths and letting the flames dance over the dying city. It was all that was left to kill.

Van looked around; he was the only Kindhrin left moving. The rest lay in shambles among or under fallen debris of what was once their home.

Everything was stolen from them. They were never given a chance to oppose it. And it was not enough to satisfy the monsters. They just kept destroying, destroying, destroying, destroying. Wiping out everything like they thought it all diseased.

"I said ..." Power raged within Van's very spirit as he usurped the barbarians' destructive intent, ready to use it on them. "STOP!" Fury and hate compelled a bitter cold wind to blow, swallowing the entire city. Ice froze over everything around him and swept throughout the land in waves of razor-sharp pillars. Everything became consumed by the devastating blizzard and shattered under the pressure of Van's malice.

* * *

The white having cleared, Van blinked frantically to find not a ruined Kindhrin city, but the very chamber the vestals have escorted him to.

What had happened? Did he pass? Or had he failed?

Silent as the vestals were, they surely would have given him a sign.

Yet they could not do anything. All four of them had fallen limp over floor. Anyone who might walk in would assume they had been attacked.

Concerned though he was for their well-being, a heavy fatigue kept Van pinned to the ground, preventing him to do more than bat an eye.

His once buried memories tormented him. It ate him alive to know he could not have done anything to save anyone, just as he could not save the friends he abandoned. Even though it was all some distorted memory, it was too real to ignore.

Failing his friends, failing his people, failing himself—the guilt ran through him so that it felt like he was being quartered.

The time for lamenting is over. Now you must press forward or risk being consumed by your own weakness.

Pruina's voices settled the ripples in Van's mind, allowing him to think clearly.

Losing one's self over what happened would accomplish nothing. He finally found significant answers to the questions he had been asking. Grim as they were, they served as a necessary catalyst.

Opposing the weight of his body, which briefly reminded him of when he almost died, Van slowly rose to his feet. He gave a staggering glance at each vestal and uncomfortably limped toward the door. Figuring out what to do with what he learned could wait. What mattered most at that moment was finding those poor women some help.

The looks of the people who watched Van step out of the cathedral without guidance rocked him to the core. They stared at him as if fearing he would attack.

Shaking off his feigned strength would have reassured them otherwise, but Van refused to lose it. Although an illusion, that strength was all he had to keep him standing.

He told Sir Charleston of the vestals' condition and watched as the knight took another to help them.

When Van asked his mother what everyone seemed so frightened of, she simply shook off the little scare she had and said it was nothing.

How it gripped at his heart's remnants to find he affected even his loving mother. It was worse than her lying to him again.

The vestals awoke three days later and were questioned by King Faustign and the Holy Knights. Van wanted to know what happened, but he was restricted to his bedchamber since the rite. Servants, mainly Lyn, brought him his meals during his confinement. Others made attempts to remove Snowflake, but only managed to get scratched and bitten before she hid behind Van. They never tried to take her away directly and left with their marks when he took notice.

Victoriah might have influenced the Estrines to not force him to give the fox up in some way.

When he overheard that the royals and nobles gathered in Lord Estrine's quarters, Van saw his opportunity. He picked the lock—as his key was taken away from him—and snuck through the halls to get to the man's study.

Getting there was easier than expected. The guards had been spread so thin since the attack, there were barely any between him and Lord Estrine's quarters. With them gone, Van could listen in at the doors.

They were not just afraid of him that day—they dreaded him. From what he overheard, the same thing happened before. During the Rite of Chivalry, while the vestals sifted through the page's memories, the spell had been broken by the one they inspirited. Each time that happened, they suffered critical conditions and occasionally death. For that reason, they feared each child who stepped from the cathedral alone as monsters who would destroy the kingdom.

And so they have dubbed Van the very same evil.

Though it remained unsaid, he thought that, under ordinary circumstances, they would have executed him. Anyone would either run from or kill monsters once they distinguished them from people.

An impulse drove him to rush inside and speak up for himself, but it passed when he heard someone else do so instead. Princess Camellia said she trusted in him, that he was not what they claimed him to be.

The farther Van went when returning to his bedchamber, the more he thought the princess' judgment misguided. But it eased his pain to know there was someone who believed in him.

Her face was the only one left unchanged by him that day. It might have been due to her condition. But perhaps she saw more than he thought.

With the answers he asked for uncovered, he silently reflected on them while waiting in his bedchamber for another. He needed to be clear of not just the past and present, but also the near and distant futures.

Only the footsteps approaching from outside managed to break his focus. Three people walked together, but one stopped several feet away from the door and the remaining two waited momentarily behind it.

"Remember what you promised." That was Victoriah.

The door opened without a response from the other. His mother walked in with, to Van's surprised, his father beside her.

Van greeted his father, confusion eminent in his voice. Jerrell barely left Russalin after getting those terrible scars. He must have been there for the rite.

Jerrell did not respond. He merely stared at his son as though disappointed.

"Congratulations, love," Victoriah said, hoping to break the awkward silence. "You passed your rite."

Her words made Jerrell's brow twitch. The man then forced a smile either to make his son or himself loosen up. "Yes. Excellent work, Vandelas. You do your parents proud, passing the rite so soon."

Van stared blankly at his father. It was easy enough to see the scarred man felt apprehensive. Jerrell's tense posture and agitated facial expressions gave that away, not to mention how he addressed him by his proper name rather than as "Van."

"I ... understand that you have chosen to fight under Ederea's flag."

There it was. That was what bothered him.

"Yes. Princess Camellia offered me something I could not refuse." Van realized his voice came across as cold and lifeless, but he did not feel inclined to change it.

"Something you *could not* refuse?" Jerrell hissed faintly.

Victoriah nudged him, ushering him to get his frustration under control, casually enough for Van to almost believe it was an accident.

She did not want him causing a ruckus, but Van thought otherwise. He wanted to see precisely where that anger had been rooted and how deep. "Yes. In allowing me the chance to join the Ederean forces and continue my training with them, I am being used to further secure the relationship between Vermalio and our neighboring country. With the Renegades' attempt to kill Princess Camellia, tensions between both kingdoms will grow high. Regardless of what the Ederean king and princess have said, I could see they were cautious about being in the same room as a Vermalian knight. If they trust in me, then I can rebuild what was lost. The stronger I become, the stronger our countries' bond can grow in entrusting them with me."

For a moment, Jerrell seemed calm, but Victoriah kept her wits about her. She could tell something was about to happen.

"So ... you're doing this for Vermalio's sake."

"No. This is solely for my own purposes."

"Wha—"

"Preserving peace between both countries will allow me to find what I need sooner. Involving myself in more fights means shying away from that task. And from what I understand, Ederea undergoes far less political, economic, and internal strife than Vermalio. It only makes sense to go to a more peaceful country than stay in Vermalio, where there is less information, less security with my identity, and fewer chances to look out for myself."

Jerrell's agitation spiked dangerously high. Listening to his son speak so self-centeredly with a voice so emotionless it almost seemed inhuman was more than he could take. "What madness are you spouting, boy!?"

"Jerrell—"

"No, Victoriah! Not this time! I won't stay quiet about this! How can you stand there tongue-tied and listen to our son speak this way?"

It was a rare sight to see anyone, especially her husband, speak to Victoriah the Wolverine with such condemnation. It even surprised Van.

"A boy striving for knighthood going to another country for his own purposes alone, without concern for the crown he was raised under? It's blasphemy! What is it that is so important that you must abandon everything that makes a knight worthy of his shield?"

Jerrell paused a moment to fill his lungs. His son said nothing, wanting to hear what else he thought of him.

"Where has your devotion gone, Vandelas? Even if Ederea is our ally, it is not the same as the kingdom you've sworn your loyalty to. You're supposed to believe in our king! You're supposed to believe in—"

"I don't know what to believe anymore!"

Jerrell's words were much too bloody for Van to endure. He bellowed his thoughts before realizing what had been said.

Even so, he did not regret it. It was the truth.

Those vehement words silenced Jerrell and made him and his wife look upon Van in shock. It was the first time their child shouted at them like that.

Now that he said that, Van needed to tell them the rest. They were his parents. They deserved to know the truth. "Father, tell me again. Tell me how it is the Kindhrin—*my people*—died out."

His voice held a critical resolve neither parents noticed before. For that reason, Jerrell ignored his outburst and focused on Van's. "I told you this before. The Kindhrin succumbed to avarice, destroying themse—"

"You're wrong. That's a lie, I know it!" Van interrupted. "I saw it... I saw it all—the weapons flying, blood staining the sand, homes burning ... all of the Kindhrin running from those who set them ablaze! It wasn't greed or insanity that destroyed them! It was genocide!"

An entirely new air filled the room, casting aside all anger and frustration and leaving only dread and anguish in place. There was so much conviction, so much disdain and turmoil in the boy's voice that neither of his parents argued with him. They began to believe it too.

"I was lied to by a man I trusted with my life. I was lied to by this country's history. Even you two lied to me about what I am—you kept my own ethnicity from me for nine years!" Van choked on how vilely he growled at his parents. It literally hurt him to address them so horrendously, but he could not contain his frustrations anymore. "...How can I believe in anything ... if there are so many lying to me?"

Silence fell upon all three of them, a silence that only added to the dread crushing them. Van endured it, as had Victoriah, but Jerrell could not bear the pressure so easily and left the room, limping and holding his right shoulder.

Victoriah painfully watched her crippled husband go, wondering which of his scars was troubling him the most. After he left, she went to the other hurting man in her life, kneeling before her son and cupping his shoulder. "Van ... who was it? Who was it that destroyed the Kindhrin?"

Van trembled in attempting to control his unstable emotions. His breathing was becoming ragged and raspy. "I don't know. Damn me for it, but I don't know!" It became so hard to speak. His chest ached and he thought his lungs would pop. He took slow, deep breaths to quell his anxieties and soon stabilized his breathing. "But ... I do know that they took something precious from me, something I can't get back. I'll never forgive them for that they've done. When I find out who they are ..."

Victoriah made no response. Van sensed neither alarm nor fright from her valsara, but instead a reluctant kinship. She felt his pain and did not wish for him to embrace those savage feelings, not so soon.

"Mother, can I ask you a favor?"

"Of course, Van."

Van stood and walked to the dresser to retrieve the empty sword hilt and its scabbard, then presented them to her. "Could you return this to Father for me, tell him I'm sorry for breaking it? It broke when I tried to protect Camellia."

His words were of poor choice. The mixed feelings of pride and guilt that sweltered in Victoriah had immediately been overshadowed by grief and a hint of anger. She kept her eyes locked on his as she stepped forward, and gripped the weapons and his hands tightly. "Van, listen to me. Don't ever, *ever* apologize for protecting or avenging someone—anyone! ...Understand?"

Van was surprised. Just as he had never lashed out at his parents before, the mother had never admonished her child like that. She did not like doing it.

He took those words to heart. Gripping whatever parts of Victoriah's hands he could, Van looked to her with resolution once again. "Yes, Mother. I understand."

~ Epilogue ~

Van left Brigadier with the Ederean royals shortly after the verdict of his rite had been passed. Preparations were already made and held for their departure days before. They waited only long enough for Van to collect his valuables.

Before he left, Van needed to take care of something important: Rubi's flower. Although he went through the unforgivable to get it, he wanted it to rest with her. Once he found the pearl orchid, he froze it thoroughly enough that it would never melt and entrusted Sir Charleston to give it to her when she was returned home. He knew the knight could be trusted with it.

For several long days, King Godefroy du Joiec and his daughter sat side by side in the same coach while Van rode in the seats adjacent to them. Van rarely ever spoke. Even when it came time to step outside to stretch their legs and eat, he remained silent and nearly inactive.

Van grew weary the closer they came to the border. It made him anxious to leave the only home he knew.

What would Ederea be like? Even though he read about the country in a few books, he pondered on how much of it was true and what was exaggerated.

Getting information from the royals seemed prudent, but before anything else, there was something far more important he had to say.

So he waited until it finally happened.

"We have crossed onto Ederean soil," said the coachman through a sliding window.

Princess Camellia lit up upon hearing she had returned home. "'Tis wonderful news, is it not, Vandelas?"

He did not respond, and only stroked Snowflake's fur to calm him. They were past the border; that was the best time to say what he needed. But now that the time came, his throat tightened.

The uncomfortable silence brought a sigh from King Godefroy. "Young Vandelas, I understand the pain of losing those precious to you. The very same pain plagues me whenever I lose a valued member of my court, or when my queen died."

Van felt guilty for staying quiet for so long, causing the king to speak up for his sake.

"But you must understand that if you grieve for too long, it'll only weaken you. Be it knight or king or fishmonger, unless this pain is put to rest, it will slowly destroy you. Strengthen your resolve to live by living for those that have passed—'tis what kept me alive on the battlefield until my coronation."

"Your words are greatly appreciated ... my king," Van said while bowing his head. "But that is not why I am hesitant to speak."

The confused looks on the king's and princess' faces showed they worried for him in an entirely different way now. Perhaps they were having second thoughts about bringing him along.

"I will speak plainly: I know the princess is blind."

Their shaken expressions confirmed his suspicions to be true. In truth, Van was skeptical about what he had interpreted from the princess' behavior, at least until the attack took place.

"And I realize you've kept this quiet from the Vermalians out of fear that they would reject a country with a vulnerable heir."

King Godefroy's countenance grew morbid, as though thinking he made a grave mistake.

"Rest assured, I told no one of this."

"And why are you telling us now?"

Van lifted his hand from Snowflake's scalp and brought it into his shirt to pull out the Shift Pendant he kept hidden, holding it plainly in view. "You are not the only ones guarding a dangerous secret."

A squeeze of the smooth gem brought the wrinkles on King Godefroy's face to broaden. The spell had broken and Van's true colors were revealed.

"As you can see, Your Majesty, I am not Vermalian, but a Kindhrin. My true existence has been concealed by this tool: a Shift Pendant. I've been living my entire life protected by this since the Vermalians deeply despise my race... But what about your people?"

King Godefroy looked upon Van with the utmost shock and awe, baffled by what he had witnessed, but then a smile drew over his shaggy face and he chuckled gruffly. "A daring lad you are, if not a tad rash," said the king. "Though you needn't worry about that. We Edereans bear no ill will toward the Kindhrin. Quite the contrary! We had once planned to establish trade with them before the Cascades had become obstructed by demonic waters."

Van clenched his teeth. Through his studies, he learned that the seas between Vermalio and Harah Krid—the Cascades—were plagued by horrendous storms and ravaging waves not long after the genocide.

While they had been talking, Princess Camellia had been eying Van's pendant—or rather, the magic within it. Her eyes were fixed directly on the charm; being able to do that while also possessing a powerful magic meant she also had magic sight. She lifted her hand to tap the Shift Pendant, exhaling in awe when it glowed in reaction to her contained power.

Small and brief though the reaction was, it reaffirmed the suspicion that it was her magic that, although inadvertently, reactivated the Shift Pendant when she healed him.

"Princess Camellia."

The princess turned to Van and seemed curious a moment, then jolted back, suspecting she was being rude, and sat straight again. "My apologies."

He slipped the Shift Pendant back into his shirt, then looked to the princess. "Forgive my asking, but why is it that you've taken such an interest in me?"

Princess Camellia's cheeks were speckled pink, but she attempted to maintain a straight face. "Ah, aye. You see, a member of Father's court also brandishes magic. He seeks an apprentice, but his expectations are rather high. The lads brought to him thus far were deemed unacceptable. Ultimately, he came to me with the request that I find him someone suitable, as he trusts my judgment."

The fact that she picked him out of anyone else did not inspire confidence given their entourage. The few Ederean soldiers they travelled with were all burly, their muscles thick as stone. Though they were all adults, it made Van ponder on how much promise their youth had.

And this man Princess Camellia spoke of—if he was not satisfied with them, what hope was there for him?

"'Twas much to ponder on, even when considering the observations of my ladies." The princess paused a moment, thoughts on those that she had lost. "I was uncertain. But when I looked upon the full brilliance of your valsara, I realized I was right. You are the one he seeks."

It put Van at ease to know someone thought so highly of him. The goals he had were so far away that they hung with the stars. If he was to reach them, he would need the strength that was expected of him.

This warrior spoken of must have been highly revered to have a place in the king's court. "Who is this person?" Van asked the king.

"A very proud swordsman by the name of Wolfram Sörrign."

"Is he strong himself?"

King Godefroy laughed heartily at the question, truly amused. "Don't wish to be trained by a weakling, aye?" A broad smile was worn across his face. "You shall see for yourself once we return. The varlet will expect to see what you can do as well."

The informality suggested he and Wolfram had a strong relationship, perhaps an old friendship.

The king's recognition was a good sign. Not only that, but this Wolfram also knew magic. With his guidance, perhaps Van would learn further control of the Second Verse than he would alone.

A haven far from Kindhrin haters, a chance to further better himself, the time to find the answers he needed—all of that had been granted to him by the Ederean royals. He never felt more gratitude in his short life.

He looked upon the venerable king and princess. After all that had happened, he still did not know if he could believe in them entirely, but they believed in him.

He bowed his head to the both of them and came back up to show a tired albeit kind smile. "I am grateful to you both for this opportunity. Know that I will go beyond every expectation you have."

Both royals wore smiles beaming with delight seeing his devotion. Energy shimmered in their eyes. If they were not inside such a small space, it was doubtless they would have let that energy run free.

"We have great faith you shall, Vandelas," said the princess.

The guards outside suddenly became livelier, shouting ambiguous cries that were nonetheless cheerful. Another sound caught Van's attention—a rather rhythmic *whoosh, splash.*

"We've arrived at the ocean," King Godefroy exclaimed.

Much of Ederea consisted of an archipelago resting in a breach between the mainland. The country began in that archipelago after the du Joiec line ceased to be that of conquerors. And after their first twenty years of friendship, Vermalio gifted land to Ederea in exchange for military aid against the Pternites and the promise that they would prevent the remaining Abioan kingdoms from making hostile actions against Vermalio.

The coachman spoke to the king through the window. He spoke in the Abioan language, so Van could not understand well. Whatever it was did not concern the king much, so it must have been a minor issue, although Van did hear the word for "storm."

The coachman moved away from the window. In the dying cries of excitement, Van heard him dismount from his seat.

"It might be a wee wait before our journey continues," informed the king.

"Might we step outside for a time?" Princess Camellia asked Van. He had been the one to escort her since her servants were killed. "I'd very much like to stretch my legs."

"Of course."

Bundling Snowflake in his left arm, Van stood and opened the coach door. When stepping outside, he became astounded by the ground sparkling in the sunlight. The sand looked very pale and crumbled easily under his weight. He turned to the water when he was nearly blinded by a glare reflecting off it. The sea stretched out vastly, much more so than any lake he ever saw. And the water rippled beautifully with the sunlight, as if dancing with it.

The water in its calm state almost appeared as a mirror taking the sun's golden glow into its own world. It took his breath away.

"Um ... Vandelas?"

In getting mesmerized by the beach, he had forgotten about the princess. He turned back to her and took her hand before she got upset.

"My apologies," he said as he led her outside.

Princess Camellia smiled. "'Tis your first time seeing the ocean?"

"Yes. It's beautiful."

"Tell me what you see."

It was an unexpected request, but Van took another long look at the beach. "Well ... the sand we are standing on is very bright and shiny, sort of like ... like, uh, glass. It's soft, though, and shines with an array of charming colors. And the water—it bends constantly but is easy to see through up close. Then there's the horizon blending with the water so far away, like it could go on forever."

"A very fine depiction indeed."

It was kind of her to say so, but Van thought he could have done better. Perhaps his words would have sounded more flattering if he had spoken in Abioan.

"I ask that question of many others, and each answer is always different. Every time, I try imagining what they see from what they say. And no matter what, even when I stand on the same beach, what I see is always different."

That sounded exciting to Van, but dejection rang in the princess' voice. It made him feel sorry for her. He could not imagine her grief.

"The world is not always a beautiful place, Princess. Much of it gets covered in the evil people spread."

"Aye, yet there is much beauty to behold; focusing only on the unsightly things distracts from that truth. Though there are those who wish to taint the world's beauty, there are also those who fight to preserve it. Surely, that only makes life all the more beautiful."

For one so young, Princess Camellia held such sage wisdom.

But her words still carried such sadness. She needed only sigh to say "I covet the sight I was born without."

Van turned toward the ocean again, desiring the same wisdom fair Princess Camellia had. "Magic in our world is dying, Princess. Fewer are able to discover the gifts within their souls with each passing generation. Even less possess the magic sight we both share."

He felt the princess' luminous eyes on him as he spoke.

"No one can see everything, so we must cherish what we do."

He felt the sadness in her dissipate as relief and comfort spread through their connected hands. Princess Camellia squeezed Van's hand briefly. "You have my gratitude, Vandelas."

The princess looked back to the horizon in content and peacefully took in the qualities of the beach with her other senses, adding to the mental tableau she was painting.

Van remained by her side, contemplating more ways to describe the pleasant scenery for her. He sought to enjoy the tranquility with her.

For that tranquility would not last long.

Vandelas' adventure has only just begun, and so has that of another young page training in Ederea.

With a past as tragic and shrouded in mystery as the Kindhrin's, Luchs struggles with his own identity crisis. Once a slave taken from his home, he suffered from a terrible trauma that gave him amnesia. Now taken into the care of a kind noble family, he wishes to become a knight so he may repay them for their compassion.

However, training for a knight's shield in Ederea is much more perilous than in Vermalio. The boys risk their very lives to prove their mettle and mature into men capable of protecting their land. Can Luchs handle the training and the trials that come thereafter, or will he die trying before he can reclaim his lost memories?

Mountaineer Page
Second Book of the Aethereal Knights' Tales

9 781734 341515